THE HOUSE FELL ON HER HEAD
BY
KATE MITCHELL

ISBN: 978-1523662180
ISBN-13: 1523662182

DEDICATION

Mum and Dad - there's something of each of you in here.

Alice

Sheffield

The first thing was the people. Forming a line across the road, blocking my way. I pulled into the kerb. They were looking away from us, up the street, towards Mum's house. That was the second thing – blue lights, flashing above their heads. Police? Fire engine? At least she was here, safe. I glanced at her, in the passenger seat, chin on her chest. A tiny bubble of air wobbled on her bottom lip for a couple of seconds, disappeared as she breathed in, then reappeared with the next breath. Even in sleep, she clutched her handbag in her arms as though she expected to be set upon by a gang of thieves. I turned off the engine and the car gave a little jolt. The bubble popped on Mum's lip, she took in a quick breath, then her fingers opened the clasp of her handbag and followed her eyes, rummaging in the depths, looking for the door key. We had caught the attention of the crowd, and faces turned towards us.

Then the third thing, when I knew for sure that something was very wrong. Rob was coming towards us. Running. Rob didn't run. But his face was red and blotchy and his specs had slid down his nose. I wound down the window. As he came alongside, pushing his specs back into place with a forefinger, I could see the twin tracks they had made in the perspiration leaking from his face. Through the space he left in the line of people, I saw the front door. Ajar. Had I left it open? Maybe Mum had been burgled? She'd only agreed to come out today after a lot of persuasion, and now, I'd never be allowed to forget it.

Putting his face close to the window, Rob stammered, 'They f-f-found – in the g-garden-' and was pushed out of the way by a plump, blonde woman.

Mum said, 'What's happening, Alice?' She was peering through the windscreen at the people who had moved in Rob's wake and now surrounded the car bonnet. The door key was in her hand. 'Who is that? Did I hear Robert? Where is he?'

The blonde had her arm through the open window, waving a card under my nose. Rob's voice came from somewhere behind her, 'I've been ringing your mobile all afternoon.'

I lifted my phone out of the door pocket. It was flashing, *12 missed calls*. I said to the invisible Rob, 'You knew where we were.' It was Mum's birthday. It had taken weeks to plan, to get her out of the house for the day while the landscape gardener performed what he called, 'a proper makeover, you know, love, one of them Alan Titchmarsh thingummies off the telly'. My husband was to supervise the gardener and make sure it was all finished by the time we got back. I felt a rush of relief – of course it couldn't be a burglary, Rob had been here all day.

The pushy woman was waving the card close to my face, so I couldn't read it. She said, 'You are Violet Ibbertson?'

Mum said, 'Yes?' and the blonde leaned across me, giving me a close-up of her grey roots, holding out the card to Mum. Now I could see it was a police ID card.

Rob's face appeared from behind her shoulder and I remembered what he'd said and asked, 'What did you find in the garden?'

The blonde woman stood up as he opened his mouth, and he closed it again. I turned my head to look at Mum.

She had an expectant look and I realised she hadn't taken in whatever was written on the card, and may be thinking this was the surprise I told her would be waiting when we got home. My mother hates surprises, so I'd been preparing her as we drove.

'I've got something special lined up, Mum, when we get you home.'

'Another treat? I think I've had quite sufficient treats today, thank you, Alice. Really, I'm a little too old to be so spoilt on my birthday.'

'Well, I hope you like this surprise. It's as much for me as it is for you.' Which was true; the main point of gardens in my view is to have a pleasant place to sit with a good book, and the time and energy Rob spent doing Mum's garden would be better spent on our own so I could do more of that.

'Mum,' I said. 'This is not the surprise I was talking about.'

I felt at a distinct disadvantage, sitting in the car with the blonde hovering above me and everyone staring through the windscreen. 'Excuse me,' I said, and opened the door so she had to step back. I clambered out of the car with as much dignity as I could and stood facing her. She was a good deal shorter than I, but made up for it with her width. I pulled my skirt straight and said, 'Can I help you?'

She spoke slowly, as though I was an idiot. 'Detective Inspector Turnbull,' showing me the ID card again. I made a show of taking it from her and reading it. 'I need to speak to Mrs Ibbertson. Could we go inside?'

I dipped my head back into the car where Mum was frowning out of the windscreen. 'Why are the police here, Alice?'

'I don't know. Let's go in the house and find out.'

As we walked around the car I looked at Rob for an explanation and he inclined his head towards the Inspector and shrugged. Mum already had the passenger door open – a man I'd never seen before was holding it for her – and was using it as a support, parallel to her walking stick, to pull herself upright. I glared at the stranger and took hold of the door firmly until he let go.

Mum, then me, with Rob bringing up the rear, made a little procession behind the Inspector. An Alsatian growled as I went by. A teenager from one of the neighbouring houses was sitting on a wall with her friends, her face half hidden behind a huge pink bubble, which burst as I passed. I jumped. She giggled. I stuck my tongue out at her. Her mouth dropped open, bits of pink gunk clinging to her bottom lip. At the gate a uniformed constable held the blue and white tape high enough for us to walk under and along the short path. His chin was a rash of yellow-headed spots. The Inspector stepped into the hallway in front of me. I noticed her hemline was held up by staples.

The door closed behind us. In the darkness of the narrow hallway, with the sun still in my eyes, I could barely see. Rob tapped me on the arm and whispered, 'The gardener…'

The Inspector talked across him. 'Mrs Ibbertson, your gardener contacted us because of a problem when he was digging.'

Mum stopped with her hand on the top button of her coat. 'Gardener?' She smiled, 'Oh, I think you have the wrong house, dear.'

My stomach turned over. This was going to be my fault. Once again, I'd set out to please my mother, and it looked as though I'd got it wrong. Then I shook my head, irritated with myself. For crying out loud, I'm a grown-up. I took a deep breath and said, 'No Mum, she's right, it's our – *my* gardener. I arranged for him to come.' I could feel her disapproval radiating along the dim hallway. 'He's putting in a patio, to make it easier to…'

Dropping her handbag on the hall table, she pushed past the Inspector and trotted down the hallway, tapping her walking stick on the thin runner, then on the brown linoleum of the kitchen.

As I followed her, the Detective Inspector said, 'Bones. Beneath the rockery. We think they're human remains.'

I stopped. The sun through the fanlight cast my shadow in front of me, long and thin. A little cry from the kitchen sent me hurrying to the kitchen door. Her tiny silhouette was at the window, her stick lay on the floor. She was gripping the stainless steel draining board so tightly that the bones of her knuckles glowed white. I went to stand beside her, looking onto the garden.

It was a moonscape, on which alien beings, hooded and masked and clad from head to toe in pale blue, walked and talked and wrote on clipboards. In an eruption of rocks and soil the privet hedge lay, uprooted. Close to the window, on an overturned wheelbarrow, a pigeon pecked at an abandoned sandwich. Where I expected to see a rockery, a white tent stood inside a yellow and black cordon. A figure reversed out of the tent, filming with a camcorder. At the back gate, a police officer guarded a blue and white tape. On the hill behind the house, a young man looked down on this activity, the ball in his hand forgotten while his dog pranced, trying to get his attention.

The plan. I needed to show Mum the plan. Opening my handbag, turning it upside down, I emptied purse, receipts, shopping lists onto the draining board. If Mum saw the ideas that Rob and I had worked on – well, my ideas really, which Rob had sketched with his usual precision – I was sure she'd like it. She would want the smart new fence and a stone flagged patio in place of the ancient hedge and moss-covered lawn. She could surely imagine new flowering plants and shrubs where Rob had drawn curls and flourishes. She would want to sit in the sun, beneath the parasol, at the table – which right now was leaning, flat packed, against the garden wall – looking out on the new pergola where her beloved roses would be transplanted directly into her line of sight. She would say, 'That's lovely Alice, well done Alice.' Here was the plan. I pushed the pile of scraps and other stuff to the side and smoothed the creases out of the paper.

'Look, Mum.' But her eyes were fixed on the ruin of the garden. 'It was supposed to be finished.' I needed to explain, to show her. 'By the time we got home. It was…'

'A surprise. So you said. It certainly is that, Alice.'

I put my hand on her arm and felt her trembling. 'Look,' I pointed to the picture, but she pushed it away.

'The rockery,' she whispered.

'The rockery wasn't supposed to – really, Mum, I was absolutely clear that…'

With a flick of her wrist she shook me off.

'Mrs Ibbertson?' I'd forgotten the Inspector was there. 'What about some tea?'

'Of course,' I said. Reminded of my manners, I made for the pantry where I collided with Rob, who had the kettle in his hand.

'Liam will make it,' said the Inspector. 'Won't you, Liam?'

The spotty constable was standing in the doorway, his hat in his hand and his hair standing on end like a character in a comic who's just received a shock. Perhaps he was shocked; he looked too young to know much about bones in gardens. I thought he might be about the age of our grandson and I'm sure we wouldn't want Adam doing this kind of job. The Inspector glanced from the constable to the kettle and back again with raised eyebrows. I could see she was used to being obeyed. He took the kettle from Rob and filled it at the sink, glancing warily at Mum who stood immobile. He looked at the back of the kettle, felt around it, underneath it, frowned. Rob took the kettle from him, placed it on the cooker and lit the gas ring.

'We'll need to interview your mother as soon as possible. You must accompany her, of course.' She kept flicking her blonde bob back with her fingers, like a nervous tic. I was already irritated by it. Coquettish, my mother would call it. She may not do it if she knew how it emphasised her jowls. Not even a natural blonde. Mid-forties, I guessed. The constable was opening and closing cupboards, locating cups and putting them on the table. Rob followed him with the saucers.

'You mean we have to go to the police station, officer?'

'Inspector. No,' she said. 'Not at this stage. We'll interview your mother here, in a little while. But she will have to move out,' I looked at Mum and when there was no reaction to this information I knew she hadn't heard. My mother had never spent a night away from home to my knowledge. 'If it becomes a criminal investigation.'

'A criminal investigation?' I might have shouted that.

An animal sound between a squeak and a scream made me look at Mum. She was pushing her fist into her mouth, biting down on her fingers. Rob passed the teapot to the constable and joined me by her side. She didn't resist when we each took an arm and guided her across to the fireside armchair.

'But it was a birthday surprise,' I said, to no one in particular. 'I told him, the gardener. He wasn't supposed to touch the rockery.' Even as I said it, I knew it sounded ridiculous, even suspicious. As though I knew there was something under the rockery. 'I mean – my mother loves the rockery.'

'Get a move on with that tea, Liam,' the Inspector said. He seemed to be wondering what to do with the teapot. He'd probably never seen a kitchen like my mother's before. I wanted to say, 'Welcome to the nineteen thirties, alive and well and living at Hurdle Hill'. The kitchen had a few mod cons such as the cooker that Mum was forced to buy in 1971 when North Sea gas came in, but otherwise it had hardly changed in my lifetime.

Rob was squatting beside Mum, patting her hand, watching her with that kindly frown that she hated, but right now she seemed oblivious. I found the tea caddy and handed it to the constable. He opened it and stared inside. I took it from him and put two level spoons of tea leaves into the pot.

'He was pulling up the privet hedge,' the Inspector was explaining, her hands gesturing what she was describing. 'Seemingly the roots went under the rockery. Pull out the roots, the rocks collapse and a hole appears.' She flung her arms outward, palms upward, as though she had performed a trick. I half-expected her to say, 'Ta-da!' But, 'Human remains,' was what she said.

The kettle whistled and Mum looked around, startled. I opened the back door. An arm shot in front of me and pushed it closed again. 'You can't go out there,' the Inspector said. She waved the arm towards the table and said, 'Please sit down.' A merry tune that sounded like the *Sugar Plum Fairy* trilled from her pocket and she pulled out her mobile phone, saying, 'D.I. Turnbull', which was useful because I'd forgotten her name. She listened intently, watching me all the while, as though she expected me to make a run for the back door. Or perhaps the caller was talking about me. I felt like a schoolgirl under the eye of the form prefect. I sat.

The constable poured boiling water onto tea leaves. He took a bottle of milk from the fridge and placed it on the table. I got up, put the bottle back in the fridge and brought out the milk jug. I stirred the tea leaves. All strangely familiar actions in a world that was becoming more unreal by the minute. I poured a cup and passed it to Rob. He lifted it to Mum's mouth, but she kept her lips closed tight, childlike, and some of it dribbled down her chin. Through the window, I saw that the dog walker had been joined by a family sitting on a blanket. It looked as though they were eating a picnic.

'Mrs Ibbertson?' The Inspector dropped her mobile phone into her pocket and knelt beside Mum's chair, placing her hand on Mum's arm to get her attention. 'Is there anything you can tell us, Mrs Ibbertson? Anything at all? It might be some time ago?' It was though Mum hadn't heard.

There was a tap on the kitchen door and a thin, young woman with spiky hair in an unlikely shade of red came in. The Inspector stood, pulling her skirt down over her hips with difficulty, and gestured to the back door. The young woman turned to me and held out her hand. She smiled apologetically. I didn't catch her name. 'Forensic archaeologist,' she said, 'I'll try not to disturb you.' Both women went into the garden. I made to follow them but the young constable had the door closed and his back against it in seconds. He looked afraid, as though I might argue with him. I smiled at him and watched the red blush creep across his spots. He reminded me of Adam when Rob teased him about girlfriends. Through the window I saw the new arrival pull white coveralls from her backpack and put them on while the Inspector talked to her. One of the figures detached itself from the group beside the tent and passed blue bags to the Inspector. I thought, freezer bags? The Inspector put her feet into them. And that simple action, of taking my assumptions and turning them upside down until they became something completely beyond my knowledge and experience, made me realise that from here on in, nothing would be certain. The Inspector and the forensic archaeologist, spikes protruding from her white hood, approached the yellow and black cordon.

As I turned from the window, I caught a movement in the corner of my eye. Mum was pulling herself out of the chair. Her hands on the arms, bent at the waist, she could have been standing on the edge of a swimming pool preparing for a dive. I stepped forward as she lurched forward and down, head first. The side of her head hit the edge of the fender with a soft crunch and she folded onto the floor.

Frank

Malkin Farm, South Australia

Human remains. A skull. The words jump off the screen and jangle around in my brain. I feel dizzy, but when I close my eyes, a shadow presses against the lids. I open my eyes to push it away. My mate, Sam, is looking at me with a worried face. Of course, it's not Sam – it's Keith, his lad. They have the same floppy blond hair.

Amy takes my elbow and steers me into the chair in front of the laptop. 'It's yesterday's *Star,'* she says. 'A friend in Sheffield sent me an email with a link. There's a photograph, look.' She presses a key and the words disappear. Now, I'm looking at blue and white tape, and a house, behind it.

Amy puts her arms around my shoulders in a hug that nearly smothers me. She's got it straight off. They know my story. I'm their family heirloom, passed down from one generation to the next. She lands a kiss on my head and clucks off.

I stare at the screen. The curtains look different. Behind me, a knife and fork hit the plate. Keith moans about coming in from shearing fifty sheep to a meal of rabbit food. Amy reminds him he needs to lose weight, says there's plenty of vitamins in salad. I reckon that door's been painted. A chair scrapes back. The fridge door opens and closes. A tinny hisses. Keith swallows noisily then belches. Amy tells him he's disgusting. The kettle boils. Yes, that door was brown. Or was it green? But it's definitely the house. I'd never forget the house.

Amy wraps my hands around a mug of tea. The sweetness makes me gag. It must have half the sugar bowl in it. I pull my eyes away from the photograph and look out of the window. I need to get a grip. There's things to do. It's been a long wait. I thought it was too late, but maybe all those years of watching the sheep, the creek, and the slope of the Wallaburra hill range rising up beyond, maybe they were all leading to this day.

It says a skull, that's one skull, which is wrong for starters. It also says she's collapsed. It doesn't say she's dead. So I've still got time. My greatest fear has always been that they would be left alone. Nobody but me would have searched for them. Nobody else believed they needed to be found.

This is the suitcase I brought on the ship: brown, peeling cardboard, held together by the stickers that I collected from our ports of call. A shipload of lads and lasses in search of a future. Except for me – I was more intent on getting away from the past. 'Ten pound poms' they called us. Sam and Doreen were the life and soul of the party as we crossed the equator – he dressed up as King Neptune in a wig made from a mop-head he'd stolen from the cabin boy and brushed with Doreen's red shoe polish. They laughed fit to burst as they watched the water going anti-clockwise down the plughole. Keith says it's not true that the water goes down a different way either side of the equator, but I told him, I've seen it with my own eyes.

As I shut the case, a hinge snaps off. Amy sees me fiddling with it and brings me Keith's blue holdall. She won't take 'no' for an answer. Half a century of memories from this parallel life fit into that holdall; my real life is in the brown canvas haversack that I lift from the hook on the door as I leave.

Amy has it all written out on a piece of paper she calls 'an itinerary'. She clips it to what looks like a supermarket coupon, but she says it's an electronic ticket which she assures me really will get me all the way to London. She goes through every detail, making me repeat it, especially the bits about changing flights at Singapore and then getting across London. When she's sure I understand, she gives me my passport – I got it to go on holiday with them five years ago but I didn't go in the end. There seemed no point in going anywhere else, until now.

Keith has brought the ute to the kitchen door. He throws the holdall in the back and waits in the driving seat. Amy wraps me in a hug that squeezes the breath out of me, then she stands at the door, waving. As we drive away, I watch her shrinking in the mirror until she's just a speck. By the time we take to the main road, the dawn is lifting from the lower reaches of the Wallaburra hills. I've often been out here with the sheep in the early morning, thinking it's not so different from what I remember of the Derbyshire moors when the heather used to glisten with mist. Today, for the first time, I allow myself to imagine the years rolling up with that purple haze, to make way for the remembering.

Keith takes me to the Qantas desk and sticks with me until I've checked in. The holdall has disappeared along a conveyor belt. They swear to me that it'll get swapped onto the right plane at Singapore without me having to do anything. It doesn't matter, it's only stuff. So long as I can keep my haversack with me. Keith checks my boarding pass and makes me go through Amy's instructions once more. At the security barrier, we shuffle our feet, not looking at one another, until Keith squeezes my hands in his great fists. 'Anything. Anytime,' he says and turns, walking away quickly through the crowd, one hand raised above his head so that I follow him until the exit doors slide closed between us.

I find a seat facing the display board. From here I can watch my flight number as it flickers off, then appears somewhere else on the screen. It makes my eyes water but I don't want to miss the gate number. I've waited too long to risk it going wrong.

Alice

As the sun rose, it was as though a curtain was drawing back and letting light fall across the garden, revealing it quiet, but ruined. I'd watched them most of the night, working beneath floodlights, taking crates full of plastic bags, and at one point a covered stretcher, round the back of the house and onto the road. Most of them had left, leaving one police officer at the front gate, and this one at the back, stamping his feet against the early morning chill.

'Still here.'

I thought that's what I heard but when I looked over to the bed, Mum's eyes were closed. The reflection of her blue and purple bruises stained the white pillow case. Maybe it was a question: *Are you still here*? Did she think I might leave her on her own? Or perhaps it was: *Am I still here*? Her body made hardly any impression beneath the eiderdown. A pink eiderdown, covered with white floribunda. As the dawn light moved across the room, it illuminated the clusters of yellow polyantha which tangled in the creases of the curtains, their thorns long ago frayed to nothing; and the roses on the wallpaper - orderly, vertical lines of tea roses, faded to the palest pink. This room had always given me that sense of being stifled, unable to breathe, roses closing in on me, brambles reaching out for me. I realised my lips were moving, silently reciting, '*Crimson Glory; French Lace; Gallic Rose...*' and I was shocked to have retained such useless information for – what? – more than sixty years!

Linoleum. Whoever used that word these days? There is laminated flooring in my house, thank you; with underfloor heating, courtesy of Rob's retirement lump sum. Here, I could trace the muddy brown path where my mother's feet had worn off the leaf pattern, from door to dressing-table, to bed, to window. Almost a century of feet – imagine that. Beside my slippered feet, the linoleum had been scuffed into two opaque circles through which the floorboard was visible. An old, old memory: I'm playing in the garden and look up to see my mother framed in the window, standing here, right in this spot, watching me. *Don't play near the rockery. You'll hurt yourself.* There was no rockery, now.

I can see no trace in this room of Joe, my stepfather, who was here for almost twenty years. When I moved out after Rob and I married, Joe moved into my old room at the front of the house. I discovered this by accident, when I was looking for a photo album; I walked into the front bedroom and there he was – not in person, but in things. An army camp bed, blankets neatly folded. A row of penny westerns lined up beside my records. Mum kept his bed made up in her room but it was a pretence; she asked Rob to move the bed out immediately after Joe's funeral. The roses had long since closed over the space that Joe temporarily inhabited and it seemed my mother had always been the only occupant, in her narrow iron bedstead, surrounded by the sight of roses and the smell of mothballs and lavender. Rob joked that we should give the house to the National Trust as a pre-war museum.

The front door closed below and Rob called up the stairs, 'Only me.'

Looking down onto the top of the white police tent, I wondered whether Mum might have viewed the rockery differently, had she known what lay below it. I looked at her; she didn't quite close her eyes fast enough. She was awake.

'I'll bring you a cuppa.'

'A cup of tea would be very nice, thank you, Alice.' Corrected, feeling fourteen years old again, I scuttled off.

In the kitchen, Rob had the electric kettle unpacked and switched on. It was my Christmas present to Mum more than ten years ago, and remained boxed, on the pantry shelf. 'Never trust anything that mixes water with electricity,' she'd said. Rob was unpacking milk, a cafetiere, coffee and a radio that he'd brought from home in a collapsible plastic crate. I was surprised to see Constable Liam sitting in the armchair. I'd forgotten he was here. He was fast asleep.

'They're camped out in the street,' Rob said. 'They probably thought I was the milkman and by the time they realised, I was past them. It's all over the news.' He switched on the radio. At the first blast of '*The Candy Man*' the constable jumped out of the chair, stumbling and rubbing his face with its surprising thickness of dark whiskers. It must be painful, shaving. Does he shave around the spots or over them, I wondered? And why doesn't he grow a beard? Perhaps, like the Army, he had to have permission. He was blushing a deep red and I realised I was staring at him. I turned away and started to prepare a tea tray, switching the radio off as I passed.

Rob pointed upwards with his thumb: 'Any better?'

'Awake and talking.'

Rob divided the boiling water between the teapot and the cafetiere. He poured two cups of tea, passed one to the constable and took the other upstairs, with a plate of digestive biscuits, on the tray. In the crate, I found a pack of croissants and my Sudoku book; bless him. Taking my coffee and a croissant through to the front room, I stood at the bay window studying the activity on the street. A man was speaking to a camera, in front of a large van with a satellite transmitter on top. Several people surrounded the police officer at the front gate while he gazed impassively over their heads. One of them caught sight of me and called out. I was trying to work out how I knew him when a camera flashed, startling me. Rob pulled the lace curtain out of my hand and let it fall back into place. 'They're very excited,' he said. 'They think it might be another Cromwell Street, with bodies in every corner.' I glared at him and he added, 'Bad taste, sorry.'

Frank

Flight QF 587 to Perth

The mighty pull as the plane lifts into the air makes me imagine a great iron magnet hanging over Sheffield, drawing me home. It's a Boeing 737-800 according to the card in the seat pocket. As soon as the captain says we can move around, I pull my haversack from under the seat, take out the parcel of black fabric, and open it carefully. Now then, it's important that I remember it in the right order, and I think this is first. It's faded with age, but I can still make out '*Robinson Crusoe'* on the cover, and I can still smell the ink on the picture of a man in a fur tunic and hat. Inside, the fancy writing says, '*Awarded to Frank Sheldon, for Attendance at Sunday School, 3rd September 1939.*' The day the War started. The day I first heard Violet's name.

It was a fine sunny morning, that Sunday. Sam and me were planning to go rabbiting in the woods. Mam was baking. I took a cake off the cooling rack and dropped it into my pocket. As I reached for the door latch, she came up behind me and caught hold of my collar.

'Back upstairs and get ready for Sunday School.'

'But it's last day of the school holidays. And Cyril doesn't have to go to Sunday School. It's not fair.'

Dad looked up from his first pipe of the day. 'Them as brings a wage in can do what they wants with their Sundays, but meantime, tha'll do what thy Mam says.'

As I reached the stair door it burst open and smacked me in the face. Our Jean jumped down the last two stairs. She saw me holding my nose and bent over me, twirling her skirt back and forth in her hands, going, 'Oh me, Oh my.' She was mimicking Shirley Temple. Our Jean was daft about the pictures and went at least once a week, then sent us all mad acting out the film and singing the songs. She pulled me to my feet and tried to kiss me. I pushed her away.

'Mardy boy.' She lifted her coat off the peg. 'See you laters, alligators. Remember Joe's coming for tea.'

'Joe the Beau is it?' Dad chuckled. Jean pulled a lump of pastry off Mam's rolling pin and popped it on his nose. Mam laughed. Jean skipped out of the door, singing, '*On the good ship Lollipop...*'

I changed into clean trousers and put on the scratchy grey socks that Jean had knitted for me. Back in the kitchen, Mam made me stand still while she rubbed my knees with the flannel until they burned. She took my gas mask box off the hook and slung it across my shoulder. She didn't know that my gas mask was under the bed. The box came in handy for carrying my marbles and other odds and ends.

As I crossed the yard, Mr Wreakes from next door came out of the privy buttoning up his fly. His face was drooped and wrinkled like a half-used candle. His pipe was clamped between his long yellow teeth and his voice whistled around the stem as he said, 'Tha scrubs up well, young Frankie.' He said the same thing every Sunday. He winked. 'Mam and Dad having a lie-in?' He said that every Sunday, too.

Sam Ainsworth, my best pal, was sitting on his doorstep, rolling marbles into the gutter. I reckoned we could still go rabbiting but he said, 'It's prize-giving and if I don't get anything, me Mam'll think I've not been going and she'll gi'me a crack.'

He had a point. So we walked together up to Chapel. As we went in, Mrs Trippett, the Sunday School teacher, waddled towards us. With her fluffy white cardigan and feathers in her hat, she reminded me of the geese that swam on the millpond. She flapped her arms, sending us into the side chapel and closed the door on us. While we waited we played marbles and I won a Cat's Eye off Ernie Culshaw.

Mrs Trippet came in and said, 'Sit down, children, and pay attention.' Like lightning Ernie Culshaw had that Cat's Eye back in his pocket. I hissed at him to give it back but he looked as though butter wouldn't melt, and Mrs Trippett frowned at me. 'There'll be no Sunday School today,' she said. 'The Minister has brought his wireless in because we're expecting the Prime Minister to speak to the nation. Then there will be a short service.'

So it was that I sat between Mrs Trippett and Sam in Chapel listening to the words, "*and so this country is at War with Germany*." Mrs Trippet cried and the organ burst forth and we sang, *Jerusalem*! as loud and fierce as ever I heard it. I could see Sam felt the same as me, as though our hearts were about to jump out of our mouths with the excitement.

Then we were back on the street and I was surprised to see the sun was still shining. Remembering our Attendance Prizes, me and Sam went back to find Mrs Trippett. She was sniffing and blowing her nose while the Minister patted her arm.

I pulled on her other sleeve. 'Miss?'

She looked at me as though she'd forgotten who I was.

‘Go away, boy,’ the Minister said. ‘Can’t you see Mrs Trippett is busy?’

I could see the pile of books on the table that should have been given out that day and I wanted mine. ‘But, Sir, it’s right there. Please, Sir, me Mam’ll skelp me if I don’t bring it home.’

Grumbling, the Minister picked up the books one by one, looking at the writing inside until he found ours, and handed them to us. Sam got *Treasure Island.* Mine was *Robinson Crusoe.* It was covered in blue cloth with a picture of a man wearing a fur hat and a red tunic. I pushed my nose into the cover to smell the ink. I thought it a right fancy book. The Minister turned back to Mrs Trippett, so we tucked our books down the backs of our trousers and ran all the way down to Beacon Street where Sam headed for his house and I charged up our gennel and through the back door. I tripped over a basin, clattering it across the floor. Water spilled everywhere and a pair of long johns flew through the air then landed with a great splosh. It looked as though my Dad had been steamrollered.

The kitchen was empty. I imagined the war might already have taken everyone while I’d been out, leaving me alone, and my innards did a somersault.

I yelled, ‘Mam? Dad?’

There was a scuffling above me in the bedroom like mice running across the floor. Mam called, ‘Whatever’s up, Frank?’

I opened the stair door and shouted, ‘Quick, there’s a war on.’

It looked like our Jean coming down the stairs, with her hair hanging wavy and dark about her shoulders. She was winding her hair up as she came down and by the time she reached the bottom step, she was Mam again.

‘There’s a war on,’ I said again. ‘They told us at Chapel. We sang ‘Jerusalem’ and Mrs Trippett was scriking like a dam-burst and…’ I took my book out of my trousers and held it up to her but she took no notice, pushing pins into her hair and looking at Dad who had come downstairs behind her.

He said, ‘It’s definite then,’ and in a few strides he was across the kitchen, pulling on his jacket, lifting his cap from the hook and ramming it onto his mop of brown curls. ‘They’ll want to sort the volunteer roster for fire watch.’ He stepped into the puddle of water and took no notice, pushing his wet feet into the boots that waited by the door, still covered in white dust and wrinkled into shape from when he’d pulled his feet out of them on Saturday afternoon. Then he was gone. Mam made me mop up the spilled water while she wrung out the long johns and hung them out. While she cooked the dinner, I cut parcel tape into lengths and stuck crosses onto the window. Licking the tape made me feel sick.

‘What’s this for, Mam?’

‘It’s to show Jerry he’ll not frighten us. He’ll fly over Sheffield, see all the crosses and know he’s wasting his time.’

‘But Mam, didn’t tha say, when we put up blackout curtains the other week, that it was so Jerry couldn’t see our lights when he flies over?’

‘Aye.’

‘So, Mam, how will Jerry see the crosses if there’s no lights?

‘Mind thy lip,’ she said.

Jean’s boyfriend, Joe, came to tea that night. Joe and Dad were talking about all the new orders coming in for steel for fighter planes and Mam had the best cups and saucers out.

My brother Cyril was full of news. ‘They’re taking on messengers at the Town Hall,’ he said. ‘If tha’ll sign to say I’m sixteen, I can get a uniform and a bike.’

This sounded a right good idea. I pulled at Dad’s arm. ‘Can I do that?’

‘There’s a job going here,’ Dad said, ‘As apprentice to thy mam. Start now and get a brew on.’ Everybody laughed.

Jean said, ‘Joe’s going to join up in the morning.’

‘He doesn’t have to join up,’ said Dad. ‘There’s plenty of work at our place if he needs a reserved occupation. They’re working round the clock already, and it’s not even started yet.’

‘He’s got a trade, Dad,’ Jean said, ‘He’s going because he wants to. They’ve told him his job’ll be waiting when it’s over.’

‘Aye well, I’m only saying,’ Dad said, turning the wireless on. The swooshing sounds as he tuned it made me think of the waves on Filey beach where I’d been with the Sunday School outing last year. We listened in silence to the news which was all about the war. I sat opposite Joe and Jean, watching them googling eyes at one another. Dad switched the wireless off and started to fill his pipe. Mam gathered the cups and saucers together. ‘Bedtime,’ she said as she took my cup out of my hand.

I dropped under the table to crawl my way out between all the legs. A piece of black material that must have dropped when Mam made the curtains was wedged into the skirting board. I was folding it carefully to put it in my pocket when I heard Jean say, ‘So we’re thinking of bringing the wedding forward.’

Mam said, 'Bring what wedding forward? I wasn't aware there was a wedding in the offing, young lady.'

This sounded interesting so I scuttled backwards under the table and up into my chair. Mam was staring at Jean, a cup hooked onto each finger and a pile of saucers in her palm.

'We've been thinking about it for a while,' Jean said.

'So what's all the rush?' Mam said. 'Has tha got a belly full of arms and legs?' Bill sniggered. Jean threw him a dirty look. Dad stopped tamping his tobacco and cuffed him round the head.

Dad wagged a finger at Joe. 'Well, lad, if that is the case,' he said. 'There certainly will be a wedding.' Joe looked down at the table, his ears bright pink.

There was a crash and I looked under the table to see one of the cups lying in pieces on the floor. Mam put the rest of the cups and saucers down and pressed her hands flat on the table. Tears ran down her face and Jean jumped up and put her arm around Mam's shoulders.

'Mam, it's nothing like that,' she said. 'It's with Joe joining up. We thought…'

Mam blew her nose on her pinafore. She picked the broken cup off the floor. 'This was Nannan's tea set. She'll be spinning in her grave listening to this carry-on.'

Jean said, 'I'm not expecting. We've decided to get married a bit sooner than we would have. That's all.'

'I can glue it, Mam.' I said it to stop her being unhappy, but it reminded her that I was there.

'Bed,' she said.

By leaving the door off the latch and sitting on the third stair, no one could see me, but I could hear everything.

Mam said, 'She's not yet twenty.'

‘We’ve been courting for months,’ Jean said. ‘Why wait?’

‘And why not wait?’ Dad asked. ‘At least until the war’s over?’

Joe said, ‘It’ll mean I get married man’s allowance and Jean will get half of it. And she’ll get a pension if anything happens to me.’

I saw Dad go to the mantelpiece, take a taper and light it at the fire. His ears wiggled up and down as he put the taper to his pipe and sucked on it. He pointed his pipe stem towards the table. ‘Upstairs,’ he said. ‘Now.’ I heard chairs scraping back and scampered up the stairs as Bill and Cyril came up behind me. Mam called after them, ‘Mind there’s no light,’ and closed the stair door.

Cyril and Bill flung themselves on the bed and in the dusk I saw Bill rolling a cigarette. Cyril picked up my book.

‘That’s mine,’ I yelled, and went to grab it, but he stood up and held it above his head so I couldn’t reach it. There was no point in riling him; he’d damage it if he thought it was worth something to me. I took my shoes off and crept onto the landing. Lying down, I could watch the kitchen table through a gap in the floorboards.

Mam said, ‘What do Joe’s folks make of this?’

‘He’s not got any,’ Jean said. ‘His Dad copped it in the last War, and his Mam went with the flu straight after.’

Dad said, ‘Sorry lad, I didn’t make the connection. Ibbertson, of course. Wasn’t your Dad with Ropers’ lads when most of them copped it?’

‘That’s right, Mr Sheldon, he was at Passchendaele,’ Joe said.

Dad was standing by Mam and he put his hand on her shoulder. ‘Ah well,’ and I could tell by the sound of his voice that Jean was going to get her own way as per usual. 'Happen we'll not stop human nature. We'll make do.'

'I don't want to make do,' Jean wailed. 'I want it to be special.'

'If tha wants it special, tha'll have to wait,' Dad said.

Mam said, 'We've a bit put by.'

'It won't cost much, Mrs Sheldon,' Joe said. 'We're doubling up with a pal.'

'How's that?' Mam asked.

'My pal, Richard, he's getting married. He says we can double up.'

'And what about his fiancée? What's her name?'

'Violet.'

'This Violet lass, then. What does she make of having a double wedding?'

No one spoke.

'Not much, by the sound of it,' Mam said.

'Richard thinks she'll be fine about it,' Jean said.

'She doesn't know?' Mam stood up, pushing her chair back so fast it fell over.

'Oh, yes,' said Jean, and at the same time Joe said, 'By now she does.'

'What does that mean?'

Joe said, 'Richard's talking to her about it tonight.'

Dad said, 'I take it they're close friends of yours?'

'Richard is,' said Joe. 'We grew up together. And Violet seems a good lass.'

Mam asked, 'And do we have a date?'

'The sixteenth,' Jean said.

'Of December? November?'

'September.'

‘September?’ Mam screeched. ‘That’s two weeks away. How can we organise a chuffing wedding in two weeks?’

‘Don’t worry, Mam. These friends of Joe’s, they’ve got it all organised.’

‘Aye,’ said Joe. ‘They’ve had their wedding booked for a while.’

‘And Sybil will lend me her frock,’ Jean added.

‘So, it’s all sorted.’ Mam sat down and put her head in her hands.

‘Well, nearly. Dad has to sign a form for me, being as I’m under age.’

Jean stood up. Thinking she might be coming upstairs to get this form, I crept back to our bedroom. Bill and Cyril were snoring. I looked out on the street. It was completely dark but for the shapes of the houses against the stars. Taking Cyril’s torch from his trouser pocket, I got under the covers and opened *Robinson Crusoe*. The print was small and the story very drawn out and I was soon asleep, with no inkling that a train of events had started which would turn my life upside down and inside out. And that I would still be looking for answers seventy years later. With this Violet at the centre of it all.

Alice

Rob said, 'I half expected you to bring your Mum home last night. Got the spare room ready, in case.'

I brought him up to date with events of the previous evening. We'd called an ambulance, but Mum refused to go to hospital. I'd offered to bring her to our house. Of course, she said no. The paramedics called the doctor who said she needed a couple of stitches really, but as she insisted, he put on special plasters to close the wound and left some pain-killers. The Inspector eventually said that so long as we had a police officer with us, we could stay here, and Constable Liam volunteered to stay on. As if conjured up by his name, the Constable appeared, still blushing through his early morning growth. 'It's just that I'm supposed to stay with you.' He was interrupted by a knock at the front door. He returned with a young man dressed casually in jeans and a jacket.

'Doctor Grahams,' he introduced himself. 'You are?'

'Alice Burgess. Mrs Ibbertson's daughter.'

The doctor took a file from his briefcase and pulled out its inner card. 'Next of kin?' I nodded. He studied the card. 'You had the locum chap last night. He left a message about…' He turned the card over, frowning, and said, 'Think a card might be missing. Nothing much on here.'

'There won't be.' I couldn't remember when Mum last went to the doctor.

'Nineteen-eighty-one?' he said, and I wondered if I'd said it aloud. 'And that's a cross reference about her husband's health. Would that be right?'

I shrugged – it was probably right. He followed me up the stairs. On the landing he stopped and said, 'No next of kin on record since Mr Ibbertson died. I'll take a note of your name. Burgess, you say?' He jotted it on the card and I gave him my telephone number.

Mum was sitting up, holding her cup and saucer, managing to look both outraged, probably because she'd heard us talking about her, and fragile.

'Well, Mrs Ibbertson,' the doctor said. 'That's quite a shiner. I wouldn't like to see the other chap.'

'This is Doctor Grahams.' I started straightening the bedclothes.

Mum put her hand on mine. I looked at her and realised she wasn't being affectionate – she wanted to stop me fussing. 'I can manage,' she said, holding out her cup and saucer with her other hand. The cup was still full. She waved at me impatiently with her free hand so I took it and left, feeling like an incompetent waitress.

For the sake of something to do I tidied the bathroom. The face flannel was on the side of the basin; it was wet. The soap had also been used recently. I listened at the bedroom door but the rumble of voices was too quiet to hear, so I took the tray downstairs to find Rob chatting companionably to Constable Liam about Sheffield Wednesday's game the following day. Rob's knowledge of football was limited to what he couldn't avoid seeing or hearing on the news. Yet his memory for detail meant he could name enough names and recount enough game results to be able to hold his own in a conversation. Clearly, he'd convinced Liam.

I poured a fresh cup of tea and passed it to Liam, 'For your colleague.' I pointed through the window to the policeman guarding the back gate. He took the cup out of the back door. When he was half way across the garden, I whispered to Rob, 'She's been out of bed.'

'She was coming out of the bathroom when I took her tea up. Shouldn't she?'

'She was adamant she couldn't move under her own steam last night. The paramedics carried her up to bed.'

Rob tapped the side of his nose. 'Crafty old hag.' Clearly, Rob was sufficiently recovered from his shock of the previous evening to insult my mother. Maybe I should be relieved by this return to normality.

'What do you mean?'

'Have you ever known your mother to stay away from home?'

Rob was right of course; even in this crisis my mother was in absolute control, and as ever had done it without me noticing. Not for the first time, I reflected that friends who had become carers to their elderly parents might actually have it easier. If your parents become dependent, you may at least feel as though you've grown up.

'I rang Judy,' Rob managed seamlessly to change the subject as Constable Liam returned. 'She reminded me she's coming up on Monday afternoon.' I must have looked blank because he added, 'To bring Adam?' Of course. Our eldest grandson would be starting university in Sheffield the next week. I was hoping it meant we'd see more of Judy. I'd missed her since she moved down south with the boys. But what a mess for them to walk in to. Rob read my mind. 'Let's hope things are sorted by then.'

The front door opened and the Inspector's voice called down the hallway for Liam. He met her in the kitchen doorway. I heard her say, 'The officer on the gate says the doctor's here?'

'Yes Ma'am. Upstairs, with Mrs Ibbertson.'

Her shoes clipped up the stairs and along the landing. I heard the bedroom door opening, then raised voices. Doctor Grahams shouted, 'Get out,' and I stood at the bottom of the stairs watching her come down, looking completely unfazed. Today she was wearing a grey pinstripe skirt suit which was probably quite smart once, but now it was crumpled and appeared to have a patch of white dog or cat hairs across the lap of the skirt.

'Get the kettle on, Liam,' the Inspector ordered, and then said to me, 'If you don't mind, that is?' The '*Sugar Plum Fairy'* started to play in her pocket and she took out her mobile phone, going into the front room. We heard her raised voice.

'Somebody's getting a rollicking,' Rob said.

Deciding that whilst my mother may reign over the bedroom, I can at least assert myself in the kitchen, I abandoned my half-eaten croissant and took the kettle from Constable Liam. He looked around, confused, until Rob pointed to a chair and he sat at the table. He accepted a croissant from Rob and laid it on his plate, staring at it as though daring it to attack him.

The Inspector came back into the room, saying into the phone, 'Use last week's gym kit, they won't notice. See you later.' She cut off the phone and dropped it back in her pocket. 'Kids,' she said, looking at me and raising her eyebrows as she sat at the table. I stared back. I wasn't going to be her friend. She leaned across and took the croissant from Constable Liam's plate. 'You get off,' she told him as she took a bite. 'Check in with the Sergeant then take the rest of the day off. But I want you back here at five.' To me, she said, 'It's very important that I interview your mother.'

'Does she need a solicitor?' Rob asked.

‘Do you think she needs a solicitor?’ she asked him.

Rob flushed and I thought he was going to let her intimidate him – he’s not at his best with bossy women – but he took a deep breath and said, ‘I only meant that if you want to question her, she should have legal advice, that’s how it’s done, isn’t it?’ She shrugged. She’s one to watch, I thought.

Constable Liam had put on his uniform jacket and was pressing his gelled hair under his hat. The Inspector said, ‘Ask the Sarge to send me a bacon and sausage roll with the next officer.’ With a hurried ‘Ma’am’, Liam was gone, passing Doctor Grahams in the doorway. I raised the refilled cafetiere to the doctor and he gave me the thumbs up.

‘Yes please,’ said the Inspector, although she hadn’t been asked. She dropped a newspaper onto the table. ‘Thought you might want to see what they’re saying.’ She turned to the doctor. ‘So when can I interview Mrs Ibbertson?’

‘I can’t say at this stage.’ He put three heaped spoons of sugar into his coffee. ‘I’ll call in tomorrow and assess Mrs Ibbertson again.’

The Inspector rolled her eyes. ‘This may be a murder investigation.’

‘Officer, this may be a murder investigation,’ – as she flourished her ID card, he glanced at it and corrected himself without pausing – ‘Detective Inspector. Therefore, by implication, it may not? I’ll remind you that Mrs Ibbertson is a lady in her nineties who is suffering from shock and has had a bad fall.’ His words made me feel guilty for criticising my mother’s need for control. She was independent. Why shouldn’t she stay that way? Most of my friends’ parents had zimmer frames, wheelchairs, commodes… She lived alone, needed no carers and asked me for very little, except some gardening. I should be proud of her.

The Inspector's lips tightened. 'We are experienced in interviewing vulnerable people, Doctor,' she said. 'It would be acceptable for her daughter, or even yourself, to accompany her.'

'No and no, Detective Inspector. Mrs Ibbertson is absolutely not to be disturbed until you get the medical go-ahead. Do I make myself clear?'

Climbing the stairs with Mum's lunch, I smelled burning and hurried, placing the tray on the top step and hauling myself up by the banister, onto the small landing. I threw open the door to find Mum standing by the fireplace, her back to me. The bottom of her nightdress was on fire. At the sound of the door, she turned towards me and I saw that the flames were actually coming from a heap of torn and crumpled papers in the hearth at her feet. She was holding a lighted match against the scorched brown edge of more papers in her other hand. I pulled the pages from her, blowing at the corner to be sure they were out, at the same time stamping on the small fire in the hearth, causing a light grey ash to stick to my slippers. She snatched the papers out of my hand.

'It's only rubbish,' she said, turning to the bed where I could see a notebook lying open. I was nearer and reached it quicker. Picking the book up, I saw that several pages had been ripped out and guessed this was what I held in my hand. The open page was densely covered with Mum's precise handwriting. Loose papers were tucked between some of the leaves and as I flicked the edges, a small rectangle of paper fluttered to the floor. The writing stopped about two thirds through the book. The next half a dozen or so pages had been cut neatly out, then the rest of the book was blank. I closed the book and let my fingers trace the faded edges of a red rose embellished on the green velvet cover.

'Your diary?'

'Some old ramblings.' Mum grasped at the book and my hands instinctively tightened around it. The book felt intimate and precious. My mother had never shared anything from her past, with me, and here was something she had kept from me, something that may concern me, and she was trying to deprive me of it.

'Why are you burning it?'

'I thought it was time I started clearing out.' She looked around the room and sighed. 'I don't want you to have all the decisions about what to keep and what-not.'

'But your diary, can I?'

'No.' She pulled at the book. I wanted nothing more than to look at this book, and I pulled back. 'If you don't mind, Alice, it's private.' I looked down at her hands with the swollen blue veins criss-crossing the liver spots. I noticed her bent fingers and swollen knuckles. She never complained, although I often moaned to her about my various arthritic aches and pains. The wave of emotion that had gripped me left as fast as it had come and I felt unaccountably selfish. Abruptly I let go of the book. She wobbled and I thought she was losing her balance, but when I grasped her elbow she shrugged me off and held the book against her chest.

'It's not the best time, Mum, to be tidying up. If you'd told me you wanted to have a clear out, I'd have lent a hand. I can bring our shredder over for you.'

Hearing steps on the stairs, I picked up the scorched pages which Mum had dropped when she was trying to get the book from me. I folded them quickly and pushed them into the pocket of my cardigan. I saw the rectangle of paper that had fallen to the floor and stood on it as the door opened and the Inspector appeared, the tray held expertly on one palm.

'Someone left your lunch on the landing, Mrs Ibbertson?'

In that interval of no more than ten seconds, my mother had managed to get back into bed and was lying against the pillows, her eyes half-closed. The green book was nowhere to be seen.

'You're not supposed to be in here, Inspector,' I said.

'Oh, no need to stand on ceremony; this isn't an interview. And call me Claire.' She perched on the bed, her skirt riding up to reveal a broad ladder in her tights; a splodge of scarlet nail varnish halted its progress. 'It's a courtesy call, really.' Mum appeared not to have noticed her, and looked so frail that I found it hard to believe that I had been wrestling with her only moments before.

I was reasonably confident after the doctor's speech that the Inspector – Claire – shouldn't be here. I suspected this may be a trick. Apart from Judy being brought home by the local beat bobby at fourteen, when her group of friends was caught smoking in the allotments, I've never had anything to do with the police. Rob might know how to deal with this pushy police woman, but he'd gone home to pack an overnight bag for me. I considered phoning him but this would mean going downstairs and leaving her alone with Mum.

I was still working out what I should do, when Claire continued, 'I'm doing a press conference in half an hour or so and it's only right to tell you what I'll be saying, before you see it on television or the papers, and so on.'

Mum was looking into the middle distance from beneath half closed eyelids. I held out my hands for the tray and waited for Claire to cross the room and hand it to me, so that I could keep my left foot on the floor. As I took the tray from Claire's hands and placed it on the dressing table beside me, she helped herself to a slice of Battenburg from the plate. I picked up the cup and saucer and Claire took it from me, saying, 'Let me'. She held the cup and saucer out to Mum who made no effort to take it from her.

'I've spoken to the forensic archaeologist,' Inspector Claire went on.

'The young woman with the red spikes?'

'I know,' Claire rolled her eyes. 'They look younger all the time. Makes me feel ancient.' She took a bite of Battenburg and sipped from Mum's cup of tea. 'She's not able to do a formal report yet but she says it's a young woman. There since the nineteen forties, she thinks.'

'How does she know that?' I asked. Mum's eyes were completely closed but her fingers plucked at the eiderdown, as though trying to pick the small, white roses.

'Clues from the site. Various bits of clothing-'

'I thought you'd only found bones. You mean there are clothes?'

Claire looked from me to Mum while she finished her snack. She passed me the empty cup. 'Not much, fragments really, you know the sort of thing – a gabardine, a bit of canvas that could have been a bag. Oh, and a gas mask. That's a pretty big clue.'

'What did you mean by 'the site'?'

'Oh, didn't I say? It's an Anderson shelter.'

'What is?'

‘Where the remains were found. The report says it’s an old Anderson shelter. Well, I should say the ruins – it’s been destroyed at some point, and buried.’

‘Under the rockery?’

‘Seemingly.’

‘Nineteen forties? So, wartime then? Was it a bomb maybe?’

‘We don’t know yet, but that’s a possibility.’ Claire stood, pushed down her skirt until the ladder disappeared. ‘You don’t know anything about an old shelter in the garden?’ I shook my head. ‘Well, your mother may remember it.’ She was watching Mum whose eyes were still closed but now she had one hand over the other as if to keep it still. ‘I mean, it isn’t the kind of thing you miss, is it? Your mum lived here all her life?’ I nodded. ‘So she was here during the War?’ I nodded again. ‘Thought so. Could you have a chat with her, hmm? When she wakes up. Find out about this shelter? When it was built – thirty-nine, forty-ish, obviously, but when exactly? And when it was destroyed, and so forth? That would help us a lot.’ At the door, Claire turned and looked at the hearth. ‘Still got a working fireplace? Nice. Burning something?’

I kept my hand over my pocket so the bulge of the papers was not visible. ‘Only a few scraps, old receipts, that kind of thing.’

Claire shrugged and said, ‘Well, let us know what your mother says?’ She turned in the doorway and looked past me to Mum. ‘Remember it’s a crime scene, Mrs Ibbertson. No more burning any papers.’

As the Inspector’s feet clipped back down the stairs, I bent and picked up the small square of thin, tissue-like paper from under my slipper. It opened with a crackle and I saw that it was a single sheet with a ragged edge where it had been torn from a notebook. Tiny handwriting crammed both sides of the page, the ink blurred as though it had been wet and had run, making it difficult to read. I made out, *"29th May, 1940, My Dear Violet"*.

'Alice?' Mum's voice made me jump. I pushed the paper beneath the crocheted doily on her dressing table. 'Could we have a fresh cup of tea, do you think?'

I came back to find Mum sitting up, and popped the tray on the bed in front of her. She ignored the tea and sandwiches and picked up the mail that I'd collected from the doormat. In the kitchen just now, waiting for the kettle to boil, I'd replayed the events of the morning in my mind. Despite her bruises, which still flashed an angry blue-pink, and the doctor's belief that she was too ill to be interviewed by the police, Mum seemed able to get to the bathroom, and could clearly hop in and out of bed when it suited her. As I watched her sifting through the post, making two neat piles, I thought that apart from being in bed – a place I'd never seen her before; I couldn't remember her being ill enough to be confined to bed – she looked her normal composed self. So I was puzzled and a little awed by her performance for Claire. The term 'passive aggressive' came to mind, a phrase that Judy told me means getting what you want by doing nothing, or acting as though you want something else. Judy said I was simply passive, by which I gathered she meant standing around like a spare part trying to think of something clever to say. As Mum passed me a handful of flyers, I came full circle, feeling mean for even beginning to question her when her life was in turmoil because of me and my grand ideas for a garden makeover. I pointed to the leaflets and the local free newspaper that she had put on one side. 'Are those for recycling?'

‘Not yet, I want to check them for vouchers.’ I lifted the tea from the tray and she obediently took it from me and sipped. I dragged the Lloyd loom chair across to the bed and sat. She had set the cup and saucer back on the tray.

‘What’s this about an Anderson shelter?’ I asked. ‘I don’t remember it.’

She picked up and studied an envelope from her other pile, turning it over and peering at the sender’s address. After a long pause, she said, ‘It was gone long before you were old enough to have noticed it.’ She waved the envelope towards the dressing table and I followed her line of sight to the bone-handled letter opener. It was a gift we’d bought her during a stopover in Qatar last year; it pleased me no end that she actually used it. Hearing the Inspector’s voice from the garden, I crossed to the window where I looked down on Claire, who was being shown the contents of a plastic bag by the spiky-haired woman. I couldn’t make out their words and I couldn’t see what they were examining. I looked back at Mum who was holding out her hand, passed her the letter opener from the dressing table and sat back in the chair.

‘But I was what, nearly five before the War ended. I’m sure I would have remembered a shelter.’

She tore the envelope open and pulled out what looked like a utility bill. ‘We used a Morrison shelter. It went under the table. Mother and I would make up a bed and that’s where we slept, whenever there was an air raid. You slept between us.’

‘I think I might remember that – was it some kind of cage? I don’t know if it’s a real memory or a photo I’ve seen. But if we had an Anderson shelter, why didn’t we use it?’ She was studying the bill as though it was far more interesting. I resisted the temptation to carry on talking and eventually she looked at me as if surprised that I was still there. 'Why didn't we use the Anderson shelter?' I repeated. Mum busied herself straightening her bed-jacket and brushing a speck of invisible dust from the sleeve. Eventually she said, 'It must have been in the wrong position. The rain running off the hill flooded it. We couldn't use it.' She put the bill on the tray. 'Bring my cheque book would you, Alice, from my bureau drawer.'

I wasn't going to be dismissed quite so easily. 'Did Joe build it?'

She looked at me as though it was the stupidest question. 'No, of course not. Daddy and Richard built it.' She thought for a moment then added, 'Your father and grandfather. The weekend the War started.' She pushed the tray away from her, impatiently, and tea sloshed into the saucer. 'Daddy was terribly upset that it couldn't be used.' I took the tray and placed it on the dressing table. I looked beneath the doily. The letter had gone.

'So how do you think this lady, whoever she is, got into the Anderson shelter?'

There was a long pause. I said nothing. That was something else Judy had taught me – don't keep talking, filling the spaces, keep your mouth shut and you'll be surprised what people say. Maybe half a minute went by, and all she said was, 'I don't know.' So much for psychology, Judy.

'Could she have been a passer-by?'

'I suppose she might. Yes, that could be it. A passer-by.'

'Is it possible that she was passing by when the air raid siren went off, and needed somewhere to shelter?' She didn't reply. My thoughts ran on; I was beginning to be intrigued by my own imaginings: what might have brought a strange young woman to shelter in our garden? Who was she? 'Wouldn't she have knocked on the door or something? Asked to use your shelter?'

I was surprised to see Mum's eyes were wet and reached across to hold her hand, but she shook me off and started again with that strange movement with her fingers, plucking the roses. 'It was quite acceptable to use a shelter wherever you could,' she said. She looked out of the window, as though remembering. 'There was so much noise those nights, with the air raids in full swing, we wouldn't have heard her.'

'But wouldn't she have noticed that it was flooded?'

She said nothing for several seconds. I found myself thinking aloud, 'Maybe she was desperate. Maybe it wasn't so badly flooded? You know, if there hadn't been any rain…' Mum looked at me, her lips tightly pressed together but her eyes shining with tears. 'What if,' I said, leaning towards her, 'What if she was passing by, away from home, when the siren went off, and she needed somewhere to shelter? She would have thought she was safe. Not knowing it was going to be the worst place. The poor lady. I wonder who she was.' Then it occurred to me, 'Surely you'd have seen her when you went out the following morning? You'd have seen that the shelter had been bombed and looked–'

Mum waved a hand at me. 'Goodness Alice, so many questions! You're forgetting how chaotic everything was.' She closed her eyes and was silent for so long that I wondered if she had fallen asleep and was about to leave when she said, very quietly, as though to herself, 'So dirty. Bricks, rubble, dust everywhere. The pavement all broken up. Gosh, such a lot to tidy up. And the smell…'

‘And you had me of course.’

She opened her eyes and looked at me for a second without recognition. Then said, ‘Oh yes, of course. You were, what? A few days old. No, we wouldn’t have gone into the garden to check on the Anderson shelter. No reason to. We could look out of the window and see it was a wreck and that was that.’

It was so unbearably sad to think about that young woman lying injured, alone and terrified in what must have been such a cold, dark place. My thoughts spoke aloud, ‘And her family would never have known what happened to her.’ I was startled to see Mum was shaking with sobs, tears pouring from beneath her spectacles, running down the two deep grooves that ran from the bridge of her nose to the corners of her mouth. She pulled a handkerchief from the cuff of her bed-jacket, took off her spectacles and covered her eyes with the handkerchief in her trembling hands. This time she didn’t resist when I reached out to comfort her. As ever, I towered over her, my arms easily circling her small shoulders. Minutes passed while I breathed her familiar perfume of tea rose. Then she pushed me away, blew her nose and put her spectacles on.

‘Do remember the cheque book, Alice.’

Dismissed, I picked up the tray, as questions fought one another for a place in my mind. I imagined a young woman sheltering in the cold and dark, unknown to us in the house, unknown for, what, seventy years, more? At the door, I turned back. Mum’s eyes were closed. She looked exhausted.

‘How did it become the rockery?’

Opening her eyes, she looked towards the window and said, 'We left it there, covered it up as best we could, Mummy and I.'

'But what about scrap metal? Wasn't that important during the War? Couldn't you have had it taken away?'

Her eyes went back to the patch of clear blue sky beyond the window. 'I suppose you're right, but to be honest, the shelter reminded me so much of Richard and poor Daddy. I didn't want to deal with it. So I put some earth over it, and a few flowers around it.' She gave a long sigh. 'I'd only been married to Richard for six months when he joined up and he didn't come home again.'

'My father?'

'I had nothing to remember him by.'

'And that's how it became the rockery? A kind of memorial?'

She pulled herself up in the bed and looked at me. 'You could say that, yes, I suppose it was. For a long time, it was a bumpy bit of the garden that we kept you away from, because it might be dangerous. One day, Joe brought some rocks back from the Peak District – I know you're not supposed to, but in those days, no one noticed if you filled your car boot with boulders. And so we turned it into the rockery.'

'Was there any bomb damage in the house?'

'No, we were lucky.'

'I thought you said there was a lot of mess?'

She tutted. 'I meant in the streets of course. Now,' she picked up the free newspaper and opened it. 'If you could bring me my cheque book and pen, Alice.'

In the kitchen, I poured the untouched tea down the sink and looked across the devastation that was the garden. I had a sense of opportunities lost. My mother was so full of sorrow for the poor woman in the Anderson shelter. Intimate conversations had never been a feature of our relationship. Perhaps I hadn't been the most sensitive daughter. She may have found it hard to communicate her needs. This is the kind of language that my daughter uses. Judy grew up in the sixties, embraced the feminist movement in the seventies and brought up her own children with a permissiveness that I found alarming. I always enjoyed a close relationship with Judy, so different from my own relationship with my mother. I don't know where I learned to be such a different parent. Even now, affection seemed more than I could offer my mother, or more than she would allow. Mum must have been utterly disconcerted by the events of the past twenty-four hours, and I reminded myself again that I had only myself to blame for this crisis. It may have been better for everyone if the shelter had retained its secrets, at least during my mother's lifetime.

Rob bustled in with the holdall he had packed and brought from home. He picked up the junk mail from the tray and piled it neatly beside the coalscuttle for burning. Over coffee, I told him about the conversations with Claire and my mother.

'There'll be a record online,' he said. I could tell he was excited to find he may have a role in this drama. Adam had often joked with Rob about being a 'silver surfer'. Rob loved the internet and liked to be up to speed with the latest technology. 'I'll have a look when I get home.'

I wondered aloud whether my mother could be persuaded to live with us.

'Invite her, by all means,' Rob said. 'But you know it's unlikely.'

He was right. I don't think she even went away for a honeymoon. I remembered when Rob and I came home after our honeymoon in the Lakes. Mum invited us round for Sunday lunch. Joe wanted to know what Rob thought about the new motorway.

'It's very fast.' Rob told him. 'Have you been to the Lakes?'

'Oh, we're not the holidaying sort,' Joe said.

'Not even for a honeymoon?' I'd asked.

'No,' Joe said, and Mum, coming in from the kitchen carrying the roast chicken, said, 'We had neither time nor money after the war, for honeymoons.'

'What about your first marriage?' I asked Joe. Before he could answer, there was a crash. Mum had dropped the meat platter. I helped her clean up the spilled juices. I knew very little about my step-father's previous life; I was six years old when he married my mother and I had few memories that didn't include him.

Unpacking the holdall Rob had brought for me, I was reminded why I did all the holiday packing. He'd put in a pair of thick socks but no change of underwear. And he'd packed the nightie he bought me for Christmas longer ago than I care to remember; had he not wondered why I never wore it? I decided to sleep in the narrow single bed that still occupied one side of the large front bedroom. The settee may have been more comfortable but I didn't want to be far from Mum. This was the bedroom I took over from my grandma when she died. It didn't occur to me to think it strange that my mother chose to stay in the smaller, back bedroom, even when she married Joe.

Pushing my clothes into the tallboy drawer, I was surprised to find a blue and white plastic flower at the back. I couldn't place it for a moment. I held it to my nose, between my index and first finger, trying to identify its distinct smell - rubber and something like bleach… chlorine. It was one of the flowers from my swimming hat. I sat back on the red PVC chair and held the flower above my ear. I could see in the dressing table mirror that even though my hair was now white, this cornflower blue was still my colour. Twizzling the flower between my fingers, I looked around at this museum of my youth, remembering.

The geometrically striped wallpaper was the very height of fashion in its time. Joe took my side and persuaded Mum that I needed something more modern than the little flowers that had adorned the walls while I was growing up. Joe and I decorated it together. He didn't change anything when he moved across the landing. I was sad that he didn't live to see Judy grow into a teenager who thought this room was a treasure trove of full circle skirts and other fifties fashions that had been created especially for her. She and Joe would have loved one another's company. It was Joe who bought the Dansette for my fifteenth birthday, and followed it with a 45 record every Friday that he bought on his way home from work: Buddy Holly, Bill Haley, all the latest sounds, and all still on the shelf above the bed, leaning against his collection of Western comics. It was Joe who encouraged me to bring friends round and try out the latest jive moves; he'd push back the table, roll up the carpet, and swing me around the front room. My friends thought Joe was the coolest stepfather ever. Mum wasn't interested; she would find an excuse to go out. Even so, she had never seen fit to clear out this room. Within days of Judy leaving home, I had turned her room into a glory hole full of hobbies, spare clothes and even the ironing, yet Mum had managed to keep this room tidy, clean and dusted.

Thinking about growing up and even growing old in the shadow of my mother's apparent immutability, and the reminder that she was now very frail, gave me a sharp tug of panic. My mobile phone rang from my cardigan pocket, bringing me back with a start. I dropped the flower into my lap and took out the phone.

It was Rob, ringing from home.'Are you on your own?' He sounded excited.

'Yes.' The clock beside the bed said seven o'clock.

'Right-oh, I thought I should tell you this straight away.' I picked up the clock and was surprised to hear it ticking. So Mum wound it regularly. It unsettled me a little, thinking of my mother caring for this room as though it were a kind of shrine – but to who? Me? Joe? I was surprised by this aspect of my mother, a kind of nostalgia that I hadn't suspected.

'Are you still there?' Rob asked.

'Sorry, what did you say?'

'I'm coming over in a while with a Chinese, but I might not get to see you on your own, so thought I'd better phone. What do you fancy? Your usual?'

My stomach growled at the thought of prawn stir-fry. 'That would be lovely.' I put the clock down and walked across to the window. Rob's opening gambit penetrated my reflections. 'But what did you want to tell me that couldn't wait?'

'That information your mum gave you? About the shelter being bombed?'

From the window, I saw the television van had left. There was no longer a police officer outside the house and the blue and white tape had gone.

Rob continued, 'I've been looking on the internet. There's a website about the Sheffield Blitz, did you know?' This was Rob in his element – despite his chit chat with Liam, people scared him; he loved facts and figures. 'There's a map,' he went on, 'with little red dots for all the bombs that fell on Sheffield. Well, the thing is, there were no bombs there, on Hurdle Hill.'

'But Mum told me…'

'No, the nearest to you would have been further over Walkley way, off Liberty Road.'

I sat down heavily on the red chair, pushing my fingers along the PVC, making it squeak. I wondered aloud, 'Maybe some bombs didn't get recorded?'

'I doubt it.' Ever the bureaucrat, Rob has total confidence in official records. 'Listen, it says here, "*nearly six hundred people killed, three thousand shops and houses destroyed*". I suppose it's feasible that one person was unaccounted for, so maybe nobody came looking for our lady. But it doesn't explain the destruction of the Anderson shelter. Every single bomb has been recorded, from the records at the time, and all the unexploded bombs found since. Whatever destroyed your Anderson shelter, it wasn't a bomb.'

Frank

Perth Airport

Amy's itinerary: *"Four hours wait in Perth. Do not leave the airport. Follow signs to 'Transit'. Stay in the transit lounge."* The stewardess walks with me. I wonder if Amy phoned and asked her to make sure I don't get lost. Even if I did, I've got four hours to find my way again. Anyway, I'm here now, quite comfortable, with plenty to eat and drink, and the newspapers. In one of the English papers, I find a little paragraph at the bottom of page seven. I don't suppose it's interesting news to most people – the world's full of bigger tales – but this is my story. If I asked any one of those fellas dashing past with their little pull-along business cases, they'd probably reckon I was fretting about things that happened so long ago that the outcome can't make a difference. But it'll make a difference to me.

'*Skeleton may be war victim'*, it says. She certainly was a war victim, but I'm not sure it was in the way they mean. *'Forensic archaeologists have established that the human remains were buried in a ruined Anderson shelter. She could have lain here unknown to the occupants of the house –'* I'm starting to think that's not likely.

I've put my watch back one and a half hours, like the stewardess explained. Now, it's the same time I left Adelaide, and there's a chunk of my life that has ceased to be. I wish I could do the same with the last seventy years and be there when Jean needed me.

It says she's still too ill to be interviewed by police. She won't have any idea that I'm on my way. She probably thinks I'm dead. I remember that Anderson shelter. I helped them to build it, while I had time on my hands with no school. Our teacher had enlisted, so they joined our class with the infants. By dinner time the teacher had enough of us and told us to go home until they could make proper arrangements. Sam and me went to the river to get on with building our dam. On the way I told him about our Jean getting married.

'Will tha get her bedroom?' he asked. I hadn't thought of that. A bedroom of my own. Suddenly there was something to be said for Jean getting wed.

We got to the river and were busy building our dam when Sam yelled out and grabbed his arm. A trail of rusty blood-red clay ran down his sleeve. There was a cheer and I spotted Ernie Culshaw's ginger head disappearing under the old bridge and heard his sidekick Billy Roberts giggling. We gathered up mud and grass with maybe a few stones mixed in, and made a pile of cannonballs which we placed on the bridge wall. We hunkered down, peering over the wall for what seemed ages before first Billy stuck his head out and looked about, then Ernie came out and climbed up the bank. As soon as they were both in the open, we jumped up and pelted them with our mud balls. One hit Ernie smack on the nose and he started blubbing. I ran over the bridge and jumped on his back. He skidded down the bank and sprawled onto his face in the river. It wasn't deep but his mouth and nose were under water and he spluttered and kicked. Billy ran off.

I chanted at him, 'Cat's Eye, Cat's Eye.' Then I pulled his head up by his hair. He spluttered through the watery blood dripping from his nose, 'In me pocket'. Sam sat on

Ernie's legs while I went through his trouser pockets. There was a penknife, three ha'pence, a half-sucked gobstopper, and my marble. Throwing the other things onto the bank, I took the Cat's Eye and stood up, letting Ernie loose. Sniffing and dripping, he picked up his bits and pieces and ran off along the river path. I held the glass marble between my fingers and watched the blues and greens glinting in the sunlight coming through the trees.

'Let's head home, I'm hungry,' Sam said. We parted company on Beacon Street. In our yard, Mam was bringing in washing. The minute she saw me, she started ranting.

'Where the chuffing hell has tha been? There's a chuffing war on and a wedding coming and look at thy chuffing clothes, all covered in mud.'

She made me strip off my jersey and trousers then and there and scrub them at the sink. I was in the yard, jumping up, trying to reach the washing line when Mr Wreakes came out of his house and leaned against his door jamb watching me, sucking on his pipe.

'Them's a lovely pair of legs, young Frankie,' he said. 'I met a mam'selle or two in the Great War that didn't have legs as good as that.' He chuckled and this started him coughing. As he thumped his chest, the pipe flew out of his mouth and straight into the drain that ran down the middle of the yard. I couldn't help laughing. His face was like a hairy beetroot. 'Cheeky little bugger', he wheezed and lunged at me. Dodging round the sheets and under his arm, I ran in through our door, passing Mam as she came out to see what the racket was.

'Pick on somebody thy own size,' she said to Mr Wreakes. 'Thy missus for a start. Or does she stick up for herself?' This made me laugh again. She followed me into the kitchen and cuffed me, saying, 'Don't be so bloody cheeky.' She grabbed the trousers from me and went into the yard, pulling the prop away so the clothes line dropped down and she reached the line easily.

Jean came home from work, gabbling the minute she came through the door. 'It's all fixed. Joe's papers came and he's off on Thursday. We met his pal Richard at dinner time and went to see Registrar together.'

Mam said, 'Still intent on rushing things then?' She was pouring boiling jam into the jars standing in a line on the table while I cut out greaseproof paper circles for the tops.

I said, 'Mam? When our Jean gets wed can I have her bedroom?'

Jean said, 'Don't be soft, I shan't be leaving home. Not until War's over and Joe comes back. Then we shall find somewhere to live.'

This seemed a long time to wait and if Joe wasn't even going to be living with us I was hard pressed to see why she was bothering getting married at all. Mam took the pile of paper circles from me and popped them on top of the jars, covering them with little cloths.

She said, 'This Violet lass. What does she reckon to the plan?'

Jean said, 'I haven't met her. Joe says she works in the Bank, a secretary or something fancy.'

Mam passed me the string and the scissors and I started tying the cloth tops onto the jars. She looked at Jean and said, 'I don't want to be a wet blanket, but I reckon the lass might not be too chuffed. Having a double wedding's a big thing even with thy greatest pal.'

Jean said, 'Well, Richard is Joe's greatest pal. They're more like brothers than friends if it comes to it.'

Mam half-turned to me and wiggled the string round the necks of the jars to show they were loose. 'Tha can do them again,' she said then turned away and said to Jean, 'Well, I reckon we should show willing and try to get along with the family. Maybe me and Dad will go up and visit them.'

Jean pushed her finger round the top of one of the jars that wasn't yet covered and pushed the jam into her mouth. She said, 'Her Dad's thre'pence short of a shilling by all accounts. I should leave it to Joe to sort out.'

Mam said, 'I reckon we'll make the effort, show our appreciation.' I scooped up a fingerful of jam from the same jar and was about to put it into my mouth when Mam slapped it out of my hand. She said, 'Tha needs to get to know this Violet a bit, see if tha can't make friends with her.'

Jean said, 'We're going up for tea on Wednesday, before Joe leaves. We need to get the licence signed and back to the Registrar before then. Happen Frank can call round and pick it up?'

I said, 'Why can't our Cyril go? He wants to be a messenger.' This earned me a filthy look from both of them.

On Tuesday Mam said that seeing as there was no school I should read my book. So I sat on the bed reading *Robinson Crusoe* and keeping out of her way. She was fussing and cleaning such as I couldn't remember since my Nannan's funeral. I was downstairs getting a drink when Cyril came in, full of his new allotment idea, telling Mam how he could get free seed potatoes from the Town Hall. In the end, she said he could go to the Town Hall and put his name down.

She said, 'Tha'll be on Shanks's pony mind. I've no money for tram fares.' Then she seemed to forget that I was supposed to be getting educated and gave me a brush and bucket. 'Go and clean the privy. And mind tha gets rid of all the spiders.'

I stood on the wooden seat to brush off the top of the wall, under the roof, where all the cobwebs gathered. I knocked a fluffy white ball and hundreds of baby spiders fell out of it onto my face, making me spit and rub my eyes so I lost my footing and nearly fell down the pan. I grabbed at the top of the wall to steady myself, pulling some of the bricks loose with one hand. There was a gap behind, where the wall met the roof. This is what gave me the idea. I nipped upstairs, got *Robinson Crusoe* and my Cat's Eye, wrapped the blackout material round them and wedged the parcel behind the bricks. As I pushed the bricks back I heard a hissing from the gennel and jumped down to find Sam peering round. I beckoned him into the privy.

He said, 'Lady from Education has been. There's to be classes in people's houses until they get air raid shelters in schools.'

'What, a teacher coming to house?'

'I think so. Any road, my Mam said quick as lightning they could use our front room. I reckon she wanted to make sure I got there. So when lady comes here, get thy name down for ours.'

Mam was calling me. We went into the kitchen.

She said, 'Hello Sam, love, how's thy Mam?' Without waiting for an answer she turned to me. 'Here's that message for Richard. Now remember, tha calls him Mr Clarke. And remember, no thees and thas, make sure tha says you and yours. Tha says "Mr Clarke, will you please give me the special licence form for my Dad to sign". Has tha got it?'

I repeated the message twice to her satisfaction, then she made me memorise the address and the directions.

She said to Sam, 'Get off home now, Sam, I want Frank going straight up to Hurdle Hill and no messing about.'

She strung my gas mask box over my head then grabbed the comb and tugged at my curls until some more teeth broke off the comb and tears came to my eyes. As I walked up the street, she called me back and pushed a jar of jam into my coat pocket. She said, 'Give that to Mrs Knowles.'

The crosses on the windows had caught on and Liberty Street looked like a row of sums after my teacher had marked my book. On Hurdle Hill I looked back the way I'd come, right down to the works along the river. Except I couldn't see that far because only one or two of the tallest chimneys were to be seen above the grey smoke that sat on top of the houses all the way along the River Don. I knew that folk walking around down there would feel cold, because the sun never reached the ground when the works were at full throttle. I jumped around on the spot to look the other way down into the Rivelin Valley. Right at the bottom of a narrow road winding between the houses, was a patch of shining water that I knew was the river. I could see up the other side, over what looked like a forest of trees, and into the countryside, which stretched as far as I could see. I jumped back to look at the grey side, then back to the colour. It was like watching *Redskins* at the pictures – when it was the white man's land it was black and white, when it changed to the Indian's land it was in colour. As I jumped around for the third or fourth time, the jar of jam dropped through the hole in my pocket and smashed on the path. I pushed the mess into the grass with the side of my shoe and went on.

Hurdle Hill Terrace was posh. There were bay windows, most with lace curtains, doors painted in bright colours, and cars parked outside some of the houses. I found number fourteen but couldn't see a gennel so I knocked on the front door. After a few minutes, I was about to knock again when the door opened a crack and a little lady peered at me through round spectacles like the bottom of lemonade bottles. She looked me up and down without smiling, from my hair to my shoes and back again, with one eyebrow lifted like a question mark.

'I'm looking for Richard – I mean Mr Clarke.'

'And you are?' She opened the door a bit more and stood in the opening, as if she thought I'd run in if she left a big enough gap.

'Frank Sheldon, Miss.' She frowned at me and I said, 'Jean's brother.'

She closed the door again. I stood, not knowing whether to stay or leave. Then I heard a man's voice from inside the house, calling, 'Bring him in Violet' and the door opened again, barely wide enough to allow me through. I thought this must be the Violet that our Jean had been talking about. She looked right snooty and she was really little, only a bit bigger than me. I walked down a hallway and into a kitchen, where a lady sat in an armchair knitting with four needles and the same scratchy grey wool that our Jean used to knit my socks. Peering at me over her glasses, her lips clenched like she'd sucked on some cod liver oil, she looked so like Violet that I had to look behind me to be sure she hadn't magicked herself into the room in front of me. But there really were two of them. Violet put her hands on my shoulders and steered me past the other woman and through the door into the yard. Two men stood looking at a pile of curved, corrugated sheets of steel. The old man turned and smiled at me, his eyes twinkling under bushy black eyebrows that wriggled up and down like hairy caterpillars. He looked so comical I couldn't help smiling back.

The younger man said, 'Frank, is it?' With his collar and tie under a brown apron, and his moustache, he looked like the manager of the rolling mill who I met once when I took a message for my Dad. He said, 'Violet, shall we have lemonade all round?' Violet smiled at him then glared at me as she turned and went into the kitchen. I worked out this must be Richard.

He said, 'What do you make of this, Frank?' pointing to the heap of metal. 'It's a new garden shed.' I'd seen the council workmen unloading a pile of such steel at the end of most of the roads in Walkley in the summer, and I knew it was an Anderson shelter, but I reckoned either he might not know this or he might have got one off the back of the council lorry and was planning to use it as a shed. So I said nothing. He said, 'Come and see where we're going to put it.'

I'd thought the yard was about the same size as ours, but stretching after the yard was grass and rows of vegetables, and a wall with a wooden gate and Hurdle Hill rising up beyond it. There were no houses overlooking the yard, and hedges separated the houses on either side. It was like being in the countryside. An area of grass was marked out with wooden pegs and string. The old man lifted a spade that was leaning on the wall and started digging up the grass.

Richard said, ‘What do you think, Frank? This is where we’re thinking of putting the shed.’

Violet came up behind us holding a tray with a white jug and three glasses. She held it while Richard poured lemonade, passed a glass to me, and one to the old man who put down the spade. He was puffing and panting.

Violet said, ‘Are you all right, Daddy? You don’t need to do the digging. We can get someone in.’

He drank his lemonade in one long swallow, looking at me over the rim of his glass. He put the glass down and stood in front of me, squeezing my arms to check my muscles. ‘Have you come to help us, young man? You look too small to dig.’

I said, ‘I’ve got to get back to my Mam, Mister.’

Richard smiled and said, ‘Would you like to help us to dig the hole for the shelter and earn a couple of shillings?’

I thought quickly. Mam would be pleased with me for earning some money. There might be no school for weeks. I said, ‘I could come tomorrow afternoon.’

Violet said, ‘Richard, are you sure?’ looking me up and down again, as though she’d not seen anything quite like me before. She stared at my shoe and I looked down and realised that it was covered in jam. I wiped it off on the sock of my other leg. She curled her lip and looked away. ‘I’m not happy about having strangers in the house when Mummy and Daddy are on their own.’

Richard said, ‘Frank might be good company for your Father,’ and took a long drink from his glass. ‘And he’s not a stranger, he’s a family friend now, aren’t you Frank?’ When he winked at me I felt right important.

Violet picked up the tray and looked from it to me as if to tell me to hurry up. I emptied my glass straight down my throat as I’d seen Richard do, but the lemonade fizzed up into my nose, making me cough and sneeze all at once. Violet's Dad laughed and slapped me on the back. Richard handed me a big white hankie.

I remembered the message from my Mam and when I could speak I said, 'Mr Clarke, has tha got a special licence form for our Dad to sign?'

'Certainly. Violet, it's in my attaché case, in the hall. Could you get it?'

She said, 'Come along then,' and walked into the kitchen with the tray.

Richard said, 'So you'll come tomorrow, after school, to do some digging?'

I said, 'School's closed. I'll come after dinner.'

He nodded and raised a hand to me. I followed Violet through the kitchen, where the other lady was still sitting by the unlit fire, knitting.

Violet said, 'Mummy, this is Frank Sheldon. He'll be coming to help Daddy and Richard to put up the new garden shed.'

Now I was close up I saw her mam had wrinkles all round her mouth and her hair was grey. She said, 'Is he with the gypsies?'

Violet said, 'No, he's from the family – you know, Jean Sheldon is marrying Joe. This is her brother.' The way she said it I thought she might rather I was from the gypsies. The only other person I'd heard using 'Mummy' and 'Daddy' for their Mam and Dad was our teacher in infant class, Miss Broadhead, who came from down South. When I'd tried it at home my Dad said Miss Broadhead was a fancy piece and might give us ideas above ourselves. I wondered if my Dad would call Violet a fancy piece.

In the hallway, Violet picked up a brown leather case and rested it on the hallstand to open it. She pulled out a piece of paper and handed it to me. I folded it carefully and put it in my back pocket. She started to close the case, then stopped, put her hand in and picked something up. It was a small, black box. She opened it, and I saw a silver watch, its face the size and shape of a threepenny bit, with a narrow silver strap. When she moved it from side to side the white stones around the face caught the light and sparkled. I thought it was the kind of precious thing that Robinson Crusoe would have packed in his trunk to take on his sea voyage. She ran her fingertip around the watch face and looked up. I saw her reflection in the mirror. All the meanness dropped off her face when she smiled and she even looked a bit pretty, though nothing like as beautiful as our Jean. Then she caught sight of my reflection beside her. The smile slid off her face, she placed the watch back into its box, put it in the case and snapped it shut. With her hands on my shoulders, she spun me around, pushed me along the hall, and I found myself on the other side of the front door which slammed behind me.

Mam thought it was a good idea for me to help Mr Knowles. She said, 'Mind tha doesn't take any money, though,' spoiling it for me straight away. 'We shall owe the Knowleses enough with this wedding caper, and if tha's seen to help out, it'll go down very well for our Jean.'

Before I could argue, Cyril came in and started on again about his allotment plan. He said, 'They've said we can dig up the bowling green on Hurdle Hill. We'll have spuds, carrots and owt else we fancy.'

I went up to Hurdle Hill Terrace every afternoon for the rest of the week, helping Mr Knowles until tea-time, when

Violet came home and made it clear that it was time for me to leave. I dug carefully along the line of string and lifted the turf, then dug down about two feet.

On the second day, we were sitting on the bench, drinking a cup of tea that Mr Knowles had made, when he said, 'They're telling me it's a garden shed, Frank.' He tapped the side of his nose. 'I know it's an Anderson shelter. They're trying to keep this talk of war from me, but they leave things lying around.' He took a pamphlet from his pocket, which had a picture of the completed Anderson shelter and a diagram of how the parts fitted together. He said, 'Don't let on, will you?' I shook my head. He gave it to me and I put it in my pocket.

The soil was like clay and heavy so it was slow going and I was glad when Richard came one afternoon to help, saying it was early closing day. By the end of that day we had a rectangular trench that measured exactly ten feet long by four feet wide and three feet deep, exactly like the instructions in the diagram, although we were pretending that it was Richard's measurements that he had on a piece of paper. When it was finally built, Mr Knowles said to Richard, 'We've saved the turf to put it on the top as camouflage.' He winked at me when he said it. I noticed after that, Richard started calling it the shelter.

On the Friday, Richard came home as I was leaving and gave me a shilling. I tried, though not very hard, to refuse. As I walked down the street, I saw two people who looked familiar walking towards me. I was about to pass them when I realised it was my Mam and Dad. I stopped and stared. Because Dad had no cap on and his curly hair was springing up all over, and Mam didn't have her pinafore or scarf on, they looked like somebody else's mam and dad. Mam said, 'Thy face'll get stuck like that if wind changes,' as they walked past me and knocked at number fourteen. Violet opened the door and she seemed to be expecting them because she let them straight in, although I saw how she looked my Mam up and down from behind, as she turned to follow them into the house.

The following Monday I was back at Hurdle Hill Terrace, and found that over the weekend Richard had put wooden ends on the shelter, so it had started to look like a proper Anderson shelter. Mr Knowles passed me the squares of turf and I laid them over the top. He was a kindly old bloke but a bit forgetful. We became good pals. He'd stop half way through a sentence, glaze over and forget not only what he was saying, but who I was. I got used to this, and would nudge him and say, 'Frank,' and he'd say, 'Of course Frank, now, what were we doing, Frank?' and we'd be away again until he wandered off to look at his marrows or some such thing. Sometimes I found him staring up at Hurdle Hill with a frown on his face. Then, I'd pick up his hand and he'd look at me and smile, and come back to sit on the bench.

I took every opportunity to go the privy while I was visiting the Knowleses. It was outside but joined on to the house, so you had to go out of the kitchen, and back in at the next door. None of the other houses on the street shared this lav. I would pull the long chain and watch the water disappear along the pipe and into the ground, wondering where it went. The paper was like sheets of tracing paper in a box, so there was no ink on my hands afterwards. Even so, if Mrs Knowles saw me coming out she would tell me to wash my hands in the kitchen. One day Richard said to me, 'We're going to turn the smallest bedroom into a bathroom so we'll have an indoors lavatory, what do you think of that, Frank?' I thought my

Mam would have something to say about having a smelly old lav in the house.

It was better to be up at Hurdle Hill, out of the way of Mam and Jean with their carry on. If it wasn't cleaning or moving furniture around, it was cooking cakes and pies. Jean was getting more hysterical every day. She would be singing and twirling round the kitchen one minute, then crying the next. The latest panic was whether Joe would get home in time for the wedding. He was at training camp and expected to arrive on the Saturday morning, which Jean said was cutting it fine.

There was a lot of busyness at Hurdle Hill Terrace, too. But a woman called Mrs Swindon seemed to do all the work, while Mrs Knowles sat by the stove knitting a grey sock that got longer every day; or at the table reading the newspaper, cutting bits out and setting them on one side.

Mrs Swindon was as wide as she was tall and wore stockings that wrinkled round her ankles and a green hat like a tea cosy even though it was still more or less summer. I liked to watch her over the window sill. One day, without even looking in my direction, Mrs Swindon said, 'I've eyes in the back of my head, tha knows, and I'll be having a word with thy Dad if tha steps out of line'. So I kept away from her. Mr Knowles sat on the garden bench and I squatted by his feet. He said, 'We're better off here, Frank, out of their way.' Violet seemed to me to be like a top that I had when I was small, winding and winding as tight as she would go, but broken, so that instead of going faster she would wind up even further the next day. I thought it seemed a strange do, with a lot of work and not much fun, getting married. One afternoon I went into the house to ask for some twine for Mr Knowles to tie up his runner beans. In the hallway, I could hear a noise from the front room, where I'd not been before. I pushed open the door and saw Violet on her knees on the carpet, with her hands covering her face and pieces of blue cloth scattered all around. She was rocking back and forth and I thought she was laughing.

I said, 'Please, Miss,' and when she looked up I saw her mouth was full of pins, her eyes magnified by her spectacles were red and puffed up, and her face was blotchy pink. It was frightening. I closed the door again.

That day, as I left, she said to me, 'I think we can do without you, from now on, Frank. The shelter is all but finished.'

For the rest of that week, Mam had me running around, helping. I said, 'Why do we need to clean up if wedding tea's at the Knowleses?'

She said, 'Jean'll be bringing her young man home on Saturday and we'll give her nowt to be ashamed of.'

I said, 'Why can't Jean go and live with Joe's family?' I was still hoping for my own bedroom. Especially now both of my brothers had boots on all day and when they took them off at night it was like sharing a bed with a dead donkey.

Mam reminded me, 'He's not got any family to speak of', which I thought sounded like a right peaceful kind of life.

Alice

I was lying awkwardly across the narrow bed. My neck cricked noisily as I struggled to sit up. The scorched and creased pages of Mum's diary were scattered on the floor.

Rob stood over me, holding out a cup of tea. 'Bath running. Bacon and eggs downstairs when you're ready.' He helped me stand upright. 'Do you think we should cancel?' I had no idea what he was talking about. 'Cyprus.' Of course – we had a holiday booked for – 'Friday,' he said. It seemed like a decade ago that we'd decided on a late summer holiday – somewhere to relax once the garden makeover project was completed. He read my hesitation as reluctance. 'Unless you think this will be all sorted by then?' He waved an arm in the general direction of the back of the house, taking in Mum and the garden.

'No, you're right,' I agreed. 'Even if the investigation is over, I don't think it would be right to leave Mum on her own.' I swallowed the hot tea fast and waved a hand in front of my mouth to cool it as I passed the cup back to Rob.

'I wonder whether we're covered by the insurance,' he said. 'The illness of a nearest and dearest and so on. I'll ask the doctor when he comes – he might give us a certificate.'

'It doesn't really matter, in the scale of things, does it?' I was irritated by his parsimony. Taking the huff, he left without another word.

I collected the diary pages together, my mind still full of what I'd read during the night. After Rob had left, I'd pottered around in the kitchen, checking on Mum every now and then, until about ten o'clock when I thought I could close myself into a room without raising Constable Liam's suspicions. In fact, when I announced, 'Well, I think I'll be off to bed,' he just shrugged and I wondered if he thought I was so old I ought to have gone to bed much earlier. Before I was out of the room he had his phone out and was texting. I was about to say something about a girlfriend, but thought this might embarrass him and left him to it.

In my old room, Joe's room, I spent a couple of hours piecing together the remnants of Mum's diary and reading it. There was some scorching of tops and bottoms of pages, pieces torn off and missing. Some entries were in shorthand. I could decipher most of it. When Mum had finally accepted I wasn't going to university and really did want to do secretarial work, she'd spent night after night trying to teach me Pitmans. I'd never been very good, but remembered enough. I'd gone to bed, but couldn't stop turning it over in my mind, and sat up and read it all again.

cotton velvet with small white flowers, and insists on making my wedding costume, despite my insistence that I don't need her help. The first time she made me a costume was for the Whit Sunday Parade, ten years ago. She sewed the blouse onto the skirt the wrong way around, so I had to wear it with the bow at the front. I'm sure I looked ridiculous. I've made my own dresses since I could use a machine and I think I make a good fist of it if I say so myself. I shall just have to let her do it, then stay up after she is asleep, to re-work the seams as necessary.

1st September 1939
The newspapers are full of the possibility of war. I hope it doesn't spoil my special day. That sounds selfish I know. Richard is a Pacifist. He says he will not enlist no matter what. I know this means he is a man of high principles but I worry what people will think if he does not fight for his country. The Bank is very strict about employing people of good character and it may reflect badly on me. Daddy says Richard is right to stand up to jingoism. I thought it a lovely word and looked it up in the dictionary but it means "belligerent national policy" which is a frightening idea. The Daily Express believes the Government is right to stand up to Mr Hitler, who is certainly belligerent, so I am not sure what to believe. I tried to talk to Mummy and she says it's none of my business, I should support my future

diary and bought me this beautiful book, green velvet with a rose embossed on the front. I have spent the evening copying into it. Mummy says 'green should never be seen' and is unlucky but I rather like it. Richard joked that it should have been a violet but roses are my favourite.

They were testing the siren as we walked past the Town Hall at one o' clock today. Such a terrifying wail. Knowles Nee Knowles Violet Clarke nee Knowles. In elocution, Miss Wilson said it is pronounced neigh, and the way she said it, rather like a horse, made us laugh. I can't believe that in fifteen days I shall be Mrs Clarke. It is raining.

2nd September, 1939
If there is a war, which is looking more likely by the day, then I hope it will all start afterwards. "As if the world can stop for you," Mummy said, which made me feel rather mean. Just two weeks to go. Mrs Violet Clarke formerly Knowles. We received a letter from the hotel in Bakewell to say my postal order had arrived safely and they have reserved a suite overlooking the River Derwent. They said 'honeymoon suite' but I would rather not think about that. Instead, I will imagine walking beside the river in the moonlight with my husband – Oh, dear, there I go again, but I can't help feeling excited even though Mummy has warned me that I will be disappointed. Today, we took delivery of the Anderson shelter. Richard has told Daddy it is a new shed so he won't be worried about the possibility of war.

furious not to have been invited, although she won't admit as much of course. Lillian told me she has been asking all the girls if they have received their invitation yet. Of course they said yes, and according to Lillian, Jane became very red in the face. I smiled and turned back to my typewriter. Surely she doesn't expect me to pretend she is a friend after all she said about Richard? If the powers that be knew her father was passing on information he might find himself in hot water. Because he's an inspector of police, he thinks he's above the law.Richard explained it all to me. I can see it was a case of mistaken identity. Whatever is the world coming to when a man can't take an evening stroll in the park without his motives being misinterpreted? In thirty six hours Mr Chamberlain's ultimatum to Germany expires. The Daily Express is full of advice about what to do in the event of war with recipes

will be ruined by this war nonsense. It is also my twenty-first birthday, so should be the happiest day of my life and it is feeling less so day by day. Mummy and I were pinning the pattern to the fabric ready to cut out my suit while we waited for Mr Chamberlain to come on the wireless. As expected, Mummy has made a hash of the bias-cut facings even though I left Elizabeth Craig open at the very page. I can hear Richard arriving.

I can't believe it. Not only is my wedding to be spoiled by the war, but Richard has decided we will have a double wedding with his friend Joe and his fiancée. Apparently because Joe has enlisted he is in a terrible rush to marry. I know Richard treats Joe like a brother, since their fathers were together in Daddy's regiment, but this really is the limit. I have only met Joe once and although he seems a pleasant enough young man, it's difficult to see what they have in common. Joe's fiancée (Jean is the name she goes by) is a lovely girl by Richard's account but that is not the point. I don't know her at all. Richard might have consulted me before making arrangements. Mummy found me crying when I was making the cocoa and she said mean by setting too much store by things'. She says I ought to be glad to have found a husband with good prospects and who is unlikely to enlist, as I will have a better life than she did as a result of the last war.

Richard and I have walked on Hurdle Hill every Sunday during the summer, watching the houses being built across the valley. I estimated we could save the deposit in six months. Now it seems the houses won't be built "for the duration", which means until after the war. I was so looking forward to having a home of our own. Richard is calm about it, but of course, anything will be better than his lodgings. I've never met his landlady but he describes her as an awful dragon. Mummy is happy that Richard will be living here, but I look around my little room and – I would rather not think of it.

4th September 1939
Daddy is in a bad way. He had an attack of what Mummy calls his 'terrors'. She says the Great War ruined her life. It was a rare confidence, although of course I have always known that Daddy's nerves have never been the same since the war. "If only he had lost an arm or a leg," Mummy said today. "It would have been so much easier than losing his mind." I think that a cruel thing to say. Richard will be here soon. He is able to calm Daddy down. He will take him into the garden and encourage him to concentrate on his vegetables.

Daddy spent all day counting the screws and placing them into neat pile. Then I found him looking at the plan for the Anderson shelter, though where he found it, I don't know. So he isn't fooled by talk of a new garden shed.

I can barely contain my excitement. I'm sure I wasn't meant to see it. I was looking for the wedding licence for Joe and Jean, in Richard's attaché case. They sent Jean's brother to collect it. I think he may be retarded from the way he stares with his mouth open. Anyway, in the case I found the most beautiful watch. It is silver, with precious stones around the face. I feel terrible to have been so cross about sharing our happy day. I had begun to feel there was no love or romance, only duty and practicalities. Mummy talks of Richard as though he is an investment rather than a son-in-law. Even Lillian said: "you've done well for yourself". Then this business with the police made me feel – but I was wrong. Richard does have affectionate feelings for me after all. The newspaper says there may soon be a shortage of coal and electricity, so I must remember to buy candles.

5th September, 1939

Jean likes the cinema and dancing. She told me the cinemas have been closed. She is sad about this. She asked had I seen "Dawn Patrol". She said there is an actor called David Niven who is the 'spitting image' of Richard. Luckily Richard wasn't listening. He would disapprove of being compared to a war character, being a Pacifist. Jean asked how Richard and I had met and when I told her, she called it a "whirlwind romance". It is true it is only eleven months since we met at the Regimental Dinner and so maybe the situation seems to have moved rather rapidly. When I see it through Jean's eyes, it does look romantic. I am truly beginning to look forward to my wedding and

Alice

I was fascinated and frustrated by these glimpses of a young woman looking forward to her marriage while everything and everyone seemed intent on ruining the romantic time that she yearned for. I'd stood at the front bedroom window, trying to imagine my mother as I had never known her. I wanted to believe her marriage to my father had been happy, even though it was short. As the trees along the Rivelin Valley started to emerge from the darkness – a line of inky blue silhouettes signalling dawn – I was still searching my memory for a single glimpse of Violet the girl in the mother I knew. I failed to find her. So I doubted the outcome had been a happy one.

On my way to the bathroom I peeked around Mum's door. She appeared to be asleep but I knew she'd wake if I went in. I'd been in a couple of times during the night and if she was dozing, she snapped awake immediately, pulling up the covers like a child hiding something from sight, so I suspected she'd got her diary under there. Clearly, she'd not forgotten that unseemly tug of war yesterday, when I'd tried to get it from her. She must have expected me to creep up on her while she was asleep in order to steal it. She wasn't wrong. I was even keener to get a look at the rest of the diary after reading those few pages. I knew I should feel ashamed at my blatant disregard for her privacy, but I justified to myself that I had already invaded her privacy by reading some of the pages. I lay in the water – bless Rob, he had brought a bath bomb from home and the musky smell filled the room –

with my mind running on in this circular fashion as it had for much of the night.

In the kitchen Claire was already seated at the table with a plate of bacon and eggs in front of her, pouring herself a cup of tea. She seemed to have a food-sensing radar. Liam was looking on rather sadly and I realised it was for him that Rob had cooked the breakfast.

'You can get off home,' Claire said to Liam and he nodded goodbye to Rob and me as he left. Claire ate heartily while I pushed the bacon around my plate and related my mother's account of how the Anderson shelter was flooded and never used. I went on to describe how a passer-by might have sheltered there on one of the nights of the air raids, and that it must have been hit by a bomb. Rob and I agreed last night that although we have a lot of questions, it was this version of likely events that we would tell the police. Claire appeared to be listening while she ate, then, reaching for a slice of toast she said, 'That's all very well, but I had one of my team do some background research and he told me there weren't any bombs here.'

Rob and I looked at one another and when I saw Claire looking at me, I blushed like a teenager.

'To be fair,' she said, shrugging, 'That's what we thought at first. But seemingly the closest bombs were in Walkley. All along Liberty Road and a good number in the streets behind, but not around here.'

'Surely not all the bombs were recorded?' Although Rob had poo-pooed this idea, I decided it was worth hazarding with Claire. 'We wondered whether it might have been a stray bomb?'

Claire shook her head as she buttered a slice of toast and took a mouthful. We waited. Rob sat down and started to eat his own breakfast. Claire spread marmalade on the second half of her toast. We waited. She seemed to be enjoying the anticipation. She finished her toast, took a sip of tea and said, 'The forensic archaeology woman – seems to know what she's doing – she reckons–' se stopped and looked from one to the other of us '–that the sheets of steel were lying across the hole.' Delving into her bag she located a little Chinese silk lipstick case, the sort with a mirror in the lid, and examined her face, checking her teeth for stray food. She carefully reapplied the scarlet lipstick, pressed her lips together, and delivered what I realised was a punch line of sorts. 'In other words, it wasn't bomb damage that destroyed your shelter. It was a person.'

I knew I should look surprised, but my mind was spinning with the details Mum gave me and which I couldn't believe she got wrong. There must have been an air raid. She was so specific about the sights and the smells that she convinced me completely that she had been there, caught up in it all. When Rob told me about his research last night, I'd said, 'But Mum remembered it. There's nothing wrong with her memory. How else could it have happened? The reports must be wrong.'

Rob had still been confident that the records were accurate, but he agreed to double-check. He said there were some first person accounts in the city archives that might give more details, and he was going to phone them as soon as they were open. Claire had arrived before he had the chance.

She closed her handbag and slung it across her shoulder as she stood up; looking at us, waiting for a response.

Rob said, 'You mean it was taken apart, not blown apart?'

Claire nodded approvingly at him. 'Exactly. "Deconstructed" is the word she uses, but you've got it. So we're not setting any store by the bomb theory.' The *Sugar Plum Fairy* burst forth from her pocket. She pulled out her mobile phone, looked at the screen and answered it as she went into the hall.

Either Rob or Claire had brought in the daily newspaper. I pulled it towards me and skimmed the first few pages to give me thinking time. Already, we'd been relegated to page seven of *The Mail* and I was relieved. Rob put a hand on my shoulder and squeezed; we read the article together, silently: *Skeleton May Be War Victim.* There was a photograph of the house, and that was probably me, looking out of a gap in the lace curtain, but it was too indistinct for anyone to recognise me, I was sure.

Rob whispered, 'Curiouser and curiouser, Alice.' It was an old joke but I couldn't smile. 'Sorry old fruit,' he went on. 'It seems we can't pull the wool over this one's eyes, and we have to admit your ma is cannier than she seems.' I nodded. 'Any luck with the diary?' An avid reader of crime novels, Rob was much taken with the idea that the diary held the clue to the identity of the poor woman. 'Bound to,' he'd said. 'Why else would she have squirreled it away?'

Rob had always been cynical about my mother's motives. Whereas I lived in awe of her wit and intelligence, Rob thought her snobbish and manipulative. Where I was used to not coming up to her expectations, he said she put me down. When I chose to go to secretarial college she made her disappointment clear. Though she did spend time helping me learn shorthand, which came in very useful. Later, I remember telling her I'd found a job with a cabinet-making firm in Sidney Street. She was furious.

'Work in a factory?' she said.

'It's in the office,' I said, thinking she'd be proud.

'Even so, Alice, a factory,' she said with contempt.

I met Rob there; he was in the accounts department and doing his accountancy exams. After we married, he started his own business, with me doing the back-office side of things, so from my point of view the job worked out well. I suppose she wanted the best for me, don't all mothers? She was a secretary in a bank, where she rose to be the manager's personal assistant. It was probably one of the best careers that a young woman of her social class and education could hope for at that time. She worked full time, and ran the house like a production line, from which Joe and I popped out neat, tidy, and on time every morning. Joe joked that she made a better sergeant major than he ever had. She was right to boast about her sewing prowess in her diary – she'd made all our clothes. Often I fell asleep to the thrumming of her sewing machine below my bedroom. Then she would be in the kitchen in the morning, with the fire laid, Joe already packed off to work and my breakfast and lunchbox on the table. At eight-fifteen on the dot, she would pop on her hat and coat and we would walk up the hill to Crookes where she caught the tram to work and I waited for the school bus. When I came home from school, Joe would be ready with tea and biscuits but he was not allowed to start cooking the supper as this was Mum's domain. We would spend a happy hour, playing card games – our secret – before I ran to meet her from the tram, to carry the shopping which she did in her dinner break.

Rob had often said he was relieved that I didn't take after my mother. She terrified him when we first met. When I talked about how wonderfully organised she was, he said I was mistaking duty for affection. I told him she was typical of mothers in the forties and fifties, but he would shrug it off. Even growing up in a children's home, an orphan of the War, Rob said he experienced more love than he thought I did from my mother.

We'd been restricted in what we could say last night with Liam present. He told us this was his first 'family liaison' role and he was thinking of applying to join CID so he could do more of it. Rob had brought enough Chinese takeaway to share and it had been like entertaining the grandchildren. We were becoming fond of Constable Liam.

The 'Joe' that Mum mentioned in her diary must have been my stepfather. I knew he'd been married before, but it seemed odd that he was my father's best friend, rather like those old customs where it's expected that men would marry their brother's widow. I wanted to know what happened to Joe's fiancée, Jean, and whether the plans for a double wedding ever came to anything. I phoned Rob from my room and read the entries to him. He reminded me of the exchange that Mum and Joe had when we returned from our honeymoon.

'If this is the same Joe, and it certainly makes sense,' Rob said, 'then Jean must have been Joe's first wife. And the wedding would have been the four of them, your mum and Richard, Joe and Jean. But in that bit you read about Bakewell, your mother was obviously expecting to go on a honeymoon. I got the impression that day, way back, when we were talking about honeymoons, that she didn't go.'

‘Maybe I could ask her, remind her of that day, and ask her what happened to stop her going.’ Of course, I knew I would never ask her and she would never tell.

We were left with far more questions than we’d started with and I found myself agreeing with Rob that the answers would probably be in the rest of the diary, and thinking up ways of getting hold of it.

‘She hasn’t been to the bathroom all night,’ I told him. ‘In fact now I think about it, I can’t remember her being out of her room since yesterday morning before the doctor came.’ I wondered whether she was dehydrated, because she’d drunk nothing but a few sips of tea and her bedtime Horlicks for forty-eight hours.

‘Or perhaps,’ said Rob the cynic, ‘She thinks you’ll nip in and take her diary if she leaves it unattended, so she’s going to the loo whenever you nod off.’ This was probably nearer the truth. We ate in silence, able to hear Claire talking in the hallway but unable to make out what she was saying, and then Rob said, ‘We could get some sleeping pills from the doc.’

‘You’ve been reading too many crime novels,’ I said.

‘It could work.’

‘She won’t take them.’ I was confident of this.

‘The doctor gets along well with her. See what he thinks. If you say she’s exhausted and can’t sleep he might give her something and persuade her to take it.’

Claire was speaking as she came back into the room, waving her mobile phone. ‘She might seem a bit brown-bread-and-sandals, but she’s got all her chairs at home’. I frowned, unable to interpret her riddles. ‘The forensic archaeologist,’ she explained, sitting at the table. ‘Seemingly our lady had no shoes.’

‘What?’

'No shoes. Now then,' she appeared to be thinking, tapping her lips with her phone, transferring scarlet blotches onto the screen. 'Going with your idea – that this person was passing by the house – though I'm not sure where you'd be going, to pass by this house, I mean, it is a bit out the way of anywhere, isn't it? But putting that on one side for a minute – let's say she was passing the house and thc bombing started, so she dodged into the Anderson shelter in your Mum's garden – where do you suppose she left her shoes?'

She smirked at us, as though she'd said something profound. Her phone rang again. She looked at the screen and this time answered it without leaving the room. After listening for a few seconds, she looked at her watch and muttered, 'Sorry, sorry, I'll be there in, oh, ten minutes. Leaving now.' She cut off the phone, dropped it into her pocket, checked her bag and started towards the door saying, 'Sometimes I think it would be easier if my son was taking drugs. At least he'd keep out of my way. I forgot it's Saturday. He's playing the local league at eleven o'clock. Here we go, Mum's taxi.' She ran along the hallway, her heels clicking, calling, 'Might be back later.'

'I didn't have her down as the mumsy type,' Rob said as she left. While he cleared away the breakfast things, I took tea and toast up to Mum and told her what the Detective Inspector said about the shelter being taken apart, 'deconstructed'.

She sighed heavily. 'Well, of course it was, Alice, I told you, Mummy and I took the shelter down, because it was badly damaged and a bit of an eyesore, so we had to make it safe. We had to move the steel sheets and we managed to get it sort of level.'

‘And you didn’t see–’

‘Of course not, Alice. It was wrecked. We made it safe and covered it up. We didn’t pick it up.’

‘If you had done so, you might have seen-’

‘We might have seen – yes.’ There was a little catch in her voice.

This seemed reasonable to me. ‘But –’ I wondered whether to give her the rest of the information and decided that on balance it could only help us to resolve the mystery, which, presumably, she was as keen to get to the bottom of as we were. ‘The police say the lady wasn’t wearing any shoes. What do you think about that? I mean, why would she be out in somebody’s garden, without any shoes on?’

I thought she was about to speak, but Doctor Grahams called from the hallway and she clamped her lips together. I met him on the landing and brought him up to date quickly. ‘She’s not eaten anything, and,’ – after a pause I decided to try it – ‘I don’t think she’s slept, since the accident. Maybe you could give her something?’

‘I’ll have a word,’ he said and went into the bedroom. I found Rob in the front room, where he was speaking on Mum’s old black telephone.

He replaced the handset. ‘I’ve made an appointment at the archives for Tuesday morning. They’re very helpful. They’ll look out the relevant records for me.’ As I said, this was Rob in his element.

We went into the garden, feeling as though someone would jump out and tell us not to, but there was no one. It looked like the aftermath of an earthquake. I wondered whether I could get the landscaper back, to fix up the garden now the police had finished, but I put the thought to the back of my mind for later.

‘Perhaps we could do the same with the allotment,’ Rob said. ‘Call the police – anonymously – say we found some bones buried there. It’d save the cost of hiring a rotavator.’

I laughed out loud, then glanced guiltily up at Mum’s bedroom window and was momentarily surprised to find she wasn’t looking down on me. I couldn’t remember ever being in this garden without her scrutiny. It gave me an unaccustomed sense of freedom, but there was nothing I wanted to do with it, so I helped Rob to gather up the plants that had been tossed from the rockery by the police diggers. Their exposed roots were shrivelled from having lain without water for two days. Rob found a stack of old pots amongst the cobwebs in the old outside lavatory that had been turned into a shed at some point. We fell into our accustomed roles in the garden, working companionably together, pushing plants into the pots and standing them in a row along the edge of the wall. He fetched the hose pipe and gave them a soaking. It was cooler, cloudy, suddenly autumn. Already the sun had passed over the house, leaving its shadow lying across half the garden. On the hill, a few dog-walkers paused and glanced our way. When they did, Rob gave them a cheery wave and, embarrassed, they moved on quickly. On the other side of the gap where the privet hedge used to stand, Mrs Barratt came out of her back door with a washing basket on her hip. I blushed at the thought that she may have heard me laughing and would think I was being disrespectful.

She raised a hand and came towards us, saying, ‘Such a shock, Alice, I can’t imagine…’

Rob acted as decoy, going across to speak to her while I escaped indoors. I was filling the cafetiere when Doctor Grahams joined me.

‘Well timed,’ he said and sat at the table.

‘How is Mum, do you think?’ I asked him.

‘Quite dehydrated. Make sure she gets plenty to drink.’ He pulled out a notebook and wrote a couple of words. ‘These are things you can get in the supermarket, glucose drinks and so forth.’ He tore off a page and handed it to me. ‘Otherwise, she’d put a lot of younger people to shame.’ Don’t I know it? ‘But we mustn’t let that fool us. I think she’s more shocked than she’s letting on. Are they putting you under pressure to allow her to be interviewed?’ I told him about the visit from Claire to Mum yesterday and he shook his head. ‘Any more of that and you give me a ring. Here,’ he took a card out of his pocket and wrote a number on the back of it. ‘That’s my personal mobile. My partner’s a lawyer, shall I ask his advice?’

Taken aback by the casual way he’d announced his sexuality, and unable to stop myself thinking ‘what a waste’, I probably had my mouth half-open for a moment. He smiled at me, no doubt knowing exactly what was going through my mind, and tapped on the card with his pen and passed it to me. ‘Ring me if you need to.’

Rob came in from the garden, looked from the doctor to me and raised his eyebrows. I nodded at him and turned my attention to pouring the coffee. He said, ‘Did Alice tell you how worried we are, Doctor? Not sleeping and eaten nothing for forty-eight hours. She seems unable to drop off at night. We think she’s exhausted.’

‘Off her food, not able to sleep, it’s all to be expected,’ the doctor said. ‘Tell you what,’ he delved into his briefcase and brought out a prescription pad, wrote quickly and handed it to me. ‘These will help your mum to sleep, should she feel the need – use your discretion. Now, how about yourself? How are you?’

I was placing his coffee in front of him as he said this, and he pressed the back of my hand very lightly and looked at me so kindly that quite inexplicably I felt hot tears burning my cheeks. I covered my face, embarrassed, but he seemed unfazed and said, 'It's a great strain on you. Perhaps you ought to see a doctor for a bit of help? Are you with our practice?' I nodded and he said, 'When I call in tomorrow to check on your Mum, we can have a word. It's important that you get plenty of rest. In the meantime, if you need to take one of those…' – he waved in the direction of the prescription as he gets up to leave.

I was aware of Rob coming back from seeing the doctor to the door, moving around me quietly, pushing a cup of coffee in front of me. He patted me on the shoulder and cleared his throat – he's not very good with emotion – and then I heard him climbing the stairs. I'd blown my nose and was drinking my coffee when he came back a few minutes later. He looked suddenly much older, perhaps because he was worried about me, or maybe I'd not noticed, before. If Rob looked old, then, presumably, so did I.

'She was in the bathroom,' he said. 'I would have had a look around, but she must have heard me because I hadn't even got to her bed before she was behind me. These are for the recycling bin,' He had the free newspaper and some papers that I recognised as the mail I took to Mum yesterday, and placed them beside the coal scuttle on the hearth, 'or for burning. But here's the thing…' his voice rose with excitement, 'I went to the loo and these pieces of paper were floating in the pan. She's obviously been trying to flush it away.'

Like a conjuror, he pulled a few soggy scraps from his pocket. 'There's no saying how much she managed to get rid of.' He pushed the damp pieces around on the draining board, trying to match them, and triumphantly placed eight together. I recognised the handwriting, the same as her diary entries.

keeps rabbits in his bedroom, would you believe? I tried not to show how appalled I was. She uses real sugar in her cooking. I have a pamphlet which explains why it is wrong to encourage the black market and I will pass it on to her. We went to the Hippodrome to see "Gone with the Wind" which is in technicolour, a (unreadable) *It was quite spoiled by what Jean said during the interval. It's made me think again that there may be something between her and Richard. She asked did I think Richard was like Ashley Wilkes? I took it that she meant the character, not the actor, as Leslie Howard does not have Richard's bearing at all. I pretended to find the idea funny and said, trying to laugh, that she probably thought I was like Melanie, (who, poor girl, was in love with the Ashley character long before he took any notice of her) and she* (unreadable) *did she see herself as Scarlett O'Hara? (who we know was infatuated with Ashley, though I didn't say that of course). She laughed and said "Oh, fiddle-de-dee, Vi." I do wish she would use my given* (unreadable)

'We'll be able to date that from the time of the film,' Rob said. 'I'll look online when I'm at home later.'

'It partly answers my question about Jean,' I said. 'She obviously became a big part of Mum's life after the wedding.'

'Maybe you should ask her to tell you about Jean?' Rob suggested.

'Only when I can admit to reading her diary. First, I need to talk to her about the shoes. We were interrupted by the doctor, remember?'

'Shall I come with you?'

I reminded him, 'You need to contact the travel agent before they close. And the chemist. And there's a few things you could pick up from home.' If I was going to be here much longer I needed some home comforts. I'd forgotten how joyless this house was. No television, no music, unless I wanted to get out my old 45s from upstairs or Joe's collection of swing and jazz records which were still stacked neatly in the radiogram in the front room. Tearing off a margin of the newspaper I scribbled a quick list for Rob. He waited with his jacket on, anxious to be off. I added the drinks recommended by the doctor, and some healthier food items for me. Rob would survive on takeaways if I let him and I was sure his waistband was already showing the effect of the last couple of days.

As I looked around the bedroom door, she seemed to be pushing something back under the covers. She took the tea from me and placed it on her bedside table, then ignored it. Her eyes looked more sunken than usual behind her spectacles, and the skin on her forehead appeared looser. It was as though she was disappearing before my eyes.

'Mum, the Doctor said you need to drink more. You'll make yourself ill. Rob's gone to buy you a glucose drink. Shall I bring you some water?' She shook her head, no, but picked up the tea again, and sipped at it. 'I was thinking about the shoes,' I said. She was watching me over the rim of the cup. 'Why do you think she'd be out there in the garden without shoes? Unless it was summer? But didn't you say the shelter was damaged in an air raid? And Rob looked it up, he said that would have been in December. Too cold, wouldn't you say, to be out barefoot?'

I thought she said, very quietly, 'Slippers.'

'Slippers?' I repeated. 'You think – what? Maybe it was a neighbour who, say, heard the siren and ran out in her slippers?' It seemed simple and obvious. 'Did one of your neighbours go missing then, after the air raid?'

She held out the empty cup and leaned back against her pillows, seemingly exhausted. 'Do you think I might have a biscuit?'

I was on my way downstairs, pleased that she wanted to eat and thinking what I could tempt her with, something more interesting than a biscuit, when my mobile phone rang. Taking it out of my cardigan pocket I saw it was Judy.

'Mum,' she said. 'Are you okay? I'm sorry, I had no idea, we've been in France as you know, completely off the grid, having a bit of a break before Adam leaves for Uni. I saw the newspaper on the ferry last night and I managed to catch Dad this morning. How is Gran?'

I should have texted her, but hadn't wanted to ruin her holiday. I gave her the official line and could tell she knew this much from the newspaper and her earlier conversation with Rob. She reminded me she would be here on Monday afternoon, with Adam, moving him in to his student accommodation, and would call round afterwards. She enthused about his city centre apartment which sounded like a modern alternative to halls of residence but a good deal more expensive. While she chattered on, I wondered how was it that in two short generations, young people seemed to have come to consider a university education and a luxury apartment at eighteen, as their birth right. Then I realised what I was thinking and was horrified that I may be turning into a moaning old biddy. I finished the call with promises to see them for tea on Monday, and went to the pantry to look for something to tempt Mum's appetite. I scraped some mould off the top of a jar of elderberry jelly that probably came from the local W.I. market years ago, spread it on bread and butter and found a selection of biscuits.

After giving Mum the tray, I tidied her room, chatting about Judy and Adam, telling her about our plans for Monday. When I looked around she had fallen asleep. I couldn't help feeling annoyed. She'd never been interested in her grandchildren. It didn't take much effort to listen. There I was again. The familiar cycle of guilt and anger. Judy would have a field day with my relationship with my mother, if I told her the half of it. Suddenly I was trembling with fatigue, and decided to lay down for a while in the front bedroom.

Frank

Flight QF71 to Singapore

There's a lot of water between Perth and Singapore. It's easy to forget how far it is. Two weeks to cross in 1966, less than seven hours today. That first time, I didn't care too much whether I made it or not. My inheritance from Tom Malkin was enough to buy a farm, and if anything happened to me, it would all go to Sam and Doreen so they could carry on with the dream. Their dream that I was buying in to. My nightmare that I was running away from. This time across the Pacific, I'm not prepared to take any risks – if there's a chance of there being an accident, I'll do my best to survive it. So I listened carefully to the instructions, watched the video, read the safety card and kicked my heels to check there was a box under my seat where the life jacket should be. The stewardess saw me do that and came along to say, 'Don't worry Mr Sheldon, if there's a problem I'll do it with you.'

When everybody's settled, she comes along with lunch. As I move stuff to make space on my table, the Cat's Eye rolls onto the floor and into the aisle. There's a bit of a palaver finding it. The stewardess picks it up and hands it back to me. The woman waiting to pass down the aisle catches sight of the rabbit's foot in my other hand and stares at it.

'Is it some kind of aboriginal ritual?' she asks in a snooty English accent. If I'd known Amy was going to buy me into the business class I'd have told her no, let me sit with the ordinary folk. This lot don't look that friendly.

The stewardess is all right, though. She's interested in the Cat's Eye and I show her how the colours change when I hold it up to the light. She asks about my trip and am I going to visit family in the UK? I say, 'sort of' and she asks me when I saw them last. 'The 1960s,' I say and, 'Goodness me,' she says, 'Will you recognise one another?' 'Oh yes', I tell her, 'No doubt about it.'

She passes the Cats Eye back to me and I wrap it up, with the rabbit's foot, in the black cloth. As I push the parcel back into the haversack, my fingers find a piece of twine. This was left over from Mr Knowles's runner beans. I popped it into my pocket at the time – you never know when these things will come in handy. And it did, for after Jean went missing, I put the curtain ring on it, and hung it round my neck for years, to keep it safe. The copper is completely green now, and the ring much thinner than I remember. It looks liable to snap. At the time, it was quite the thing, although Jean moaned and said her finger might get infected.

'I'll get that gone-green' she said, 'and have to have it cut off.'

Joe laughed. 'You mean gangrene,' he said. 'It's only until I save up. Then I shall buy you a jewel fit for a princess.'

On the day of the wedding, Dad and Bill were on early shift and as soon as they left Mam pulled Cyril and me out of bed and had us running hither and thither. I went to the corner shop to get orange boxes while Cyril went up to Dixon's butchers to borrow their spare delivery cart. Jean and Mam wrapped pies and cakes in cloth and clipped the caps onto bottles of ginger beer. We packed these into the boxes and put them on the cart, and then Cyril went off, pulling the load up to Hurdle Hill. At half past ten, I was polishing boots and shoes while Mam starched the collars, and Jean was taking the curlers out of her hair and throwing them into the sink, when there was a knock on the door and I opened it to find Sybil, Jean's mate, standing there with a brown paper parcel.

Jean said, 'Tha's cutting it fine.' She left her hair frizzed all over and ripped the parcel open, holding up a frock with pink and blue flowers that looked big enough to make a pair of curtains.

'It'll fit where it touches,' Mam said.

Sybil said, 'We can pin it.'

Jean stripped off to her petticoat. She said to me, 'Don't stand there like piffy on a rock bun. Carry on getting them shoes polished.' She pulled on the frock and pinched the waist together. Mam got the pins out of the sideboard and Jean stood on a chair while Sybil pinned the frock.

Sybil said, 'These won't show under the jacket.' She took a pale pink jacket out of the parcel and passed it to Jean. She pointed to a smaller parcel. 'Josie's sent you her gloves.'

Mam opened the parcel and dangled a white glove from her finger. She said, 'Will thee look at these.' There was an orange stain across the palm and one of the fingers had worn through at the end. 'Has she been polishing brass in them?'

Jean looked down from the chair and her mouth dropped. She wailed, 'I'll not be able to marry without gloves, Mam.'

'Happen we'll have time to get into town early and buy some new ones at C and A Modes.'

Jean jumped off the chair, pulling the dress so that one of the pins stuck in Sybil's hand. Sybil yelped. I laughed which brought Mam's attention back to me.

She held out the iron and said, 'If tha's finished polishing, put that back and pass me the hot iron.' She laid out the jacket ready for pressing.

Sybil said, 'They reckon she's a bit la-di-da, this Violet.'

Jean said, 'Pass me the brush, Frank. Aye, I'm not sure it was such a good idea, having a joint do with the Knowleses.' Jean did a twirl around a chair and Sybil checked the pins, and Jean started to brush out her curls. 'I wish we were having a private family do.'

Mam said, 'Wouldn't we all like a sit-down dinner at Marples Hotel at five bob a head?' She sprinkled a handful of cold water onto the jacket, and as she pressed the hot iron onto it her face disappeared in a cloud of steam. 'Tha wants to be grateful to the Knowleses for having the wedding tea at their house. Thy Dad's already putting in double time to pay our share.' She saw I'd stopped moving. 'Frank, get kettle back on to boil ready for thy dad. He'll be home any minute.'

Jean said, 'I'm sorry, Mam.' She climbed down from the chair and sat on it, propping a mirror up on the table. She scraped orange powder onto her nose. 'Everybody's gone to a lot of trouble. But nothing seems to suit that stuck up lot. There I was this morning helping lay the table, and first they want it set this way, then that way.' Jean pulled her mouth wide open and pushed bright red lipstick around it. Sybil said, 'Too bright,' and handed Jean another lipstick. Jean rubbed the bright lipstick off and painted her lips in a pink that matched the pink stripes on her frock, talking all the while. 'And when I look round the chuffing ham's disappeared. That Violet, she looks me up and down as though she thinks I've slipped it under me coat. She took out a pen and drew black lines round her eyes. 'It turns out the queer old bugger has only put it in the chuffing Anderson shelter, along with half the pork pies. So there he is, at the kitchen door, mithering on about securing the quarter-master's stores.' She stood back on the chair and passed Sybil the pen.

Sybil was laughing so much she was shaking and Jean said, 'Stop laughing or it'll go all over the place.' Sybil pushed the pen into the back of Jean's knee and started to draw a black line down the back of Jean's leg. This wedding lark was beginning to seem very peculiar.

Mam said, 'Let's hope they can keep him under control. They've no cause to lord it over us when they've got Colonel Bonkers in their own back yard. He'll –'

I shouted, 'Stop making fun of Mr Knowles. He's my friend.' They all looked at me with their mouths open.

Cyril came in. He said, 'No flowers for buttonholes. Flower shop on Infirmary Road's got a notice up that says it's closed for the duration. I've been right up to Hillsborough Corner with no luck.'

Jean said, 'Aw, Mam. I saw they'd got buttonholes up at the Knowleses. We'll look like poor relations.'

Mam said, 'There's some things we'll have to do without and be grateful for what we have got.' She nodded to me and Cyril. 'Get moving and get that bath ready.' To Jean she said, 'Why don't the two of thee get into town early and get them new gloves.' She went to the sideboard and took out the cocoa tin which I knew she kept the money in for rent and such. She handed Jean a couple of bob.

Jean said, 'Thanks Mam,' going to give her a hug.

Mam said, 'Be careful. Tha doesn't want to get messed up. Meet us at Registry Office, in plenty of time mind.'

Jean and Sybil went off and Cyril and me got the bath off the privy roof and set it down on the kitchen floor. The second kettle started boiling as Dad and Bill came in. Mam went upstairs to get herself ready. Dad stripped off and got in the bath. I poured water over his head with a jug, watching the white dust turn to a sludgy river that ran down his back and into the water as his hair turned brown again. He wrapped a towel around himself and shaved while Bill bathed. When they'd done, Cyril and me dragged the bath outside and emptied it into the drain. As we were lifting it back onto the roof, it slid through my wet fingers and onto Cyril's head.

He said, 'Clumsy sod,' and slapped me on the shoulder. I yelled for my Mam. Mrs Wreakes burst out of the privy. The door cracked against my legs and made me shout out loud.

Mrs Wreakes said, 'Frightened life out of me, little buggers. I thought it were Mester Hitler come calling. Tha's a couple of hooligans what'll end up in approved school before long.'

The bedroom window flew open and Mam stuck her head out. She shouted, 'Oy, thee owd witch, leave my lads be, else I'll clock thee one.'

Mrs Wreakes snorted and waddled across the yard. Her frock behind was tucked up into her drawers. I nudged Cyril and pointed. We folded up laughing.

Mam said, 'Get inside now and get dressed, I can't leave thee alone for two chuffing minutes.'

When we were all ready, we lined up in the kitchen while Mam checked our shoes, our ears and our collars. She threw some water on my hair to try to make it lie down. With his hair all springy and even a cigar in his top pocket, my Dad looked like Harpo Marx. When she'd finished pushing and pulling us about Mam led us out like a Sunday School parade and marched us down to the tram stop on Infirmary Road.

The tram came. The conductor called, 'Room for two,' and Mam shoved me and Cyril on, then pushed in herself and pulled Dad after her.

The conductor said, 'I said room for two, missis. The rest of thee can get off.'

Mam said, 'Get on wi'thee, the four of us together don't make up the size of her.' She pointed to the lady whose backside I was crammed against. 'If tha wants to make some room, happen she could walk. She could do with a bit of exercise.'

The conductor said, 'There's no need for that, missus, this lady's paid fair and square and is entitled.'

Mam said, 'And has she paid extra to bring that arse with her?'

The lady turned her head and I saw it was Mrs Trippett. I ducked my head down so she didn't see me. Mam gave me an extra shove, pressing my forehead right into the clasp of Mrs Trippett's handbag. I thought I'd be marked for life.

The conductor said, 'One more word from you, missis' but then he squeezed his way through the people and disappeared.

I couldn't see and could hardly breathe and felt a bit sick with the swaying of the tram as it rattled along, until the conductor shouted, 'Snig Hill'. Somebody got hold of the bottom of my jacket and pulled me out from between the bodies like a plug popping out of a full sink. Then

Mam had hold of my hand and marched me up the hill to the Corn Exchange.

A lot of people were milling around outside. I saw Violet and Mr and Mrs Knowles. Someone ruffled my hair and I looked up to see Joe in his uniform, standing beside Richard. He winked at me which made me feel pleased to know him.

He said, 'Where's Jean then? Has she changed her mind?'

Richard laughed.

Mam said, 'Is she not here, yet?' standing on tiptoes, looking down the street.

A tall man with half glasses perched on the end of his long nose came out waving a watch in his hand and said to Richard, 'We have a strict rotation of marriages every fifteen minutes. We must start in five minutes exactly.'

Mrs Knowles pushed between Richard and the tall man. 'My daughter has had this ceremony booked for months, on the understanding that we would have the full services of the Registrar for half an hour.'

'It's our busiest day this year, Madam.'

She said, 'It's a wedding, young man, not a bargain basement sale.'

The man said, 'Tell that to all the young people who are rushing to marry,' and he snorted so that his half glasses wobbled and nearly fell off.

Richard took the man aside and I heard him say, 'I'd appreciate it if…'

There was a loud 'Coo-eee' and I turned to see Auntie Eileen coming up the street, pulling a buck-teethed girl with bony knees sticking out from a frilly pink skirt. Auntie Eileen's hair was as wild and curly as mine and my Dad's. Her hat looked about to topple off. She fussed around Cyril and Bill, until they had matching pink spots on their cheeks, then she looked around and spotted me.

She said, 'Is that Frank? By, he's getting a big lad.' Pushing the girl towards me, she went on, 'Does tha remember thy cousin Mildred?' Mildred had the same springy hair, tied down with a pink ribbon which met in a large bow on top of her head. 'Here Mildred, stand with Frank.' She turned back to my Dad. 'Where's the blushing bride?'

Mildred was looking up at me with a silly grin so I stood behind one of the pillars in case anyone I knew came past. Mildred followed me. I went over to stand beside my Dad and he laughed down at me. Mam was still jumping up to look over people's heads, to see if Jean was coming.

The official man came out again. I was sure it was less than five minutes. He said, 'I'm very sorry, sir,' to Richard, with a little smirk that made him seem not sorry at all, 'I really cannot wait any longer.'

Some ladies standing near us began squealing and I saw Jean and Sybil puffing towards us, waving their hands to show their new, bright white gloves.

Violet said, 'Come on, Mummy,' before they'd even reached us, and took hold of her Mam by the arm. As they passed me, I heard Violet say, 'This was supposed to be the happiest day of my life. She's ruining everything. She doesn't even have a hat.'

Her Mam said, 'Just grin and bear it, my dear.'

Joe and Jean started canoodling.

Mam got hold of Jean's arm and said, 'Get on, else tha'll miss it.' She shooed Joe and Jean through the enormous wooden doors and pulled me after them.

Our shoes made no sound on the corridor of thick, red carpet and wood panelling. A lady with a big leather book under her arm pointed us into a room. Mam pushed us into one of the rows of chairs. Mildred was sitting with Auntie Eileen in front of me and she looked round at me then giggled into her hands. I pinched her elbow. She squealed. My Dad gave me a clip on the leg.

Jean and Joe, and Richard and Violet, stood at the front with the official man. I thought Joe looked really smart in his uniform.

I whispered to my Dad, 'Why isn't Richard in the Army?'

He said, 'He's a conchie.' I puzzled over this because it made me think of a shell that the Minister had shown us when he told us about being a missionary in South America. I wanted to ask more but Mam leaned round Dad and shushed me.

The official man was talking down his nose in a drone that reminded me of the noise flies make when they're trying to escape from the flypaper in the butcher's window. The ceiling had pictures of cherubs in clouds with leaves around the edges. I counted two hundred and seventy-three leaves around the ceiling and twenty-two people in the room. I was dividing the leaves by the people in my head when there was a ripple of laughter around me. Joe was patting all his pockets then, as though he'd suddenly remembered where he put it, he pulled a ring out of his inside pocket. He made a great performance of putting it on Jean's finger, and then kissed her hand.

She said, 'Soft ha'porth.'

Auntie Eileen leaned back and said to my Mam, 'I see somebody's been at the curtain rings.'

Mam laughed and whispered, 'They've not got two pennies to rub together. He reckons he'll get her a proper ring with his first pay.'

Richard was laughing along with everyone else. Violet wasn't laughing.

Mrs Knowles said, 'Let's have a photograph of the signing of the register,' and a man with a tripod under his arm came forward and started to set it up.

Auntie Eileen said to Mam, 'Inside pictures? No expense spared, eh?'

The official man said, 'No time for that, the next couple is waiting,' and he flapped across the room with his elbows out and his head stuck forward like a drake running into a puddle. He stood with the door open and waved us through as though he couldn't get rid of us fast enough.

I heard Mildred say, 'Can I have me photograph with Frank?' so I nipped behind the door until she was well ahead, and came out behind Richard and Violet.

Violet was saying quietly to Richard, 'But Mother paid for inside photographs and she has the album ready. If she hadn't been late we wouldn't have had to rush like this and we would have got the photographs.'

Richard put his arm under her elbow and said, 'How about if I arrange for the photographer to come back next week, especially to take the photographs? We could do it in my dinner hour?'

Violet smiled up at him and said, 'Can you do that?'

'Of course. You could meet me in town.'

'Now that I'm a lady of leisure.' Violet looked at Richard in a way that reminded me of the day she'd found the watch and seemed really happy. She stopped so suddenly that I stepped on the back of her shoes. She didn't notice.

I looked round her and saw Jean waving her hand, saying, 'Only the best curtain rings for my husband.' Everybody was laughing.

Joe saw Violet and shooed everyone away from the doors. He got hold of Jean and danced her around. People walking past had to step off the pavement but they laughed and slapped Joe on his back. The man with the box camera organised us into families to take photographs, then he took one of Jean and Richard and Joe said, 'Oy, mate, you've got the wrong couple,' and everybody laughed except Violet, who stared at Jean even when Richard stood beside her and they posed for the photographer. She smiled but her lips were thin and pressed together and as soon as the camera flashed, her mouth became a straight line again. Then Joe and Jean had their photograph taken.

Taxis were lined up along the pavement ready to take us to Hurdle Hill Terrace. My family got into a blue Austin Low Loader. I was squashed between Mam and Dad while Bill and Cyril had the fold down seats behind the driver.

I asked the driver, 'Can we open the top?'

He said, 'No, it's fixed. We take the seats out and convert it to an ambulance at night.' This was a pity because it was my first time in a car and we'd have looked right swanky driving through town with the top down.

Dad said, 'He's done well to get petrol for this.'

Mam tapped the side of her nose and said, 'Money talks.'

At the Knowles's house, we went into the front room, where I'd seen Violet looking all strange and puffy a few days before. Now, there was a table pushed against the wall next to the piano and chairs stood around three sides of the room. Mrs Swindon was bringing food from the kitchen. Mam started to help her but Jean told her to sit down. Richard carved meat while Jean and Violet filled plates and passed them around. Mr Knowles poured dark brown liquid into glasses which Joe and Richard passed to the grown-ups, and then there were more glasses, this time with ginger beer, for me and Mildred who were the only children. Every time Jean and Joe passed one another they got soppy all over again, and every time they did this, the group of noisy ladies went 'Woo-ooh!' and laughed. Violet handed out the plates with her eyes on the ground. She had a look on her face as though she'd swallowed a cupful of cod liver oil.

I sat on the settee which was rough on the backs of my knees and made me itch. Mam pulled my hand away to stop me scratching. Cousin Mildred sat beside me so I got up and stood by Cyril and Bill, but they pushed me away. I ended up stuck between the piano and the table. This meant my elbow was on the piano and I couldn't hold the plate straight, so the blancmange slithered off the plate, down my trousers and onto the floor. I pushed it under the piano with the toe of my shoe. Mrs Knowles came past and snatched my plate away before I could ask for more.

There was a great performance of cutting the cake. The photographer set up his tripod and camera and Richard and Violet posed for ages with the knife on the cake before he was satisfied and there was a mighty flash. Then they pushed the cake back together to make it look like new and Jean and Joe cut it while they had their photographs taken. Finally they handed slices round, but the icing was too hard to bite into. I ate the fruity part, then licked the strip of icing until it was soft enough. I put my head back and was about to drop it into my open mouth when it was whipped out of my hand by Mam who said, 'Mind thy manners.'

Richard and Joe came to stand by the piano. They were speaking very quietly. Richard took a box out of his pocket and passed it to Joe. I was sure it was the same box that Violet had found in Richard's attaché case. I remembered the beautiful watch inside.

Joe said, 'This means a lot. I'll pay you back.'

Richard said, 'No need. It's a privilege, being able to help out.'

I remembered the look on Violet's face when she'd found that watch. I should say something to Joe. Across the room, Jean twisted the curtain ring on her finger while she laughed with Sybil and her other friends. Violet looked at Jean's finger, and then down at her own ring. I had a feeling that something bad was about to happen, like the time I broke the window with my football and Mam made me wait in the bedroom until my Dad came home. My belly turned over.

I pulled Joe's sleeve. 'Joe, there's something…'

He ruffled my hair. 'Alright, scamp? Want some more ginger beer?'

Then it was too late because Mr Knowles was tapping a glass with a knife to make a sound like a bell and everybody stopped talking. Joe winked at me and walked across to stand behind Jean's chair. Richard stood behind Violet. Mrs Knowles passed Mr Knowles a piece of paper.

He read, 'I am a very proud father today, welcoming this fine young man into my family.' He stopped and looked around the room. Under his caterpillar eyebrows, he looked puzzled as though he wasn't sure who all these people in his house were. 'In these dark days of war,' he wasn't reading now, 'When our world is in trouble and we depend on young men such as … such as …' He looked around and saw Joe. 'This brave young man, going off to fight…' Mrs Knowles tapped Richard on the arm and he started to move towards Mr Knowles. 'Mud and noise, young man,' Mr Knowles was saying to Joe.

Richard put his arm around Mr Knowles's shoulder and started speaking. 'Ladies and gentlemen,' he said. 'I'm proud to describe myself as the son-in-law of Mr Knowles, who, as everyone knows, distinguished himself at Passchendaele in the last War. My wife and I' – at this there was a chuckle around the room – 'are looking forward to having a family and I'm sure you will all agree with me that Mr Knowles will make a very fine grandfather.'

Jean's friends started to cheer, then went silent when Jean shook her head at them. Violet's face was blotchy pink, and she twisted a handkerchief in her hands. Richard introduced my Dad who stood up. I thought how smart he looked in his suit. His neck was purple and he fidgeted with his collar.

Dad said, 'This is my only daughter, and I'm thankful for that since one wedding is enough to be going on with.' There was some laughter at this. He went on, 'I wanted to say that although it's a quick wedding it's not what tha thinks.'

Mam laughed, sounding like a firecracker in the silent room. She put her hand over her mouth. Dad's collar had come undone at one side and stuck up under his ear. He looked at my Mam, stood up straight and said, 'I'm right proud of our lass. She's the loveliest girl I set eyes on since I married her Mam. And if she's anything like her Mam then Joe'll have the best wife in Christendom.'

Joe put his hands on Jean's shoulders and kissed her on the top of her head. Dad went on, 'And I want Joe to know that he's part of our family now. Even though he could've claimed a reserved occupation, he wanted to fight for his country and we're right proud of him.'

Mr Knowles stood up and seemed about to speak again, but Mrs Knowles pulled him back into his chair and Richard said, 'Ladies and gentlemen, will you please raise your glasses and toast this lovely lady who is now my wife. Violet Anne Clarke.'

Everyone said, 'Violet Anne Clarke' and for the first time that day I saw Violet smile properly, showing her teeth which were very white and even and which had made a faint line on her bottom lip. She looked happy but I knew it wouldn't last. I wondered whether I had time to stop what was going to happen, but Joe was already speaking.

'Ladies and gentlemen, please raise your glasses for my sweetheart who is now my lovely wife, Mrs Jean Ibbertson.'

Jean's friends cheered and stamped and Mrs Knowles stared at them with her mouth open as though they were Red Indians.

Joe took the box from his pocket and handed it to Jean. I closed my eyes. Jean squealed. I opened my eyes as she jumped to her feet, throwing her arms around Joe and giving him a sloppy kiss. She lifted the silver watch out of the box and held it up. I was afraid to look at Violet.

Auntie Eileen said in not such a quiet voice, 'Happen he could've got a ring for her if there's money for watches.'

Mrs Knowles said, 'Come along, Violet, dear, open your gift.'

Violet was holding a box. It looked the same. I let my breath go. There were two watches and it would be all right. Violet smiled at Richard as she opened her box and looked into it. I expected her to lift the watch out, but she kept looking.

Mrs Knowles looked over her shoulder and said, ‘That’s beautiful, dear, do show it to everyone.’

Violet lifted a silver locket and chain out of the box and dangled it from her fingers. Richard leaned across and unclipped the locket so it fell open. There was a heart shape on each side.

He said, ‘We’ll put our pictures in there as soon as the photographs are developed.’

Violet smiled, reminding me of the times when I got a present I didn’t like and tried to look pleased. If I were Violet I’d rather have had the watch, too. But at least she had a present, so I thought she should be happy. Richard closed the locket and put it around her neck. Joe put the watch on Jean’s wrist.

Jean said, ‘Come on Sybil, give us a song.’ Sybil stood up and started to sing in a voice that made the glasses on the table shiver:

For years and years I’ve been alone, a spinster on the shelf,

I’m right fed up with spendin’ all me money on meself,

I’m all prepared for married life, its secrets I’ve been taught –

Auntie Eileen called across the room, ‘So, our Jean, does tha reckon tha’s prepared for married life?’

Sybil said, ‘I can give thee a few pointers, Jeanie.’

One of the other ladies said, ‘Aye, there were no secrets for thee on thy wedding day.’ There was much laughter. As Sybil threw her head back to carry on singing, her little brown hat that looked like the lid on a meat and potato pie, with twisted pastry all around the edges, fell onto the floor. Bending over to pick it up she lost her balance and stumbled into Joe, who put his hand under her elbow and helped her back to her seat, laughing.

Mrs Knowles came over to the piano, shaking her head. ‘Violet, darling,’ she said, pushing back the cover. ‘Shall we have a little Peer Gynt?’ Violet crossed the room to join her. Pulling out the piano stool she lifted the lid, picked out a sheet of music and settled with it in front of her. Sybil pushed her nose in the air with her forefinger and sniffed loudly, then sat down again, whispering to the lady next to her. Jean put a hand on her shoulder and squeezed it. Violet started to play.

Mam was going out with an armful of plates so I ducked under the table and slipped through the door and followed her into the scullery. In the garden Richard and Joe stood with my Dad and some of the other men, smoking cigars. Mr Knowles was sitting on the garden bench, nodding and smiling.

He said, ‘Coming to join the escape committee, Frank?’ I was surprised he remembered my name. ‘Have you seen the shelter since it was finished?’

We walked down the garden and I saw the shelter now had a door. Two steps led down to a strip of brown linoleum between wooden benches that ran along each side, a blanket neatly folded on the end of each. On a low table at the other end stood a Kelly lamp and a pile of magazines and newspapers. Mr Knowles closed the door behind us, making me blink in the sudden dark. I heard him fumbling, then a match struck, and when I opened my eyes he was lighting the lamp. It spluttered then caught, and a dim yellow glow filled the space.

We sat on the benches opposite one another, our knees touching. It smelt as warm and damp as a rabbit hole on a summer’s day. Mr Knowles put his hand under the bench and pulled out an Ovaltine tin. Inside were ginger biscuits. We sat munching, and I thought how lucky Mr Knowles was to have a den like this. There was a thump and sunlight flooded in, making me squint at the shape in the doorway.

Bill's voice said, 'It's like the Black Hole of Calcutta in here. Dad says if tha wants to stop and help Mam with washing up and what not, tha can, but we're off.'

I gave the Ovaltine tin back to Mr Knowles and followed Bill. Mam had a pinafore on that wasn't hers and was bustling about, cleaning up with Mrs Swindon. Dad and Cyril were waiting at the front door. As Sybil came out she bent over and wrapped her arms round me, smelling of talcum powder which made me want to sneeze. She said, 'If I wasn't already spoken for, I'd wait for thee to grow up a bit,' and tried to kiss me. I wriggled away and stood next to my Dad. She said, 'As handsome as thy dad.'

Mam was suddenly behind us, tucking Dad's collar down. She said, 'Aye, and he's spoken for.' Sybil joined the rest of Jean's friends and they pushed one another out of the gate, giggling.

Auntie Eileen said to my Dad, 'Don't be a stranger.' She pulled Mildred through the gate. Mildred gave me a little wave over her shoulder. I pushed my tongue out as far as it would go.

Dad said, 'I reckon I'll stay a stranger while tha lives in that godforsaken hole.'

'Get off, it's only Tinsley, it's the end of the tramline, not the end of the world. Bobby's got to follow the work.'

Dad said, 'Tell Bobby there's plenty of work at our place so he can move back over here as soon as he wants.'

Jean came rushing out of the house, her eyes sparkling and talking fifteen to the dozen. She said, 'Mam, Dad, tha'll never guess what? Richard has got us a hotel for the night in Bakewell. We've to get the trolley bus at half past six in town.'

Mam said, 'Well that's grand. Are Richard and Violet going?'

'No, that's the thing. It was their honeymoon and they've only gone and given it to us, being as Joe's pay hasn't started to come through yet and he's got to go back to camp on Monday. Richard says they can go away anytime.'

Dad said, 'Well, it's more than kind of him. He's done our family proud today, there's no doubt.'

At the same time Mam said, 'Richard's idea, eh? Does tha not think tha'd better check with Violet? She might not be feeling so generous.'

Mam got hold of Dad's arm and led him over to where Richard and Violet were waving to some people leaving. Dad spoke to Richard and shook his hand. Violet stared at Mam and Dad and said nothing. Jean bounced out of the gate and joined them, putting her hand on Richard's arm and chatting away. Violet turned and walked quickly into the house with her head down, knocking into Bill who was leaning on the gate.

Bill said, 'What's up wi' Lady Muck?'

Dad called over to us, 'Come on, let's get off.'

It seemed Jean wouldn't be bringing Joe back to the house until Sunday so all the cleaning and scrubbing had been for nothing. I didn't mind. I was pleased as Punch to be walking down the hill with Dad and the lads.

Joe was as good as his word and when he came home on leave he had a wedding ring for Jean. She put it on and threw the curtain ring on the table. I picked it up and put it with my marble, my book, and my piece of twine, in the gap under the privy roof.

Alice

There was a loud crash somewhere in the house and I sat up, my heart racing. The little clock said almost four o'clock, so I'd been asleep for more than three hours. I rolled off the bed and rushed into Mum's room. She was standing at her window, leaning on the frame, looking down at the garden. At the sound of my voice, she looked round, her face pale and drawn. How tiny she seemed, standing there in her long cotton nightie, more like a child than a woman.

'I've been asleep.'

'Clearly,' she said quietly, her eyes on my hair. I put a hand up and found my curls were sticking up in all directions. I pressed them as flat as I could, and tried to straighten my crumpled clothes.

'Can I get you anything?'

'A chair if it's not too much trouble.' I looked for sarcasm but couldn't find it. Her voice seemed to be diminishing with her frame. I started to drag the Lloyd loom chair across but she shook her head and said, 'There's a straight chair on the landing'.

With the chair in position by the window, she sat and resumed her customary position, which I now thought of as sentinel of the garden or more precisely, the rockery. I brought her a glass of water from the bathroom and she set it on the floor.

'Would you like to join us downstairs?' I thought she must be feeling lonely up here. She shook her head, no, and waved a hand, dismissing me.

Rob was in the kitchen, all of Mum's saucepans around his feet.

'Can't find anything big enough for this,' he said, waving a handful of long spaghetti which he started to break in half in order to fit it into the largest pan. 'I was shopping at the Co-op,' he told me, 'And the girl at the till pointed at my basket and said, "A little pot of cream and you've got a carbonara there." Some promotion they've got on, a 'meal deal' she called it, she gave me the recipe. Oh, and it worked out that the wine came free.' He pointed to the recipe card propped up against a bottle of sauvignon. 'Thought it sounded a good idea.' He broke eggs, patiently separating the whites into a bowl. 'Sit, relax.' He still had the ability to surprise me.

He poured a glass of wine for each of us and I sat in Mum's armchair in front of the dead fire. There was a small patch of dried blood on the corner of the fender which I rubbed off with a tissue.

While Rob cooked, I recounted my conversation with Mum and explained my idea of someone, a neighbour or somebody living not far away, rushing out to the shelter, panicked by the siren, with no time to put her shoes on, maybe wearing slippers. When I finished, the bacon pieces were sizzling and spitting in the frying pan. Rob took it off the heat and turned to me, shaking his head.

'I think if you tried that one on the Detective Inspector, she'd laugh you out of town.' I stared at him. He waved the spatula at me. 'Don't you think someone might have noticed if one of the neighbours went missing? It doesn't stack up as a hypothesis, does it?'

And he accused my mother of putting me down. Of course, he was right, it was illogical. This terrace of houses, standing on the side of the hill, looking across the valley, was not a through route to anywhere; the neighbours all knew one another and no one could have gone missing without being noticed.

'No, old fruit,' Rob said, turning back to his spaghetti, 'Your ma's pulling the wool over your eyes.'

I jumped to defend my mother. 'She didn't say…' and stopped, realising that it's true, she didn't say anything of the sort, this was all my own idea.

'By the way,' he said as he drained the spaghetti and dropped it back into the saucepan. 'Two pieces of news. I didn't only do the shopping. I've been online.' I could think of a number of jobs at home that he might have done if he had time on his hands, but before I had time to tell him this, he said, 'I found the date of "*Gone with the Wind*". It was April 1940 when it came to Sheffield.'

The door knocker banged heavily and Rob signalled to me to stay seated while he went. I heard Claire's voice in the hallway, her food radar no doubt clicking.

'Something smells good,' she said as she came into the kitchen.

'How was the football?' I asked.

'Rugby. They won. He's happy. Now then,' she sat at the table where I joined her. She opened her notebook, held her pen poised and said, 'Did you think any more about the shoe problem, Alice?' I felt like one of her team, as though my contribution was vital to the investigation, though I suspected this was a technique she had. Use of first names. It was subtle, I'd give her that.

'As it happens,' Rob said, from his position at the cooker, 'We did. And what we want to know is, could she have been wearing slippers?' Claire put her chin on her hand, nodding to encourage him. 'For instance, she could have heard the siren and rushed out without putting shoes on. It's possible, isn't it?'

I was irritated that after pouring scorn on my idea, he was making it sound like his own. Claire put her finger at the side of her mouth for a moment then shook her head. 'Mm, now, if that were the case, you see, we'd find fabric remnants, wouldn't we? By the feet?'

Good, I thought, at least if she thought it a daft suggestion, she wouldn't think it mine. But there was a gleam in Rob's eye that meant he was enjoying an argument for argument's sake, and wouldn't much care about the outcome.

'I don't know,' he said. 'Maybe not. Depends what kind of fabric, surely? I saw on *Time Team* once –'

'Well, it's an idea, I'll give you that,' Claire interrupted. 'I'll make a note of it.' She didn't. 'But I suppose I'm more interested in how come the body was moved? You sure I can't see your mother?'

'The doctor says Mum still isn't fit to be interviewed,' I said, glad that Mum had decided not to join us.

'What do you mean, the body was moved?' Rob asked.

'Pity,' Claire said. 'It would save all this to-ing and fro-ing and I could get it from the horse's mouth, if you'll excuse the expression.' She turned to Rob. 'The angle of the head. Makes us think she died somewhere else and was moved into the Anderson shelter. Then someone covered it over –'

'Mum and grandma,' was out of my mouth before I could stop myself.

She looked directly at me.

'What I mean is…' I rushed to explain what sounded like an admission. 'They found the shelter in ruins and decided it was dangerous, so they covered it up. Mum told me about it. They thought it was bomb damage. Of course you say it wasn't, but they thought so at the time. They had no idea there was a body in there.'

'Ah, well,' Claire picked up the wine bottle and studied the label. I ignored the hint.

Still studying the bottle, she said, 'Yes, I can see that a casual observer wouldn't have seen the body. After all, it was under the bed.' I was relieved to hear that something seemed to be matching up to my mother's account. Rob served up the carbonara on to two plates.

Then she said, 'Which more or less scotches your idea that the lady was sheltering there, doesn't it? I mean, why would she shelter under the bed?'

Rob put the plates into the oven and sat at the table. 'So, Detective Inspector, if I've got it right –'

'Claire,' she said.

'If I've got it right,' Rob repeated. 'You have a body you believe died somewhere else, then was put into the shelter. You think someone then took the shelter apart deliberately. We've explained why the shelter was 'deconstructed' – your word – and you can hardly think Mrs Ibbertson is capable of moving a body? You've seen the size of her after all. Do you have any idea how big the lady was?'

'Big,' Claire said, 'That's to say she was a large lady for her time. Seemingly people are taller now than in those days, so she was unusual in being about five feet six or seven, and she was probably quite well built. Probably' – she pointed to the wedding photograph of Rob and me which was on the mantelpiece and then at me – 'about your height, Mrs Burgess.'

Rob said, 'So, we'd agree that it wouldn't be very easy for Mrs Ibbertson to move the lady if, that is, Mrs

Ibbertson was involved in any way, in the lady's arrival at the shelter?'

Claire leaned conspiratorially towards Rob. 'I didn't say that Mrs Ibbertson might have moved the body, Mr Burgess. You did.' She looked straight at him for several seconds, watching him blush a deep pink from his chin to the roots of his hair. Then she sat back and said conversationally, 'It's a good opportunity to bump somebody off and get rid of a body, though, don't you think? Dark nights, bombs going off all around. I'd say it would be a pretty good bet that you wouldn't be discovered.'

'You're not a believer in the wartime spirit then, Detective Inspector?' Rob said. 'Everyone helping everyone else?'

'Not me, Mr Burgess,' Claire laughed. I noted her use of formal names. 'My granddad was a policeman during the war and he told me a few tales that would surprise you. He used to say they were the darkest days in more ways than one. You wouldn't believe all the crime that went on.'

'You said 'bumped off', Rob said. 'Are you suggesting this was a murder?'

Claire waited for a few seconds – she was definitely a woman who enjoyed creating suspense – then said, 'It's looking that way.'

I asked, 'What makes you think so? What evidence do you have?' and she looked sharply at me.

'Well, now, being a police officer, I like asking the questions. So let's see what questions we have so far…' Claire fiddled with the wine bottle, looking at it as though the questions she sought were written on the label, and then casually started to count on her fingers. 'One, why is the gabardine draped over her? Wouldn't she be wearing it? Two, why is she lying under the bed if she's using it as a shelter? Three, why is she lying in water? In wet soil in actual fact. You confirmed that the shelter wasn't in use because it was flooded, so why would she lie there of her own accord? Oh and of course, four, why is she not wearing any shoes? You think maybe slippers, I ask where's the fabric to suggest there was anything on her feet? And, you see, we know this because the fabric that's been in the waterlogged soil is pretty well preserved. As is the skin on the back of the lady – sorry…'

My hand was over my mouth. I was feeling a bit queasy. She was half-smiling, not sorry at all, she was thoroughly enjoying the impact of every word. 'So, where were we?' She checked her hand, counted her fingers then tapped her thumb. 'One, two, three, four, aah, five. Who moved her? If she died somewhere else, she must have been moved afterwards. After all, if she died naturally, wouldn't they call for help? Oh,' – she grasped the index finger of her other hand and added, as if it was an afterthought – 'Six. How did she come by a broken leg and seven blows to her skull?'

I felt winded and struggled to get my breath. Whatever I'd thought about the dead lady over the last two days, it hadn't occurred to me that we were involved in a murder investigation. Rob looked as though he'd been taken by surprise too, and I thought that this was the effect Claire had been playing for when she stood up suddenly and said, 'Well, I must let you get on with your meal. But I'm sure you appreciate that this is now a criminal investigation. And we're getting to the point that we must ask Mrs Ibbertson some questions.' She looked from one to the other of us and picked up her handbag, swinging the strap over her shoulder. 'You see, just because it was seventy years ago, we don't take it any less seriously. The problem is, of course, although forensics can tell us most things, we really could do with a witness. And seemingly nobody else from that time is still around in the neighbourhood. Apart from your mother.' She was fiddling in her bag, pulling out and checking her phone, while we remained motionless. 'We may have to bring in the police surgeon for an opinion if your doctor keeps insisting we can't see Mrs Ibbertson. I'd rather we didn't have to, but I'm sure you can appreciate how we're fixed. Well,' she put the phone away and moved to the door. I followed her down the hallway, watching her square heels click along the linoleum towards the door, 'I'll be back tomorrow.'

'On a Sunday?' I asked.

'No peace for the wicked,' she said. I didn't think she meant herself. 'I've got something to show your mother.' Standing on the doorstep, looking up and down the street, she said, 'Liam's not coming tonight. The Chief Super seems to be satisfied that there aren't any more bodies buried around the place and sending in the team wouldn't come up with any forensic evidence given the lapse of time. Anyway,' as she walked down the path, 'My budget's overspent as it is.'

The spaghetti had suffered from waiting in the oven and was brittle wherever it wasn't covered with sauce, but it went down very nicely with a couple of glasses of the sauvignon. We offered Mum a small plate and she refused, but she handed me back an empty glass and agreed to eat a biscuit and drink some of the Lucozade Rob had bought for her, which we left on her bedside table as she settled back into bed.

Over supper we talked about Claire's droplets of information and tried to match them with Mum's account. Increasingly, I tended to agree with Rob who was convinced Mum knew much more than she was letting on, that there was much more to it and we didn't yet have the full story. It seemed remarkable to think a ninety-odd year old woman might be an important witness to something that had happened over seventy years ago. We were worried about Claire's not-so-subtle threats and agreed it was time for legal advice, so we would contact the doctor's friend tomorrow.

We were washing up together when I remembered. 'What was the second piece of news?'

He stopped in the act of drying the saucepan and slapped his hand against his forehead. 'Stupid of me, sorry. It's – well, not sure how you'll take this, old thing–'

'What?'

'Maybe sit down?'

'Don't be a drama queen, out with it.'

'All right. It's about the family tree, you know the one that Judy started?'

I remembered. Judy had asked all of us for dates of birth and all manner of details to put into the family tree, then suddenly she'd stopped working on it. 'Mum refused to give her any details. Called it silly. She said – what was it, now? I remember – "what's the point of knowing all that, how does that help anything?" Judy said she couldn't do any more without that information.'

'OK, but when all this online family history lark started, I said to Judy that I'd have a look at it for her, maybe we don't need your mother to give us the information. She sent it to me and it's on the computer at home. I never got around to doing anything with it, but with all this going on, I decided to pull it out again. I thought, you never know, if your mother's keeping secrets–'

'And what did you find out?'

'Oh, nothing.' My husband really is very infuriating sometimes. I glared at him and he added quickly, 'I just thought it might be worth sending it to Shirley.'

'Shirley? You mean the Shirley you used to work with?'

'That's her. So I sent it to her.' This Shirley had been Rob's PA for a few years after I retired. Since Rob retired, she was constantly contacting him for references for jobs she didn't get. 'She's started doing online genealogy. Says there's quite a demand for it.'

'And how did you know this? I can't remember you mentioning it.'

'I met her the other day, in town. Probably didn't mention it because I know how you feel about her.' I decided to let that one pass. 'You have to admit, she's a trier. She went to college, did a course, learned all about computing, and now she's set up this home business. Doing quite well by all accounts.' He meant by her own account, probably.

'And you asked her to get involved in our family affairs?' Rob pulled off his glasses and polished them on the tea-towel. 'The same Shirley who you told me could never be trusted with personal information?'

'I don't think I exactly said that.' Rob put his specs back on, decided they were still dirty, took them off, started polishing them again. 'I've no evidence to suggest Shirley was, well, indiscreet. No, it isn't that. It's more that she makes a bit of a meal of knowing something personal about you. I'm sorry, I thought it would help.

Move things forward. It being the weekend, and Tuesday being the first chance I can get to the archives.'

I recalled a couple of phone calls when this Shirley said she couldn't put me through to Rob, but had been secretive about why he was not available. Most people would say, 'in a meeting' or something like it, but Shirley seemed to enjoy inferring there was more to it. The truth was that there was nothing to tell – so I believed, anyway – and it seemed Shirley was just relishing her position as his right hand woman.

'Correct me if I'm wrong, but I'm sure I heard you say once, that "with Shirley, a trouble shared is a trouble doubled"? Are we talking about that Shirley?' He nodded and pushed his glasses back onto the bridge of his nose, making a bit of a performance of it to avoid meeting my eye. 'And you sent her… what did you send her?'

'The stuff Judy had done, asked if she could look into it for us, get any more information. Sorry if I've done wrong, but she seems to know her way around these things and is certainly more *au fait* with the technology.' So he'd been impressed by someone who knew their way around the internet. Typical.

'And?'

'She said she'd seen the news and understood it might be urgent. She was fishing. I didn't tell her anything. She said she'd get onto it right away. She's got the landline and our mobile numbers and said she'd call as soon as she knew anything.'

'You don't think you might have consulted me, since this appears to be about me, before involving a stranger?' If it could fall any further, Rob's face did. In the silence, he busied himself putting the pots and pans away, then moving them around again, until I went across to him and, hugging him from behind, and said, 'Sorry, I know you're trying to help.'

He patted my hand and reached for the pharmacy bag, taking a blister pack of sleeping pills from it. He pressed four into his palm and looked at me.

'We could crush them into her Horlicks.'

'Isn't that going a bit far?'

'Do you want to read that diary or not?'

Yes, I did. I was ashamed that I did, and maybe Rob intuitively knew this for he said, 'She hasn't eaten or slept in two days. She must be exhausted. And she'll need her wits about her if Claire gets her way.' I nodded slowly. He added, 'Don't worry. I'll make the Horlicks. And I'll stand by her while she drinks it.'

Frank

Changi Airport

Amy's itinerary: '*Singapore: two hours wait. Follow signs for 'Transit', stay in transit lounge. Do not leave Airport.*' No chance of me getting lost, the stewardess brought me right here and settled me in. It's a VIP lounge, apparently. I daren't think how much Amy paid for all this. There's a shower, and I can help myself to food and drink. Not that I need anything, I've eaten so much on the plane. How do they do that thing with food at 38,000 feet? I had stew and dumplings, and then I asked for ice cream just because I wanted to see whether it really was frozen. The stewardess laughed at me. It's dinner time in Sheffield. I wonder what's going on there. The young ladies here couldn't have been more helpful. They looked up the *Sheffield Star* for me on the internet, and found the latest news.

Forensic investigations have found that death resulted from a fractured skull and other injuries which police say are not consistent with an air raid. The police spokeswoman told the Star that a murder investigation is now underway. The young woman has yet to be identified, and police say this may take some time as a large number of people went missing during the Blitz.

Not an accident. If I worked it out at all, in my ten-year-old brain, I thought about all manner of reasons why Jean had gone missing, like she'd got lost, or run off, or had an accident. I was sure that Violet was covering something up. Murder though? That never occurred to me. Sixteen hours to go. It doesn't say whether Violet's recovered. If she has, she could be telling the police anything. She certainly had everyone fooled at the time.

I check my haversack. It's important that I remember things in the right order. I think it's going to be important to other people to have things in the right order. Next up is another book. This one is a thin textbook covered with grey cloth and in faded type on the cover it says, *German for His Majesty's Forces*. It has dog-eared corners and pencil marks all through it, faded now and impossible to read. It takes me straight back to Hurdle Hill Terrace in the week following the wedding.

Richard had popped in to see if Jean was all right the night after Joe had gone back to training camp. He sat down and chatted to my Dad as if they were old mates. As he was leaving, Richard asked if I could go and help Mr Knowles to dig the garden over, to put in some special winter root vegetables.

Afterwards my Dad said, 'He's a nice chap and no mistake.'

Cyril said, 'If tha wants to do some digging tha can help me on the allotment.'

Mam said, 'Charity begins at home.'

Whatever that meant, it sounded like work so I decided not to risk it by hanging around. The next day, and for the following week, there still being no school, I headed off to Hurdle Hill straight after breakfast. By going in through the back gate, I avoided meeting Mrs Knowles. Mr Knowles was usually pottering around the garden. Violet brought out tea and bread and butter for us though she didn't speak to me. One day, while I was digging, Mr

Knowles wandered off into the house and came back with this grey, cloth-covered book.

He said, 'Now then, young man,' – he'd probably forgotten my name again – 'this could come in useful.' He sat on the garden bench and waved me to sit beside him. 'We had to learn German you know, in the last lot. It might come in handy this time. You need to be prepared.' He opened to a page with a picture of soldiers in a pub, and underneath it had the German for saying hello, ordering a glass of beer, and saying goodbye. He turned to a page showing British soldiers marching, and we tried to pronounce the German words. Mr Knowles marched up the garden and shouted out, '*Links um!*' and turned to the left. I caught on and called out, '*Rechts um!*' and he turned to the right. I found some canes leaning in a corner that made do as rifles. I marched beside him and then he shouted, '*Umdrehen!*' and I turned to the left and he turned to the right and we bumped into one another. We laughed until Mr Knowles was bright red in the face. He leaned on my shoulder, wheezing.

Mrs Knowles came out of the door and shouted, 'Arthur! Stop that at once and come indoors.' She tutted about him being in the garden in his carpet slippers and told me to go home.

On early closing day, Richard spent the afternoon with us in the garden. He asked how Jean was, and if we'd heard from Joe.

I said, 'She's not heard from him since he left on Monday. She's right mardy.' He laughed. I asked Mr Knowles if he was going to go to war and he chuckled and said he'd already been.

Richard said, 'He means the last war. Did you know Mr Knowles is a hero? Maybe he'll show you his medals one day.'

I remembered my Dad had said there was a reason Richard wouldn't join up and decided to ask him if he would go and fight with Joe.

He shook his head and said, 'It's complicated' and then the rain came bucketing down and the three of us took cover in the Anderson shelter. The rain hammered against the wooden ends of the shelter. The German book was on the small pile of magazines on the little table. I picked it up and was looking through it, rolling my tongue around the strange words, when I heard Richard saying, 'It's over, we're at home,' very softly and I looked round to see Mr Knowles with his hands over his ears and his head on his knees, rocking back and forth and talking very fast. I made out odd words: 'John... going over... don't...' and then he lifted his head and pointed to the edge of the shelter where it met the ground. I could see muddy water seeping under the side of the shelter where we had dug it into the ground.

Mr Knowles said, 'Mud.'

Richard said, 'It's only a bit of rain from the hill.'

Mr Knowles said, 'Rain coming in the dugout. Mud.'

Then the rain stopped and Richard held Mr Knowles under the elbow and led him out of the shelter. Violet was calling, 'Daddy' and she ran through the rain to the other side of Mr Knowles, and together they helped him into the house. I left, seeing they wouldn't be doing any more digging, and was nearly home before I realised I still had the book in my hand.

I went to take the book back the following day, but Mr Knowles wasn't in the garden. Peering through the kitchen window I could see Violet sitting at the table, sticking something into a book. When I tapped on the window she jumped as if she was frightened. Seeing it was me, she slapped the glue pot onto the table and came to open the door.

She said, 'You can't see my father. He's ill.'

She was about to close the door when I heard Mr Knowles say, 'Is that Frank? Bring him in, Violet,' so she opened the door to allow me in. He was sitting in the armchair on the opposite side of the fireplace to Mrs Knowles, who was still knitting what looked like a very long sock, but with dark green wool this time. As I passed the table where Violet had been sitting, I saw writing and pictures on the page. I liked cutting out and sticking, and leaned across to read it. She'd drawn a picture of a bar of soap with *"Lux"* written across it and underneath in very neat handwriting it said, *"Make your soap last longer, never leave it in water"*. Violet snatched the book away and closed it.

I turned to Mr Knowles who smiled at me. I offered him the German book and said, 'I'm sorry, I took it home by mistake'. Violet tut-tutted behind me as if she didn't believe me.

He said, 'Keep it, Frank, you might need it, you never know.' Violet stood at the door watching me so I gathered I shouldn't stay, and said goodbye to him.

I could hear her following me down the garden path, to the gate. As I closed the gate behind me, we looked at one another across it. Glancing back at the house, she said, 'I know Richard thinks you're good company for my Father, but he gets far too excited, so I'd be obliged if you didn't come again.' I felt too sad to say anything, and she added, 'And if Richard should ask, you'll oblige me further by saying you're too busy with your schoolwork.' I looked down at my shoes. 'Do you understand?' I thought she might ask for the book back, so I pushed it down the front of my trousers and ran off up the hill.

I showed the book to Dad at supper. He said, 'We shall be safe with thee, then, when Jerry comes calling,' and they all laughed, so I took it into the privy and wrapped it into my parcel of treasures.

Some days later, I was filling the coal bucket in the yard when I heard that tut-tutting from the gennel and looked up, expecting to see Violet. She came head first, wearing a pointed hat with a dent in the top of it, her handbag held out in front of her and watching her feet as though she expected to walk in dog mess. I remembered the book and thought I was in trouble. I ran in the house, slipped in to the understairs cupboard and pulled the door almost closed.

There were three sharp taps at the door and Mam came thumping down the stairs above my head. I heard her say, 'What is it now?' in a cross voice as she came into the kitchen and opened the door. Then her voice changed. 'Violet love,' she said, 'Bring thyself in. Sit down.' I heard chairs being shifted around. Mam said, 'Jean's not home yet. Shall I make a cup of tea?'

Violet must have sat at the table, in the chair nearest to the cupboard door, because I could hear her really clearly. She said, 'No need to go to any trouble, Mrs Sheldon,' in her prim little voice. 'Richard asked me to call. He works at Burtons, you know. The men's outfitters.' Mam said nothing. 'Well, it seems they have some end of line items, some shirts and… erm, other men's garments. He thought they might come in useful.'

Mam still said nothing and I thought it wasn't often she was lost for words. I was glad to hear Jean approaching, up the gennel, singing as usual:

Of all the girls that are so smart,
There's none like pretty Sally,
She is the darling of my heart,
And she lives in our alley.

Jean squealed as she came into the kitchen, 'Vi,' she sounded really pleased to see her. 'I was thinking of you – Sally in Our Alley – it's showing at the Oxford…'

Violet said, 'On Upperthorpe?' as if she was talking about Timbuctoo.

Jean said, 'On Friday night. Shall we go?'

'Well, I shall need to ask Richard.'

'Oh we don't want him coming along and spoiling it for us. Let's make it a girls' night out. Two married women, out together. It'll be fun.'

Violet said, 'I don't know.'

I heard Jean filling the kettle as she said, 'Think about it and let me know. Anyway, to what do we owe the pleasure? Richard all right?' She whispered to Violet, 'Isn't married life marvellous?' Violet took a sharp breath and said nothing.

Mam said, 'Violet came to give us something.'

Violet said, 'It's only a few…' She sounded unsure of herself. 'Richard wondered whether you wanted any of the… erm…'

Mam said, 'Stuff they're chucking out of Burtons,' really sharply and I could tell she was vexed. 'Charity cases, he thinks we are.'

Jean lifted the boiling kettle off the coals. 'That's a nice thought, tell him thanks, if our boys don't want it I'm sure Joe will appreciate it.'

I heard Mam puff loudly and then her feet pounded as they went up the stairs above my head.

Violet said, ‘I think I’ve offended your mother. I didn’t mean…’

Jean said, ‘Don’t worry about it, Vi. So, this film, it’s Gracie Fields. Isn’t she grand?’

Violet said, ‘I’m not sure about Gracie Fields. I mean, Mother says she would be such a good opera singer, but instead she makes these *musicals*,’ she almost spat the word out.

Jean said, ‘That’s what I like about her.’

Violet said, ‘Oh, I didn’t mean, oh dear, no offence?’

Jean said, ‘None taken.’

I wiped my nose with my sleeve and the coal dust made me sneeze. The understairs cupboard door opened and Jean pulled me out, shouting, ‘What’s tha doing in there, nebbin’?’ She called, ‘Mam.’ As I heard Mam’s feet on the stairs above me I pushed Jean away and ran out of the back door. I decided to lie low until they’d calmed down.

Without school, and now I wasn’t going up to Hurdle Hill any more, Sam and me more or less ran wild. It all seemed a bit of a lark. In due course, we had lessons for a couple of hours in the morning in the front room of Sam’s house but it was nearly Christmas before a letter came to say a new teacher had been found and we were to go back to school in January. Cyril was in his last year at big school and due to matriculate, so his class had carried on. Mam was working at Fergusons with Jean and they were both doing double shifts. If Jean saw anything of Violet I didn’t know about it, and I didn’t see anything of the Knowleses. Then it was Christmas, and Jean was all of a dither because Joe was due home for forty-eight hours on

Boxing Day. I was excited too, because he'd written in a letter to Jean that he'd got me a Hawker Hurricane pin. On Christmas morning, I woke up early, excited, and dashed downstairs where Mam was banging about in the kitchen. Our stockings hung over the fireplace.

I asked, 'Can I take mine down?'

Mam said, 'No, tha can wait until everybody's had breakfast.'

So I went back upstairs and jumped on Cyril and punched Bill to wake them up. They were too sleepy to catch me and I ran downstairs. Eventually, everyone was up and had their breakfast, and Mam handed out the stockings. We all got a packet of raisins, a sixpence and an orange, then we each had a different game of cards. The lads got a pair of socks and a balaclava each and Jean got some talcum powder. Jean gave me a box of Liquorice Allsorts. It wasn't like a proper Christmas, because Dad and Bill had to go to work after breakfast, and Jean was moping around with nothing to do but wait for Joe.

He came on Boxing Day and stood in his uniform, inside the door, looking half asleep. Jean fussed around him, sitting him down to pull his boots off and not even complaining at the stink coming from his feet.

I asked, 'Has tha brought the Hurricane pin, Joe?'

Bill asked, 'Has tha been in France? It says in this week's *War Illustrated* how they've built pillboxes and anti-tank ditches all down the–'

Jean said, 'Bugger off and leave him alone,' and she helped Joe upstairs where he slept until tea time. When I found him standing with his back to the fire, talking to Dad, he seemed to be back to his lively self.

Joe said, 'That's for you, Scamp,' nodding towards a little brown paper bag on the table. It was the Hawker

Hurricane pin. I put it on my jacket lapel and put on the jacket to admire it. I wanted to go round to Sam's straight away to show him.

The curtains were closed. I was tapping on the door when a woman stuck her head out of the next door along and said, 'Young Sam's round his Nannan's while his Mam's at hospital, love.' She could see I didn't know what she was on about so she went on, 'Mester Ainsworth, he were knocked down by a car last night.'

'Sam's dad? Is he dead?'

She said, 'It's touch and go. Happen we'll know more later. Who shall I tell him was asking?'

I ran back round to our house and burst out, 'Mam, Mester Ainsworth's in hospital from being knocked down.'

She said, 'Well I'm sorry for their troubles. There's more folk been killed in accidents caused by the chuffing blackout than in this War to date and that's a fact.'

The following afternoon Jean was at work, so Joe took me to the pictures to see the latest Tarzan film, and we went into town on the tram. Joe paid to sit in the stalls, so I was surrounded by grownups. I looked up to see if there was anyone I knew in the gallery who might notice I was there with Joe, but the cigarette smoke was so thick I could barely see. Joe let me rummage in his greatcoat pocket and I found a packet of fruit gums. The heavy red tasselled curtain opened and we watched the Pathe News.

The voice said, '*On the Baltic coast, the German people are starving*,' while grey women shuffled across the screen, wrapped in coats and head-scarves, and joined long queues outside shops. I thought it didn't look much different to the High Street on a Saturday afternoon. Then there was a family sitting at a table with two children smiling broadly, with a steaming plate of food in front of them. The newsreader sounded excited when he said, '*While in Britain the start of food rationing in January will ensure that everyone continues to get their fair share.*'

The curtain closed. I looked around for the usherette with the sweet tray but no one came and the lights didn't go up. After a few seconds the curtain swung back again and band music was filling the picture house when there was a great banging and I thought the walls were going to explode. Someone shouted, 'Air raid,' and people started screaming and pushing their way out of the rows. A man in a suit ran onto the stage and started to shout and wave his arms but no one was listening to him. Lights came on. We moved with the crowd, pressed in on all sides. As we passed the stage, my feet were lifted off the ground. Joe grabbed me under the armpit and held me close. The emergency side door had been opened and I could see the sky above the heads of the people in front. The fruit gums I'd been eating a few moments before had become a solid lump in my throat, making me gasp to get my breath. As the woman in front of us half-turned, something about the way her hair swept up from her forehead, into a wave, put me in mind of Jean and I swallowed hard to try to clear my throat. As we reached the outside, people in front of us stopped moving but those behind us were still pushing, squashing us.

I said, 'Joe, what about Jean, will she get to the shelter?'

Joe said, 'They've got a shelter at Fergusons, she'll be alright, Scamp.' He pushed a way through the crowd and I saw the shelter built into the side of Atkinsons store. At the door of it was an ARP man.

The woman with the wave in her hair said, 'So tha's not letting us in, then?'

The ARP man said, 'It's not an air raid, love. I think I'd have heard if it was.'

I looked up at the empty grey sky.

Joe said, 'False alarm. Let's get back to the pictures.'

The man in the suit was standing at the side door. He said, 'The boiler has burst. I'm afraid we're closed for the day now.'

Joe said to me, 'You look as though you've seen a ghost. Let's get you home.'

More than anything, I wanted to see that Jean and Mam were alright. It might be a false alarm but what would happen if there was a real air raid and we weren't there? With Sam's dad's accident, and the funny smell Joe had brought home with him, and now almost an air raid, I was suddenly full of fear and the war didn't seem so exciting. As we walked back to the tram, I felt proud to be with a soldier in uniform. People stopped and talked to him and said things like, 'Give 'em hell, son,' and patted him on the back.

That night, Jean and Joe went to a dance at the Marples Hotel. She made him wear his uniform even though he had other clothes. She said, 'I want everyone to see my handsome soldier husband.'

Joe said, 'It'll need a bit of spit and polish,' and he let me help him shine his boots and his buttons. They looked grand as they headed off, our Jean with her hair done up in curls and Joe shiny and clean.

I was awoken by voices. It was such an unusual sound that it took me some time to realise it was coming from Jean's room. Whispering rose to talking, then dropped back to a whisper. Bill and Cyril were snoring beside me. I got out of bed and put my ear to the wall.

Jean was saying, 'Stuck up little cow and no mistake. All I did was call him Tricky Dickie. If looks could have killed, I'd be mincemeat.'

Joe said, 'She doesn't mean it, Jeanie. Richard says she's as shy as a mouse and she's awkward around people. You could perhaps make a friend of her, bring her out of herself?'

'Well, isn't she the charity case? With her posh house and her piano, and all her fancy elocution lessons, it's me that has to be kind to her?'

'She's not like you, Jeanie. She doesn't have any friends.'

'Why does that not surprise me?'

'She's never had the chance. Her mother's kept people away because of her dad. You've seen how he is when he gets confused. So Violet's had a very quiet life. Could you not spend a bit of time with her?'

'Well, happen I could see if she wants to go to pictures from time to time, it wouldn't harm.'

'You're a good girl, Jeanie.'

'At least in pictures, we won't have to talk.'

'Even if you are on the sarky side.'

The bedsprings creaked and I heard Jean giggling as I climbed back into bed and drifted off to sleep, thinking of Violet, and thinking maybe if Jean could cheer her up that would be a good thing.

Jean and Joe were leaving for the railway station when Sam called round. Jean said, 'Come on in, lad. How's thy Dad?'

Sam said, ‘He’s right bad. His leg’s crushed and Mam says he’ll not walk straight again. He’ll not be able to drive the crane either so he’ll happen lose his job.’

Jean said, ‘Well, give thy mam our best,’ and she and Joe waved to us all as they left.

Mam called from the table where she was making pastry, ‘I’m right sorry to hear that, Sam. I’ll go round and see thy mam this aft.’

Sam pulled a newspaper parcel from under his jacket. It was stained with blood. ‘Mam says does tha want some pigeons?’

‘Tha’s not having to get rid of his pigeons, surely?’

‘Aye, Mam says he’ll not be able to look after them and she’ll not have money to feed them. This is first lot. Mam says will a tanner be all right?’

Mam went to the cupboard and lifted down the cocoa tin, took out a shilling and gave it to Sam. She said, ‘Make sure thy mam gives me first refusal of next lot. Mr Sheldon’s fond of a bit of pigeon.’ As we left, she gave Sam a bag of potatoes that was hanging on the back of the door. ‘Here, tell thy mam we’re overrun with spuds if she won’t mind taking some of our hands. They’re what Cyril’s grown on his allotment.’

I said, ‘Cyril’s spuds haven’t –’

She pushed us out of the door, saying, ‘Make sure tha’s home for six.’

So it was pigeon pie for supper. Jean was on lates and without her or Joe there seemed to be too many empty chairs at the table. Bill and Dad talked about where Joe might be headed. I’d heard Bill talking to Joe over breakfast, about being in France. Joe had been talking about walking past graveyards full of fallen soldiers from the last war.

'To think my Dad's in there somewhere.' Joe had said.

'Passion Dale, wasn't it?' Bill asked, and his voice was full of wonder. I remembered Richard saying something about this at the wedding.

I'd asked, 'Where's Passion Dale?'

Bill said, 'Belgium'. He puffed up his chest and leaned his head back as if he was about to deliver a sermon. 'Third Battle of Wipers. Summer of 1917.'

Joe said, 'It was one of the main battles of the last war.'

Now, Bill pulled a copy of *The War Illustrated* from his pocket and unfolded it onto the table. He turned the pages until he found what he was looking for, putting his finger on a photograph of soldiers digging trenches, up to their ankles in water. He said, 'They need all the hands they can get. Happen I shall join up when I'm eighteen, if it's not over by then.'

Dad's face flushed purple as though he might burst.

I asked, 'Did tha fight in last war, Dad?'

Dad looked over to Mam, lifting his eyebrows and she shrugged. He pushed his plate away and pulled out his tobacco tin. 'Happen I shall tell thee this because it might give thee an idea why I want my family to stay in one place and in one piece.'

We all leaned across the table to hear him better. 'I joined up soon as I was old enough. Couldn't wait to get a rifle in my hand.' Cyril and Bill looked at one another. 'My Dad, thy Granddad, was out in Flanders and I had some fancy notion about fighting alongside him.' He stopped and looked at Mam and she winked at him. 'He was in the field hospital when I landed. He never made it back.'

I remembered the photograph my Nannan always had on her sideboard, of a man in uniform, and wondered if that was my Granddad, but nobody had spoken of him before.

Bill's eyes were shining. 'So tha was in Army at eighteen then, Dad? And Granddad fought as well?'

Dad put his palm up towards Bill. 'Whatever's in thy mind, forget it. I'm telling thee what war's all about, none of that fancy nonsense they put out on the wireless. We had the same idea, me and my pals, we all wanted to be in the thick of it.' Bill was nodding. Dad tamped tobacco into his pipe. 'As it happened, it was all over when we got there. We was the clear-up mob, bringing them back from the fields, one bit at a time and not knowing which bit belonged to who. Happen one of them was Joe's dad.' He paused to light his pipe, then pushed his head back and blew out a smoke circle. I stood on tiptoe to blow it higher. 'So think on that for a minute.'

I looked at the photograph in Bill's paper and imagined an older Joe, lying in the bottom of the watery mud that I could see there. It made me think of Mr Knowles, crying about the mud coming into the Anderson shelter, and how he must have been thinking about the same thing.

Dad pointed his pipe stem at Bill, then Cyril. 'So listen up. None of my lads is going to be cannon fodder for this government.' He paused a while, sucking on his pipe, then said, 'Tha's in a reserved job with good money. I want my family here, not scattered across half of Europe, after this lot's finished.'

'Well, I reckon that was then and this is now and…' Bill turned the page of his magazine and pointed to a photograph of young lads in uniforms doing something with a model aeroplane. 'See, our Cyril.' and Cyril leaned over to look. 'Happen we could be Air Cadets.' He stopped talking as he registered the look on my Dad's face. Dad pulled the magazine from under Bill's hand and rolled it up. He held it out to Mam who was stoking the fire under the kettle.

He said, 'That's only fit for burning,' and she took it from him without a word. He looked at Bill, as if daring him to do anything about it. Mam put the rolled up magazine behind the clock on the mantelpiece and continued stoking the fire. Dad and Bill stared at one another across the table like cock bantams raring for a fight.

Mam said, 'That was a good bit of pigeon. Mind, I'd rather have gone without than profit from poor Mr Ainsworth's bad luck. They're saying it'll be months before he walks again, if at all.' I could see she was trying to change the subject, and Dad broke off staring at Bill to look at her.

Cyril said, 'Aye, but it's worked well for our Jean, eh?'

Dad said, 'What's that?

Cyril said, 'I saw that great pudding, Sybil, this aft and she said our Jean had only gone and got Mester Ainsworth's job, driving crane at Ferguson's.'

That sounded right good. I imagined our Jean sitting on top of a crane.

Mam's head swivelled round and she pointed the white-hot end of the poker at Cyril. She said, 'She never has?' Cyril nodded, looking pleased as Punch to have told her something new. 'Would she jump in his chuffing grave as quick? Whatever am I to say to Mrs Ainsworth when she finds out?' She pushed the poker back into the fire, making red-hot coals fall onto the grate. 'I'll be having a few words with Madam when she gets in.'

Dad had left the table and was sitting in his armchair by the fire. He said, 'I'd not fret about it, our lass. Happen we'll be a lot safer with our Jean driving that crane than we ever were with Ainsworth. It frit the life out of us to watch him swing that jib around on a Friday after downing four pints at dinner time.' He tapped out his pipe and started to refill it. 'Hit by a car? Not bloody likely. I reckon he was three sheets to the wind and jumped on top of that car, thinking he'd get a lift home. Pity the poor sod who was driving. Imagine the whites of Ainsie's eyes plastered against the windscreen.'

We were all laughing now, even Bill. It was true, Sam's dad was more often drunk than not. Mam wagged a finger at me and said, 'Tha's not to repeat one word of that to young Sam or his family, mind.' Taking the kettle from the fire, she poured it into the sink ready for washing up.

I sat on the fender and nudged Dad to get him back to the point. 'So what about Wipers, then? Did Mr Knowles go there?'

'Oh, aye, he were Sergeant Major. Tha'd not think it to look at him now, but he were one of the bravest, by all accounts. He's got medals for it. Left him for dead under a pile of bodies of his men, most of them from Roper's down in Netherthorpe. Only him come back alive. Lost his marbles, mind.'

Bill asked, 'Isn't that where Joe's dad were killed?'

'Aye, Joe's dad, Richard's dad, a whole gang of them, all from Roper's works and all of them in same regiment. That was how they did it then. There was supposed to be some kind of glory in marching off together with the whole town seeing them off.'

Mam stopped washing up and stared out of the kitchen window. 'I'll be buggered if I can see any glory for the folk left behind, bringing up a family with no money coming in. Like Joe's poor mam.'

'What happened?' I wanted to keep this story going. It was rare to have Mam and Dad telling us about the old days.

Mam said, 'She died, poor soul, with the flu that killed off more after the war than died in it.'

Cyril asked, 'Is that why Joe grew up at Richard's house?' and I wondered how he knew that.

Mam said, 'Aye. Richard's mam took him in and brought him up.'

Dad had his fresh pipe lit now, and he leaned back, the pipe resting against his lips. He said, 'So tha sees what damage war does to ordinary folk,' and closed his eyes, which meant the end of the conversation. Bill checked that Dad's eyes were closed, then slid his magazine from behind the clock. He signalled to Cyril to go upstairs with him.

I lit a candle with a taper from the fire and, with my hand shielding the flame, slipped out of the kitchen door and into the privy. Taking out the German book, I put my head against the cold bricks and closed my eyes. I thought of Mr Knowles with his face in the mud and soldiers piled on top of him. I pictured my Dad walking across a muddy field, holding a pair of legs and calling for Joe, while bombs exploded all around him. I knew my Dad was right and our lads shouldn't go, and that Joe was right and he should go. Then I didn't know what to think about the rights and wrongs of war.

We're on the way to Heathrow now. They put me on first, with the old crocks. I'm not sure what I think about being lumped together with the wheelchairs and whatnot. On the other hand, I don't think I could be doing with all that standing about and queuing, it's a long haul and I'm feeling a bit tired if truth was told, so I mustn't grumble. There's a new stewardess – this one's called Simone – she's looking after me – and she tells me they're called cabin crew now, that stewardess is a bit old-fashioned. I settle into my seat as the plane lifts off and I can feel that magnet as powerful as ever. Don't worry, I want to tell them, I'm on my way and I'll make sure everybody knows what's what. At least they know it wasn't an accident. But something's not right. They're only talking about one body. Surely they can tell that some of those bones belong to a baby.

I see her there, clear as day, standing on Chapel Hill, her back to the sun. She's a lumpy, bumpy black shape made up of gas masks, haversack, and with the baby wrapped into her coat for warmth. I wonder if – yes, of course, that'll be it. Jean was wearing her gabardine. Well, if she's still got it on, the baby will be wrapped inside it, of course she will. They'll have found her by the time I get there.

Alice

I listened at Mum's bedroom door. She was snoring with a slight catch in her throat that couldn't be faked. I crept across the floor and stood over her for what felt like several minutes. Her bruises were a dusky brown in the late evening glow that came through the thin curtains. Even in sleep, her hands plucked and smoothed the tiny flowers across the quilt. 'Mum?' I touched her arm. There was no change to her breathing. Patting around her legs, I felt cotton, soft and unresisting, then something harder near the bottom of the bed, and slid both hands under the eiderdown. Slowly, slowly I drew out the book and walked backwards, holding it in front of me like an offering. Only when the door was closed behind me did I allow myself to breathe freely. With shaking hands, I felt the thinness between the faded velvet covers.

Opening the book on the kitchen table, I ran my fingers along the thick wodge of torn edges. Just a few pages remained. Rob leaned across me and thumbed the corners.

'Assuming she kept a regular diary, she's managed to get rid of quite a bit of it,' he said. 'If the part you saved from the fire was before her wedding, in September 1939, and the bit about going to see '*Gone with the Wind*' was the following April, then I'd say the six months that covered her wedding and afterwards, and the part from April to August – she's managed to get rid of most of the year, some of it probably down the loo before I got there. What have we here?'

He turned the book round to face him and flicked through, handing me some loose papers. A typing proficiency certificate dated 23rd July 1937. A certificate of achievement in elocution: *Violet Anne Knowles, Recitation of Shakespeare's Sonnets, 15th May 1938.* A sheet of music for *Peer Gynt, Op. 23.* A scrap of paper with '*Richard's arm and chest measurements*', probably for knitting. A recipe for sausage and sultana casserole, cut neatly from a newspaper, with '*4th February, 1940*' handwritten above and an advertisement for Bovril on the reverse. A shopping list, or perhaps it was a housekeeping budget: *a bag of flour, seven pence; tea, three shillings.* I remember pounds, shillings and pence as though it was yesterday. And I criticised my mother for living in the past. But what caught my eye as I turned it over onto the growing pile by my elbow, was a note on the back of the shopping list. In the familiar cursive script: *oh what a tangled web we weave when first we practice to deceive Mummy keeps repeating those lines as if she knows I wish Daddy was here he'd know what to do.* I set it aside and pulled the green velvet book round to face me. Ran my fingers over the faded rose on the cover. Rob went up to check on Mum.

Violet and Alice

17th August 1940
The park was full of little boys this afternoon, trying to shoot sparrows with their catapults. The Sheldon boy and his friend were there of course. I'm sure the Ministry knows best but birds stealing grain is hardly a problem in the city, surely? It seems to provide an excuse for small boys to get up to mischief. It's certainly far too dangerous to walk there at the moment. Mummy has had notification that Daddy's pension has stopped, although she will receive a small widow's pension. Richard's pension has not yet been paid. It never rains but it pours. Mr Armitage asked me today, with a great deal of nervous clearing of his throat and his cheeks quite pink, when I was going to give up work. I didn't know what he was talking about, and then I realised. I haven't mentioned it to anyone. He must have noticed, which is very embarrassing. Thinking quickly, I said 1st September. Well, I mustn't cry over spilt milk. We shall have to live off our savings.

'Life must have been hard,' I said to Rob who came back at that moment, signalling with his head on one side, resting on his hand, that Mum was still asleep. He emptied the rest of the bottle into our glasses. 'My grandfather died, my father died, she's expecting me, and of course there was no maternity pay.' Another part of Mum's life that I knew nothing about.

Rob looked over my shoulder and said, 'She certainly had a time of it.' He pulled his chair alongside. 'Don't you think her style of writing is odd?'

'It's all like that,' I said. 'Young people did speak and write rather differently in those days. You can almost see where she's put her finger after each full stop to get the spacing exactly right. I think this is how they were taught to write.'

'I remember grammar lessons in my day,' Rob said. 'They don't seem to bother much these days, with all this text-speak and instant messaging type of communication. Adam's generation wouldn't be able to imagine life without even a telephone. Even so, it's a bit stilted to say the least. Look at this – "*a great deal of nervous clearing of his throat*" – it's like reading a novel. When she was writing about meeting Richard, I almost expected her to exclaim when that chap walks in – what's his name? That serial we've been following on TV?'

'Pride and Prejudice?' He nodded. 'You mean Mr Darcy? I suppose that reflects her life at the time, very insular, with romantic dreams. She doesn't cross anything out which makes me think she must have drafted a rough copy, and made sure this notebook was perfect.'

'You think she had a rough book?' Rob laughed. 'Like at school?'

'She may well have,' I said. I pulled the notebook towards us and we read together.

20th August 1940

Jean offered me a box of bent tins. She said they came from a grocer who was bombed out. As the bomb dropped on the other side of town, I think it unlikely. I refused. Joe is on pre-embarkation leave. He thinks he is going to Italy although he shouldn't say. Jean came with him. I saw Mummy looking from one to the other of us and frowning.

30th August 1940
My last day at the Bank. Mr Armitage gave a short speech which was very complimentary. He gave me a gift of a Bond for the baby. Jane has knitted bootees. She has never stopped currying favour after saying those awful things about Richard last year. A year gone. Looking back at what I wrote then, I feel so much older. Not more grown up, but really old, worn out. What am I to do? A bomb fell on Sheaf Street yesterday. I wish it had fallen on Hurdle Hill. It would be a relief. Sometimes I want to run up onto the hill and scream. Who would hear me? Who would care? I thought Richard did, but I was wrong. It didn't matter how hard I tried to be a good wife. He did not want me. I want to tell Joe because he's to blame; it would wipe the smile off his face. The butter ration is to be reduced to 4oz from Monday next. As I use margarine I shan't be affected. I wonder whether any of the vegetables Daddy planted earlier in the year are fit to eat. I haven't been in the garden since Daddy became ill. Another Dig for Victory leaflet came through the letter box today, so I suppose I should make an effort. I will. Tomorrow, I shall start to re-organise the garden.

2nd September 1940
The potatoes and root vegetables are quite edible and will probably last the winter if I'm careful. Mummy came out and said I shouldn't be gardening in my condition, whatever will the neighbours think? She was smiling when she said this. I do believe she knows. Mrs Allnutt came to visit and asked Mummy to start knitting for the troops

again. 'If you have time,' Mrs Alnutt said. 'I expect you're very busy knitting for your grandchild.' Mummy laughed and said no, she had plenty of time on her hands. I did think that if she believed I was expecting she would be knitting for the baby, so maybe she does know.

'I don't understand this,' I read the last entry again, aloud.

Rob said, 'She's suggesting she's not pregnant. Or maybe she's saying that her mother doesn't believe she's pregnant, and is teasing her about it? Interesting, how she goes off into practical things, when she's in the middle of an emotional outburst. And that she hasn't re-drafted that, just left it in.'

17th October 1940

Went to tea with Jean and her mother. The boy and his funny little friend were pushing one another around on the pavement and bumped into me. They stood and stared as I went by. When I looked around they were behind me, waddling like ducks and giggling behind their hands. Jean told me I should have a green ration book as an expectant mother. I didn't know this. She is coming to take me to the doctor in the morning for a certificate. I shall ask Mummy to tell her I am out. At last Richard's pension has come through, it is pitifully little but we can manage if we are careful.

23rd October 1940

Jean called on Friday, and on Monday and Tuesday. Today she caught me at the window, so I had to see her. 'Joe made me promise to keep an eye on you,' she said when she came in. I told her I'd collected my green ration book. She said I looked pale. She brought an almond cake she has baked. I suspect it's made with butter and real sugar, but it is very tasty. I'm afraid I finished it all after she left.

28th October 1940
Jean says it's an old wives' tale that expectant mothers should stay indoors and it's far healthier to get lots of exercise. She started to tell me how exercise helped and was speaking very plain. She laughed at my blushing and said I shouldn't be embarrassed to talk about my condition. If it is a girl she will call her Elizabeth and if a boy she will call him Philip. She asked me what names I had thought of and was shocked that I hadn't. Then I caught sight of "Alice's Adventures in Wonderland" on the bookshelf, and said, 'Alice'. She said that was a lovely name. People stare so, the women smile at me in a way that makes my face burn with shame. How women go through this all the time I have no idea. Last week when I was passing the Town Hall a young woman despatch rider pulled up on a motorcycle. She was in uniform with a jaunty little cap, and looked quite the thing. I was very envious. If only I had not started this, I could be doing something like that now. Or even join the WVS. They have a very smart uniform.

3rd November
I think my original idea was probably correct. Why else would Richard have bought her a silver watch – even though he pretended it was a gift from Joe – and why would he let them have our honeymoon? And he kept the photograph, the one of the two of them outside the Registry Office. The more I think about it the more I can see that he

was besotted with her. That other thing, that disgusting idea, that he tried to make me believe, was to put me off the scent. Well, it hasn't worked.

'That solves one mystery,' Rob said. 'She didn't have her honeymoon because Richard gave it away to Jean and Joe.'

'That's awful,' I said. 'She was so looking forward to it. She really is brooding on my father and Jean. I wonder if there was anything going on between them. And what has Richard said to her that is so disgusting?'

7th November
The newspaper is full of the latest raids. It feels as though it's getting nearer every day. Today's tip from the Daily Mail: It is easier to cut bread into thin slices if you dip the bread knife into boiling water before each cut. I think I'm onto them. It came to me in the night. That baby is Richard's baby. I also think Joe doesn't suspect a thing. I believe he is as innocent as I am. It makes perfect sense. Richard certainly wasn't interested in me and I don't believe for a moment that he was

Rob and I looked at one another. 'You know,' he said, 'I think I might have been right – that your mum wasn't pregnant at all.'

'Don't be ridiculous,' I said. 'I was born, what – less than four weeks after this entry? That's a fact. She sounds lonely, frightened. It's barely a few months after my father was killed. She must be grieving. Maybe this is all part of, what do they call it? Feeling angry towards Richard for abandoning her. We should ask Judy; she knows all about bereavement.'

13th November

She laughed at me. I am tired of people laughing at me. The boy sniggering behind his hand. People in the street. Richard must have been laughing at me when he wrote those awful things. I'm glad he didn't come back. I couldn't stand living with such deceit. I had it out with Jean. I didn't say it straight out of course, as I don't know the right words. I asked if she remembered going to see 'Gone with the Wind' when she had said Ashley in the film reminded her of Richard. She said yes, and I asked her if this was because she liked Richard? She said of course she had liked him. I said, I mean really like him? She said, what are you saying Vi? I said, after all, he did visit you after Joe had left. Yes, she said, because Joe was his friend, he came to see how I was. I said, is that all that went on? She stared at me for a long time. Then she laughed. She said 'You don't think - me and Richard?' I said nothing and she said 'You do'. She had the grace to blush. 'I'm not going to stay here to be insulted,' she said and marched out. Well, she didn't deny it, so I think I'm on the right track.

18th November

Mrs Sheldon visited today. She said she was sorry I had fallen out with Jean and hoped we would make it up. Luckily I had my coat on as we need to be careful with the coal, so she thought I was about to go out and did not try to come in. She brought a box of vegetables which she said were left over from her son's allotment, and a dozen eggs. I told her we had plenty, but she pushed them through the door anyway. She kept saying 'Are you sure you're alright, love?' I've always liked Mrs Sheldon and wonder whether

I might talk to her. Though I couldn't bear it if she laughed. The newspaper is full of the latest bombings. The poor people of Coventry; they say there was scarcely two minutes between Thursday and Friday morning when bombs were not falling. There is a shortage of wool now. Mrs Allnutt popped a note through the door to say she needs to look a little further afield for supplies.

26th November
Mrs Sheldon came. Jean has gone into Jessops Hospital for the baby. His baby. She said you look peaky Violet are you taking your vitamins? I nearly told her. I called to her as she walked down the road. Mummy said 'Violet' in that warning tone of voice like when I was little. Like she knew what I was thinking. I called 'Give Jean my best' and Mrs Sheldon smiled and waved. Then she was gone. Maybe she thought I wanted to make it up with Jean.

28th November
It's a girl. Elizabeth. The boy brought a note. Peeping through the letterbox. I think I know what to do. Jean will see reason. It is my baby. She can't deny it.

3rd December
Mummy makes me stay indoors. She says 'you can't go out in your condition, Violet' and 'we must make sure you get your vitamins' in a sarcastic tone of voice. I think she is teasing me, daring me to tell her.

Over the page was an undated entry:

Mummy: 'Violet is not feeling herself.'
Mrs Sheldon: 'It can't be long now can it?'

Mummy: 'Oh, any day now.'
Mrs Sheldon: 'Jean and Elizabeth have left hospital early because they're worried about air raids. But I'm worried that it isn't any safer at home'.
Mummy: 'I'll tell Violet you called'.
My door is locked.

Rob started to say something and I shushed him. I needed to let this information start to sink in before I could trust myself to speak. Strands of my mother's life were wafting around me like threads, and when I tried to grasp one, it flitted away and another strand floated near, only to disappear as I reached for it. One – my mother believed Jean was having an affair with my father. Another – Jean's baby was Richard's baby and so should be her baby. Another – she was expecting me, but for some reason her mother, my Grandmother, didn't believe her. I was born on fourth December, but there was no mention here of her going into hospital. I checked the dates again. Yes, she was at home on third of December. If the undated entry was written on the same day, she may have gone into hospital later, or on the fourth itself.

I was disappointed that the end of her diary was the beginning of me. I would have liked to read about myself. Then I reasoned that keeping a diary was something a young mum would not have time for during wartime. I was selfish for being disappointed. I kept a baby's first year book for Judy and always wished there had been something similar from my own babyhood. Even a few photos. There was nothing and this diary, which ended with so many questions, the very day before I was born, somehow emphasised my loss. I wondered whether Mum had been as excited as I was to be a new Mum, whether she ever regained the anticipation she had described in those days leading up to her wedding. Did she ever make up with Jean, did they spend time together with their babies? Somehow, I think not. Too many questions, too few answers.

Rob broke into my thoughts. ‘She’s become very insular; it’s got quite an oppressive feel. There’s a lot of tension in those last few days. See, how her writing becomes more fragmented and rushed, but more normal in a way.’

‘Yes, oppressive is a good word,’ I agreed.

‘Your mother and your grandmother together in the house, just the two of them, day in, day out, trying to keep warm–’

‘Or even obsessive. A year ago, she’s looking forward to her wedding–’

‘Then she’s dreading it, and she doesn’t like Jean–’

‘Then Jean’s going to be her best friend. And now she’s barely going out, terrified of people looking at her, too embarrassed to talk or even write about being pregnant.’

‘And her mother has locked her in her bedroom.’ Rob was turning over blank pages. ‘It’s like reading the beginning and the end of a novel, without the middle. And that’s where the information is, that would make sense of it all.’ He pointed to a line of very small writing along the margin of the last page, which looked almost as though it was trying not to be seen.

She leaves food outside the door. Why am I being punished? They should be punished.

‘I wonder whether there was any truth in the Richard and Jean thing,’ Rob said.

‘Who knows?’ Perhaps none of us knows much about how anyone else lives their life, really. I tended to think my mother’s generation was very prim, but that didn’t mean they wouldn’t have had the same sort of romantic preoccupations we thought we invented in the fifties and which our children thought they invented in the seventies. ‘After all, Mum ended up with Joe, after my father was killed. So it is possible my father and Jean had a thing going. Maybe Jean and Joe got divorced and he got together with Mum.’

‘Swingers, eh?’ Rob joked and I glared at him. He was articulating my own thoughts. He shrugged and changed the subject. ‘Your mum seems to have had an odd relationship with your grandma. She wants to talk to her, then she’s frightened of her... You were, what? Four, when your grandma died?’

‘A bit older, nearly six.’

‘You’ve talked about her before. She didn’t sound like your typical gran. A bit of an old harridan if you ask me.’

He took the book off me and was re-reading the last few entries. I stood up, stretched, walked across to the sideboard and picked up the photograph of my grandfather and grandmother with my mother between them. She was dressed up and smiling, and looked so young. This was the girl who had written the diaries. It must have been taken before she married. Maybe at the Regimental Dinner that she wrote about, where she met my father. There were no other photographs of my mother or of her with my father. Not even a wedding photograph.

I looked at Grandma more closely. ‘How small she is.’ It was obvious, looking at the photograph; she’s the same height as my mother. 'I always think of her as very tall. Maybe that's just because I was little. I remember her standing over me and…'

It was a shadowy memory.

'Angry,' I remembered. 'Always angry. She knitted a lot.'

Rob said, 'You didn't tell me that. She knitted your clothes?'

'No, I don't remember her ever knitting anything for me. I expect it's like my mother says here, she was knitting for the Front. Whatever it was, it was always grey. She used metal needles – the kind with points at each end, they use them for knitting socks. She'd poke me with them. And at the table, she'd rap my knuckles with a knife, or a fork, whatever was in her hand. Always slapping, prodding…'

'Shhh,' Rob put an arm on my shoulder and I realised my voice had risen. 'You'll wake your Mum up.'

I sat beside him but couldn't take my eyes from those of the woman sitting on the sideboard. It was a long time since I'd looked at that photograph and I realised I avoided it whenever I was in the room.

'She hated me.'

'She certainly sounds very fierce. I mean what kind of mother would lock a pregnant young woman in her room? But 'hate' is a bit strong.'

Yes, she did, she hated me. I had her now, large as life, in my mind, standing in front of me, telling me I am – 'A guttersnipe,' I said, seeing her lip curl as though I smelled of something unpleasant. I could hear myself snivelling, trying not to, and the more I tried, the more I sniffed and the more she despised me. I knew this but could not stop it. I didn't even know what she wanted from me, what I could do to be the person she wanted me to be. 'There was no music or singing in the house,' I remembered. '*Let's have some peace and quiet,* that was all she'd say, whenever I made any noise. Even laughter. I wasn't allowed to laugh out loud when she was around.'

'But when we met you used to love dancing and singing to the latest records.'

'That was Joe. He encouraged me to be up to date. For Mum, if it wasn't classical she didn't understand it. She let me get on with it, though. She and Joe took me to the cinema to see musicals when I was little and I think she quite enjoyed them. But grandma disapproved, we weren't allowed to sing. *Tell her to be quiet,* she'd say to Mum. I remember going to see the Wizard of Oz. Coming home on the tram, I asked Mum, if I wished hard enough would Grandma turn into colour? Like the part in the film when everything changes from grey to technicolour. Grandma always seemed grey to me. Her clothes. Her hair. Her knitting. I thought if I sang *Over the Rainbow* she would turn into colour.'

Then I remembered the visitor. It was a man, and he was smiling at me, and Mum was smiling at me, and I was so happy, that I stood up and started to sing, *'Somewhere over the rainbow,'* and he clapped his hands. Then Grandma came in and said, *'Stop that racket',* and Mum raised her voice, I hadn't heard her do that before, and said, *'Leave her alone.'*

I turned to Rob.'It must have been Joe.'

'What was?'

'Our visitor, he was wearing a uniform. It must have been Joe. I wanted to sing for him, and Grandma and Mum had a row about it. Then later that evening, when I was in bed, I heard... Shouting. I was frightened, it was

Grandma's voice and she was angry.' I thought, what have I done now? 'The voices were on the landing. I got out of bed and tiptoed to the door…'

'Doughnut,' Rob said affectionately, wiping my cheek with his thumb. 'She can't get you now. She's dead.' He patted my arm. 'She's dead.'

She's dead, she's dead. Lying at the bottom of the stairs, her head on the carpet where her feet should be, she's upside down. 'The house fell on her head.'

'What?'

'Then the house fell on her head, Ding Dong! The Witch is dead. Which old Witch? The Wicked Witch! Ding Dong!'

Rob was shaking my arm, half laughing but when I looked at him I could see fear in his eyes. 'Shhh, you'll wake your Mum up. Why are you singing that?'

'I don't know. I remembered Grandma lying at the bottom of the stairs.'

'Your voice was really strange.'

'What do you mean?'

'Like one of those little characters in the Wizard of Oz. The Munchkins?'

'I remembered… I think, I must have heard raised voices, and I came out of my room – I slept in Mum's room when I was little – and Mum was standing at the top of the stairs with Grandma. I ran towards her. Then she fell.'

'You told me before, that's how she died, falling down the stairs.'

'Yes, but I'd forgotten that I was there. They must have been arguing, that's what woke me up.'

'You don't think your mother pushed her down the stairs?'

I stared at him. 'I never thought – surely not. You don't think for a minute that my mother would harm anyone?' I looked at the photograph. 'I think I might have pushed her.'

'And you're remembering this now?'

'I must always have known it, somewhere in the back of my mind.'

Peeping through the gap in the bedroom door. Grandma has one foot on the top step as though she's just coming upstairs, and Mum is above her, on the landing. *'I'm her mother, I know what's best.'* Grandma is poking at Mum the way she pokes at me when I do something wrong. I run towards them and Grandma turns her head to look at me, then she is falling.

I heard Rob saying, 'Oh dear, oh dear. Let's leave this, it's upsetting you. We can do it another time.' He carefully placed the loose papers back between the pages. Never at his best with emotion, I could see he didn't quite know what to do with all the feelings that this evening had stirred up. Maybe I could talk to Judy about it. He made for the door. 'Shall I put the book back?'

I took it from him. 'I'll do it. I know exactly where it was.'

I listened at the bedroom door for the pop-pop of breath to tell me she was still asleep. Sliding one foot slowly in front of another, so I didn't trip over the rug in the pitch dark, I felt the bed bump softly against my thighs, lifted the eiderdown and pushed the book underneath. It pressed against her foot and her eyes opened. I stopped breathing. She stared at me for a long moment. I made a play of smoothing the eiderdown. 'Are you okay Mum? Can I get you anything?' but she was asleep again.

Frank

Flight QF319 to Heathrow

This is not my pocket torch – I left mine under the bunk at the shelter. This is Cyril's. I borrowed it, though he never knew it. It's red, like mine, and at one time it had one of those black metal hoods that fitted over and made the light point downwards so that it kept to the rules of the blackout. Of course, it made the light so weak that often as not we bumped into somebody who was also walking along with a hood over their light. My torch – the one I lost – I got for my tenth birthday. 23rd March 1940. Which was also, that year, Easter Saturday. It was the next time Joe had leave. And Cyril had left school.

I remember Jean, standing over the fire, cooking up a stew ready for a big family supper to celebrate Joe being home. As Mam passed her, she caught hold of Jean's wrist and said, 'It's a bit risky wearing thy fine watch around the house. I should have thought it'd be locked away safe.'

'I reckon it's safest on my wrist. Then, if there's an air raid, I shall have it with me.'

'Don't say I didn't warn thee.'

Jean twirled across to the sideboard, picked up a stack of plates and waltzed to the table, singing,

'When my dreamboat comes home,
and my dream no more will roam,
I will meet you and I'll greet you,
when my dreamboat comes home.'

She was so carried away that she didn't see Joe's head appear round the door. He put a finger to his lips to shush

Mam and me. It was hard to keep quiet when my belly did such a lurch at the sight of him. He slipped round the door and stood watching Jean, smiling, a thin cigarette stuck to his lower lip. As she turned from the table, singing,

'Moonlit waters will sing,
Cause that tender love you'll–'

she saw Joe, squealed, and ran to him, jumping up to wrap her legs around his waist.

Mam said, 'Come on, Frank, get knives and forks and finish laying the table.'

When she'd finished canoodling, Jean took Joe's coat from him, hung it on the door and pulled him by the hand up the stairs.

It was the first time in weeks that we'd sat down together for supper. The rolling mill was working round the clock, everybody was doing double shifts, and Dad and Bill were out two nights a week doing ARP duty. As Dad pushed his empty plate away and pulled his tobacco tin towards him, he turned to Joe and asked, 'So what does tha reckon to this war?'

Joe said, 'It's not quite what we were expecting. It's been quiet. They stopped sending lads out to France and set them on to shovelling snow, then filling sandbags to help with the floods.'

Dad nodded as he filled his pipe. 'Aye, well, it's been the coldest winter on record, so they say.'

It had been a good winter. Sam and me had earned a lot of pocket money from snow shifting. We couldn't spend it because toffees were rationed. We'd gone up to Hurdle Hill and done all the houses on the Terrace. Sam had knocked at the door of the Knowleses and it was opened by Violet who told us to go away.

Dad said, 'But it's not all bad. We're working all hours so between us we're bringing in a good few bob. See, my missis there, she's putting away half our wages every week.'

I knew this, for I watched Mam each Friday night, collecting in the wage packets from Bill and my Dad. She'd give them their spends – five shillings for Bill and a ten bob note for Dad - and she'd put the rest into a Rowntree's Cocoa tin which sat in the cupboard between the tea caddy and the semolina jar. She'd said to Jean, 'If I should cop it, remember where it is and make sure everybody's looked after.' Jean was the only one allowed to keep her wage packet on account of being married. She paid Mam five shillings a week for her board.

Dad put his pipe between his lips and pushed the tin to Joe, saying, 'Sorry, lad, I've only got pipe tobacco today.' Joe shook his head and pulled his own baccy out of his pocket along with a packet of rolling papers. Jean cleared the table and Mam mashed the tea. I got a taper from the mantelpiece and lit it at the fire, and walked across to Dad, shielding the flame with my hand. He held my hand to bring the flame to his pipe, then, when it was lit, he let go of my hand. While all this was going on, he was telling Joe, 'There's steel piling up for new boats and planes. But what's going to happen, I'd like to know, if the politicians sort it out and none of it's needed? I read that the Americans are calling it the Phoney War.'

It was true that everything seemed to be happening a long way off and mostly at sea. There'd been no bombs and the Germans hadn't invaded. We'd stopped carrying our gas masks around again, and we hadn't had an air raid practice at school for weeks.

Joe said, 'I think things are about to change. There's a lot of us had notice of being shipped abroad soon, so something's in the offing.'

Dad was leaning back, his eyes half closed, enjoying his pipe as he asked, 'And where's tha off to?'

Joe shook his head. 'We're not told. I've to report to London Victoria Station at twelve noon on Monday.'

Bill piped up from behind his latest copy of *War Illustrated*, 'It'll be France, I reckon. The boat train goes from Victoria Station.' Bill was in the know when it came to the ins and outs of the War.

Dad said, 'I reckon Joe knows that, clever bugger, but unlike some, he's not got a gob the size of Totley Tunnel. Has tha not seen that poster, *Loose Lips Sink Ships*?'

Bill's ears were pink as he looked down at his magazine. Cyril nudged him and said, 'Happen tha could join up on t'other side, our Bill?'

Bill grabbed Cyril's arm and was about to thump him when Mam came up behind and cracked their heads together. She said, 'That's enough.'

Joe said, 'The lads are keen to get out there and see some action.' He'd rolled a fag so thin that he had trouble pushing a match in to press the tobacco down. I watched him lift it to his lips and when he inhaled the entire first half of the fag disappeared. He went on, 'If something doesn't happen soon I might join the Navy or the Royal Air Force and get out to the Atlantic. They're having it tough out there and they need more pilots.'

I asked, 'Will tha be allowed to fly a Hurricane?'

Bill had perked up again. He said, 'I've read about that. They catapult a fighter plane off a merchant ship, he drops his bombs on the enemy then ditches into the sea.'

I thought this sounded right exciting. I asked Joe, 'Can tha swim?'

He chuckled and said, 'I'd learn pretty fast if I had to.'

Bill said, 'They reckon the survival rate's about twenty-five percent.'

Jean started to pull the cups towards her, crashing them into a pile. She got into a tug of war with Bill who was trying to pull his cup back.

He said, 'I've not finished.'

Jean said, 'Tha needs to spend more time filling thy gob and less time letting rubbish out.' She walked across the kitchen and pushed the cups into the sinkful of water, washing them roughly and almost throwing them onto the draining board. Soap bubbles flew onto the window, popped and left a slimy trail.

Mam said, 'Oy, miss, I'd like them cups for another day if it's all the same to thee.'

Jean said, 'I've a mind to kill him meself rather than let him go out there and get shot down and swim around in them freezing waters, hoping a ship might pass before he gets too tired and drowns hisself. Then not even a body to look at because he's at the bottom of the chuffing Atlantic.'

Joe got out of his chair and went across to the sink, putting his arms round her from behind. She slapped his hands with her wet ones and shouted, 'If they can catapult a fighter plane off a ship to drop bombs, I'm damned sure they can send it without a pilot.'

Bill said, 'Tha's talking soft. Who does tha think would press the button to drop the bombs if there were no pilot?'

Mam chipped in, 'I think our Jean's got a point. Happen if they get better catapults they can shoot the bombs straight from the ship without any need for planes.'

Dad chuckled and said, 'That's best idea I've heard this year. Happen we'll send thee off to London to tell Mr Churchill how to do his job.'

Cyril laughed. 'Aye Dad, I reckon it's a good job they don't let women into the War Cabinet.'

Dad shook his finger at him. 'There's no call to disrespect thy Mam. Tha's not too big to get a crack.' Bill smirked at Cyril, who went into a sulk.

Jean had thrown the dish mop into the sink and stormed across the kitchen, flinging the stair door back and stamping up the stairs. Joe followed her. I heard their shoes clattering across the floor above, and their voices, Joe's speaking softly, then Jean, high and excited. There was a creaking as they sat on the bed, then she was bawling while Joe still talked softly. I looked up at the ceiling, wondering if Joe would come back and talk to my Dad some more about the War. Cyril pushed me off my chair and I landed on the floor on my bottom.

He said, 'Don't sit there, go and help Mam finish washing up.'

'Aw, Dad, tell him he can't push me around, I'm nearly ten.'

Dad said, 'Tha'll be tall enough to reach sink then,' and chuckled.

The next day was my birthday. I was wide awake with excitement and went downstairs before it was properly light. Sure enough, there was a box on the table with my name on it, and inside, the red pocket torch with its special black hood. I put the battery inside and ran back upstairs to nudge Cyril awake, but he pushed me away. I went into the yard. I could hear Mr Wreakes puffing and panting in the privy. Putting the torch against a knot hole in the wooden door I flashed it on and off.

He said, 'What the bloody hell is that?' I hid round the corner in the gennel as he rushed out, buttoning up his fly as he stumbled across the yard, nearly tripping over the drain. He reached his door, shouting, 'Here, missis, has siren gone? What's them lights?'

Back in the kitchen, Mam was getting ready for work.

I asked, 'Can I go and show Sam my torch?'

'Go on then. But be home for dinner time.'

Cyril came downstairs and Mam said to him, 'Tha's to be at works' gates at nine. Dad's fixed up an interview with foreman.'

He winged, 'Aw, Mam, do I have to? I don't want to work in the rolling mill. I reckon I shall have enough growing at allotment to bring in a wage this summer.'

She said, 'Tha'll have a proper job like the rest of us, and bring some money in.' She had her hands on her hips which was a warning sign but Cyril had his back turned, lifting his seed potatoes out of the understairs cupboard and didn't notice.

He said, 'But Dad said last night there's more money coming in and tha's got plenty put by.' He put the box of potatoes on the table.

'And what's makes thee so chuffing special that tha can prance about gardening while the rest of us is working our arses off? Tha can pay thy way like everybody else round here who's of age.'

Cyril stayed quiet, inspecting the chits on his spuds very closely. I liked to see him told off. She turned to me and said, 'And tha needn't look so smug. There'll be less gallivanting for thee and more to do at home, with everybody out at work.' Cyril smirked at me. I wished I was fifteen today, instead of ten, and could go out to work with the lads and have a wage packet to give Mam on a Friday.

In Sam's gennel I made a noise like a cat squawking, which was our special signal because he wasn't allowed out to play. Since he was made lame by the accident, his dad made Sam fetch and carry for him all day while his mam was at work. After a few minutes, Sam came out of the door. I showed him my torch. 'Can tha come out?'

He said, 'For a bit. Me dad's asleep.' Then, as we were walking along Liberty Road, 'Where shall we go?'

It had started sleeting and my ears hurt with the cold. I thought of the Knowles's Anderson shelter, which would be warm, and there may be biscuits in the Ovaltine tin. And I would be able to use my torch.

We cut through the gennels behind Liberty Road past the library, and crossed over to Hurdle Hill Road. The sun shone cold and the sleet had turned to a wispy snow that blew up my sleeves and down my neck. We took a short cut across the hill, me telling Sam about Joe maybe becoming a fighter pilot. With our arms outstretched, we became fighter planes, humming up and down the side of the hill, sputtering at one another, until we collided and fell, laughing, onto the soggy grass, rolling into a hot and sweaty heap of arms and legs. Sam landed on top of me and my nose was in a molehill. This made me think of what Dad had said about Mr Knowles being left for dead underneath his soldiers. I didn't want to play any longer. I led Sam along the narrow lane behind the gardens, peering over the wall to check there was nobody at the back of the Knowles's house. I waved Sam to follow me through the gate and over to the shelter. It didn't bother me that Mr

Knowles or Richard might be around. I didn't think they'd mind us visiting. It was Violet and Mrs Knowles that I was keen to avoid.

The shelter was empty and dark and smelt of turf and paraffin. I pulled out my pocket torch and we looked around. The Ovaltine tin was on the table and we sat side by side on one of the wooden benches, eating ginger biscuits and looking through a magazine with pictures of different kinds of cars. I heard a man's voice. Thinking it was Mr Knowles coming in, and it would be a nice surprise for him finding me here, I stood up, ready to say Hello. But it was Violet's voice I heard next, saying, 'Let's sit inside the shelter, out of the cold.'

I whispered, 'Quick, under the bed,' switched off my torch and squeezed underneath the narrow wooden bench on my belly. The door opened. I saw Violet's feet step down, and stand inside the door, then Richard's feet walked past my face, to the table.

Richard said, 'I'll light the lamp.'

A freezing draught from the open door blew under the bed. I had my back against the steel edge of the shelter where it met the earth, and could feel water soaking into my jersey and seeping up the skin of my back. I heard Richard take the glass off the lamp and strike the match, then smelt paraffin and heard the pop of the light. Violet's shoes came across the floor and stopped about three inches from my face. She sat above me so I was staring at her calves. Richard's shoes walked across to the door. When it closed it was almost dark but for a dim glow from the lamp.

Violet said, 'Won't you think again? Daddy will be so upset.'

Richard said, 'I can't go on like this Violet. Everyone has to make sacrifices, and we're having it easy compared to most.'

He sat beside her and the wood of the bench dipped and pressed down hard against my shoulder so I couldn't have moved if I'd tried. My right ear was now under water and I was starting to shiver from the cold, trying not to because it might make the bed shake. Between Violet's legs I could see Sam under the opposite bed, his eyes shining yellow and scared. If either of them looked down, they might see the corner of his jacket that was sticking out.

Violet said, 'If you leave, I shall have to go back to work and Mummy will struggle to manage Daddy on her own. I thought you were quite definite that you wouldn't enlist.' She was whingeing. My Dad hated whingers and I could hear from Richard's voice that he felt the same.

'I've already explained. I've had to change my mind. It's all very well having a political viewpoint but I can see now that it's a moral issue.'

'Is this because of what happened on Friday, when that man called you a coward?'

'No. Well, I'll admit that was probably the final straw. I don't want to be thought of as a coward. And I am, if I sit at home while my friends go off to fight.'

'You mean Joe.'

'Yes, I mean Joe, but there are others. Most of the men at Burtons have joined up.'

'Sometimes I think Joe is more important to you than I am.' Richard said nothing. 'You see, you won't even deny it.'

'No, Violet, I won't deny it. Joe and I have been friends for a lot longer than I've known you. More than friends.'

She started shrieking. ‘Don’t say any more, I don’t want to hear it. You forget you have a wife to think of.’

He said, ‘Very well. There’s no more to be said.’

Violet stamped one of her feet and it splashed in the water.

Richard said, ‘I thought we’d managed to divert the water, but it’s still coming in.’ He stood up and I thought he was about to look under the bed.

Violet was crying. ‘I don’t know how I’m going to tell Daddy.’

Richard sat down again. ‘I’m sorry. But my mind’s made up.’

She blew her nose. ‘What shall I do?’

‘I’m sure Jean will keep you company. You should visit her.’

‘Oh, I’ve tried but I haven’t anything in common with her.’

‘You should give her a chance, Violet. She has a lovely personality.’

‘She certainly seems to have succeeded in impressing you.’ She sounded vexed and I thought it was about Jean but couldn’t work out what she meant.

Richard said, ‘This war may be over within the year. We’ll have a life afterwards. And a family. I promise.’

Violet took a sharp breath and when she spoke she clipped the words off at the end, reminding me of Mrs Trippett in Sunday School when she was cross with us. ‘Well, if you’ve decided, there’s no more to say. I shall write a letter to Mr Armitage at the Bank to see whether he has a secretarial position available.’

‘It’s not absolutely necessary. You will get half my pay.’

‘That will hardly be sufficient. Will you tell Daddy?’

‘Let’s go and join them, and tell them together.’

Richard stood beside the Kelly lamp. Suddenly he bent down and again I thought he was going to look under the bed. I held my breath. But he scooped up a soggy ginger biscuit that I must have dropped on the floor. He said, ‘You must check your father doesn’t keep food in here, it will encourage rats.’ Thinking of rats being near made me shiver harder and I was surprised the bench didn’t shake. I heard Richard blow the lamp out. As the door opened a cold wind blew under the bed.

As soon as the door had closed behind them, we rolled out from our hiding places. I was soaking all down my left side and my shoe was full of water. I was shaking with the cold. Slowly, I inched the door open, and when I was certain Richard and Violet had gone into the house, we sneaked along the path, out of the gate, and ran across the hill. We were back on Liberty Road before I realised I’d left my pocket torch under the bed in the shelter.

On Easter Monday, Joe sat at the table in his uniform, his jacket on the back of the chair and his cap on the table. I knelt in front of the fire, holding the bread on the toasting fork against the red hot cinders. Mam, Dad and Cyril had gone to work and Bill was in bed after the night shift. Jean was quiet for a change as she mashed the tea. She didn’t even shout at me when the bread caught fire. She lifted it off the toasting fork, dropped it in the swill bucket, and passed me a fresh slice. When I next looked, she and Joe were canoodling and she was wailing. The bread caught fire again. They went upstairs and I was able to finish making and eating my toast before they came back.

Jean said, ‘Right, Frank, I’m off to the station with Joe, then to work.’

'Can I come?'

'Whatever for?'

I wanted to see Joe for as long as I could but I knew she'd think I was daft if I said that. I said, 'I've never been to station. I'll be no trouble. I'll go with thee to Ferguson's after and walk home by meself.'

Joe said, 'That'd be grand, Frank,' before she could refuse.

Jean shrugged as she put her coat on. 'Don't make a nuisance of yourself. Happen you could make yourself useful and bring my good clothes home after I change at work.' I'd noticed how she'd started speaking posh since she was married, though not quite as snooty as Violet, and sometimes she got her new way of talking, and her old way, mixed up.

I asked, 'Will Richard be there?'

'Why would he?'

'Well, he's joining up isn't he?'

'Don't be daft. What make you think that?'

I realised I wasn't supposed to know this, and shrugged.

We took the tram all the way to Midland Station. The tram was full and the station approach was heaving with men and women in uniform and old people and women with children and everybody seemed to be kissing or crying or laughing. Jean and Joe started canoodling so I moved away from them and clambered onto a large crate and stood on the top, with a good view over all the heads and up the track.

The shiny green and gold engine rushed towards me, its brakes screaming as it pulled into the station. Whistles blew and people shouted. The racket reminded me of the noise of the rolling mill, when I went to meet my Dad from work and stood at the gates listening to the giant steam hammers dropping onto steel. As the train squealed under the station roof, its steam cloud rolled along from the far end of the platform, folding itself around people, so it seemed they were being lifted into the sky, head first. As the steam cleared I could see faces peering out of windows for the whole length of the train. It was so full that surely the people waiting on the platform would not fit in. Doors opened and hands appeared, pulling people through them. The kissing and canoodling couples seemed to take no notice.

A voice cut across all the noise, booming out, 'All aboard for the sunny south coast. Free bed and breakfast, a free postcard home every weekend, and we'll even pay you while you're enjoying yourself.' There was some cheering and others were shouting, 'Get him off!' I saw it was quite a young man in uniform, sitting on the shoulders of other men, who now carried him to one of the doors. Some hands came out and pulled him into the train with much laughing.

I looked for Joe and couldn't see him. I couldn't get my breath for fear that I might not say goodbye to him, then I spotted Jean's hat, saw Joe beside her, and jumped down to run up to him. There was more space now on the platform, and those already on board were shouting to Joe and the other men who were still saying goodbye to their families. The guard blew his whistle, and Joe pulled away from Jean. He saw me, ruffled my hair, gave her a last kiss and jumped onto the step. He was sucked into the bodies at the door. His face reappeared for a second then he was gone. Jean was calling his name and waving like a mad woman but the train started to move off and we were blinded by the cloud of steam. When we could see again, we were looking at the very end of the train disappearing through the tunnel. It was as though everything was frozen for a moment as we stared at the empty track. The platform was silent.

Jean said, ‘Come on,’ sounding as though she had a bad cold. ‘I’ll get me pay docked if I don’t get a move on.’

We ran for the tram and jumped on as it started to pull away. At Shalesmoor we got off and walked round to Ferguson’s. Sybil was standing by the gates with Jean’s overalls in her hand. Sybil got bigger every time I saw her. ‘Happen that’s where all the butter’s going,’ Mam said the last time Sybil came round to our house.

Sybil said, ‘I’ve sorted it with Dennis, he says tha can use his office to change.’

‘Thanks, Dennis,’ Jean shouted to a little man with thick glasses under his peaked cap, and went into the office by the gates. I waited outside, with Sybil and Dennis.

Sybil put her arm round my shoulders and said, ‘Tha’s growing up nicely, young Frank. Don’t forget now, I want first refusal when tha gets to courting age.’ I ducked out from under her arm and moved well away.

Dennis took off his glasses and stretched his arm up so the lenses were pointing through the window of the little office. He rolled his upper lip back and smirked. The men standing across the yard whistled and laughed.

Sybil said, ‘I’m laughing fit to burst, I am.’

One of the men called, ‘Don’t be a wet blanket, Sybil. The owd lad doesn’t get a lot of fun.’

Jean came out with her overalls on, a scarf tied at the front of her head. She was rolling her frock and shoes into her jacket to make a parcel which she passed to me. Without looking back, she trotted across the yard. I wanted to wait and watch Jean get into her crane, but Dennis shooed me off and I made my way home.

The house was so quiet and empty that I decided to call for Sam. His head appeared at the kitchen window. He pointed behind him with his thumb.

I heard his Dad's voice calling, 'Sam, who's at door?'

I asked, 'Shall I come and keep thee company?'

Sam pushed the window open and whispered, 'Best get off. He'll be cadging for pennies, then he'll be sending one of us down the pub for a jug of ale. Mam said not to let anybody see him while he's raring to get a drink inside him.' Sam's dad had made him spend all the money he'd earned from snow-shifting, on beer. His Dad yelled again and Sam ducked back inside. I heard him call, 'Nobody, Dad, it's some folk in street tha can hear.'

I walked down the street, fingering the marbles in my pocket. Then I remembered my pocket torch and decided to try to get it back. As I let myself into the Knowleses garden from the back gate, there was no one around, but when I approached the shelter I heard a low sobbing sound. I listened at the door for a time until I was certain I wasn't listening to Violet or Mrs Knowles, and then pushed open the door. Mr Knowles was sitting on the bed, his head in his hands. I pushed the door shut and sat beside him. He looked at me with tears running down his face.

'See the mud?' He pointed down to the water on the floor of the shelter. I didn't want to say I knew because I'd lain in it only two days ago. Already I could feel my toes getting wet where my shoe had worn through into a hole.

I said, 'It isn't muddy, it's only a bit of water. Happen we can bail out.'

‘I’ve been trying.’ He picked up a jam jar that was on the bed beside him. ‘This is how it starts. First the rain. Then the water. Then everything turns to mud.’

I said, ‘We can sort it out,’ wanting to make it all right for him again.

‘It’s the water table, you see, that was always the trouble. You’ve got to avoid low lying land. That’s why I built the shelter into a hill. I thought that would avoid the water table, but now you see, we’ve got the problem of the rain running off the hill.’

I said, ‘I’ll get a bucket from the house and if we both go at it–’

‘I should have known better. All I had to do was bring them home. Good lads, every one of them. They should have come home to their mothers and girlfriends.’

The door opened and Richard came in. His head touched the top of the shelter and he had to stoop. I saw he’d shaved his moustache off and this made him look very different. He peered into the gloom and saw me. ‘Hello, Frank, I’m afraid my father-in-law isn’t very well.’

Mr Knowles looked up at Richard. ‘Is that Harry?’

Richard said, ‘I think you’d better get off. Perhaps come back in a few days, when Mr Knowles is feeling better.’

I stood up but couldn’t get around Richard and sat down again while he moved across to the other side of Mr Knowles. As I was going out of the door I had a thought and rummaged in my trouser pocket to find my marbles. I selected my best Cat’s Eye and held it out to Mr Knowles. He took it, peered at it in his palm, and closed his fist tightly around it. I was back on Liberty Road before I realised I’d forgotten my torch again.

I never did get my own torch back and I had my backside skelped good and proper over losing it. That was how I came to borrow this one, which was Cyril's. By rights, I shouldn't have taken it. I've had cause to wonder, many a time, whether, had I not taken it, things would have turned out different?

Alice

Cool, clear, heavy with dew. The kind of morning that would get us out of bed at dawn when Judy was young, to walk along the river and up through the meadows, looking for brand new, white mushrooms for breakfast. Rob had been right, I needed to 'home in' as he called it; he stayed with Mum so that I could sleep in my own bed. Sound and images had spun around in my head, making me feel drunk: the voice of my mother, and the very different voice of the young Violet, calling out from her diaries and colliding with shadowy images and fragments of speech that I knew belonged to my grandmother, but were always slightly off the edge of my memory. In the small hours I took one of the sleeping pills and fell asleep quickly, waking refreshed to the sound of the cat purring in my ear.

Breathing in the soft, damp air, I walked through the wet grass to the bottom of the garden, stopping to admire the perfectly round hole drilled by the woodpecker in the sycamore. The leaves were edged with gold, but surely it had been summer when I last stood here. Time seemed to be speeding up. I heard the newspaper crash through the letterbox back in the house. Smudge meowed and rubbed against my ankles in search of food. I followed the track of shining footprints back across the lawn to the patio door. The mixed fragrance of chrysanthemums and gladioli drifted into the house with me. These familiar, reassuring sounds and smells of Sunday morning made me want to sit in an armchair, close my eyes and think of trivial, everyday things like when to put the geraniums away for winter, or what to have for lunch.

I decided to call Judy. She was delighted to hear from me. 'How are you? How's Nan?' I quickly brought her up to date on the police investigation and Mum's health. 'Don't worry about food tomorrow,' she said. Tomorrow? 'Monday? Adam?' Of course, I'd completely forgotten. 'Don't do anything for tea. I'll bring something.' Calm. Practical. Like her dad. I decided to tell Judy about reading the diary. She listened without interrupting while I gave her a summary.

'I don't blame you at all,' she said, when I paused. 'It sounds as though there are some family secrets that you need to know about, whether or not they relate to this skeleton.' We were both silent, probably for more than a minute, then she said, 'You'd think she wasn't pregnant,' mirroring Rob's comments.

'But we know she was because here I am.'

'Yes, but you could almost believe she'd had a miscarriage, you know? She was pregnant, then she wasn't, she hasn't told anyone and doesn't know how to.'

I fed Smudge, collected the wodge of Sunday newspaper from the hallway, poured myself a coffee and skimmed the news section. Disasters. Politicking. Dramas. It all seemed so irrelevant. Pottering around, skimming the pile of mail on the kitchen worktop, listening to messages from family and friends on the answering machine, I realised how much Rob had been doing, quietly, keeping people away from me during the last few days.

The phone rang. It was Shirley. 'I've done it,' she announced, sounding full of the joys. Already? It was – I checked my watch – nine o'clock. She must have been up all night. 'But,' and her voice dropped several octaves, 'there's something – I'm sure you know...' I recognised this as Shirley's 'empathy' voice, the one that said, 'I feel for you'. Again, I felt angry that Rob had consulted her about family business. Yet there was a possibility that she might help, so I urged her on. 'You didn't tell me you were adopted.'

'What?'

'Sorry, is it a family secret or something like that?' She didn't sound sorry at all. She would be delighted to have uncovered a family secret.

There were a few seconds in which I battled between shrugging off this shock news as if either I knew or it wasn't important, and wanting to cry out, 'Tell me, quick.' My impatience won. I knew I'd live to regret it but I said, 'What do you mean?'

'I couldn't find much information in the online archives. All I can tell you is that there's a record from 17th January 1941, which states you were adopted by Mrs Violet Clarke, of – well, it's your mother's address.' While she had been speaking, I'd walked into the conservatory and sat beside Smudge who now rolled onto his back and presented me with his stomach for stroking. 'Alice, are you there? Alice?'

'I'm here.'

'I'm so sorry, Alice, you didn't know, did you?' Shirley's sugary sympathy oozed down the telephone. 'What can I do to help? I could come over?'

The idea that she might pop round to offer support in person horrified me. 'No, really, it's fine,' I said. 'A bit of a surprise, but that's life. I'd better get off now, Rob will be wondering where I am.' I was about to say goodbye when I thought, and said, 'Can you print off the – whatever it is – record? Or email it to Rob?' and put the phone down rather quickly.

I don't know how long I sat, staring out at the garden, absently stroking Smudge's tummy, until he grasped my wrist in all his front paws and started kicking my hand with his back paws. It hurt. It brought me back to the present. I needed to get to Hurdle Hill Terrace.

The Co-op was opening as I pulled up outside. It took some time to get round the aisles, where it seemed that every third person knew my mother, me, or Judy. Usually I enjoyed the feeling of belonging to a small community, but as one person after another quizzed me about the news, I had the urge to shout, 'Leave me alone,' and run home to hide until it was over.

The doctor's car was outside Mum's house and I pulled into the kerb behind him. Mrs Barratt waved from her window where she was rehanging her net curtains. Doctor Grahams was in the kitchen with Rob. I remembered the sleeping pills and worried that we may have given her too many.

'Has something happened? Is Mum all right?'

'Seems okay,' Rob said. 'Took her tray up, she didn't ask where you were. Doc's telling me' – and I could tell from his voice that he'd learned some new and interesting facts – 'that the police can't question your mum if he says she's not fit. They have to arrest her to interview her formally.'

'We don't want her to be arrested.' I pictured her being pushed into a police car, in handcuffs.

'Even if they did,' said the doctor, 'They couldn't move her without a medical say-so.'

'Claire said they might bring in the police doctor for a second opinion,' I remembered. 'We were going to phone your friend, the solicitor, first thing on Monday morning.'

The doctor shook his head. 'The police surgeon is a GP on overtime. I'm sure he or she would be of the same opinion. It's standard practice. The police are used to it. She's trying it on.'

Rob nodded enthusiastically and added, 'Trying to get under the wire, so to speak, and persuade your Mum to answer questions. Then if she drops herself in it they'll say it was voluntary.'

I flinched at his inference that Mum might have had something to hide from the police. 'Are you sure they won't take her to the police station?'

'Sure as I can be. I think the Inspector is under pressure to resolve the case and without your mother, she can't. In any event it would be pretty controversial, taking a sick, ninety-plus woman to the police station against medical advice. I'm prepared to gamble they won't even try.'

I asked, 'Claire wants to show Mum some things she thinks might help them to identify the body. Can she do that?'

'No,' the doctor said. 'If it's critical, perhaps you can show them to her? We don't want to obstruct the police but they can't talk to her.'

'So we don't need a lawyer today?' Rob said and before the doctor could answer the door knocker sounded loudly.

I hadn't locked the front door so Claire had let herself in and arrived in the kitchen before any of us had moved. She was dressed for the weekend in jeans and a boho shirt with pumps, her hair tied back. Perhaps she was planning on some line-dancing later.

'How is Mrs Ibbertson today?' she asked.

'Poorly.' The doctor nodded towards her hand. 'Is that what you wanted to show her?'

Claire placed two large, plastic zip-lock bags on the table. All I could make out was soil and dirty pieces of metal, one more rusty than the other.

'No questioning of Mrs Ibbertson,' said the doctor. Claire raised her eyebrows and shrugged as if the thought had not occurred to her. 'Mrs Burgess can show them to her, if you agree?' Claire looked from me to the doctor, and I thought she was going to object, but then she shrugged again. 'I'll come up with you,' he added. I knew he was spending much more time with us than he should, and I was grateful. I didn't think I was mistaken in thinking Claire was threatening us last night. I'd always thought people being questioned by the police only need a solicitor to help them wriggle out of it. Why would anyone need legal help if they were innocent? I was changing my opinion.

'I'll put the kettle on,' Rob said and Claire gave him the thumbs up.

Mum was sitting up in bed, reading the article about the discovery of the skeleton that had dominated Friday's newspaper. I presumed Rob had brought it up for her and made a mental note to have a word with him. She seemed to be disappearing before my eyes, shrivelling away, although the bottle of Lucozade was almost empty, as was the cup she handed to me. I was glad the Doctor was with me, as I would have found it difficult to talk to her without spilling out questions about the diary, or Jean, or the stunning news that I'd heard from Shirley, and not even had a chance to discuss with Rob, yet. I still could not reconcile the anxious young woman of that diary with the self-contained mother who, even now, although increasingly fragile, was looking at us with dignity, mixed with a little trepidation.

‘The police would like to know if you recognise anything,’ I said, placing the bags on the bedspread. Mum frowned at them. Not surprisingly, I thought, realising that they must look like bags of rubbish. I brought the tray from the dressing table and placed the bags on it.

‘No pressure,’ the Doctor said. ‘If it means nothing to you, just say so.’

He shuffled one of them flat, so that I could see that the rusty metal was in fact a torch. A patch of dull red paint showed amongst the brown rust.

Mum had stopped frowning and looked at the Doctor and at me and said, her voice a croak, ‘No, I’ve never seen it before.’

The Doctor slid the torch along the tray and pressed the other bag flat with both hands. It was a chain or perhaps a bracelet. Mum peered through her spectacles, took them off and polished them on her handkerchief, put them back on and looked again. She seemed to be having trouble focusing.

‘Shall I hold it a little closer?’ I asked and picked it up, holding the plastic bag in such a way that the bracelet was dangling from my fingers. I could see that it was a tiny watch face with a narrow metal bracelet, very tarnished.

Mum was shaking her head, no.

The Doctor touched the bag, looked closely and said, ‘Looks like silver.’

Silver. Now I remembered. Mum talked about a silver watch in her diary. A watch that Richard bought her, with a narrow silver bracelet and little precious stones around the face. I looked closely at the blackened band but it was hard to see any resemblance to the description.

‘Claire’s going to get it cleaned up,’ I said. ‘On Monday.’

Mum turned her head away. 'I've never seen it before.' Her speech was slurred. She looked at me briefly then down at her hands, and again I saw that movement, placing one hand on the other as if to hold it still. I recognised the look in her eyes. It was there when she was taking in the destruction of her rockery from the kitchen window on Thursday. Now, it reminded me of something else.

A memory: I don't know how old I was when I bought her a purple heather for Mother's Day, and got up early to plant it for her. She ran out of the house in her nightdress, pulling me away from the rockery, dragging me along the path until Joe, my stepfather, heard me screaming and ran downstairs thinking there'd been an accident. My mother was a calm, measured person who never raised her voice or laid a hand on me. It was a shock to have her grabbing, scratching, screeching at me. Neither of us mentioned it again. Some days later, I noticed she had planted the heather on the rockery.

Another memory: only a few years ago, Mum and I were watching from the kitchen as Rob cut the privet hedge and mowed the lawn. He started weeding the rockery and one of the granite rocks became dislodged and Rob went to lift it, to replace it more securely. Mum banged on the kitchen window with her stick, so hard the glass cracked. On both occasions I was astonished by what I assumed was temper. Now, I realised it had been fear, for this is what I now recognised in her eyes.

'Do you think Mum looks a bit dehydrated?' I asked the doctor.

'Are you drinking plenty, Mrs Ibbertson?'

I said, 'I wouldn't say 'plenty'. She's drinking and eating but only when we stand over her and insist.'

Mum tutted to let me know she was cross that I was speaking for her.

'More confused than usual?' I nodded. 'Mmm, I'll do a quick check.' He took his stethoscope and blood pressure monitor out of his case. I left them and joined Rob and Claire downstairs, where they were drinking coffee. I looked for the muffins I bought at the Co-op and realised the shopping was still in the car. Mrs Barratt was sweeping her front path.

'How is Mrs Ibbertson?' she asked.

'Getting better by the day, thank you.' I kept moving, collecting the bags from the boot of the car. Mrs Barratt leaned on her broom stale, nodding and smiling with her head on one side as I passed, and I heard a 'Hm!' as I closed the door on her.

Claire had finished her coffee. She picked up the zip-lock bags containing the torch and watch, from the table, collected one of the muffins as I put them down, and headed for the door, saying, 'Got to take the kids to see the in-laws, Sunday lunch and all that.' This was another detail from a normal family life that did not fit with my image of Career Claire.

I waited until the front door closed behind her, then asked Rob, 'Did you give Mum the newspaper?'

He shook his head. 'I thought you must have left it with her yesterday. Do you think she came downstairs in the night?' It's entirely possible. Rob could sleep through an earthquake. In fact, he did, when we were in Hawaii a few years ago. I unpacked the vegetables and placed them on the draining board. Rob took the hint and got the potato peeler out of the drawer. While I tidied, and he peeled, I told him about my conversation with Shirley. I should have liked him to be more surprised. He just said, 'Well, that makes sense, answers a lot of questions.'

Before I had time to challenge him on this remark, I heard Doctor Grahams coming downstairs. 'You're right to be worried,' he said as he pulled out his prescription pad and started to write. 'Pulse is not so good, but she insists she's drinking and eating. Dehydration. You need to keep a close eye on her, it can be serious in a woman of your mother's age. Keep her topped up with drinks.' He handed the prescription to me. 'This is a supplement, it helps retain the fluids. Give her some of this straight away and every three hours for the next couple of days.'

I held the prescription out to Rob who gleefully put down the peeler and picked up the car keys.

The doctor said, 'I'll call in tomorrow,' and was about to walk out of the door with Rob when I decided I needed to say something. My momentous news seemed not to figure in anyone's mind but mine. Rob had more or less dismissed it, and seemed not to have considered that it might have had an impact on me. I needed someone to listen, to recognise that this was a significant moment.

'Doctor,' I said to his back, and he turned, surprised, as I realised that my voice had been rather loud. 'Could I check something with you?' He stepped back into the kitchen, frowning, and I felt guilty that I was holding him up for something entirely ordinary. Rob looked back from the hallway, and must have picked up that I was upset as he came back, saying, 'Your ma will be okay, old thing, the doc says–' and I interrupted him and started to tell the Doctor about Shirley's research. 'Is there any way you could check this, you know, on your records?'

Doctor Grahams nodded and opening his case lifted a very small computer onto the table. Rob's eyebrows raised, his attention caught by this new technology.

'We could have a look at your records?' he suggested and when I nodded he opened the computer and did something with a small gizmo from his pocket. 'Security', he said, and looking at the little gadget he tapped some numbers into the computer, moved the mouse around, then tapped at the keyboard. 'This is the database for all the records in the practice,' he explained to us as he worked. 'Your mother's records are still on paper,' he reached into his briefcase for a record pouch and pulled from it two handwritten file cards, 'and haven't been converted to electronic yet. We prioritised regular patients you see. As you said the other day, your mum's not spent much time at the surgery.' As he turned the cards over I saw that the typical spidery crawl of doctor's handwriting had not changed over the years, only the faded ink and the change to biro gave a clue as to the age of some of the entries. 'Anyway, first things first, let's bring up your records.' He asked me to confirm my date of birth, address, while he tapped into the computer, read, tapped some more, and explained, 'Ah, yes.' He turned to me. 'Bang up to date. You're on the waiting list for a knee operation?' I nodded and he pressed the up and down arrow keys for a few more seconds. 'The advantage with this new system is that we can navigate right back, pick up patterns and so on.'

'Does it have a search facility?' Rob was leaning over him. 'For example, if I had, say, angina, could you tell whether that's something hereditary?' I glared at Rob, understanding what the phrase 'stealing my thunder' meant. He did his 'what now?' look with a little shrug.

The Doctor said, 'Yes, it has a lot of advantages over the old handwritten records, and you're right, we could compare family histories to find out whether there is a genetic link.' Rob looked smug. 'That would take a lot of time, though, so we'd only do it in special circumstances.' He turned the screen towards me. 'It can be useful for finding your childhood records at a glance, without ploughing through mountains of paper. You'll have seen your records?'

'No,' I said. He looked surprised.

'We wrote to all our patients, invited you to view your records at the surgery before they were converted to electronic.'

I remembered vaguely but it hadn't been a priority. He turned the screen towards me and pointed. The entry read: "*Child fretful. Mother killed air raids, Mrs Clarke to adopt. Teething powder.*"

'This is not my record,' I said, and realised that I hadn't believed what Shirley had said. It was a mistake.

The doctor swivelled the computer back and tapped at the keyboard. 'Really? Let's check that.'

Rob read over his shoulder. 'Could the files have got mixed up?'

The doctor shook his head. 'It's unlikely. Some areas had trouble with the private firms that moved the records on to computer, but we've had no complaints. So far.' He read aloud, '*Seventeenth January, nineteen forty-one.* No previous entry.' He picked up Mum's cards, searched and found what he was looking for. 'No, it's correct. It says here, "*Alice, 8 wks, adopted from Mrs Clarke's cousin, deceased.*" Clarke was your mother's first married name, yes?'

The ground had shifted again. Rob put an arm around me, led me to a chair.

The doctor said, ‘So your friend who did the research was correct.’

‘Did you know your mother had a cousin who was killed during the war?’ Rob asked.

I didn’t even know my mother had a cousin. If she had a cousin, she must have had an aunt, an uncle, there may be other relatives. I thought my mother was an only child. I’d often wished I’d been part of a large family. Another thread floated free – Judy and Rob were right; she was not pregnant. Who am I?

‘But I have a birth certificate.’ I’d seen it often enough during my life to know that my mother was Violet Clarke, and my father was Richard Clarke, deceased. It was all a mistake. They were talking about someone else. But who? I needed to ask my mother.

Frank

Flight QF319 to Heathrow

The little lad in front of me is having a tantrum. His dad's trying to tell him it's time to sleep and he's having none of it. It's a long time for kiddies to sit still. They're going for a walk around the aisles. It'll give me a bit of peace but probably wake everybody else up. I don't know much about children apart from having been one myself. Sam and Doreen had an idea that it would be good for me to have a family of my own. They used to leave little Keith with me, probably thinking if I got some practice in, I might get to like the idea. They were forever trying to fix me up with young ladies. Doreen's sister for one - I think she hoped we'd make a go of it and she could come to Australia with us. Then Doreen tried to get me interested in the young women on the ship and, after we arrived, while we were looking for land to buy, she started rounding up any likely lasses in our digs. As soon as we settled in Gulawalla, she began inviting the neighbours around. Nobody lives nearer than two miles from our farm. I liked being well away from everything, but Doreen could always find an excuse for a party, especially if there was a daughter or a sister that was single. I didn't mind, I was always civil, but I was determined there would never be another family for me. This stewardess – she's called Hermione, I said that's unusual, I've not heard that name before, and she told me how to pronounce it. She says, 'You don't have grandchildren who read Harry Potter then?' and I told her I don't have any children. She says she can start up a film about this Harry Potter chap for me to watch, so I could see for myself. Maybe later. I reckon I've got a deal of thinking to do at the moment. Right now, I'm thinking about my family.

I know life at our house wasn't always as cosy and kind as I choose to think. My mam and dad wouldn't have put up with half the backchat parents seem to tolerate these days. Oftentimes in our street, we'd hear somebody's mam or dad shouting, 'I'll gi'thee a crack upside thy head', and plenty were the times I felt the carpet beater on my backside. I don't think it did us any harm. And being part of a big family isn't always a good thing. Brothers – and sisters – can be mean to one another. But there's no joy in thinking badly of them. Even so, remembering Cyril's shenanigans sorely tests my good intentions towards his memory. Take the rabbits, for instance. This rabbit's foot might be a bit shrivelled, and it's more grey than brown, but I keep it because it reminds me of that time with Cyril. I can see now what his plan was, all along. He fixed it so I'd spend my pocket money and my spare time looking after those rabbits until they were nice and fat, and then he planned to sell them on and make a few bob for himself.

It must have been April when Cyril brought the rabbits home, because I recall that's rabbit season. He dumped the small wooden crate on the table and stood back, looking very pleased with himself. Jean had just taken a tray of buns out of the oven and put them onto the table and she swore at him and moved them to the draining board. Inside the crate was a sack that appeared to be moving. Cyril put his hand in it and pulled out the smallest rabbit I'd ever seen, no longer than four inches from its tail to its ears. As he dangled it by its ears, its legs ran through the air.

'And how many of us does tha reckon to feed with that?' Mam laughed.

He pulled out another rabbit, swinging one from each hand. 'I'm going to rear them. I might even start breeding,' he said. 'I got them off Foxy Riley.' Foxy was a wild man who lived in a hut he'd built himself out of fallen branches, in the woods down by the river. His ginger hair and beard were so long and straggly, it was said he wrapped them round himself to keep warm, instead of wearing a vest. People said he lived off the chickens that he stole from the farms around Sheffield. I was surprised that Cyril knew Foxy. Sam and me often went near to where Foxy lived but as soon as we set eyes on him we'd scarper.

I leaned across to look under the sacking and saw another rabbit. It shivered in a corner of the crate, looking up at me with its huge brown eyes.

Mam said, 'Best check they've got all their legs if they're from Foxy.'

Jean said, 'I'm surprised old Foxy's still alive after the winter we've had.'

Cyril said, 'He lost all the toes on his right foot. Frost-bite. Had to go to Infirmary to have them amputated.' I stared at him. Sam would be right impressed with this information.

I asked Cyril, 'How much did tha pay for them?' I put my hands around one of the rabbits and Cyril let go so that I was holding it. I ran a finger along the soft brown fur on its spine and felt it tremble.

Cyril tapped the side of his nose. 'I swapped that old coat that was in the ragbag for them.'

I asked, 'Where shall we keep them?'

Mam said, '*If* we keep them. It'll be months before they're big enough to eat. Who's going to pay for their food? And who's going to look after them?'

Cyril dropped his rabbit back into the crate and said, 'Our Frank can take care of them. He's got nowt else useful to do.' I didn't agree with him and was about to say so, but Cyril had never given me anything before so I kept my mouth shut.

Jean said, 'Mind they're not in the house when Violet comes to call. We'll not have her thinking we live in a farmyard.'

Mam looked at her and said, 'When's that then?'

'Tomorrow night. She's coming for tea.'

'All this way for a cup of tea,' Mam said.

'No,' Jean said, with her nose in the air. 'For a proper tea. I thought I'd do a bit of ham salad. And we could have these buns.'

'Since when have we had tea in this house? Why can't she have supper like everybody else?'

'I told Joe I'd make an effort, take her out a bit, with Richard gone. We're going to see *Gone with the Wind*. It's showing at the Hippodrome.'

Mam said, 'Well, tha'd best hide them rabbits, else she'll have Ministry on us.'

I put the rabbits in the crate under the bed. Their scratching woke me up early. I used Mam's ear syringe to put water down their throats, and put in a bit of lettuce that I found in the kitchen. When I told Sam about the rabbits, he had the bright idea of fixing up his dad's old pigeon shed, turning it into a hutch. So the following day after school, we hefted it around from Sam's house to ours and with a bit of a to-do got it down the gennel. I shovelled the coal higher to create a space and we set the shed against the privy wall. We'd almost finished knocking out the perches when I heard Jean's voice.

'What the chuffing hell's going on here?'

I turned round and saw Jean, very pink in the face, standing with Violet who looked me up and down, then Sam.

Mrs Wreakes's door opened and she said, 'What's all this banging and carrying-on?' She stood on the doorstep with her hands on her hips, and said, 'I hope tha's not thinking of setting up with pigeons, I can't stand the stink of the bleeding things.'

I said, 'We're making a rabbit hutch.'

Jean shouted, 'Mam, come and look at what he's doing.'

Violet said nothing, staring up and down at us from behind her glasses, and I thought the cat must have got her tongue.

Mrs Wreakes said, 'Well it looks like a pigeon shed to me.'

Jean said, 'It looks like a scrapyard.'

Mrs Wreakes said, 'And tha'd best make sure it stops on that side of yard, else I shall consider it my property and I shall be having them pigeons or rabbits, or whatever they may be, in my oven.' She walked across to the privy and banged the door closed behind her as Mam came out of the house.

Jean wailed at Mam, 'Look at him, Mam, he looks like a hooligan.'

Mam grabbed me by the elbow. 'What the chuff... Tha knew our Jean was having a visitor, and look at the state of thee.'

Jean said, 'Come on, Violet,' and marched into the house. She seemed to be very stuck up suddenly. A bit of mess never used to worry her.

Mam said, 'Get off home, Sam. Though what thy Mam's going to say when she sees the state of thy school clothes, I don't know.'

I saw Sam was covered head to toe in coal dust and pigeon droppings and realised I must look much the same. I made for the door. Mam pulled me back and stripped off my jersey and trousers. 'I shall get thee a bucket of water and tha can clean thyself up out here.'

'But Mam, it's starting to rain.'

'Then tha'll get washed a bit quicker, I dare say.'

When I'd washed down as best I could, Mam sent me upstairs to put clean clothes on. I had to walk across the kitchen to reach the stairs, with no trousers on. I saw Violet's coat was hung on the peg my Dad used for his work coat, and she was sitting on my Dad's chair at the table. I reckoned there'd be trouble if he knew that. None of us was allowed to sit in his chair. I lay down on the landing where I could see the kitchen through the gap in the floorboards. Violet sat at the table and Jean was putting eggs into the small pan and pouring boiling water over them from the kettle. My Nannan's teapot and the matching cups and saucers were on the table.

Jean said, 'I don't know what you must be thinking of us, Vi.' I knew she was in a temper by the way she banged the pan down on the hob.

'Oh, it's nowt to fret over,' Mam said. 'Boys will be boys. I expect Violet understands that, don't you, Violet love?'

I heard Violet laugh, not a proper laugh, more like a hiccup that she was trying to stop coming out. 'Well, Frank certainly seems to be very boisterous.'

Mam laughed. 'Boisterous, eh? A boy-sterous boy. Well, that's one word for it.' She seemed to think this was very funny. I couldn't understand why Violet and Jean were best friends after the mean things they said about one another behind their backs, and why Violet was allowed to eat the rock buns and poke fun at me.

Mam said, 'Right, girls. I wish I could come to Hippodrome with thee but I must get to work.' She got up and I scuttled as quietly as I could to the bedroom. She shouted up the stairs to me, 'No more fun and games, my lad. I want to hear tha's been on thy best behaviour when I come home.'

I heard the door close behind her, put on some clean trousers and crept downstairs. Jean was looking through bags and opening cupboards. She looked in the larder cupboard and in the meat safe. 'I swear I had a lettuce, Vi,' she said. I slid along the wall towards the back door. She heard me as I lifted the latch, spun round and got hold of me by the shoulders. 'Don't tell me tha's fed it to them chuffing rabbits,' she said, and when I didn't answer she pushed past me, stamping up the stairs. Violet was smirking at me. She looked really pleased that I was getting wronged. I thought I could slip out but when I opened the door the rain was coming down so hard that it was bouncing back up and over the doorstep. I shut the door. The buns looked very tasty. I sat down opposite them. Violet kept smirking at me so I decided not to take one in case she told on me. We stared at one another until Jean came back and waved a lettuce leaf under my nose. She was about to have a go at me when Violet said, with her eyes as big as the lenses of her glasses, 'You keep rabbits in the bedroom?'

Jean's face went red as she said, 'Yes, well, no, of course not.' She looked as though she was going to cry. 'It's to keep them out of the way while Frank gets the hutch ready. Isn't it, Frank?'

I could see she needed me to be on her side, so I said, 'Oh, aye, we don't keep rabbits in the house. Can I have a bun now?'

Jean said, 'No, they're for later.' I thought this was right mean when I'd stuck up for her. She bustled about, opening a tin of sardines and sharing them between three plates, taking the pan off the fire and spooning out the boiled eggs, yelping when she splashed her fingers, holding them with a dish-towel to shell them and slice them into quarters.

Violet asked, 'How on earth do you find eggs, Jean?'

'My friend Sybil gets them for us. Her father knows a farmer.'

Violet said, 'Isn't that black marketeering? I read in the newspaper that it undermines the economy and we should all fight it.'

Jean said, 'It's a few eggs that the farmer has to spare. If we didn't use them, they'd go bad and that'd be a waste, wouldn't it?'

Violet opened her mouth as though she was going to argue, then looked down at her hands in her lap. She had this way of holding on to one hand with the other as though she wanted to do something and was trying to stop herself. I got up to help Jean but she lifted a finger at me and said, 'Don't even think about it.' Setting out beetroot and radishes on the plates she then put one in front of each of us, sat down and nodded at me to start eating. Violet popped a radish in her mouth. I watched her, trying to work out how she could chew, with her lips pressed together. When she'd swallowed, she said, 'There's a new information pamphlet with ideas for cooking without eggs. Would you be interested if I could get a copy for you?'

I knew my Mam would have said Violet was being sarky but Jean said, 'That would be good of you, thanks, Vi.'

Violet said, 'Actually, could you please not call me Vi?' Jean looked up from her plate, her fork midway to her mouth. 'Mother feels very strongly that we should use our given name.' Jean said nothing. 'Please don't take offence,' Violet added.

Jean might have started a row, but the door crashed open at that moment and Cyril came in, bringing with him a wet gust of wind that blew across the room and wrapped itself round my knees.

Cyril asked, 'What's happening in the yard?' He shook himself like a dog, scattering rain across the floor. I looked at Jean but she didn't tell him off, though I was sure she would have done if it had been me.

'Sam and me are making a rabbit hutch.'

'That's a right good idea.' Cyril nodded at me. 'I might find time to gi'thee a hand at weekend.' I was thrilled to bits. He said, 'Happen we shall start breeding. We could get a bit of business going. And tha can make a bit of pocket money.' I decided that having Cyril pleased with me more than made up for Jean being cross about a bit of muck and an old lettuce.

Violet was very red in the face. She said, 'Oh, dear, I–' then she looked at Jean and said, 'I'm very much looking forward to the film, Jean. The manager's personal secretary told me she was too afraid to go into town at present in case there is an air raid, and she thought I was terribly brave to go to the pictures.' She was gabbling away. Cyril looked at me and rolled his eyes up into his head. I laughed. Jean leaned over the table and cuffed me on the head. Violet looked shocked. She took a deep breath and then carried on talking fast. 'I read that it has stereophonic sound. Richard said in his letter that he thought it was the first film to use the new technique. He was quite envious. He wants me to write to him as soon as I get home, and tell him all about it.'

Jean poured tea from my Nannan's teapot and passed Violet a cup and saucer. Cyril picked up a cup, his hand wrapped around it, and poured the tea into the saucer, then slurped it. Jean frowned at him and shook her head but he wasn't looking at her. I picked up my cup the same way, and was about to pour it into the saucer when she grabbed my wrist and held it down. She stared at me until I put the cup back in the saucer. I looked at Violet who was holding her cup by its curly handle with her little finger in the air which looked right comical. Cyril put the saucer down and reached across to take a rock bun. Violet put her cup back in her saucer and watched Cyril eat the bun with her eyes narrowed and her lips together, concentrating like I did when I was watching an ant or a beetle gathering its food. Jean held out the buns and Violet took one, nibbling at a corner as though she was frightened it would bite her.

She said, 'Lovely,' putting it down after a couple of little bites, so it didn't look as though she thought it was lovely at all. 'You must give me the recipe.'

Jean said, 'It's my Nannan's recipe,' then added quickly, 'Without real sugar of course.' She looked straight at me as if daring me to say a word. I put my tongue out at her and snatching a bun off the plate, pushed it whole into my mouth, daring her to say something, but she turned away and started stacking the plates.

Cyril rubbed his hands together to knock off the crumbs and said, ‘If we put some wood across where that perch used to be’ – he reached across the table and pulled my exercise book towards him – ‘We could separate the top and bottom and make two hutches.’ Opening the book to a clean page, he took a stub of pencil from behind his ear, licked it and started to draw. ‘Like this.’

Jean said, ‘Come on, Violet, let’s get going. Frank can clear the table and wash up.’ Looking at me, she said, ‘Make sure it’s done before Mam gets in.’

That night, I lay listening to the rabbits rustling in the crate beneath the bed, thinking about the plans we’d made for building the rabbit hutch and feeling right proud that Cyril wanted to go into business with me. I heard Jean come in from the pictures. She was downstairs talking to Mam. Squeezing myself out from between Cyril and Bill who were snoring and puffing like a pair of steam engines, I crept across the landing and laid down to look through the gap in the floorboards into the kitchen. Mam was sitting right below me, her feet soaking in the basin. I knew Dad would be by the hearth in his chair, his pipe hanging from his loose mouth and the newspaper sliding down his legs as he snoozed.

Jean was making cocoa, chattering about the film. ‘Technicolour, Mam. I’ve seen it before of course, but this was the best. There’s this part where Atlanta is burning. It’s like it’s all happening right outside the window, in real life.’

Mam asked, ‘What did her ladyship make of it?’

‘It’s hard to say. She says to me at the intermission, “Doesn’t Ashley remind you of Richard?” and I didn’t know what to say. Well, he did have a bit of the look of Richard, with that wavy hair and a longish nose, but he was blond where Richard’s brown, and perhaps they are of a height, but –’

‘Happen the lass is missing Richard and it’s maybe like they say, after somebody’s died, tha keeps seeing them in street. She was maybe minded of Richard in that way.’

‘Mmm, she did seem right taken with this Ashley Wilkes character. So I said to her, joking, “Do you see yourself as a bit of a Melanie Wilkes character then, Violet?” and right off she says, “Well yes, actually, I do think we have similar characters in many ways”. I laughed but she was serious.’

Jean handed Mam a beaker of cocoa and stood beside her so I was looking down on her head almost close enough to touch her. I could smell her perfume, which reminded me of walking along the allotment paths in summer.

Mam asked, ‘So what’s this Melanie like then?’

‘She’s a right goody two shoes and no mistake. I’m more for Scarlett myself.’ Jean put her hands on her hips and said, ‘“Fiddle-de-dee.” That’s what Scarlett says, whenever she doesn’t like the way things are going. “Fiddle-de-dee.”’

Mam asked, ‘And does she often not like the way things are going then?’

Jean took her own beaker and sat at the table, stirring it. ‘Whenever anyone doesn’t see things her way, I should say. Anyway, I says to Vi – oh, fiddle-de-dee, silly me, I mean Violet,’ she laughed and I just stopped myself laughing in time. ‘I says to Violet, wasn’t it romantic how the women make a sash for their fellows to wear over their uniform, so the men will think of them as they go off to fight, and perhaps we should do the same for our men. And she says, quick as lightning, "But Scarlett gave a sash to Melanie's husband, and that can't be right, can it, Jean?"'

'What did she mean by that then?'

'Well, she seemed to be having a go at me, the way she looked at me while she said it, but I couldn't think what for. Anyway, the film came back on so I didn't have to speak to her again until we were on the tram coming home. Then, I ask if she's heard from Richard and she looks at me and says in that way she has –'

Mam said, 'With a face like a slapped arse?'

Jean laughed and walked below me to put her empty beaker in the sink. 'Aye, that's about right. She says, "Of course I've heard from Richard, Jean. He writes to me every week. I can absolutely depend on the Tuesday post. Why do you ask?" I was being friendly, and she spoke to me as though I'd asked the colour of her knickers. So I gave up and I don't think we said two words to one another the rest of the way.'

I wanted to tell her that Violet wasn't a real friend and she shouldn't be troubling with her, but I decided she didn't deserve to know what Violet said about her behind her back, not after the way she'd been with me that night. Mam leaned her head back and looked up at the ceiling so she was looking straight at me. I closed my eyes so she wouldn't see the whites of them, and stayed very still so she wouldn't notice any movement.

Mam said, 'Well, tha's done thy duty, as promised to Joe.'

‘Oh but Mam, if tha’d seen the frocks they wore. Tha wants to get Dad to take thee. It’s on all this week and next. It’s right romantic.’

‘Get on will thee. Dad and me, we’re beyond a bit of romancing.’

I heard Dad grunt, ‘We’ve to be up at five so there’ll be no romancing round here the night.’ I opened my eyes and saw Jean whisper something to Mam. Mam giggled. If they were going to talk soppy, I’d rather be asleep. I crept into the bedroom and climbed onto the bottom of the bed, wriggling back up between Cyril and Bill, forcing them apart where they’d rolled into one another. As I drifted off to sleep, I thought *Gone with the Wind* didn’t sound like my sort of film, but maybe I could persuade Cyril to come with me and Sam to the new Laurel and Hardy.

On Sunday, while Mam was cooking tea, Dad stood in the yard having a fag, watching Cyril and me putting the finishing touches to the rabbit hutch. We’d put in a shelf and nailed the wire to a frame to make a door in the top half. The bottom half we’d left, and planned to use it as a second hutch when the first lot had babies.

Dad chuckled. ‘Has tha checked tha’s got at least one lad and one lass?’

Cyril’s ears were dark red. ‘Foxy told me one was a buck.’

‘Tha’s not taken a look to make sure, then?’

I asked, ‘How does tha tell?’ and Cyril pushed me. Dad laughed.

Bill came out, waving the newspaper. ‘Here, Dad, they’ve started a volunteer brigade at the Dog and Duck. They’re taking sixteen and seventeen year olds.’

Dad said, 'Aye, I've heard some talk about it. They say Mr Churchill's thinking about a proper volunteer army. He seems to be getting ready for an invasion.'

Bill said, 'It's no wonder. This week's *War Illustrated* says the German Army's moving a hundred and twenty-five miles a day. It says they'll probably invade Holland and Belgium, now Norway's fallen, and then keep moving to France. They say if they're not stopped it's only a matter of time before they get to England.' Bill sat on the step with the newspaper on his knee. He carried on, 'They do say the lads in Norway didn't stand a chance. Not enough artillery. And what they had they couldn't move because of deep snow. Not a chance.'

I asked, 'Is Joe in Norway, Dad?' as pictures of deep snow replaced the mud that was always in my mind when I thought of Joe. I remembered when the Rivelin Valley Road had been blocked during the winter. The snow had come up to our waists and we couldn't lift our legs high enough to walk through it. I imagined the Army stuck in snow that deep. 'Will Joe get frostbite, like Foxy Riley, and have to have his toes cut off?'

'No, lad, he's in France, at least that's where Jean got the last letter from.'

Bill said, 'So can I join the Dog and Duck brigade?'

Dad fished around in the corner of his baccy tin to catch the last strands and push them into his pipe. He said, 'I reckon if it satisfies thee, and if it'll keep thee at home, I'll be able to talk thy Mam round.'

Mam stuck her head out of the door. 'Has tha nowt better to do than sit there putting the world to rights? There's some onions want peeling if tha's got empty hands. Frank–'

I said, 'Dad, shall I pop to corner shop for some baccy?'

He looked in his tin. 'Aye, get us half an ounce of Erinmore.' He pulled a pile of coppers out of his pocket and handed them to me and I was off down the gennel before Mam could stop me.

Over the next weeks, Bill was either at work, or out with the Brigade. When he was home, he was full of himself, talking non-stop about how they'd been taught to drill and muster, though they hadn't got rifles and he took the stale out of Mam's broom to practice with. One night after supper, he sat in the yard wearing his vest and trousers with his braces hanging down. I noticed that he had whiskers and muscles, and had turned into a man. I brought my German book out of my hiding place and showed it to him.

He said, 'That's right good, our Frank. Happen I could learn some of this, then teach it to the lads.' He was in such a good mood that he let me and Sam play at being Germans, against him and Cyril, taking it in turns to tackle one another.

Mrs Wreakes yelled from her upstairs window, 'What's all the bleeding racket. I thought Germans had landed. It's enough to give Mr Wreakes a heart attack. Tha's old enough to know better, Bill Sheldon. I'll come down there and gi'thee a crack meself since thy Mam's not able to keep thee under control.'

Mam came out of the kitchen and waved a dishcloth up at Mrs Wreakes. 'I've told thee before, keep thy tongue to thyself. And tha can keep thy hands off my lads. Happen tha's not getting enough from that owd trout indoors.'

Mrs Wreakes yelled back, 'Watch thy step. I'll be on to Corporation about that rabbit farm them lads as got there, and they'll be down on thee like a ton of bricks. Tha'd be looking for a new address.'

'Cut off thy nose to spite thy face if tha wants,' Mam said. 'If the rabbits go, so does thy Whitsun dinner.'

Mrs Wreakes slammed the window shut.

Bill said, 'Good one, Mam, that sorted her out and no mistake.'

Mam waved the dishcloth round, taking us all in. 'Just spare her a bit of thought. They've got grandsons at the Front, and they must be worried sick. Not everybody's as lucky as us, with our lads at home.'

Jean screeched from inside the house, 'Our lads at home? Well I must be imagining things because I could have sworn my husband was in France and where's that if it's not the chuffing Front?'

Mam rushed back into the kitchen and I heard her say, 'Sorry love, I wasn't thinking, I could bite my tongue off.' Jean cried and Mam made shushing noises. Cyril and Bill looked at one another and rolled their eyes. I didn't want to play the invader game any longer.

Miss Malkin brought the *Daily Sketch* to school and copied a map onto the blackboard. She allowed the boys that did best in spelling that morning, to draw thick arrows with blue chalk, showing the Germans advancing, and the girls at the top of the class drew green arrows, showing the British Expeditionary Force moving towards the same point. She said, 'We'll keep this map up to date so that we can think about our troops and support them to the best of our ability. Now, does anyone have fathers, or brothers, or any other relations, in the Armed Forces?' Most families worked in the steel industry, a few in the coal mines. I thought for a second, and then put my hand up. Daisy Biggin, Ralph Williams and myself had relations who were fighting in France. 'Daisy, Ralph and Frank, we're going to put your relations here.' She put three stick people on the dotted line where France met Belgium. 'And we'll think of them as we follow the progress of our troops.'

Miss Malkin marked Sheffield on her map. We were separated from Holland by barely a few inches of the North Sea, and a tiny strip of English Channel divided England from France, where the stick figures stood along their dotted line. Miss Malkin asked for volunteers to cut out plane shapes and she stuck these onto the sea around the coast. To see them so close gave me the shivers, and I had to wrap my arms round myself to stop anybody noticing.

That night, when he came in from work, Dad walked straight across to the table and slapped the newspaper down in front of Mam, who was chopping onions. He said, 'Look at this, our lass.' I left off peeling spuds to lean across and read the headline: *Nazis Invade Holland, Belgium, Luxemburg. The Dutch have opened their floodgates*.

'Happen they think they'll flood them out,' Dad said. I remembered a story Miss Malkin had read to us of a boy who put his finger in a dyke to stop his town flooding and wondered whether it was possible to flood the Germans out of Holland, and if they did, would the water run down into Belgium and France and cause more mud for Joe and Richard. This made me think of Mr Knowles sitting in his shelter with the water coming in.

'Can I go up and visit Mr Knowles, Mam?'

'Tha's going nowhere.' Mam lifted the pan of spuds off the draining board and carried it across the room to put it on the fire. The bottom was wet and it sizzled and hissed on the hot coals for a few seconds.

Dad read aloud, '*You must carry your gas mask. The Minister of Home Security states that all civil defence and A.R.P. services should be on the alert.*'

'Where's our Cyril?' Mam asked.

'He's working till eight.'

Mam said, 'Happen I'll go down and meet him. We want everybody safe at home while this is going on.'

Dad said, 'I'm on fire watch tonight. I'll go a bit earlier and make certain he comes straight home.'

A few days later, I came home to find Mam standing in the street, looking up and down. When she saw me she shouted, 'Where the chuffing hell has tha been?'

'With Sam.'

She said, 'There's no messing about after school from now on,' and pushed me up the gennel and into the house. 'Tha's at school, or tha's at home, and tha's not anywhere in between unless thy Dad or me knows about it.' I opened my mouth but she shushed me and nodded her head towards the table, where Jean was sitting with her head in her hands. I walked across to the table and read the headline of the newspaper in front of her: *British Troops Fight down Narrow Corridor to Dunkirk.*

Alice

Mum was still reading the newspaper. She held it a couple of inches from her nose, and I made a mental note to take her to the optician. I pulled the Lloyd loom chair closer to the bed, ignoring her frown as its feet squeaked across the linoleum, and sat facing her, my arms folded. She was watching me over the newspaper with what I'd come to recognise as trepidation. What was she afraid of? That I would discover she had been lying to me all my life? I decided not to beat about the bush.

'You didn't tell me I was adopted.'

Surprise flitted across her face and I realised this was not what she expected me to say. As she folded the newspaper with excruciating slowness and placed it tidily on her bedside table, I remembered where I'd left it – on the dressing table in the front bedroom. So she must have been looking around, presumably this morning when Rob was busy downstairs. In which case, she'll have seen the burned pages from her diary that I popped beneath it, and she would be anticipating some of my questions. She would have no idea how much more I knew.

She took off her spectacles and cleaned them with a corner of the bed-sheet, no doubt playing for time. As she tucked the arms back around her ears, she said, 'Who told you that?' She spoke quietly, almost whispering, with a new croak in her voice that reminded me of what the doctor had said about dehydration, but I felt determined to get to the bottom of this.

'Someone's done a family tree for me. And it's on my medical records.' I let this sink in. 'And yours.' She looked up sharply at this invasion of her privacy. I carried on, 'It says you adopted me from your cousin' – did I imagine the long exhale, as though she'd been holding her breath? – 'who was killed during the war.'

Seconds passed before she nodded, slowly, and whispered, 'Yes.'

'Why did you never tell me?'

Again, the long hesitation. Her lips looked dry and cracked. I had to lean across to hear. 'Surely all you need to know, Alice, is that I brought you up to the best of my ability.' She paused then added, 'Wouldn't you agree?'

'Well, yes, of course.' She nodded and closed her eyes, clearly letting me know there was no more to be said. This had always been one of her skills, quashing an argument by simply removing herself from the discussion. 'But…' She opened her eyes and looked at me with raised eyebrows as though surprised to find I was still there. I hesitated, and then reminded myself that this was possibly more important than anything I had dealt with in my life. With a deep breath, surprising myself by the firmness in my voice, I said, 'I think I have a right to know. You didn't mention having a cousin. What was her name?'

She looked around as though expecting to find the answer somewhere in the room. Although aware that Jean was not her cousin, it was the only name I knew from that time, and I half expected this to be the name she gave. So much so that I had to stop myself supplying the name for her, dropping it into the silence. My mouth may have actually dropped open when she finally said, 'Rose.'

Not sure I'd heard properly, I repeated, 'Rose?' Questions ran around my mind and out of my mouth. 'Was she younger or older than you? How old was she when I was born? When she died? Who was my father? What happened to him?' It was another, lesser shock to realise that Richard, who I'd always considered to be my father, may not have been, but this was less important somehow – after all, I'd never known him. 'Why do I have a birth certificate that says you and Richard are my parents?'

I thought she said, 'So long', and leaned back against her pillows, closing her eyes. She looked very, very frail and not at all well, but I was surprised not to feel guilty about badgering her. Instead, I felt a slow, burning anger that was unfamiliar to me. She had kept so much from me for so long – if she thought I was going to leave it at that, she could think again. My mind was spinning as it tried to absorb the new information. I didn't know who or what I was any longer. She was not my mother, Richard was not my father. What question could I ask that might get a straight answer?

'Why did you adopt me?'

There was no hesitation when she said, 'Your mother was killed during the War.' So I thought this must be true.

'That's what the medical record says. But why you? What about other relatives?'

'Killed. In an air raid.'

'All of them?' A slight nod. 'I have no other surviving family?' A single sideways movement of her head. 'What about my father?'

'Lost… Dunkirk.'

'Like my – I mean Richard?'

'Like Richard, yes.'

'And I was born on the fourth of December nineteen-forty?'

'No.' This short answer was as big a shock as any other revelation.

'That's not my birthday?' She shook her head slightly. 'When is it?'

'Twenty seventh … November.'

'And when did my – my real mother,' At this, her milky eyes suddenly cleared and focused sharply on me. 'Rose, when did she die?'

'Air raids. In December, there were air raids.' She followed my eyes to where her plucking fingers had created a little peak in the bedspread and patted it down, smoothing it. She held her hand out towards her glass on the bedside table, and I reached across and passed it to her. Taking the smallest sip of water, she flicked her tongue across her dry lips.

Something clicked in my mind as one of my questions was resolved. If Mum was suddenly left in charge of a baby, it made sense that she wouldn't have had the time to continue to write her diary. I pushed away, for the moment, my questions about whether Mum was pregnant, and why Grandma locked her in the bedroom.

'How did she die? Why wasn't I with her?'

'I was looking after you.'

'Why? Where was she?'

'Maybe … she liked to go dancing.' The way she hesitated made me wonder whether she thought there was something to be ashamed of, and maybe there was, if a young widow left a new-born baby to go dancing.

'So she wasn't at home, with her family, when they were killed?' She shook her head slightly. 'She was killed by a different bomb? At a different time? How long was it before you knew what had happened?'

'I knew … when she didn't come for you.'

'But it was definite – that she'd been killed?'

'She was never found.'

‘So it’s not certain?’

‘No other reason she wouldn’t have come back for you.’

‘But where might she have been, dancing?’

‘I think… The Marples Hotel?’

‘Why do you think that?’

‘Marples Hotel… direct hit.’

‘Didn’t you think she might be somewhere else? Maybe wandering around, injured?’

She slurred but I thought she said, ‘I was sure she was dead.’

‘But she wasn’t necessarily there? At the hotel? She could have been somewhere else?’ I repeated myself as an idea started to form in my mind.

She pushed her head back against the pillows. ‘So many questions. Such a long time ago.’ She closed her eyes.

‘Not for me, Mum, for me it’s now, it’s happening now.’ The old, obedient Alice in me knew I was being unfair, harassing an old lady, and my intuition was to leave it at that, but the new Alice was egging me on to solve this puzzle that was my story. I decided to risk it. ‘Do you think it could be Rose in the Anderson shelter?’ Mum’s eyes flew to mine, wide open. Surely she’d thought of this herself? She was usually so much faster thinking than I was. ‘Well, could it?’

I was warming to this idea. I grew up in the aftermath of the war and as a teenager I watched the builders digging new foundations in what had been the Marples Hotel, taking great care in case they discovered bodies still buried from that air raid in December, 1940. I’d started to accept that my real mother was someone I didn’t know, and that she was dead. But I couldn’t feel any kind of connection with the Marples Hotel. I knew Rob would harrumph if I was to say it, but I did believe, now I thought about it, that I had an affinity, even a bond, with the body in the garden. The feeling was growing on me and I felt a knot of anxious excitement growing in my stomach. 'It makes sense,' I said. 'The lady in the Anderson shelter could be my mother. Don't you think?'

Mum's bob of stone grey hair dipped as she nodded. Eventually, she slurred, 'I suppose so.'

I could hear myself prattling but couldn't stop. 'Like we said before, perhaps she came back and you didn't hear her – because you weren't expecting her and you'd have settled down for the night, under the table – as you explained – and she might have gone into the shelter.'

There was a long pause as we both absorbed this new train of thought and the possibilities, then her shoulders slumped and her head dropped onto her chest as she said, 'Oh dear,' and I found myself leaning across, my arms around her. My anxiety turned to tears and as they ran down my face and off my chin, I was dimly aware that I would make the sleeve of her bed-jacket damp. She was patting my back, like she used to when I was a child and was upset about something. It was an acknowledgement that I was being emotional, rather than sympathy for what I was upset about. I pulled away and when I saw that she was dry eyed, felt a little foolish.

I stood to look out of the window, blowing my nose. It was pouring down and the garden was a series of mud pools. I watched Rob splashing about in his wellingtons, beneath his golf umbrella. From this perspective he looked like one of those Shirley Hughes cartoons that the grandchildren had so much enjoyed, of a child playing on a rainy day. The crater had new meaning for me now I believed it may have been my mother lying there for seventy years. It was strange that I'd never heard Rose's name before, not even in passing. There was no mention of her in Mum's diary. Which was odd, since Rose would be having a baby – me – around the time Mum was having a baby. If Mum adopted me, what on earth happened to the baby Mum was expecting? Did she, as Judy suspected, have a miscarriage? Watching Rob below me, I heard his voice in my head – in for a penny, in for a pound, old girl.

'So did you have any children?' I turned to Mum.

Her head reared back as though I've said something really shocking. 'You were an only child.'

That wasn't really an answer. I was shivering. 'It's turning cold. What about joining us downstairs? We could light a fire. It might do you good to be out of bed for a few hours.' She looked uncertain and I said, 'The police won't be back today.'

She may have agreed in the hope I wouldn't talk about this in front of Rob. She seemed dizzy when she stood, and had trouble walking, but she wouldn't hear of coming down in her nightwear and dispatched me to wait on the landing while she got dressed. When she joined me at the top of the stairs, she stood for a few moments looking down, and then swayed as if she'd lost her balance. I was afraid she would fall and grasped her elbow but she shook her head, turned, and started the slow process of going down the stairs backwards.

Rob had laid the fire and put the roast dinner in the oven. He was still in the garden, piling up the sheets of rusty metal that the police diggers had left lying around. The box of supplement was on the table and I mixed a drink for Mum. Neither of us seemed able to make small talk and I switched on Classic FM to fill the silence. She sat in her usual chair at the fireside while I put a match to the kindling and pressed the bellows against the grate until there was a good blaze. I watched Rob working in the garden while I stretched my back against the pantry door jamb in a Pilates exercise that Judy taught me. The rain had stopped and the clouds were disappearing fast behind the hill, leaving a clear blue sky.

I went to the bathroom and was relieved to find Mum had finished her drink and popped her cup on the draining board by the time I got back. Rob was taking off his wellingtons at the door. 'We need to get a few tons of soil to fill the hole,' he said as he washed his hands, 'Unless we buy some hard-core to fill it and turn it into a patio.'

'Maybe a memorial garden?' I suggested. 'What do you think, Mum?' Rob looked at me questioningly and I whispered, 'Revelations. Later.' Mum was staring into the flames and didn't answer.

The chicken and roast vegetables were delicious. I told Rob, 'Mum has explained it, the adoption.' He raised his eyebrows and I told him the story. Mum toyed with her food, pushing it around her plate, eating nothing.

'That's all very well,' he said when I finished. 'But she wasn't sheltering was she? The police have established that.' Mum looked at both of us and I coughed and shook my head at him to try to stop him saying it, but he was concentrating on cutting his butternut squash into smaller cubes as he continued, 'She was murdered.' Mum's knife crashed onto the floor. He looked up and saw the expression on her face and said to me accusingly, 'You didn't tell her what Claire said?'

I couldn't explain why I hadn't. Maybe it was because I was so completely wrapped up in finding out about the adoption and my real mother. It was nagging at the back of my mind throughout the conversation with my mother, but the right moment never came. Rob had often accused me of putting information in boxes and deciding which to open and which to put into storage, and he may have been right on this occasion. There were enough secrets in the box I'd opened today, without giving Mum yet another revelation. Or perhaps it was selfish motivation – I wanted to find answers to my own questions before thinking too much about the lady in the shelter. Part of me hoped Claire was wrong, that there was an explanation short of murder. After all, until a week ago it would have seemed incredible that Mum was not my real mother, or that I was adopted. Yet it appeared there was a perfectly rational explanation for those facts. So why should there not also be a reasonable explanation for Rose being in the shelter? The police could be wrong.

Rob was saying to Mum, 'Well, I'm sorry you had to hear it like that', looking crossly at me, 'But I shall have to tell you now. It might be your cousin Rose. She could have been in the shelter because she got back late and couldn't raise anyone. She might even have had dancing slippers on which could explain why there are no shoes. As far as it goes, that makes some sense. But the police are certain she was killed, deliberately, by a person, not by a bomb.'

Mum was slipping from her chair and I rushed around the table to help her. She didn't resist as Rob and I together manoeuvred her up the stairs. Even in this state she would not let me help her undress, and I left the room until I thought it had been long enough. When I put my head around the door, she was sitting on the edge of the bed, struggling to put on her bed-jacket. I held it out for her, feeling the birdlike thinness of her arm as I guided it into the sleeve.

Head on the pillow, eyes almost closed, her bruises were lost in the darker pigment of the shadows around her sunken eyes. She was exhausted but I had one more question. 'So why do I have a birth certificate with yourself and Richard as my parents?'

I held my head close to her lips to hear, 'Had to have one, to get you a ration book.'

'So you pretended that I was your baby?' I thought she nodded. 'How did you do that? Didn't they need proof of identity?'

'The maternity hospital was badly damaged. A lot of records destroyed. It was easy. They believed me when I said…'

It was astonishing that she could have got away with this, considering the number of times I have had to provide written evidence of having been born, photographic proof that I am the person who was born, documents to prove I live where I say I live, and so on. I reminded myself that this had been wartime and, as she'd said before, chaos.

'But – why didn't you explain? Why pretend I was yours?'

She turned her head from side to side fractiously and said, 'You had no family. I wanted you to… to have a real family.'

'As simple as that?' I asked.

'No fuss in those days. We didn't bother about family trees and so on.'

It sounded very rational and acceptable. A thought bounced into my mind. 'Could she – Rose – could she have brought someone back with her? What if she was out dancing, with a man, maybe, brought him back, and – he could have been in the shelter with her and…' She said nothing. 'I'll have to tell the police. This is really important. Have you any idea who she was with that night?'

She whispered and I put my ear to her mouth. I thought she said, 'I tried to – good life Alice. I – sorry.'

'You did, Mum, you've been a good mother.' It was true. She was strict, she'd had expectations that I had failed to meet, I could never be like her, and now of course I understood why. But she was kind, gave me everything I needed, and yes, she had been a good mother. 'Really, the best,' I said, and kissed her cold cheek. She was asleep.

Downstairs, Rob was finishing the washing up. 'Brace yourself, old girl,' he said.

'What now?'

'Earlier, when I was lighting the fire, when you were with your mum, I was going through the old newspapers and circulars.' He nodded towards the coal scuttle and I saw the neat pile of paper screws. 'Some of them are what I cleared out of your mum's room the other day. Do you remember she asked me to put the junk mail in the recycling? I kept it for fire lighting.' He dried his hands on the towel and took from his pocket a rectangle of notepaper which he unfolded carefully and handed it to me. I recognised the letter that had disappeared from beneath the doily. On closer inspection I could see it was a page torn from a notebook, the tiny, spidery words squashed together to fit exactly to the narrow page, with odd abbreviations, wasting no space, covering two sides.

29th May, My dear Violet, if I don't make it, Joe will bring this message t/you. If he dsnt make it then vice-versa. I tell him t/go bt he won't leave me. I mst make him go on th/nxt ship. 1 boat has been to th/beach 17 times in th/last 3 days. Today I watched a mine floating twrds it & cdnt shout loud enough or run t/warn them. Men swim to th/boats & fight to get on board & are thrown back in th/water in case they make th/boat sink. I must make Joe go. He's so happy since getting th/letter frm Jean th/day before we evacuated Poperinghe, t/say they are starting a family. I wsh I cd have given you this bt it was not to be.Violet I am truly sorry it's not yr fault. Find someone who can give you proper marriage & family. I shd not have married you knowing I cd not. I will die here & have not fired a single shot at th/enemy. Greatcoat, haversack, rifle, hat – that is the order for embarkation. I gave my greatcoat to a soldier to cover his eyes frm the crows so cant embark. I nevr loved Joe more than now. He brings sea water in empty sardine tins, to clean my wound, but it is a race against the flies. No water to drink. Flies on my damnd leg. Whistle pop like a wet paper bag ths time I keep my eyes open & th bomb hits th sand men tumble into new crater sand drops back covers them flat they shot th/horses. We could have eaten them bt now they are fly-blown. Like me. Joe says would sir like sardines a la dunes or sardines ooh la la? He tries to make me laugh. I said, yr children will come here with buckets & spades & find this tin in th/dunes & they will know we were here. Like archaeologists who fnd mummies in th/pyramids. If I shamed you I am sorry for that, too. I have never confessed to Joe how I feel abt him

Alice

Rob popped home to feed the cat and pick up the air-bed. I didn't want to be alone here, or at home, overnight. Mum appeared to be asleep, but opened her eyes when I leaned over her. I pointed to the glass of supplement in my hand – it looked like thin custard but no doubt it was nutritious – and placed it on the bedside table. I wandered around the house, then into the garden, neither able to find something to keep me busy, nor sit and do nothing. Shattered fragments of speech and images tumbled over one another in my memory. Looking down into the hole with about four inches of muddy water at the bottom, I thought about my real mother ending her days in fear and agony. I still didn't feel grief, only confusion. I decided to call Judy again and pulled my mobile phone from my cardigan pocket. My pragmatic daughter could be relied upon to be unruffled by the information that had turned my world upside down, and to give me an objective opinion.

She was surprised I'd never looked at my medical records before. 'The receptionist hands them to us when we go in,' she said, 'And we take them in to the doctor. People sit reading them in the waiting room.' Then she said, 'When I think it through, it makes a lot of sense that you're not that closely related to Gran. Is it alright to carry on calling her 'Gran'? I've often thought, you don't take after her at all.'

'What do you mean?'

'Well, there's no resemblance either physically, or in your personalities. She's always been a cold fish.'

‘She had a hard life.’ I was defensive, uncomfortably aware that Judy was playing back to me the very words I had often used to criticise my mother. I’d walked into the kitchen and from where I now sat at the kitchen table I could see a trail of wet clay that I’d brought in from the garden. As we talked, I found the floor cloth under the sink and wiped my shoes and the floor.

‘That may be so, and I know she always put you first, made sure you had everything you needed, etcetera, etcetera. But, for instance, she didn’t come near us when I was little, not like a real granny. She only wanted to see me when I was dressed nicely and sitting quietly. Whereas I couldn’t keep you away from your grandchildren when they were born. If I’d wanted to, I mean.’

I had to agree. ‘Some people don’t get along with babies. Your Gran is one of them.’

‘Too right. Remember Adam’s christening, when I handed him to Gran? She looked terrified, almost dropped him. I had to take him back, quickly.’

I did remember. Despite my attempts at arranging family celebrations, Mum would find a good reason not to attend and never had much to do with my daughter or my grandchildren. It hurt, when Judy was young, but by the time the grandchildren came along, and Mum was no keener on visiting or being visited by them, I accepted that she wasn’t interested and stopped making the effort. But there was much more to Mum than this, and I felt I needed to put the record straight.

‘She’s very generous,’ I said. Breath-taking generosity. She paid the deposit on our first house, in cash which she handed over in a carrier bag. Guiltily, I knew this was the result of many years of scrimping and saving. When Judy wanted to fund herself through social work training, Mum handed her an envelope stuffed with cash, almost two thousand pounds. 'It's no use waiting until I've gone,' she said to Judy. 'Have it while you can use it.'

'Yes, I know she's generous,' Judy said. 'I didn't mean to sound mealy-mouthed. But she was never the jolly, round and cuddly grandma that – well, like you are for instance.' This was a backhanded compliment if ever I heard one. 'Gran is all sharp corners and edges. I overheard my two giggling on the way home from a visit once, joking about getting a splinter if they hugged her.'

Judy reassured me the sudden change in the family history would not upset the grandchildren. 'They've been brought up on *Eastenders,*' she said. 'They love a family drama.'

I told her about my mother saying she'd never been pregnant.

'I was thinking about the whole pregnancy mystery after we spoke earlier,' Judy said. 'When I was at college, we studied parenting. Nowadays, everyone's very explicit about the whole childbirth process – some of my teenage mums even put their scans on *Facebook* for heavens' sake – but back then, when Gran was that age, women didn't even say the word 'pregnant' in polite company.' She was right, of course. Thinking back to Mum's diary entries, when she talked cryptically about 'expectant mothers', as though the term didn't concern her, and her humiliation if anyone should mention it or even look at her, I connected this with the day I told her I was pregnant. She'd blushed to the roots of her hair and never mentioned it again. Judy was still talking. 'You remember I said it made me wonder if she'd had a miscarriage? If she had, she might not have been able to talk to anyone about it.'

I thought this one through for a moment. It would tick off a few of the questions. 'You might have a point,' I agreed. 'Say she was pregnant in the spring, and my fa– Richard was killed in early June. Then her father died in the August. If she lost the baby –'

'Which would be understandable,' Judy butted in, 'Given the stress.'

'And then she got that awful letter from Richard.'

'What letter?' Judy asked, and I pulled it from my handbag, pressed it flat on the table and read it to her.

She exhaled noisily when I'd finished. 'Crikey. Not a very nice letter to get from beyond the grave, is it? He more or less says he doesn't love her. And what do you make of the bits about Joe?'

'I don't know.' I wasn't ready to speak an idea that was forming in my mind. Judy had no such qualms.

'Maybe Richard was gay?' she said.

'What makes you say that?'

'Those comments about not being able to give her a family and a proper marriage – that's what he's saying isn't it? He seems to be into Joe more than Violet.'

She was giving voice to the suspicion that was nudging my brain. 'Do you remember I told you about her complaining that a girl at the Bank was spreading tales about Richard? Something to do with the police?'

'Do you think he was cottaging?' Judy asked.

'Cottaging?'

'Going to public toilets to meet other men for sex.'

'Is that what it means? I often wondered. It's a homely sort of term for what sounds a pretty unsavoury practice.'

'Oh Mum,' Judy laughed. 'You couldn't blame them. In those days, there was nowhere legal they could go to meet men. I'll bet that's what Richard was up to. That'll be what this colleague of Gran's was referring to.'

'And Mum wrote something about this "disgusting idea".'

'Was that the whole letter or do you think there was more?'

'It's a page torn from a notebook, so there could well be more of it.'

'I think if you put what people were saying about Richard, and what Gran was saying in the diary, together with the letter, you'll find Richard was probably in love with Joe. It might have been one-sided. I mean you've no evidence that Joe returned Richard's affections.' I was quiet, thinking over the implications of what she was saying. 'Poor Gran,' she went on. 'She may not have been able to say to anyone that she'd lost the baby, and everybody would assume she's still expecting, and it would get to the point where she couldn't say anything.'

'But this bit in the letter from Richard about not being able to give her a family – I assumed that meant they hadn't done it.'

'You mean had sex, Mum? Even if Richard was gay, and it's sounding very likely, it doesn't mean he and Gran never had sex.' We were silent for a moment, then Judy said, 'I know it's a horrible thought but it makes you think he married Gran to make himself respectable.'

I thought about this. It sounded plausible. And Grandma thought Richard was a good investment. Perhaps Grandma knew it wasn't a love match, even though poor Mum thought it was. Grandma may have wanted to have someone to look after her in her old age, if her husband was unable to work. So she was pleased to have him in the family.

‘Are you still there?’ Judy prompted me.

I shared my thoughts with her. ‘It must have been awful to have her dreams shattered. She would have been very upset by this letter. Finding out he never loved her, and had more or less used her.’

‘Do you think it was too hard for her to believe, and easier to think he was having an affair with Jean?’

‘It could be.’ I had another thought. ‘Richard must have gone to France not knowing she was pregnant. He talks about Joe knowing Jean is having a baby, but no mention of Mum’s pregnancy.’ How tragic, I thought, if Mum was going through all that and couldn’t even talk to her husband. Or her mother. Or her friend. I wondered how it resolved itself. Surely there came a time when she had to admit that she wasn’t pregnant, that there was no baby? Perhaps that part at the end, when her mother locked her in, was because Grandma realised she’d miscarried and she needed looking after? So why did she think it was a punishment? Did Grandma blame her for losing the baby? ‘And even now, she can’t talk about it,’ I said to Judy as I heard Rob coming in. ‘Anyway, here’s your Dad, do you want a word? I’ll hand you over, and see you tomorrow, about four.’

Mum had drunk the supplement. She didn’t open her eyes when I cleared away her empties and refreshed her glass of water. Maybe tomorrow, once we’d talked to Claire and made a statement - whatever the process was - she would be able to relax and start eating properly again. Then we could get back to normal. I wondered what normal would look like, when all this was over.

Rob set up the air-bed alongside the camp bed in the front bedroom and we went to bed early, exhausted from talking. We thought we had pretty much worked out what happened here over seventy years ago, and we felt ready to tell the police.

Rob suddenly said, 'Doesn't it make you wonder how our daughter came by this expert knowledge?'

'She's a social worker,' I reminded him. 'They see all sorts.'

After another long silence, I wondered aloud, 'I still can't work out why Grandma locked Mum in her bedroom.'

'It's what they did, in those days, when their daughters were out of control,' he said. 'We should have done it with ours. It might have stopped her mixing with those undesirables.'

I threw a pillow and it must have hit him, because he chuckled. 'This is fun. It reminds me of when we went camping when Judy was little. Do you think Adam would come camping with me?'

'No. I think he's far too cool to go anywhere with his grandad. Anyway, you hated camping. That's why the camp bed is forty years old and as good as new.' He'd brought my bottle of sloe gin from home and we were both a little tipsy. I thought it might help me to sleep. It didn't. As soon as I laid my head on the pillow a montage of pictures started running: Richard sitting on a sand dune at Dunkirk, injured, confused, writing his last letter, while bombs fell on the beach around him; Rose, who looked like myself but smaller, lighter on her feet, danced along the tideline, laughing up at Richard; Mum, young, frightened, pregnant then not pregnant, sat in front of Grandma, who loomed over her, tall and forbidding, daring her to speak.

Rob lay on his back, snoring. It was too far to reach and prod him into turning over and I couldn't be bothered to get out of bed. Now, I was wide awake, rehearsing my conversation with Claire in the morning. It all made perfect sense. My real mother was Rose, Mum's cousin, who was killed by person or persons unknown, as they say, and left in the Anderson shelter. Mum assumed she had been killed in the air raid and adopted me.

Frank

Flight QF319 to Heathrow

Suddenly the war seemed very close. One day we heard that our fighter planes were driving the Hun back and the next we walked into school to find the arrows on the blackboard had moved nearer to that thin strip of water. Air raid practice was every week and we got sent home if we didn't carry our gas masks to school. We let the infants play with us so long as they would be soldiers because we were always pilots, zooming around them and knocking them down.

Sam was away from school with measles, so I called round to see him on my way home. His mam called out of the kitchen window, 'Best not come in, lad. We can't risk passing it on, what with Jean expecting. Measles might make the baby blind.'

This was the first I heard about Jean expecting a baby. I was miffed that Mrs Ainsworth knew before I did, so I was ready to sulk about it, but when I got home Jean was crying, and Mam was busy comforting her, so neither of them paid me any attention. I stood behind Dad's armchair and looked over his shoulder at the newspaper, reading the headline aloud: '*We Never Surrender*'. Jean burst out crying again.

A couple of scrawny rabbits lay on the table, their necks bent backwards and blood caked around their nostrils, but their legs were stretched out, making them look still alive and running. This rabbit's foot is from that very day. I can see why the snooty looking woman turned her nose up when she saw it. It doesn't smell, and I can still make out the tuft of black hairs above the third claw, but the white's more of a dirty grey, and it is a bit shrivelled. Looking at it brings the summer of 1940 right back to me – Dunkirk, the Battle of Britain, the first bombing raids on Sheffield, and all the turmoil at home.

With all the seventieth anniversary events on television, I know more about the war now, than I did at the time. We didn't know much about Dunkirk until it was over. We knew Joe and Richard were somewhere in France and Joe hadn't written for two weeks, so everybody was worried. Then, as the news came out of what had happened, and still we heard nothing from Joe, we were all on tenterhooks.

Dad pointed to the newspaper and said, 'See, it says here, *Thankfulness at the escape of the B.E.F.* Look our Jean, it says *escape*.'

Jean said, 'And what else does it say?' She wrung her handkerchief into a tight ball and pushed it into one eye. '*Our losses are considerable,* is what it says. Now what does that mean if there aren't…' and the rest of her words were cut off by hiccups.

Bill came in then and I could tell he was full of news from the way he stood and looked around until we were all looking at him. He spent most of his spare time at the Dog and Duck Brigade and since he'd heard it was about to be renamed the Local Defence Volunteers and he was to get a uniform, he thought himself very important.

Dad said, 'Been putting the world to rights?'

Mam looked up from picking onions out of the bucket of veg our Cyril had brought home, and said, 'If it was women it'd be called gossip.'

Bill puffed up his chest and announced, 'Four thousand.' He looked around for effect. When he had everybody's attention, he said, 'That's how many they left behind to hold the fort so the rest could get clear.' Jean screamed and threw an onion at him. 'What's up with her?' He seemed puzzled that she wasn't impressed by this information. 'I thought she'd be glad of a bit of news.'

Jean took a handful of potatoes out of the bucket and lobbed them at Bill and he danced around in his hobnail boots trying to dodge them. It was so comical I burst out laughing. Dad cuffed me on the head. Mam moved the veg bucket out of Jean's way.

Jean shouted, 'And if Joe is with them left in Dunkirk, how does tha reckon he'll get out, tha stupid lummock? It says in the paper they've bombed the chuffing harbour.'

Mam grabbed Jean's arms and pulled her into her pinafore so that I couldn't hear what else she was saying. Bill looked at Dad and rolled his eyes to the ceiling. Dad jabbed his finger at a paragraph in his newspaper and said to Bill, 'Tha wants to watch thy clack. See this fellow got himself charged with rumour-mongering, and he lives just down the road in Mansfield.' Bill's ears were pink as he looked down and started to unlace his boots.

Mam nodded at me over Jean's head, saying, 'Stop gawping and clean them rabbits for me.'

I looked again at the blood coming out of its nose and said, 'I don't know how.'

Jean said, 'I'll show him.' She blew her nose and tucked her hankie up her sleeve. She opened the drawer, chose a knife and brought the whetstone from the window sill. After a few strokes to sharpen it, she handed me the knife and, picking up the carving knife for herself, pulled one of the rabbits towards her. Her eyes were red and puffy, and her voice sounded as though she was talking through wet wool as she said, 'Take the other one and copy me,' and, 'Get on with it,' when I hesitated. She chopped off the feet and dropped these onto a sheet of newspaper on the floor. I was looking at the black tuft of hair on the white foot, and must have made a noise because Jean said, 'What?' and looked sharply at me.

'It's my rabbit.' I was barely able to get the words out.

'And?'

Dad looked up from his newspaper and said, 'What did you think? That we were feeding them for fun? Nothing's for nothing, lad.'

I looked at Mam, who was picking up the potatoes from the floor. She raised her eyebrows at me, daring me to argue. I ran my finger along the fur on the rabbit's spine. It didn't spring back. This wasn't the same rabbit I'd coaxed out of the hutch that very morning. I watched Jean hold her rabbit's head in position and slice its stomach from end to end in one smooth movement. She nudged my arm. 'Get a move on,' she said.

It took a bit of sawing but one by one the feet dropped off and lay together on the newspaper on the floor. I cut through the belly until it flopped open showing the inside, pink and steaming. Jean nudged me and I watched her push her hand up, under the ribs of her rabbit, and pull the intestines away in one handful. I pressed my hand into the hot insides and grabbed the soft, slippery innards. They came away with a slurp, and I dropped them onto the newspaper where they wriggled and coiled together like fat worms. My fingers were glued together with blood that turned to webs of melting liquorice as I pulled them apart. I watched Mam from between my fingers as she sliced onions. Jean tutted and grabbed my rabbit. She peeled its coat away in a long furry rope, leaving it as pink and shiny as one of the new-born babies in the bottom hutch. She sniffed and I saw tears running down her face.

Mam put her onion down and leaned over the table to rub Jean's cheeks, saying, 'Time enough to fret when we know more. What we don't know won't hurt.'

Jean was struggling to speak and I realised she was crying but also laughing, pointing at Mam and saying, 'It's the – stop it,' and then I got it and I said to Mam, 'It's the onions that's making her cry,' and Mam looked at her hands, and started laughing too. Even Dad was chuckling behind the newspaper. Bill came back downstairs, looked at Mam and Jean and shook his head. He pushed his feet into his boots and laced them up. Jean chopped the rabbits into pieces which she tossed into the stewpot.

Bill said, 'Rabbit stew?'

Jean wagged the knife at him and said, 'Jugged hare, if you don't mind, young man,' in that pretend posh voice she used when she was mimicking Violet. So I knew he was forgiven.

Mam reached for the kettle. 'Cup of tea before going out?'

Bill said, 'No, I'll have a pint at the Dog and Duck.' He opened the door, said, Visitor,' over his shoulder, and was gone.

Hoping it was Sam, recovered from his measles, I ran to the door. Violet stood in the teeming rain, her hair flattened to her head and water running down her nose, onto her chin and then onto her dress. She was as wet as a water rat and shivering. Jean nudged me aside and brought Violet into the kitchen, pushing her into a chair and sitting beside her, holding Violet's hands in her own. There was dried blood under Jean's finger nails.

Mam turned from stirring the stewpot and said, 'Oh, Violet love, is there news?' She took the towel from the hook by the sink and started to rub Violet's hair. Mam and Jean talked posh whenever Violet was around but today Mam seemed to have forgotten. She said, 'Has tha had news of Richard?'

Violet stared down at her hands, wrapped in Jean's hands. Jean's eyes followed hers and she dropped Violet's hands and jumped up, went to the sink and started to scrub at her hands with the nail brush.

Mam said, 'Shift that, Frank,' nodding to the pile of offal lying on the newspaper on the floor, close to Violet's shoes. I looked at Violet but she seemed not to have noticed, so I knew something really bad must have happened. I thought about Mr Knowles and Richard and my stomach felt heavier as the feeling of being about to lose something grew inside me. I picked up the rabbit's foot with the black tuft of hair and put it into my pocket, rolled up the blood-soaked newspaper and took it out to the yard, where I dropped it into the swill bucket.

As I came back into the kitchen, Violet said, 'He won't survive the shock. The shock of…' and she started sobbing such as I'd not seen before. Jean had her arms around her while Mam patted at her with the towel.

Mam said, 'Frank, bring a blanket from our bedroom.'

I ran upstairs, not wanting to miss anything. As I came back, carrying Mam's eiderdown, Jean's hands flew to her face and she said, 'You mean it's not your Dad, it's Richard? When did you hear?'

Mam wrapped the eiderdown around Violet. Dad passed a cup of tea to Mam and I realised he'd brewed up. I didn't know he could do that. Mam pulled one of Violet's hands out of the eiderdown and folded her fingers around the cup. Violet put both hands around the cup as though it was the middle of winter and she was trying to warm herself. Mam put her arms around Violet and said, 'I'm so sorry, love, first Richard, and now your poor Dad.'

Violet's cup tilted and the tea spilt on the eiderdown. Jean took it from her and placed it carefully on the table. Violet's teeth were chattering and the words came out shaking. 'When the telegram came, he said nothing… then his face... and he... the doctor says he had a stroke.'

Jean said, 'When was this telegram?' Mam shot her a warning glance, but Jean took no notice. She knelt in front of Violet and held her elbows to get her attention. 'What time was this telegram?'

Mam said, 'Get on round to Sam's for a bit, Frank.'

I knew this was a way of getting rid of me, so I was glad to be able to say, 'Sam's got measles and Mrs Ainsworth says I'm not to play with him in case I catch it and our Jean's baby gets born blind.'

Violet stopped crying and stared at me. She hiccupped. Jean kept her hands on Violet's elbows and said, 'I meant to tell you.'

Violet jumped up and stepped backwards, away from Jean's hands, nearly tripping over the eiderdown which fell around her feet. She was breathing fast.

Mam said to me, 'Tha's got a big trap and no mistake, upsetting everybody.'

Jean said, 'I only found out a couple of days ago.'

Violet stood up straight and pulled her shoulders back and said, 'So am I.'

Jean was saying, 'Joe doesn't even know–' when she realised what Violet had said and added, 'But – really?'

Mam stepped between them and looked at Jean. She said, 'Of course "really",' in her warning voice. Then to

Violet she said, 'Well, Violet, love. It's a tragedy and no mistake, having lost your Richard, but a baby's a blessing all the same, and you'll remember Richard all the better for having his son or daughter.'

Jean had put a smile on her face and said to Violet, 'I'm right pleased for you,' and she put her hand out to Violet, but Violet pressed herself back against the sink so Jean couldn't reach her. She took some deep breaths and seemed to become much more like her normal self, straightening her dress and pressing her hair down. She pulled off her specs and wiped them on her hankie, although it was wringing wet so they were all smeared when she put them back on. As if she wasn't soaking and hadn't been scriking her eyes out a few seconds before, she said, 'Well, I'll be off, now. Thank you for the tea, Mrs Sheldon, Mr Sheldon. I'll see you soon, Jean. I shall hope for good news of Joe.' She pushed her specs up her nose, turned and almost ran out of the back door. I heard her quick steps down the gennel, and Jean and Mam stood with their mouths open, looking at the door.

It was three days before we had news of Joe. Every day Mam said, 'No news is good news', and Dad said, 'It'll be alphabetical, wait and see. There's a lot to get through before they get to Ibbertson.' On the Friday teatime, at the end of a hot day, Mam was at work and Jean was baking. Bill was sitting on a stool outside the back door, smoking with Dad. Cyril came skidding round the corner of the gennel and pulled up quick to stop himself falling over Bill.

Bill said, 'I can tell tha's not used to working up a sweat, our Cyril.' It was a joke of his that Cyril was still an errand boy at the works.

Cyril said, 'Where's our Jean?' She came running out of the door, her face as white as the flour that was stuck to her forearms. 'Telegram lad's on his way up street. I asked if he'd got anything for Ibbertson and he says, "Not at liberty," but he winked and –'

Jean knocked Cyril out of the way and ran down the gennel, me behind her, reaching the street as the telegram boy – it was John Culshaw, Ernie's big brother – was leaning his bike against our front wall. She was trembling so much I had to take the telegram. It seemed the street was full of people who had stopped whatever they were doing to watch. Mam came round the corner of the street, saw us, and started to run. Jean hadn't moved when Mam pulled the telegram out of my hand and put her arm around Jean to lead her up the gennel. The lads and Dad stood silently in the yard. Mrs Wreakes leaned from her upstairs window.

In the kitchen, Mam held out the telegram but Jean shook her head and Mam ripped open the envelope. Jean jigged from one foot to the other, her hands over her face. Mam pulled out a sheet of paper. I watched her eyes move across it twice, and then she held it out to Jean. 'It's from himself. He's on his way home.'

Jean opened her eyes and snatched the telegram from Mam. Her eyes moved along and up and down the piece of paper for so long that I thought Mam must have read it wrong. Then she squealed, and ran out into the yard waving the telegram, whooping, and Mam laughed, and they hugged and kissed, and Jean kissed Dad, then Bill who said, 'Ger'off.' She tried to grab Cyril but he ducked into the kitchen and I heard Mrs Wreakes say, 'Thank God, happen we'll be hearing soon.' I reckoned if Dad was right, and it was alphabetical, it would be a very long time yet before she got news of her grandsons. Jean put her arms around my head so I could hardly breathe and said, 'He's coming home, Frank, he's all right and he's coming home,' then she ran down the gennel and I heard her in the street, shouting, 'He made it, he's coming home.' and I heard somebody shouting, 'Hurrah', then she came dancing back into the yard and Dad rubbed his stomach and said, 'Is there going to be any supper tonight? My belly's beginning to think my throat's been cut.'

Although I was looking forward to seeing Joe, it seemed a peculiar thing that even though our Army had lost, everybody was cheering, as if they'd won. Jean had been at the station all afternoon waiting for his train to come in, and I ran back and forth watching all the buses coming along Liberty Street, looking for them. After what seemed a very long time, one stopped and as soon as I caught sight of them, I ran full tilt back to Beacon Street, shouting, 'Mam, they're here.' By the time the two of them turned the corner, it seemed all the neighbours were hanging out of windows and peering from gennels. Even people Mam had fallen out with came forward and clapped Joe's shoulders as he went past, and somebody sang, 'For he's a jolly good fellow'. But Joe didn't lift his eyes from the ground and I swear if Jean hadn't led him up our gennel, he'd have gone right past.

This was not the Joe that I remembered. Something had changed deep inside him. He sat at the table, staring at his hands or gouging the table with a dirty fingernail. I looked at Mam, half expecting her to tell him off but she told me to stop pestering him. Jean fussed around, making him tea which he drank in great thirsty gulps, and cooking him a meal that he picked at then pushed away. I rolled him a cigarette, put it in his hand, and brought him a taper to light it, all of which he barely acknowledged. Every so often his eyes would droop, then close, he would sway, then, as it seemed he was about to fall forwards onto the table, he would give a little jump and his eyes would snap wide open. He'd look around as though he didn't recognise where he was or who we were, and he would see me looking at him and smile, but in a weary sort of way. Jean led him up to bed, but I heard him in the night, walking around on the other side of the wall.

The next morning, Jean said to Mam, 'He's not slept a wink.'

Mam said, 'Poor lad, he'll be scared of going to sleep because of the dreams. Dad was the same when he came back.'

Joe wore his ordinary clothes - he called them civvies - while Jean washed his shirt and his underwear and scrubbed at his uniform. He said he'd lost his kitbag and had to apply for new kit, and until such time as it arrived he had to make do with this one uniform. After he washed and shaved, he said, 'I must go to see Violet.'

Jean said, 'I'll come with.' She gave Cyril a note to drop in at Fergusons, to say she wasn't coming to work today. This was very unusual. Jean wouldn't do anything that risked losing her job. She loved driving that crane. Once or twice Mam had said, 'It can't be good for the baby, hanging over that hot steel all day. Is there not a shop floor job he can put thee on?' Jean said, 'If I give it up, I'll never get it back after. There's a waiting list for that job.' Mam said, 'Happen tha'll not want a job after the baby's born, tha could stay at home.' Jean said, 'And who'll keep me?' Mam reminded Jean that there was enough money coming into the house for her to stay at home. Jean admitted it wasn't really about money. She thought driving her crane was doing her bit. 'I couldn't stand being cooped up indoors, watching the war happening out there, Joe and all the lads doing their bit and me sitting on my backside.' So that was the end of it. But she didn't seem to mind sitting on her backside when she came in from work while I waited on her hand and foot under Mam's directions.

'I want to come,' I said to Jean, as she and Joe set off for Hurdle Hill.

'No,' she said. 'This is private.'

'I don't want to see Violet,' I said. 'I want to see Mr Knowles.'

'Why?' Mam said. 'Tha barely knows him.'

'He's my friend. He's poorly and sad and I'll be able to cheer him up.'

It took a lot of pleading but eventually I was allowed to go with them, provided I stayed clear of Violet. I needn't have worried. Violet's mother opened the door and walked away, taking no notice of me at all. Jean and Joe followed her into the parlour, the room I remembered from the wedding tea, where I could see Violet's back, bent over the piano, but she seemed not to be playing it, just staring down at the keys.

Jean said, 'Don't be a nuisance now. If Mr Knowles is tired, leave him alone and wait for us in the kitchen.' She closed the door, leaving me in the hallway.

I looked for Mr Knowles in the kitchen and the garden. His runner beans were shrivelled, turning brown at the edges. I opened the door to the air raid shelter and stepped inside. Water sloshed over the top of my shoe. It was half way up the legs of the beds. The magazines sat on the little table between the beds, the edges curling. I closed the door and went back into the kitchen. On the table was the book with the green velvet cover that I remembered Violet writing in last summer. There were pages and pages of neat handwriting, with little curls on the tails such as Miss Malkin wouldn't allow us to do. On the last page, she had written: "*Butter or margarine for spreading will go further if mixed with a little plain flour, salt and milk*". Beside the book was a blue and white striped bowl with a thin yellowish paste in the bottom which made me think she'd been trying out this idea. It didn't look very tasty. There didn't seem to be any cooking going on in the kitchen, although my stomach felt like it was nearly dinner time so I looked in the meat safe. There was nothing I recognised. Back in the hallway I put my ear to the parlour door and heard Joe's voice. I reckoned Mr Knowles must be upstairs. The stairs were carpeted with a flower pattern and I climbed them slowly so that my foot didn't squelch in my wet shoe. There were three doors on the landing. I peeped around a half-open door and saw two narrow beds with flowery counterpanes. There were flowers on the wallpaper too, so many that just looking made me feel dizzy. I heard mumbling and snoring behind the next door, and as I pushed it open there was a smell such as I remembered from my Nannan's bedroom when she was ill, so I knew the lump in the bed must be Mr Knowles. His eyes were closed, his mouth drooped downwards at one side, and a little trail of something like gravy ran down his chin. It looked like him but not like him and as I peered close to be sure, one eye suddenly opened, making me jump backwards. My arm knocked a glass off the bedside table. It smashed on the floor by my foot. His eyeball swivelled round and met mine, and his teeth pressed onto his lips as though he was trying to say my name, but the only sound to come out was like a bee buzzing.

I said, 'It's me, Frank,' to help him out. The droopy side of his mouth twitched and I thought he was trying to smile. I felt fingernails digging into my shoulder and looked up to see Mrs Knowles. She steered me towards the door. Glancing back over my shoulder, I was sure Mr Knowles's eye was on me, so I waved and I thought he winked.

At the bottom of the stairs, the door to the parlour was now open and I could see Joe and Jean sitting either side of Violet, who was staring at her hands. Mrs Knowles left me in the hall and went into the kitchen, so I went into the parlour and perched on the arm of the settee. Joe was passing a narrow, black book to Violet who looked at it, turning it over and over in her hands. He said, 'We gave one another our diaries. That way, if one of us didn't make it, the other would have the diary to give to relations, whereas if we each kept our own, everything would be lost.' He reached across to open the front cover of the book and pointed inside. 'See, his name and number are here, and he told me he'd written a letter to you on one of the pages.' Violet turned a few pages over, and stopped at one that said, *29th May, My Dear Violet.* She snapped it shut before I could read any more.

Joe went to join his new unit the following day. Jean was particular about inviting Violet for tea and she came every Thursday. For all that had gone before, I started to like Violet that summer. I asked her every week about Mr Knowles and she told me he was no better, and sometimes he was a bit worse, and always she seemed pleased that I had asked. I reckoned that if she was so sad about Mr Knowles being ill, she couldn't be a bad person.

All Mam and Jean seemed to talk about was babies, but Violet would blush bright pink if they mentioned babies to her. One day, Mam asked whether Violet was hoping for a boy or a girl.

Jean said, 'Mam, you're embarrassing Violet. Leave her alone.'

Whenever Cyril came home with an offering of veg from his allotment, Mam would put some aside for Violet, since she said Mr Knowles wasn't able to get into the garden. If we weren't going to see Violet for a few days, she would make up a parcel and send me with it to Hurdle Hill Terrace. It was at the start of the school holidays that I arrived there to find the curtains closed and no one answering the door. I went around the back and through the garden gate, and as I approached the window I saw Violet inside. She was at the table, writing in her book. I tapped on the window and she jumped, then saw me and came to the door. Taking the parcel from me, she mumbled something. I decided that after all she was moody – friendly one day and miserable the next. I was half way up the garden path when she said, 'Please tell Mrs Sheldon that my father died in his sleep last night.'

I was so sad that I couldn't even be bothered to punch Ernie Culshaw when he called me a 'cry-baby'. When I told got home Mam asked what the matter was, and said, 'The poor lass. She'll have nobody now.'

I said, 'She's got her mam.'

Mam said, 'Some mother she is,' in disgust, which surprised me. I'd always thought that it was Violet's father she thought was strange.

One night Sybil came round and she and Jean were getting dolled up for a night out. Jean stood on a chair while Sybil drew a line down the back of her leg. I watched them applying a thick orange cream to their faces. Sybil painted bright red lipstick around her mouth and then smacked her lips together. She caught me watching and leaned over the table.

'Gi'us a kiss, then, Frankie.' She smiled at me. A lump of red lipstick was stuck to her teeth, making her look as though she'd taken a great bite out of somebody. I pulled backwards to get away from her and she laughed loudly.

Mam came in from work. She looked Jean up and down and said, 'And where might thee be off to?'

Jean said, 'There's a dance up at Marples Hotel.'

'I hope tha's not thinking of going dancing, in that condition?'

'Of course, Mam, don't be so old fashioned.' Jean laughed, but Mam was really angry. She threw her dinner tin on the draining board with a clatter that made Jean and Sybil stop what they were doing and look at her.

'Tha's got a bun in the oven and a husband away fighting. Tha'll be the talk of town. Wipe that crap off thy face and make thyself decent before Dad gets home.'

Jean faced Mam with her hands on her hips. I made myself as small as possible, in the corner where the table met the wall. Jean said, 'I've not been out for months. It so happens that my husband would be very pleased if he knew I was having some fun.' With that she picked up her coat, said, 'Come on, Sybil,' and walked out of the door. Sybil quickly gathered up her bits and pieces that were all over the table and dropped them into her handbag, glancing at Mam as if she expected her to have a go at her next, and followed Jean.

Mam sat at the table with her head in her hands. I thought she hadn't noticed me but then she said, 'Don't go growing up, Frank.'

At school, Miss Malkin started a Spitfire Fund. Sam and me went out looking for scrap metal to help the RAF to fight back. Down by the river in the ruins of an old mill we found a length of rusty railing which we dragged up the hill.

Sam said, 'Keep it at yours. If my Dad sees any scrap metal he'll sell it.'

Dad watched us haul it into the yard. 'What's going to do with that?'

Sam said, 'Miss Malkin knows a bloke who can make it into parts for a plane.'

Dad laughed like a drain. Mam came out and said, 'What the chuffing hell is that?'

Dad said, 'Sam reckons they can make it into a part for a plane.' Mam looked at Sam, then at Dad, and she started laughing too.

I asked, 'What's so funny?'

We thought our world was going to end the first night Sheffield was bombed. That weekend, Mam cut the list of public air raid shelters out of the paper, and made me write it out five times, so that everybody had a list in their pocket in case the siren went off while they were out. She made me and Cyril sleep in the cupboard under the stairs, while she and Dad set up their bed under the table. Bill and Jean were working nights, so Mam fretted that they might get caught out, but at least they were able to use their own beds in the day. It was something and nothing. There were no casualties. But a lot of families panicked and decided their children had to be evacuated. I saw Billy Roberts being taken to the railway station by his mam and dad. He wore long trousers and had his name on a piece of card pinned to his jacket. After a couple of nights without the sirens going off, we were allowed to sleep in our bedroom again and I was even allowed to go into town with Sam on the Saturday afternoon. On the way, we went to the park and joined some lads from our school who were trying to shoot sparrows with their catapults. Then we went to the Central Picture House to see one of the Tarzan films. I'd bought our tickets and we were in the queue when I heard Jean's voice. She was passing the cinema, with Violet.

'Where you off to?' I called to her, and they came across.

'We're going to see *The Bluebird* with Shirley Temple, at the Don. Sure you don't want to come with us?' Violet looked terrified, and Jean said to her, 'Only joking, Vi, he wouldn't be seen dead in a Shirley Temple film.' Violet gave a little giggle.

Sam was staring at Violet's stomach. She saw him looking and coloured pink, and looked away.

Jean said, 'Stop staring, Sam. Did nobody tell you it's rude?'

Sam said, 'Mam says tha can't tell she's expecting.'

Violet caught her breath and looked as though she might faint. Jean clipped Sam round the ear and said, 'Cheeky little bugger. I shall have words with your mam.' She linked arms with Violet and they walked away.

Sam whispered, 'Mam reckons it's a ghost.' When I didn't understand, he said, 'I heard her saying how sometimes people want a baby so much they have a ghost baby.' It was true that Jean's belly was much bigger than Violet's but I could scarcely credit this notion of ghost babies and told Sam he didn't know what he was talking about.

We watched a film of the RAF gunning down the Luftwaffe while the newscaster called out, '*Hour after hour through the day and the night, our fighters are sweeping against the huge raiding squadrons of the Luftwaffe*'. Children wearing woolly hats with labels around their necks, like Billy Roberts, marched towards a train.

A couple more bombs fell, a bit closer, and although Dad said, 'Happen it was a left over one they dropped on their way home,' some people died and some were injured. But it was nobody we knew, and by now, the scared feeling had stopped and we were back to thinking the war was becoming right exciting.

We had rabbit stew at least twice a week that summer and I got to be a dab hand at cleaning them out. We had to give one to Mrs Wreakes every now and then to stop her moaning about the mess in the yard. So by the time school started again in September, we were down to a couple of rabbits and I was arguing that we shouldn't eat them because we'd want them to breed again next year. This rabbit business with Cyril had taken up a lot of time and not earned me any money, since mostly the family had eaten them.

When we went back to school, Sam had new shoes and long trousers. He said, 'Mam went to WVS and told them we got bombed out, so they gave us all new clothes.'

I asked Mam if I could go down and get some long trousers, but she wouldn't have any of it. Later, she told me to take the last two rabbits round to the Ainsworths which I thought was unfair since they'd already got loads of free stuff. Mr Ainsworth was on a single bed in the front room, where we'd had our lessons when school was closed the year before. He beckoned me to him with a long fingernail and said, 'Here, Frank, does tha have a couple of bob to spare?'

I said, 'I've only got a tanner,' holding it out, and like a flash it disappeared under his blanket.

He said, 'Good lad.' Then Sam called me and we left.

So that's the story of the rabbit's foot. Happen I shall see rabbits on Hurdle Hill. It won't be so long now. I've turned my watch to Sheffield time and it's three in the morning. The little lad's fallen asleep at last. It seems like I'm the only person awake. Except for the stewardess. She sees me nip to the lavatory and when I get back she's there with a glass of water for me.

Frank

Flight QF319 to Heathrow

The sun shining straight into my eyes wakes me up. They say there's a journey you can do where you fly from one side of the world to the other and it stays dawn all the way. It feels a bit like that, a never ending journey with time going backwards and forwards – at Gulawalla it's the middle of Monday and yet below these clouds I should think most people are still asleep. They put the lights on and in a few minutes there's more food. I can see what they're doing, making out it's breakfast time when really it should be dinner time. Hermione brings me an omelette and wants to know do I want a Buck's Fizz? A cup of tea is enough for me, to put me on. Below me, the pink tips of mountains are peeping through the clouds. I'd never have thought of seeing such a sight. The Alps, says the captain. Not long now, then. Amy's itinerary: '*Arrive Heathrow 0535, follow signs for Passport Control, queue at the desk marked Commonwealth Citizens.*'

Checking everything is wrapped and back in my haversack, I find the carved piece of wood. About ten inches long and three inches in diameter, it has two small eyes, a coxcomb, and the start of a wattle on one side. I know what's missing. It has no beak. Bill was working on it with his new penknife with the silver and blue Mother of Pearl handle. Mam and Dad gave him that knife for his eighteenth birthday in November 1940. He was right chuffed. Whether he was whittling odd bits of wood or cleaning his nails with it, the knife was rarely out of his hands when he was at home. I knew where he left it when he was at work and borrowed it whenever I could.

Jean's baby's birthday was also in November, but a couple of weeks after Bill. Nobody would talk about Jean expecting in front of me. But helping Cyril with the rabbits over the summer had taught me something of the facts of life and there wasn't much that Sam and me couldn't work out. And we were both sure things were not quite right with Violet. The next time we saw her, she looked as though she'd been blown up with a football pump. Sam and me were playing on the pavement when she waddled up the street towards us. We followed, mimicking her. It was mean, but we were youngsters and she struck us as right comical.

Mam had put her foot down and made Jean stop work when her belly was so big that she could barely climb the ladder into her cab. The same night, we sat round the table after tea, listening to the Princess Elizabeth on the wireless, saying, in a voice that was posher than anything Violet could manage, *'we are trying to bear our own share of the danger and sadness of war...'*

Jean had tears in her eyes. She said, 'If it's a girl I shall call her Elizabeth.'

Mam said, 'Let's hope it is. Then, if there's any more war after this lot she won't have to go and fight.'

Jean said, 'I wish there was a medicine I could take to make sure it's a girl.'

Bill said, 'And how would they have babies if everybody did that?'

Mam nodded towards me and said, 'Little jugs have big ears.'

Jean got up from the table where she'd been writing to Joe. She handed me a sheet of notepaper and a pencil so I could write my usual few lines to go in the envelope. I drew a picture of Chad with whiskers, saying, '*What! No razor blades*?' I licked the pencil and asked Jean, 'Can I tell him about naming her Elizabeth?'

Jean laughed. 'Aye, why not?'

Bill said, 'I shall be joining up now I'm of age.'

Mam said, 'Can it not wait until after Christmas? What with baby coming, Joe should get leave, and it'd be nice to have a proper family this time round. Who knows when we might be together again.'

Bill shrugged and said, 'Happen. But no longer than that. Come New Year, I'm off.' Mam ruffled his hair and he said, 'Ger'off'.

We'd become used to Violet coming round once a week. Jean would arrange it on a night when Dad was on fire duty, and Cyril and Bill would make themselves scarce. Jean would hide the eggs and butter and meat and we'd have baked cardboard with gravy, and something Jean called Mock Buns which I was sucking off the roof of my mouth for hours afterwards. Violet usually brought a cutting from the paper with a recipe, or a leaflet about how to make something out of nothing. Jean would make out she was very taken with these ideas, and would pop it in a drawer in the sideboard 'to look at later'.

One day Mam said to Violet, 'You're looking pale, love. Have you been getting your extra rations?' I could see Violet didn't know what Mam was talking about. 'Oh love, it's important. Come on, show me that ration book.'

Violet took out her ration book and held it out to Mam who said, 'No, love, the green book.' She called Jean, who was sorting out the rag bag to find woollen clothes to take apart and knit up for the baby. 'Violet's not got the green book.'

Jean said, 'It's a bit late, Vi,' coming over with an old grey jumper of mine that had holes in the elbows. 'Did the doctor not tell you? He must have given you a certificate so you could get extra rations?' She and Mam looked at one another, their eyebrows raised. 'Don't worry,' she said. 'I'll take you down there, first thing in the morning.'

So it was settled. But Jean came back the next day, saying Violet hadn't been at home when she called. And the next day. Some days later, Jean said she'd seen Violet and had been told she'd got it sorted. She said to Mam, 'I'm not sure, she's a bit vague about hospital and midwives and all that, and time's getting on.' Mam and Jean were changing the beds and I could hear them nattering while I was getting changed into my playing clothes after school.

Jean said, 'I've heard they keep it at the bottom of the bed in a crib and I'm not allowed to go to it, even if it cries.'

Mam said, 'It'll be safer in hospital. We couldn't even get thee down the stairs if the siren went in the middle of it.'

As I searched for my socks, and found them in a corner, under Cyril's clothes, full of muck from the allotment, I reckoned maybe I could sleep in Jean's room if she was going to stay in hospital.

The next time Violet came round, looking as though she'd been pumped up so much she was about to burst, Mam said, 'Where are you getting the baby, Violet? Home or hospital?'

Violet's face turned a deep red and she stammered, 'I haven't decided yet, Mrs Sheldon.'

Jean looked amazed. She said, 'Not decided? What did the midwife say?'

Violet said, 'She said I could make arrangements nearer the time.'

'But that means there's no bed booked,' Jean said. 'That won't do. Which midwife is it? Mrs Goodwin?'

'No, it's Mrs - Oh, I can't remember. But not Mrs Goodwin.'

Mam looked at Violet. 'Have you been going to ante-natal?'

Violet said, 'Yes, of course.'

I was sure Violet was fibbing. Only the week before, Miss Malkin had asked me how my writing book came to have pages missing. Sam and me had been making paper Hurricanes. When I said I'd spilled ink on it and had to tear them out, she looked closely at my fingers, and the desk, and said, 'When people are not telling the truth, they tend not to look you in the eye.' Violet was looking at the ceiling and not at Mam or Jean.

Mam pulled a packet of tea out of the cupboard. 'Here, Frank, take that round to Mrs Ainsworth.' When I stared, she added, 'Tell her it's the one I owe her.'

Later that night Mam and Jean talked in whispers while they cleared up. I sat at the table, looking at the fighter planes in Bill's copy of Picture Post.

Mam said, 'It doesn't sound like she's been to ante-natal at all. That mother of hers is neither use nor ornament. She ought to be looking after her.'

Jean said she would have a word with Mrs Goodwin and see whether she knew Violet's midwife. They talked about Violet's nerves and perhaps she was worse than they thought, since losing Richard.

'I reckon we should do more to help,' Mam said.

Jean said, 'She's not an easy one to help.'

'I know, love, but do it for Joe, eh?'

A few days later, I heard Jean crying in her room. I told Mam and when she went up to her, I crept in to my room and put my ear to the wall. I gathered Violet had said something to upset Jean. I heard Richard's name, and something about *Gone with the Wind* which I remembered was a film they'd gone to see a long time ago. Mam must have asked Jean if she would make it up because Jean shouted, 'She can come on her bloody hands and knees and beg me and I might consider it,' so I knew it was serious because it took a lot to rile our Jean.

The next day, Mam told Jean she'd been up to see Violet, and that Jean should try to make it up. She said, 'That lass has got nobody and I reckon she's in a mess. It's not a nice house to bring a babby into.' Jean shrugged and shook her head.

Mam wouldn't allow me to sleep in Jean's room when she went into hospital. She had all us lads making a crib with some wood she'd brought home from work, while she sat at the sewing machine and made the bedding. When Jean brought baby Elizabeth home – early, because the hospital was trying to stay as empty as it could in case of raids – she was right chuffed with the cradle. There was no end of palaver over that baby. She was rolled up like a caterpillar so I could only see her face. But I could certainly hear her, squawking nonstop for so long that I started to wonder whether I should volunteer to be evacuated.

When Joe's next letter came, Jean read it aloud to the baby. He said he was looking forward to meeting her, but things were hotting up and it might be a while before he could get leave, so he'd written to Father Christmas to ask for a lift home on his sleigh. Jean didn't read the next part out loud, and sat biting her bottom lip. She put the letter into her pinafore pocket and brought the writing pad to the table. I thought she was replying to Joe, but when she'd put it in the envelope, she told me to take it up to Hurdle Hill Terrace.

Sam came with me. It was raining hard and cold and we were soaking wet by the time we stood outside number fourteen. I thought I saw the shadow of a person behind the lace curtain at the front window but nobody answered the door. 'Get a reply,' Jean had said, so we knocked and waited some more, but nobody came. I peeped through the letter box and saw a movement in the dark hallway, so I knocked again, but still there was no answer. I pushed the note through and we left.

A week or so later, Jean decided to visit Violet herself.

Mam said, 'I'm glad to hear it, but tha'll not be taking a baby anywhere in this weather,' because it was sleeting. The next morning it had stopped, so Jean wrapped baby Elizabeth in about four blankets and put her in the pram.

Mam said to me, 'Go with her. Help her push the pram up the hill.'

At Violet's house, I stood on the pavement holding the pram while Jean went up the little path and knocked on the door. Mrs Knowles looked down on us from the front bedroom. I waved to her and she disappeared. Jean knocked again. I pulled my sleeves over my hands to keep them warm on the cold steel of the pram handle. The door opened a few inches and Mrs Knowles looked through the gap. She looked past Jean to where I stood with the pram and said, 'I'm sorry I can't invite you in, I don't think the pram will fit.'

Jean said to me, 'Look after the pram a minute. If she wakes up and cries, knock on the door and I'll come,' and she turned back to the door. As she lifted her hand to push it open, Mrs Knowles said, 'Violet is resting,' and closed the door in Jean's face. Jean stood with her mouth open for a few seconds, then came down the path, grabbed the handle of the pram from me and pressed it down to lift the front wheels and turn it around on the narrow pavement. She marched off so fast I had to run to keep up with her. Jean swore under her breath, all the way home. Every so often, she would sniff and push the back of her hand to her nose. We were home in no time. Jean pushed the pram through the door into the kitchen.

Mam looked up from the table where she was mixing cake and said, 'That was quick. No joy then?'

Jean shook her head and busied herself unwrapping baby Elizabeth. I ran my finger round the mixing bowl, sucked on the sweet, fruity mixture and said, 'Can I go to Sam's?'

Mam said, 'Tha can practice some spellings. I saw that letter tha'd writ to Joe. First up thee can find out how many z's there is in razors and Elizabeth.'

I went up to the bedroom and took Bill's new penknife from his hiding place, and had a go at whittling the bird's head that he'd been working on. The knife slipped and cut off its beak. I put the knife back and took the carving down to my hidey-hole in the privy. Bill looked all over for that carving.

Frank

0855 Midland Mainline to Sheffield

Amy's itinerary: *'Follow signs for Underground (Piccadilly Line, see blue line on map enclosed). All trains go to London. Buy ticket to Kings Cross – money in envelope. Get off at Kings Cross, follow signs to St Pancras station. Take escalator to station concourse. Put pink ticket in machine to exit (machine will keep ticket). Seat is booked on 0855 train to Sheffield, look for Coach A, seat 2B. No problem if you miss it – there's one every hour, you just won't have a seat booked.'*

Green Park – Piccadilly Circus – names I've heard and seen on television. The train is getting fuller, bodies are crammed against me, it's hot and stuffy, I can hardly breathe. As I get off the train at Kings Cross, the smoky hot metal smell catches me in the back of my throat, and when I close my eyes to breathe I'm at the works gates, looking for my Dad amongst the people who are rushing, pushing me backwards and forwards. I can hear the steel rollers screeching and feel the heat blasting from the furnace. A hand under my elbow steers me along, through the people, and I open my eyes expecting to see a man, covered with sweat and dust, but it's a young woman. 'You've had a bit of a turn,' she says. 'Shall I get some help?' And when I shake my head, she asks, 'Do you have a ticket?' and I hold it out to her. Her hand cups my elbow all the way up the escalator and across to a kind of ticket barrier where she puts my ticket into the machine and two flaps snap open making a little gate. 'Go on through,' she says. The swoosh of the steam hammer makes me jump but her hand on my arm is firm and when I look round we're passing a café bar and I realise it's only the coffee machine. 'There's a first aid place over there,' she says, 'Shall we go across?' But I can't stop now. I tell her I have to be on the train. So she looks at my piece of paper and brings me to the train and finds my seat. It's in first class with my own table. The waiter's here with a cup of tea. He's promised me a full English breakfast later. He won't take any money, he says it's included. It's as well. After paying the fare for the underground, I only have a few quid left from the stash that Amy gave me. She told me I can use my ATM card here, but I'm not going to risk that until I'm in Sheffield, in case there's a problem with it. I've no time to waste. I feel better already but when I look round to say thank you to the young lady, she's nowhere to be seen. I hope I wasn't rude.

So here I am, a couple of hours from Sheffield. This is the last thing in my haversack. Turning the yellow and red tin in my hands I ponder whether I'm doing the right thing. It won't bring any of them back. The lid is starting to rust, making it difficult to unscrew. But here I have it – the smell and the taste of my Dad. It's Sunday, the fifteenth of December 1940. I'm awake early, lying in the pitch dark of the cupboard under the stairs, listening to Cyril snoring like an ack-ack gun while the baby wails like a siren.

That was the second night we'd slept in the cupboard after the bombing on Friday. The greatest adventure of my life was happening out there and I was missing it. Mam stuck her head round the door to wake Bill who was on earlies. Even though it was easier to breathe when he left, taking his cheesy feet with him, the moving around had started baby Elizabeth wailing again, so it was easier to get up. Anyway, I was keen to get out and see what was going on.

Mam was folding up the bedding from where she had slept under the table. Jean had her arms in a bucket of soap suds and from the pong I reckoned she was washing the baby's nappies.

Mam told Jean, 'I've got bad news. They've give thy job to old man Biggin.'

Jean dropped a nappy into the bucket and water sloshed onto Mam's feet. Mam said, 'Here, Frank, get that mopped up,' and didn't even tell Jean off. 'But they say there's a place on the line, with me.' Jean looked daggers at her. She took no notice and carried on, 'It means we can make sure we get different shifts and take turn and turn about, minding the babby.'

Jean said, 'I was planning on putting her in the nursery.'

Mam said, 'Why let strangers look after her when there's family that will do it?'

The door opened and Dad came in from the night shift. He hung his haversack and coat on the back of the door, pulled a ragged newspaper out of his pocket and snapped it open as he sat down by the fire. Mam pulled his boots off and he put his feet on the fender. Jean passed him a mug of tea. He patted his waistcoat pocket and swore under his breath. 'Here Frank. Get down the shop and get me some baccy.' He rustled in his pocket and found a shilling. 'Half an ounce of *Erinmore*, and mind tha brings the change.' As I was leaving, he added, 'And pop round to Mester Ainsworth and see if he'll lend us yesterday's paper. This is last week's.' He threw the paper into the scuttle and concentrated on his tea.

I was pleased to have an excuse to see Sam. I found him sitting on his front door step, with little George. Mrs Ainsworth had taken up child-minding but it was Sam who looked after George most days. He thought it was better than being stuck indoors with his dad though. He was having a contest with George, seeing who could throw stones furthest across the road.

Sam said, 'Want to come missioning? We could look at the bombed houses and happen collect some aluminium for the Spitfire Fund.' That sounded a right good idea. 'If we take the most to school on Monday, we'll win a badge.'

Little George said, 'Can I come? My dad's getting me a Spitfire kit for Christmas.' I rolled my eyes at Sam. We both knew George didn't have a dad. He shouted, 'He is too.'

'He'll have to come,' Sam said. 'Mam's looking after him all day.' I didn't mind. George was a bit of a mardybum but he was handy for fetching and carrying.

I ran round to the shop and back home with the tobacco. I filled Dad's pipe, tamped it down and handed it to him. I put the rest of the pack into his tin and pressed the lid back into place.

He asked, 'And the paper?' I'd forgotten.

'I'll go round now.' I grabbed my muffler off the peg and ran back out.

As we walked down the street I asked little George, 'What's tha got in thy pockets?' He pulled out some bits of candle, a piece of string, and a thre'penny bit. We stopped at the corner shop and sent him in to buy aniseed balls which we could get without coupons.

We turned the corner into Gelsthorpe Street and stopped and stared. The sun was low and shone through a line of empty windows, many of which had torn pieces of curtain hanging from broken panes. It reminded me of the manger we'd made at school. Miss Malkin had brought in a cardboard box and we'd cut holes in it to make stable windows. We glued a few bits of grass and sticks onto the front and stood it in the window to dry. The sun had glinted through, like a holy light. Gelsthorpe Street looked like this, a cardboard box with windows cut out and a holy light shining through. With the icy puddles glinting, it made a right good Christmas scene. We squeezed under the fence and wandered across the rubble. Walking over a door that lay flat on the ground, we found ourselves inside, which was really outside, surrounded by a tangle of furniture and clothes. There was a bed on a table, with bricks, chimneys and toys scattered around. I recognised this as being something like the diagram in my Dad's Air Raid Precautions book.

'It's called a Pancake Floor Collapse,' I said.

George asked, 'Shall we find some bodies?'

'I reckon we might.' His mouth dropped open.

Sam said, 'Or ghosties.'

George started scriking. He rubbed his eyes with my sleeve, leaving a trail of snot up my arm. I pushed him away. He started walking back to the fence, sniffling, 'I'll tell my Mam.'

Sam looked at me and shrugged. We ran over to George. Sam said, 'Come on, Georgie. Tha knows we can't manage on our own. We've got to get enough scrap metal for a wing, at least.'

George said, 'I want to go home.'

'Come here and I'll tell thee a rhyme', Sam said. 'It's rude,' and when George came over and sat with him, he chanted, *'Auntie Mary, had a canary, up the leg of her drawers, and when she farted, it departed, to a round of applause'.*

George was giggling fit to burst. He was happy again. 'That's right good,' I said. 'Where did you get it from?' Sam was grinning, pleased as Punch. We hunted around for metal. George found a black pan that he could hardly lift with both hands. We told him it was iron but he was happy enough hauling it around behind him. We moved a door that was laid flat, half under the rubble, and found a gap. Pushing the door aside we saw some stone stairs.

Sam said, 'Come on, it's a cellar.' We wriggled into the gap and down the stone steps. When we got to the bottom we were able to stand up and move around. It was a coal cellar. We dragged the door back across the entrance. Enough light came in through the grating to show us that apart from a pile of coal, the room was empty. We jigged around.

I said, 'This is right good. We can find stuff to turn it into a proper den.'

George asked, 'Can we live here?'

It wasn't such a bad idea. It would be better than under our stairs, at any rate. I had an idea starting to form in my mind about how we might be able to camp out here.

After three or four trips around the bombed out houses we had gathered chair cushions, a cot mattress, and an eiderdown that was hanging off a beam. We collected up wood from broken chairs and piled them ready for a fire later. The cellar looked right cosy. Sam came across a meat-safe, its door hanging by one hinge, and inside was a brown paper package tied with string containing four sausages. Then we went searching for aluminium, taking it in turns to be lookout in case the police or wardens came near. There were signs everywhere about looting. Although we weren't stealing anything, there was no knowing what people would think. Everyone had been acting peculiar since the bombing had started a couple of days ago.

We were on Liberty Road when I heard my name called but when I looked up the road all I could see in the dusk was a giant potato on legs.

'Where's thy gas mask, our Frank?'

As it got closer, I realised the potato was our Jean with a balaclava on and her gabardine tied up tight across her middle and bulges sticking out all over. Then I saw she had baby Elizabeth wrapped under her coat and a haversack and both their gas masks hanging from her arm.

I said, 'I'm off home in a minute, I'll get it then. Where's tha going?'

'To see Violet, to ask if me and Elizabeth can stop with her.'

I said, 'I thought you said she was too far up her own backside.'

'Mind thy lip.'

It was true. That was what Jean had said about Violet after Mrs Knowles slammed the door in her face. Why Jean would want to visit her was beyond me.

Jean said, 'Get on home. Mam's been looking for thee. They say there's more raids on the way. And Sam Ainsworth, tha'd best get young George home.' She stood and watched until we were on the corner of Beacon Street. Then she waved and turned into Chapel Hill. I was going to say to Sam that we could get back to our den, when

Mam saw me. She must have been looking for me because she shouted to me to come in.

I said to Sam, ‘Tell thy Mam tha can stop at ours tonight. I’ll tell my Mam I can stop with thee. Bring some grub.’

Sam went off to his house with little George who started scriking about his pan that he’d left in the den.

Dad said, ‘Where’s the paper?’ and I daren’t say I’d forgotten it again, so I said, ‘Mester Ainsworth says he’s not finished reading it and can I go and get it later.’ Dad nodded and went on tuning the wireless.

I made Mam a cup of tea and asked her if she wanted any errands doing. She said, ‘What’s got into thee?’

‘Can I stay at Sam’s tonight?’

‘I think his mam has enough on her plate.’

‘She says it’s all right,’ I lied.

‘Does she now?’

‘They’ve got a new Morrison shelter that she says I can sleep in with Sam.’ I was shaking now, thinking she’d be bound to see that I was making it up.

‘Has she now? Well, if she’s sure. It would be handy having one less, since Cyril and Bill are both home tonight and it does get a bit crowded under them stairs.’

During tea, I put some bread and a couple of cooked potatoes in my pocket. As soon as we finished, I shouted to Mam that I was going, and was out of the door.

Sam was on the corner. He hadn’t had any tea so he ate the bread and potatoes while we made our way through the gennels to Gelsthorpe Street. It was very dark now but we still dodged about in case we were seen going in the opposite direction to our houses. My stomach felt like a hundred sparrows were flying about in it. I was excited that we would get to see the action, if there was any tonight, and if there wasn't then we would go home in the morning as usual, go to school, and do it again another night. I was also scared about being found out in the biggest lie I'd ever told to my Mam and Dad.

The moon shone on the puddles of ice, so we could easily see our way across the rubble. I picked up a two-foot length of pipe. Sam found a chair leg and we had a sword fight. I jabbed my heel into a sheet of thin ice in one of the ruts, breaking it into long slices. We took one each. We were RAF pilots whose plane had crashed over Holland. We baled out and attacked the enemy with our long, sharp steel daggers. 'Hande hoch!' we shouted, lunging at pretend German soldiers until our icy knives went mushy and dripped from between our fingers.

The siren screamed. We looked at one another.

Sam said, 'Best get home,' but at the thought of the cupboard under the stairs, I said, 'Come on.' I got Cyril's torch out of my pocket to light the way to the entrance of our den.

We squatted on the stone steps to drag the door across, then went down to the cellar. After a bit of a performance with damp matches, we managed to light the bits of candle we'd emptied out of George's pocket earlier, and set them around. We built a lively fire. Lying across the chair cushions with the sausages on sticks, we held them over the fire to cook, then bit into them, burning our lips and tongues. Afterwards, we put more pieces of coal on the fire, and lay on the mattress, side by side, telling one another what we could see in the flames.

I said, 'We'll cop it in the morning.'

Sam said, 'I shall get the strap if we're found out.'

I said, 'Happen we should go straight to school. When Miss gives us a Spitfire badge, I'll show it to my dad and he'll be right chuffed and forget about it.'

Sam reminded me, 'We've not found any scrap metal yet.'

I said, 'We'll get up early and find some on our way to school.'

Sam brought the sticky bag of aniseed balls out of his pocket and we shared them. I took the hood off Cyril's torch and balanced it on the heap of coal so we could play shadow puppets in the beam. We lay down, stood up, climbed onto the coal heap to look out of the grating, and sucked some more sweets.

Sam said, 'This is boring.'

It was. And even with the fire, it was cold. I said, 'Let's go home.'

A deep humming sound was above us and moving closer. It reminded me of the time we'd been messing about in the allotments and we'd knocked a bee's nest out of a tree - the swarm had chased us up the path until we dodged into an open shed and hid until they'd gone past. We looked at one another. Sam's mouth was open, his lips brown from the sweets and greasy from the sausages. Together we rushed to the stairs, shoved the door aside and stuck our heads out of the gap. I shone Cyril's torch upwards, criss-crossing the distant searchlights as they lit up the little planes. We laughed out loud.

A man's voice shouted, 'Who's over there?' I switched the torch off and we ducked down. I imagined it might be my Dad on fire watch, or looking for me. He'd be wearing his greatcoat from the last war, his curly hair sticking out either side of his cap, the straps of his haversack and gas mask criss-crossing one another on his chest. The voice called again. It wasn't my Dad.

Sam nudged me and I looked up to see that in the sky, one black dot had moved away from the others. It turned to a spot, a blob, a boulder, and was coming towards us. Sam grabbed my sleeve and pulled me down. I closed my eyes. The ground shook above my head and beneath my feet. I opened my eyes and looked up to see a bright orange light had filled the sky. I pushed my head out. A ball of flame leapt into the air behind the ruined houses. The whites of Sam's eyes glowed yellow with the reflection. His lips moved but I couldn't hear anything. We pulled the door across to close the opening, and dropped down into the cellar, throwing ourselves onto the cot mattress and pulling the eiderdown over ourselves. I thought maybe it wouldn't be so bad, tomorrow night, having Bill's cheesy feet up my nose.

I opened my eyes to see a reddish glow filtering through the grating. Turning my head at the sound of scratching I saw a rat, the size of a cat, chewing on what was left of one of the sausages. I jumped up, but my leg gave way with cramp and I fell onto Sam who yelped and flung his arm out, smacking me in the mouth. By the time we'd untangled our bodies, and I'd rubbed my legs to get rid of the pins and needles, the rat had gone. We clambered out of the cellar and stood on the rubble, watching black smoke curling up from the valley.

I said, 'Happen we'd best go home before school.'

The only sounds as we walked was of water hissing out of broken pipes and the popping that came from a line of blue and yellow flames beside the broken pavement. A man sat on the kerb with a baby lying across his lap, its eyes wide open and staring at us from a face that was the colour of smoke. We turned the corner into Beacon Street, and stopped, lost. I looked behind me to check I'd made the right turning, and then back to the crater. A small fire was burning in the bottom. A beam lay across the top and young John Culshaw was helping a man to shift it. There was a smell like roasting chicken. Puzzled, I looked along the street. A line of faces stared back at me. There was Mr and Mrs Wreakes, standing next to a green door, with the number 89 painted in white on it. I remembered Mr Wreakes painting that number, last summer, and was puzzled that the door was lying flat on the ground. Mrs Wreakes held a plant in one hand, its flowers flashing scarlet against the grey dust. Under her arm was a brown teapot. She nudged Mr Wreakes and nodded towards me. I realised that I'd not yet had a wash and Mam would have something to say. I rubbed at my face with my sleeve. Mr Overton held a piglet tightly against his chest. Mrs Platt's three children hung onto her coat, all staring at me with their mouths open. Mam always said they were a gormless lot who'd make a good living catching flies. As young John Culshaw and the man moved the beam, a fountain of water came hissing and spurting out of the ground. The man shouted at us, 'Get out of the way, boys.' Young John whispered something to the man and they both looked at me and then looked away. Mrs Wreakes was beside me. She put her hand on my shoulder. I thought she was holding on to me until my Mam got there. I shook her off and moved away. There was a squeal from the piglet and I looked across to see it wriggling out of Mr Overton's arms. It landed on its snout, its backside waved in the air for a few seconds, and then it fell sideways with a thump, squealed, jumped to its feet and ran in and out of all the legs. Nobody moved. As it came past me I grabbed and caught a few inches of its tail. Its feet carried on running, scraping up the dust. I thought the tail would come away in my hand but then it stopped struggling. I picked it up, wrapping my arms around its belly and rubbing my face on its pink, hairy neck. I liked its warm softness, because I was shivering.

Another squeal made me look up the street, expecting to see Mam or Jean coming to give me what for. But it was Sam's mother running down the road, tripping over pieces of brick, her arms outstretched, her hair standing on end. She looked like a madwoman. She came up to us, yelling, 'Where's tha been, tha daft bastard,' and started beating Sam around his head, then she squashed him against her, making him wriggle. She looked at me over his head and let him go. Sam's eyes through the coal dust were pink and staring. He was looking into the hole that was appearing as young John and the man swung the beam further away from the crater. I followed his eyes and saw broken pots, a twisted fender, a shoe, white fingers holding the corner of a yellow and red tobacco tin. I couldn't make out the writing, but I knew it said '*Erinmore*' on the lid.

Alice

Smudge wrapped himself around my legs, threatening to topple me over. Poor thing, he must be missing the company. I'd woken early and come home to freshen up and feed him. I was at the health centre when it opened at eight o'clock, but Doctor Grahams was on an urgent home visit. I felt guilty, demanding all his time when he had people with greater emergencies to care for. The receptionist offered me one of the partners but I preferred to wait until this afternoon when, she said, he had a visit to us already in the diary.

At Mum's house, I found Rob cooking porridge. Comfort food. The sleeping pills were not on the mantelpiece where I left them. This reminded me that I hadn't seen the painkillers the locum doctor had left, since Friday morning. Before I could ask Rob where he'd put them I heard the door knocker. I met Claire in the hallway. She came into the kitchen and without preamble sat down. Rob had laid an extra place at the table. He passed her a bowl of porridge and smiled at me, obviously feeling very pleased with himself.

'Are those cranberries? Never tried that,' Claire said as she set upon it.

I felt well-disposed to her. She was only doing her job. She was no threat to me or to Mum. We had nothing to hide. Things were about to be resolved and then we could move on.

Rob passed me a small bowl of porridge which I took up to Mum. She looked exhausted, barely able to pull herself up against the pillows. It must have been almost four days since she'd eaten a proper meal. She picked up the spoon but seemed not to have the strength to hold it and dropped it into the bowl. I picked up the spoon and held it towards her, but she waved it away, saying, 'Leave it with me, Alice, I'll manage it in my own time'.

Claire had finished her breakfast and pulled out her notebook when I re-joined them. 'Mr Burgess – Rob, tells me you have some news for me?'

'Mum's very weak,' I said, in case she had any idea of disturbing her. 'I had a talk with her yesterday, as a result of some information we found – a friend, researching our family tree. Mum told me about her cousin Rose, who may be the - the lady in the garden.'

Claire stopped writing and looked up. 'Rose? Do you have this cousin's full name? Address?'

'No, but I can ask her later, when she's strong enough.'

'So this cousin - Rose - why does your mother think it's her body?'

'She disappeared on the night of the air raids, and she didn't come back. Mum believed she was out dancing and I think it was thought at the time that she was a victim of the Marples bomb.' I wondered whether Claire knew what I was talking about, then remembered she'd done her research, so she probably knew more about it than I did. 'But when were talking – Mum and I – she was thinking that Rose might have come here, late, not been able to get in, and decided to sleep in the shelter.' Claire wrote 'Cousin Rose' in inverted commas. 'She may not have known the shelter wasn't in use. We wondered if maybe she'd brought someone back with her. A man.'

Claire wrote, '+ man?' next to Rose's name, placed her pen across the page, folded her arms and looked at me. In the face of this scrutiny, my confidence in Rose's story started to fade, and when she said, 'I don't suppose she gave you a name for this… boyfriend?' I shook my head, feeling stupid. Rob looked over from the sink, his eyebrows raised, as she finished with, 'And am I right in thinking this is guesswork, rather than something your mother knows happened?'

I could see that Rob expected me to say more, but I decided not to mention the adoption unless I had to. I couldn't see that it mattered at this point. With just a few words, Claire had made me doubt my belief in Rose as my biological mother, and I needed to gather my thoughts and feelings in privacy.

Claire put her pen and notebook back in her bag. 'So when can I see Mrs Ibbertson? To get this down as a statement?'

'But why? We've told you everything she knows.'

'What you've given me, Mrs Burgess, is a little bit of hearsay and a lot of imagination. No use to me. If your mother witnessed something that is material to the case, then it's your mother I need to take a statement from.'

'She's far too ill.'

'Mmm,' Claire stood up. 'But you must be keen to get it sorted?' I nodded. 'If this information about her cousin Rose will help us to identify the body and move things forward, it needs to come from your mother. If it's a cousin, then there's going to be some DNA that will help. How about this – I'll tell you what to ask her, but I won't say anything, I'll sit quietly and take notes. That sound okay to you?'

So, even though she'd poured scorn on my story, she thought it was a good enough excuse to get her in to mother's bedroom. I was beginning to see through her tactics.

Rob shook his head. 'Doctor Grahams was very clear. No police near Mrs Ibbertson. We'll phone and check if you like.'

Claire let out an exaggerated sigh and said, 'It's really in everyone's interests to get this cleared up. I'll be back this afternoon. I should have the watch and the torch by then.'

When Rob came back from seeing Claire to the door, he said, 'I don't think we're going to get shot of the Detective Inspector as easily as we thought.'

I heard Mum's stick tapping on the floor above and found her in the middle of her bedroom, looking as though she was about to collapse. She allowed me to hold her under the elbow while she walked to the bathroom.

While I was waiting, Rob joined me on the landing and said, 'There's something leaking through the kitchen ceiling, in the corner.'

The bathroom door opened slightly and Mum's four fingers clasped it. There was a clatter and her stick fell across the opening and wedged the door closed. As I stepped forward and pushed the door slightly, to get a purchase and put my arm in to help her, she must have lost her balance for she fell across the doorway so it was jammed. Rob, nimbler and a good deal thinner than I, managed to squeeze through the gap.

'I've got her,' he said, 'Push the door open now, slowly.' He lifted Mum and together we took her back to bed where she collapsed against the pillows, closing her eyes. 'Nothing broken,' Rob said. 'But we should call an ambulance to be on the safe side, get her checked over.' Mum was shaking her head, saying in a whisper, 'No, no, no ambulance. Leave me.'

‘It’ll be a repeat of Thursday,’ I said. ‘She won’t go with them. Best to wait for the doctor later this afternoon.’

‘All right,’ said Rob, ‘But we’re not leaving her alone. You go and make us all a hot drink.’

When I came back, I couldn’t see Rob. Then his head appeared from the corner behind the bed and he stood, holding a brown envelope in his hand. Mum was watching him from the bed.

‘Not a good place to keep your drinks and food, Ma,’ he said to Mum, wagging a finger at her. The fact that she didn’t give him a sharp retort for being so patronising was an indication of how poorly she must be feeling. ‘Look at this, Alice.’ He stepped out of the way so that I could walk round between the bed and the wall. He’d lifted the linoleum away from the corner, and beneath it a short length of floorboard had been removed. ‘Not me,’ he said. ‘The piece of floorboard is missing’. In the gap between the joists I could see a glutinous yellow puddle. ‘That’s what’s leaking into the kitchen,’ Rob said. ‘Four days’ supply of tea and toast mixed with a little Horlicks. And I do believe the attractive yellow hue is the supplement the doctor recommended. I’ll bring something to mop it up.’ He handed me the envelope, which had my name on the front, in my mother’s writing. ‘This was tucked under the lino.’

In the envelope was a black and white photograph. A young couple stands behind a wedding cake. She is holding the knife in the classic pose, as if about to cut the cake. He has his right hand on hers, over the knife, and his left hand round her shoulders. They are looking at one another, not at the camera, and smiling. The young woman – with a start, I recognised Judy. Then I thought, it can’t be, for all Judy’s wedding photographs are in colour and this is not my son-in-law. It is Joe. A younger, thinner version, but definitely Joe. A handsome young man in uniform. There was a piece of paper in the envelope and as I pulled it out, Mum tapped my hand and held her palm towards me. Thinking she was going to explain, I passed her what looked to be a couple of folded pages similar to those from her diary. She pushed the papers under the bedclothes as Rob came in with a roll of kitchen towel.

Frank

0855 Midland Mainline to Sheffield

The fields fly past, bright green patches of life that make me wish myself back at the farm. It's early evening in Wallaburra. Keith will be out doing the last few jobs before settling down. Amy will be clucking around the kitchen, cooking up a treat for supper. The steward has brought me a breakfast, but it doesn't compare to Amy's cooking. All those years of hankering after an English breakfast and I have to admit it's a bit of a let-down. It makes me wonder what other memories I've been wasting my time hanging on to. I feel out of kilter with the world. It's much the same feeling as I had in those days after. After that day.

I remember how my brain played games with me that night. Back in the cellar, curled up, under the eiderdown, I smelled our Cyril's feet and flung my arm out. But my hand only found the cold flagstone. Then I heard Bill rattling and snorting in his sleep and turned the other way but there was nobody there. I squeezed my eyes shut, put my thumbs in my ears and my hands across my nose. A line of people started to move across the inside of my eyelids. There was Mam, laughing and pushing her hair up, under her scarf, as Dad snapped the newspaper open. Mam laughed. Dad snapped the newspaper. It was like being at the pictures but the film kept stopping and starting again at the beginning. Then I heard my name being called and the film skipped to the dark, lumpy shape that was

Jean standing on the corner of Chapel Hill, the sun dropping down behind her. As she came nearer, my heart beat faster and faster until I thought it would jump out of my mouth. I sat up, breathing fast, sure I'd forgotten something important but not able to remember what it was. Then, in the frosty glow from the morning light coming through the grating, I saw those fingers wrapped around the tin of Erinmore, and I remembered.

The door scraped as it was moved away and something or somebody dropped heavily into the opening and down the steps. I scrabbled backwards, against the wall, into the shadows. Sam appeared, a thumb stuck into the top of a beer bottle, his other hand pulling a hunk of bread out of his pocket. Grabbing the bread from him, I pushed the whole piece into my mouth, then took the bottle and drank the cold tea. He shivered and wrapped his arms around himself.

'Mam says if I see thee I'm to say, come and stop at our house for a bit.'

'Has tha told her about this place?'

'Course not. She made me stop in my room all yesterday, but I didn't tell. She let me out this morning with strict instructions to come straight home after school. She's got her eye on me so I can't stay.' That meant I'd been here for more than a day. He pushed his hand around inside his pocket and held out a pile of brown, sticky crumbs. 'It's me Mam's parkin.'

I drank more of the cold tea and then I knew what it was that I kept trying to remember. 'Our Jean and the baby? They must have missed it?'

Sam shrugged. 'Mam says all thy family copped it. Jean and the baby and all.'

The parkin turned solid in my throat and I leaned over, retching. The dark shape of the rat scuttled in front of me and disappeared behind the coal heap. I thought for a minute then said, 'But she wouldn't know our Jean was at the Knowleses. We saw them, didn't we?'

He shrugged again. 'I'd best go. I shall get a leathering if I'm late.'

I jumped up. 'I'm going up to Hurdle Hill to look for our Jean.'

We walked up to Liberty Road. People had their heads down and caps so low I couldn't see their eyes. The sign outside the library said, 'Rest Centre'.

Sam said, 'That's where they go, them that's been bombed out. They have mattresses on the floor. Miss Malkin told us, she works there when she's not at school. They have a list. We could ask about your Jean.'

'They'll be at Violet's.'

We parted on the corner of Chapel Hill, and as I turned to walk away, I saw it was the very spot where I'd seen Jean last. I thought how I would explain to her what had happened and what she might think of me for hiding when I should have been at home. An invisible hand gripped my belly and made me retch again.

At the Knowles's house, as I lifted the door knocker, a baby cried and my innards did a somersault because it meant Jean and Elizabeth were here and they were safe. I dropped the knocker and waited, then knocked again. I thought I heard footsteps in the hallway but the door didn't open. I shouted through the letterbox, 'Hello-o-o'. The lace curtain moved but I couldn't see anybody at the window. I knocked again. The door opened a crack and Violet's mother looked down on me.

'What is it?'

'Is our Jean here please?'

Her eyes were enormous through her thick glasses. She looked at me as though I was mad. 'Jean? Why would Jean be here?'

'I saw her coming here yesterday – I mean the day before.'

'You're mistaken. Jean hasn't been here'. She started to close the door.

I was turning away, thinking maybe Jean had said another name that she was going to stay with, perhaps Sybil, or – when a great wail came from above and I knew it was Elizabeth. I turned back and pushed at the door. Mrs Knowles squealed and jumped, letting go of the door so it swung open. I had a foot over the step when she put her hands on my shoulders to stop me.

'That's our Elizabeth.'

'I beg your pardon?'

I'd been listening to Elizabeth squalling for nights on end so I reckoned I knew her yell when I heard it. 'Our Jean's baby, that's Elizabeth crying.'

'Don't be ridiculous, that's Violet's baby,' and while I was thinking about this she pushed me back over the step and closed the door.

I didn't believe her. I went to the end of the street and took the little path behind the row of houses, coming round to the gate and into the Knowles's garden. I don't know what I was thinking but I saw the Anderson shelter and was walking towards it when Violet opened the back door.

I called across to her, 'I'm looking for our Jean.'

Violet said, 'She's not here.' Her face was red and blotchy and her voice was thick and cracked as if she'd been crying.

I said, 'She was coming here to stay. I saw her on Chapel Hill and she said so.'

Violet's voice was trembly when she said, 'She was on her way home when I last saw her. I'm sure you'll find her at home.'

Then I heard the crying again, from inside the house, and ran to the door, saying, 'That's Elizabeth crying.'

Violet put an arm across the door to stop me going in and said, 'No, that's Alice.'

I wondered if all babies sounded the same. 'Alice?'

'Yes, Alice. I'm sure you'll find Jean at home.'

I said, 'There isn't no home. It's gone. They've all gone.' As I said it, I realised that tears were pouring out of my eyes and my nose. I tried to rub them away with my sleeve.

Violet said, 'Pardon me?'

'Mam, dad, everybody – they've all copped it.' I thought those were the words I was saying, but she was staring at me as though I was talking a foreign language. And suddenly it was true. There had been a shadow in the corner of my mind while I'd lain in the cellar, and when I thought it was Jean, I came to find her. While I thought Jean was here, I believed everything could go back to normal, but if Jean wasn't here, if she had gone back home…

I felt someone grabbing me, but couldn't see and when I rubbed my eyes with my sleeves the coal dust made them sting. Words were falling over one another as they rushed out of my mouth. I realised Violet had her arms around me and she was crying too. I pulled away from her and stepped backwards.

She said, 'Won't you come…'

Suddenly, Mrs Knowles was pushing Violet backwards into the house, saying, 'Jean left here to go home, so we really can't help you.'

She closed the door and I stared at it, not knowing whether to knock again. Mrs Knowles came to the window and waved at me to go away. From the gate, I looked back, up to the bedroom window where the wailing had turned into little hiccuppy sobs. I stood at the gate for a long time. Then the door opened and Violet was there, beckoning me to come to her. I thought she must have remembered where Jean was, after all, and I ran up the path. She was holding out a brown paper bag and a pound note.

'Where will you go?' she said. I stuffed the bag under my coat and the money into my trouser pocket and shrugged. 'Don't you have relatives? What about your Aunt?'

Until then, I'd completely forgotten Auntie Eileen and cousin Mildred. I remembered the library and what Sam had said about lists of missing people. I reasoned that if Jean had come home after visiting Violet, she would have found the house gone, and would have taken Elizabeth to Auntie Eileen's at Tinsley. She would have thought I was at home with the rest of them, so she wouldn't be looking for me.

I stood outside the library, looking at the 'Rest Centre' sign and wondering what to say. Women wearing green uniforms and red berets rushed past me. One of them said, 'Hello, Frank, we've been looking out for you.' It was Mrs Trippett. With a hand on my shoulder she steered me in through the door and stood me beside a desk that was piled high with papers and tins and blankets. Somebody called her name and she said, ‘Stay there, Frank, I won’t be a minute.’

Around me, people stood looking at notices on the wall. One lady pinned up a list of names and the people crowded around, reading it. Another lady handed out cups of tea and pieces of cake. Babies were crying somewhere. It occurred to me that Jean might be here and I walked along the corridor, looking into rooms, taking a cup of tea from a trolley as I passed. In every room people were lying or sitting on mattresses. A nurse was tending to a woman who was screaming in one corner and I thought she must be dying, then the nurse held up a baby, as pink and wrinkled as a newborn rabbit. She swung it by its feet and the baby cried. I expected somebody to shout at her to put it down but there was a lot of clapping and cheering.

Mrs Trippett put her hand on my shoulder and turned me towards another room. She said, ‘If you sit in that room with the young folk, Frank, I’ll ask someone to come and take your details.’

I helped myself to a slice of bread with corned beef off the trolley and stood against the wall while people went back and forth passing around enamel cups and plates. A woman wearing the green uniform came rushing through the main door and said, ‘I’ve brought a van from HQ. Anything you can spare for Tinsley?’

Mrs Trippett pointed to the piles of stuff on her desk and asked, ‘How are things there?’

‘Worse, if that’s possible,’ the other lady said. ‘Not yet got everybody out.’

I pictured cousin Mildred’s silly pink bow sticking out of a pile of rubble, like Mrs Wreakes’s plant, a bright flash against the grey dust. This brought to my mind the crater, and I dropped the bread back onto the trolley. There didn’t seem any point in mentioning Auntie Eileen or Tinsley, given what the lady had said. I remembered watching the rows of evacuees on the Pathe News and thought of Billy Roberts leaving his family. I sidled out of the door and made my way back to the cellar, taking shortcuts in case Mrs Trippett came after me.

The torch battery was dead, so I lit a candle and looked inside the bag Violet had given me. There was bread, fruit cake, and a piece of cheese. I wasn't hungry and wrapped myself in the eiderdown, wondering what it felt like to die and not much caring. At some point in the night, the scuttling of the rat caught my attention and I watched it finish off the food, bag and all. In the dim light from the stub of candle, it looked brown and soft which made me think of the rabbits. I had a yearning to hold them and wondered if Sam's mam would let me have them back.

There was a bright light shining through the grating when I opened my eyes. The rat was looking up at me and I remembered the rabbits. The door wouldn't budge. Standing on the stone steps I pushed up against it with my back until it shifted an inch or so. Snow fell through the gap and down my neck. I managed to fit my fingers round the edge of the door and wriggle it until there was enough room to climb out.

My toes burned with cold as I walked to Beacon Street. The sun was shining but there was a strong wind blowing the snow off the roofs and stinging my face. A fence surrounded the crater. One wall of the privy was still standing, but the other had partly collapsed and the roof had caved in. Dropping onto my belly I wriggled under the fence and slithered across the frosty bricks. I moved the roof slates until I saw the corner of the black cloth, then pulled the parcel out and opened it. It was all there - Robinson Crusoe, the German book, my Cat's Eye marble, the curtain ring, the rabbit's foot, and Bill's carving. I saw the tobacco tin on a pile of stuff heaped beside the fence and pushed it into my pocket. The Rowntree's Cocoa tin was there too, so dented that the lid wouldn't come off, but when I shook it the coins rattled. Dad's haversack still hung on its nail on the back door which lay on top of the rubble. I put everything I'd gathered into the haversack, thinking Robinson Crusoe must have felt like this after the shipwreck, returning to his ship to collect up anything that might be useful to him on his desert island. I heard a phlegmy cough behind me.

Mr Wreakes was standing on the other side of the fence. His voice whistled around his pipe. 'Now then, Frankie, we've all been fretting after thee. Will tha come and have something to eat? Tha's looking a bit peckish.' He pulled a cone of newspaper out of his pocket and held it out. I smelt aniseed. I slung the haversack over my shoulder and wriggled under the fence. When he smiled, a black tooth wobbled in his gum. Mr Wreakes had never smiled at me. I grabbed the cone of aniseed balls and ran.

I came to a tangled mess of tramlines and watched the workmen for a while before one came over and told me to sit by their brazier and get warm. He gave me a mug of tea. Looking around, I realised this was Infirmary Road and remembered the last time I'd been here, when I'd gone to Ferguson's with Jean after seeing Joe off at the train station. Thinking of Ferguson's made me wonder if I might have been wrong and Jean hadn't gone to stay with Violet at all. Happen she'd come home, seen what had happened, and had found somewhere else to live, such as with Sybil. She'd have no money and would have to go to work. I'd be able to give her Mam's savings from the cocoa tin. Pulling the haversack tight against me, I ran round the corner to the great iron gate. The jib of the crane swung high above me. A tap on my shoulder made me jump. It was Dennis. I asked if Jean Ibbertson was at work and he gave me a queer look and stammered a bit, but then he said I should sit in his office by the gate while he sent for somebody.

From Dennis's little window, I watched him limp across the cobbled yard, and a few minutes later he reappeared, with Sybil wobbling beside him. She opened the door and stared at me. Her lips looked blood red in her white face. I thought she hadn't recognised me, so I said, 'It's me, Frank.'

She dropped onto her knees in front of me. 'It is, isn't it? It's really Frank.'

I said, 'I'm looking for our Jean. Has tha seen her?'

She pulled me into a great, warm hug. 'Oh, Frank. Come on home with me.'

I could have laughed out loud. 'Is she there then? Our Jean?'

Sybil stepped back and shook her head. 'No, Frank, Jean's gone.'

I ducked under her arm, pushed past Dennis who stood at the door, ran back through the gates and up the road. I ran until I slipped on the ice and fell over, and I might have cried for a bit. Not knowing where to go next, I followed the broken tram lines into the city centre. My ears ached with the cold. I saw the Bank and wondered if it was the one where Violet worked, but it was gutted, the windows bare and the sign hanging off. A workman walking past said, 'If tha's thinking of tunneling into the vaults, join the queue,' and went off laughing. A digger moved back and forth, clearing the rubble that had been *C&A Modes*. There was a shout and the digger stopped. Men ran over and looked in silence into the hole. Then somebody held up a manikin, the legs broken off at the knee and its head hanging down. Everybody cheered.

On West Bar the doors of the Don Cinema were open. The thought of sitting in the smoky, warm darkness with the smell of people around me carried me to the ticket desk where I held out Violet's pound note. The woman said, what was I doing with that much money and she would call the constable, so I ran away, up the hill to the Cathedral where I leaned against a headstone to get my breath back. Watching the vicar hanging holly around the door brought to mind that it was nearly Christmas.

I lost track of time. One day, I decided to go back to Violet's house and was walking along North Hill Road when I saw her pushing a pram and followed her to the Post Office. She left the pram outside and I peered in. The baby had the same tufts of black hair, and the same turned up lip, as Elizabeth. But I didn't recognise any of the clothes she was wearing. Violet came out and stood stock still, staring at me. I ran away, down the hill towards Liberty Road. It was getting dark and my legs were shaking so much I could hardly walk by the time I reached Gelsthorpe Street.

Coming round the corner with my chin tucked into my coat and my hands up my sleeves, I collided with a woman standing in the middle of the pavement with her back to me. When she turned I saw it was Miss Malkin. Then I saw Sam walking towards me with a soldier. I tried to run, wondering where I could go now, if Sam had betrayed me and the cellar was no longer safe, but my legs wouldn't move fast enough and I was grabbed by the elbow and spun around until my nose was crushed up against a smelly brown greatcoat. I pushed against the soldier's body, kicking with one foot and hitting bone a couple of times.

The soldier said, 'Oy, stop it, scamp,' and loosened his grip, allowing me to pull free. I turned away and he grabbed me backwards around the waist and held me tight. Miss Malkin stood in front of me and I thought she would tell him to get off me, but she smiled. The soldier said, 'Settle down, Frank, it's me, Joe.' Then I recognised his voice and stopped fighting. He kept hold of my collar until I convinced him I wouldn't run off. No way would I. If Joe was here, it would be all right. He would find Jean. He rubbed his shin and said, 'The Regiment could do with you on their side. I'll volunteer you for unarmed combat.'

Joe's boots were covered in dust and a stale, sweaty smell came off him that reminded me of my Dad coming home from work. He said he was on seventy-two hours' compassionate leave on account of Jean being killed. This was his second day and he'd been looking for me. He'd gone to Miss Malkin and she'd made Sam tell. He said '*killed*'.

I said, 'But she's not,' and tried to explain.

He said, 'I know, Violet told me you'd been there.' He wouldn't listen to me. 'We have to accept that Jean copped it, Frank, one way or another. She might have been caught somewhere around Chapel Hill, or maybe she'd gone home and was at Beacon Street. She couldn't have missed it unless she went into a shelter on the way. And if that had been the case, she'd have turned up by now.'

‘What about baby Elizabeth?’ Joe looked down at his boots. ‘Did tha see the baby that Violet has? Did tha get a look?’

‘What’re you saying, Frank?’

‘I reckon it’s not Violet’s baby, it’s our Elizabeth.’

Joe wouldn’t look at me. ‘Now come on, Frank.’

‘But it is.’ I remembered that Joe had never seen the baby so he wouldn’t know what she looked like. ‘They’ve got our Elizabeth.’ When I said this aloud, I realised it was what I really believed, that something bad had happened to Jean and Violet was pretending that Elizabeth was her baby.

Joe was still looking at his boots.

I shook his arm. ‘She cries the same.’ I tried again with, ‘I saw our Jean on Chapel Hill, she was taking Elizabeth up to Violet’s.’

Joe looked at me. ‘Now Frank, stop that. Nothing’s going to bring Jean and Elizabeth back, no matter how much we might wish for it.’

I said, ‘What if maybe Jean left the baby with Violet and then couldn’t go back for her, and Violet decided to keep her and pretend she was hers?’

‘Now, why would Violet do such a thing, Frank?’

I was flummoxed. It did sound a daft idea. For the life of me I couldn’t think why anybody would want a baby if they didn’t have to have one. Joe obviously thought so too.

Then came the biggest surprise. We were walking towards Hurdle Hill.

Joe said, ‘Violet says you can stay there tonight.’

I thought about running, but my spirit was down and a great tiredness had come over me. All I wanted was to stay close to Joe’s greatcoat, and that smell. If Jean wasn’t here – and Joe was certain she wasn’t – then Joe was all the family I'd got and I must do what he said or he might leave me as well.

Violet was kind to me. I said, 'Where's the baby?'

She said, 'Alice is asleep.'

Joe gave me a warning look so I decided not to push it.

They had a bathroom inside the house, just like Richard had told me, and I never thought I'd like hot water so much. Joe peeled my clothes off me. Afterwards, I sat wrapped in a sheet, on the sofa in their parlour, in front of a coal fire, drinking Bovril. I felt a bit of a nancy but I was so warm that even though the material on the sofa made me itch through the sheet, I was past caring and soon fell asleep. Once, I woke, thinking I could hear a baby crying, but it stopped, and I might have imagined it.

In the morning we were eating breakfast when Joe said, 'Miss Malkin's got an idea. While we were looking for you yesterday, we got to talking and I was telling her how we'd got the bus up to Loxley that time.' I remembered. Joe had taken me out for the day. It was the first time I'd seen sheep and I thought them the funniest looking creatures. 'You said you'd like to be a farmer.' I'd forgotten that. 'It turns out Miss Malkin has a brother with a farm out Derbyshire way. She says since he's got to take in an evacuee he'd likely be willing to have somebody she recommends. At least you'll not be with total strangers and she says there's a village school you'd like.'

Joe went to the Rest Centre to get me some clothes. Left alone, still wrapped in the sheet, I slipped out of the back door and stood looking at the Anderson shelter. It had been flattened. The sheets of steel lay all higgledy piggledy. The turf had been thrown on top of the pile and some soil on top of that. I heard a rapping and looked round to see Mrs Knowles standing at the kitchen window, making shooing signals at me.

As I went through the kitchen, I asked her, 'What's happened to the shelter?'

'Flooding,' she said. 'Run-off from the hill, so we can't use it.' I remembered Mr Knowles talking about that.

Joe came back with a parcel of clothes. They were short trousers and when he saw my face he laughed, saying there weren't any long ones small enough for a skinny-rib like me. Though the boots were far too big they were grand and I'd grow into them, so I thought it best not to say anything in case he took them back.

Violet gave me a package of bread and cheese and said goodbye to me on the doorstep. As we walked down the street, I looked back and saw Mrs Knowles at the upstairs window. I hadn't seen the baby in the time I'd been there, and looked up at Joe, about to say so, but he looked so sad that I decided against it.

From this end of town where there'd been no bombs, we were able to take the tram to the bus station where Miss Malkin was waiting. The crowd parted like the Red Sea for Joe in his uniform and as we passed, people patted him on the shoulder which made me proud but at the same time sad that he was going away again. On the bus, I knelt on the back seat and waved to Joe until we rounded a corner and he was out of sight. I sat beside Miss Malkin, hugging my haversack, watching Sheffield slip away, turning into fields and walls and empty roads.

Miss Malkin nudged me awake. The bus was pulling up and we got off. An old man sat on top of a tractor beside the road. He nodded but said nothing. Miss Malkin climbed up behind him and perched on the mudguard and told me to do the same. I wrapped my fingers around the cold, steel rim, and we rattled and bumped down a long cart track and into a farmyard.

Mr Malkin – he told me to call him Uncle Peter – showed me around the farm. Loud bleating came from behind a stone wall, and I climbed up to find the black faces of at least a hundred fluffy white sheep looking at me from the other side. I dropped down and disappeared amongst them, snuffling my nose into the warm, soapy smell.

The man on the Information Desk says, 'The tram? Not to Hurdle Hill. You'd be better on the 95 to the bottom of the hill, or take the 52 to the top and walk across.' There isn't a thee or a thou to be heard. Outside the station is a glittering steel plate with water running down it – I think it's what they call a 'feature' – and a walkway to a new bus station. The last time I walked this road, to catch the train to Plymouth and the ship, it was a city wrapped in a sooty fog that dropped black spots onto your clothes and hair. A lot of money must have been spent on prettifying the place and the air is definitely a lot cleaner, thought it could all do with a good scrub. Burger trays are heaped up against the boarded up Post Office, pigeons have decorated the façade of the Elephant Inn which is now a charity shop, and men and women sit amongst the fag ends at King Edward's feet drinking from paper bags. Where the Marples Hotel once stood is now a store with a German name. The Hole in the Road has disappeared beneath shiny new tramlines and signs saying 'Supertram'. *C&A Modes* is now called *Primark*, and while I'm looking around, a loud trilling draws my attention to one of these so-called supertrams gliding past. A concrete block has replaced the bombed-out Bank, but there, in much the same place I remember, the 52 bus is pulling in. She says, ‘Bus pass, love?’ I shake my head and hold out the remaining few quid, like so many little brass buttons.

I get off on North Hill Road and walk along the path, passing the bowling green, lush and still dewy in the shade, watching the Rivelin Valley unfold in front of me. As I set off down the narrow path, I look to my right, towards the Don Valley, expecting to see black smoke rising from the factories, and am surprised to be able to make out what seems to be a glint of water where the sun is shining on the River Don.

Alice

Rob says, 'There's a chap outside, looking at the house,' and I leave him cleaning up and go through to the front bedroom, to the window, and look down on an elderly gentleman standing on the other side of the road.

Beneath an unruly mop of curly, snowy hair, his face is like well-worn leather. He is frowning intently, as though he has the worries of the world on his shoulders. As though aware of my eyes on him, he pulls his shoulders back, adding another few inches to his height, and looks up, directly at me. He is thin and wiry, and, judging by the sinews which stand out on his forearms below the turned up sleeves, very strong. A battered canvas haversack hangs from his shoulder. There's a blue holdall at his feet. There is something very familiar about this man. I feel that we have met, though it could have been long ago.

In the time it takes me to go downstairs and open the front door, he's crossed the road and now stands with a hand on the gate, seemingly unsure whether to come through. I call, 'Hello, can I help you?' and as his deep brown eyes meet mine, we definitely know one another, but I can't think how. 'We saw you watching the house and I wondered…'

He opens the gate and walks towards me with his arm outstretched. 'We met, but you were a youngster, you'll have forgotten?' As I take his hand he grips mine in both his large fists. I feel a deep tremble, as though his body is shaking and the vibration is coming up through his limbs into his arms, to his hands, transmitting to me. Neither of us lets go.

He says, 'Frank Sheldon?' I think it's a question and am about to say, no, I don't know anyone of that name when he continues, 'I saw in the news about the body being found? In the Anderson shelter?' and I realise it's an accent, this upward tilt at the end of his sentences, turning a statement into a question. My hand is still in his. 'I wonder, would Mrs Clarke – I mean Ibbertson? Would she agree to see me, do you think?'

'Are you… a relative?' I'm still trying to place him. His eyes are locked to mine. My hand in his is hot but my arms have goose pimples.

He points to the photograph in my other hand. 'That's my sister, Jean.'

I'm glad to find Rob beside me, holding out his hand, so politeness requires this man to release my hand and take Rob's. I hear him say the name again, Frank Sheldon, but don't recognise it. Rob introduces himself and invites Frank in, tells us to go through to the garden, while he makes coffee. He picks up the blue holdall and holds his hand out for the haversack, but Frank wraps his arms around it protectively and walks past Rob, then follows me along the hallway, through the kitchen, and into the garden.

Frank walks across to the hole and stares into it for maybe a minute, then turns and, looking up at Mum's window, says, 'So, can I see her?'

Rob brings out a kitchen chair and gestures Frank to sit down, saying, 'Thing is, she's asleep just now. Have a coffee first. Take the weight off your feet.'

Frank joins me near the door, but remains standing, looking around. I sit on Mum's old garden chair and almost immediately he sits down. It would never occur to Rob to wait for me to be seated and I'd forgotten that kind of chivalry in the older generation. Frank rests his elbows on his thighs, his hands hanging loosely between his knees, saying nothing while long seconds pass. He appears deep in his thoughts and I don't want to interrupt them. This, I think, is a man used to waiting. Somehow I know he is bringing me answers and I'm not sure I'm ready to hear them.

Rob brings a tray with cups and cafetiere and puts it on the table. It's the table I bought for the new patio, which Rob must have put together at some point over the last day or two. I hadn't noticed. The chairs are still flat-packed, leaning against the wall. 'Want me to stay?' Rob asks, and I nod, so he brings another cup. 'Come a long way?' he asks Frank in an offhand, chatty fashion as though they've just met in the pub.

'Australia,' says Frank, startling us both. And as if he'd been waiting to be invited to speak – that old-fashioned courtesy again – Frank starts talking. Rob carries out another kitchen chair for himself, I pour coffee, and we all drink while Frank tells his story. He tells it backwards, starting with his sheep farm in South Australia, his friends Amy and Keith and their family, and his late friend, Sam, who emigrated with him in 1964.

'That's when I last saw you,' he says. 'You were standing right there.'

I remember now. 'There was some shouting,' I say. 'You and Joe were angry with one another.'

'It goes back,' he says, 'right back. To that night.' He nods towards the hole. He takes the photograph from me and studies it, talking about his sister, Jean. 'This is her wedding day,' he says. When he describes her, I wonder if he's confusing me with her, but then he says, 'That's how I know you're Elizabeth, Jean's girl. Peas in a pod. I had my suspicions, many a time. Was a time I thought Violet and Joe had an affair, so you looked like him, but later, when I thought about it, I knew that'd never be so; it was always Jean you favoured, not Joe. And that day I came round and you were – what? In your twenties? I could see it right off. They tried to tell me she' – he flips a thumb up, in the direction of Mum's bedroom window – 'was your mother, and' – he puts his cup on the table and his hands over his face. Through his fingers, he says, 'I thought I was going mad with all those thoughts jangling about in my brain.'

Rob leans forward and puts a hand on Frank's shoulder. 'One thing at a time,' he says to him. 'You said it goes back to that night. Tell us about it.'

Frank

It was near the end of the war when I saw Joe or Violet again. Joe wrote to me. He sent me pocket money. He told me in his letters I could live with him when the war was over. As time went on, he stopped talking about people and things I knew about, and his letters became those of a stranger who was travelling to countries I'd not even heard of. He didn't come home on leave. I thought about him less and less. Uncle Peter, and Miss Malkin – Aunt Bridget – they became my family. Aunt Bridget retired from teaching after the War and came to live with us on the farm. It was a quiet life, with only old folk and sheep for company, but it was quiet, and calm, and so different from what I'd known before that I would go for days and then weeks without remembering. When I did think of the family, it was in my sleep. Joe stood at the back of a queue that disappeared into thick fog. In front of him I could see Cyril, Bill, Dad, Mam. I couldn't see the front of the queue, or what they were waiting for, and they were all looking away from me. Jean wasn't with them.

In the spring of 1946, I got a letter from Violet.

Dear Frank,

Joe and I are getting married on 13th April and I would very much like it if you came to a small family celebration at the house at four o'clock in the afternoon. I know you and I have not always seen eye to eye, but you are Joe's brother-in-law, and therefore you are an important family member, and I would like to think you will include yourself in our family. Alice is quite a big girl, and I should like her to meet her Uncle Frank.

Yours sincerely,
Violet Clarke (Mrs)

The 'Uncle Frank' confused me. I thought perhaps Violet was saying this was Elizabeth, and so I decided to go, to find out what was happening. Joe looked smart in his uniform. He was a sergeant major and about to be demobbed. The house looked different. There was still the same furniture that I remembered but the parlour and the hallway had been redecorated and everything was much brighter. I could hear music. Then Alice came in. At five or six years old she was a little beauty. Joe swung her round in the air and winked at me. I was a gawky sixteen-year-old, all arms and legs, and didn't know where to put myself so as not to knock things over. I expected the old lady, Violet's mother, to jump out at any minute and tell me off, but she wasn't anywhere to be seen. I was very confused as to how Joe came to be marrying Violet. I still remembered how horrible she'd been to Jean, even though she now seemed intent on being nice to me.

Joe called Alice and Violet said, 'Go to Daddy.'

It dawned on me then. What I hadn't been able to understand at ten, I saw very clearly at sixteen. Alice was Joe's daughter. She was also Violet's daughter. That's why she looked like Elizabeth when she was a baby – because they both looked like Joe. In a flash I realised that Joe must have been having an affair with Violet, while he was married to Jean.

I stamped out of the house and into the garden. The place where the Anderson shelter had been was now a mound of soil, with a few plants in it.

Joe had followed me. ‘Frank, what is it?’

I couldn’t bear to see him looking so happy and well. By marrying Violet, he was making sure that Jean could never come home. I knew this would sound crazy, and I couldn’t begin to say it to Joe. My throat was full.

He put his hand on my shoulder. ‘Are you missing the family?’

I shouted at him, ‘I don’t think tha’s missing the family. I can see what’s been going on here.’

Joe looked shocked. ‘What do you mean?’

‘Aye, I can see it all now.’ I was tongue tied and could say no more.

I ran off across the hill, not stopping until I was at the corner of Liberty Road where the sign for the Rest Centre was looking the worse for wear.

On the spur of the moment I decided to look Sam up. His mother answered the door and didn’t recognise me until I said, ‘It’s Frank,’ and she said, ‘Of course it is. By, tha’s grown into a long lad. Come on in, love.’

Sam was as broad and muscly as I was tall and scrawny. We were awkward with one another, not knowing what to say or do. Mrs Ainsworth said, ‘I’ll leave tha to it, happen there’s plenty to talk about,’ and went into the kitchen. Sam and I sat grinning at one another for a full minute until he said, ‘So, what’s tha think of farming?’ and I was on to my favourite subject. He said, ‘Is there any chance of an opening?’ He told me he was apprenticed at Ferguson’s, but hated it. We settled that I’d ask Peter if he could take Sam on.

This is how Sam and me came to be together again, living and working on the farm. We visited Sheffield from time to time, to see his mam. His Dad was still invalided and giving her a hard time, what with the drink and spending all her money. Sam made sure she had something put by. I kept away from Hurdle Hill Terrace and heard nothing but for a Christmas card and birthday card, always 'from Joe, Violet, and Alice'. I never replied.

Sam met Doreen, a Land Army girl at the next farm. When we came back from National Service, which we did together, they got married. By then, Aunt Bridget had died and Uncle Peter wasn't able to look after the farm any longer so he pretty much left it to me and Sam. Doreen took care of the house and all of us. Wool was in demand following the war, so sheep farmers did well. Except for that dark shadow that followed me wherever I went, it was a good life.

Peter died in 1963, leaving the farm to me. It was a hard winter and I think that was what gave Doreen the idea of emigrating to Australia. There was nothing to stop me. I still had questions, but by now I knew there were no answers to be had. I did want to make my peace with Joe though, before I left. We drove to Sheffield and went shopping for the things Australia House said we needed to take with us, and then I left Sam and Doreen with the car, doing the rounds to say their goodbyes, and made my way to Hurdle Hill.

It was a fine evening as I walked across the hill and in by the back gate. I was pleased to see vegetables growing and the garden arranged much as Mr Knowles had it all those years ago. Where the shelter had been, there was now a rockery, covered with the brightest yellow and blue and pink flowers flowing down between the rocks.

I heard 'Hello?' and turned to see Jean in the doorway, her head on one side, smiling at me in the old way. It took my breath away. She was wearing different clothes, of course, a short skirt and a tasseled blouse. But she was just as tall, with the same eyes and dark, curly hair and as she smiled with her lips parted I saw her front teeth overlapping like they always had. She walked towards me.

I said, 'Jean?'

She frowned. 'Who are you?'

Violet's voice said, 'Frank?' and I saw she had come out behind Jean.

Jean turned to Violet and said, 'Why did he call me Jean?'

Violet looked as though she might faint. A bald, portly figure stepped around her, taking a pipe from his mouth. He shouted, 'Frank! Well, well. Come in, lad, come in. Violet, get the kettle on, let's sit down and have a catch up,' and holding my elbow he steered me towards the house.

Violet said, 'Alice, come inside', and that same cold emptiness that I remembered from looking into the crater all those years before, began creeping out from the centre of my body. My legs shook and I pulled away from Joe's hand.

Joe frowned, then said, 'Oh no. Frank, you don't still think…?'

Jean said, 'What's the matter, Mum? Dad?'

Violet got hold of Jean by the arm and pulled her over the doorstep. As I reached the door Violet closed it in my face.

Joe put his arm around my shoulders. 'Frank, Frank, this has got to stop.'

I sank onto my knees, my forehead against the door, hammering my fists against it. Joe squeezed my shoulders. I turned round and sat with my back to the door, my face in my hands. Joe sat beside me. I was embarrassed to realise that the strange noises were coming from me. For what seemed like minutes I was unable to speak. Then I said, 'Elizabeth'.

Joe said, 'No – no – Alice. Violet's daughter, Richard's daughter. Alice.'

I stood up, still shaking but able to hold the tears back, and made my way down the path, Joe following me. At the gate, I said, 'I'm emigrating on Tuesday. Australia.'

He said, 'It's perhaps for the best, lad.' I ignored his outstretched hand. 'Keep in touch.' A few yards up the hill I turned to see Violet and Elizabeth standing side by side at the window, watching Joe walk back towards them.

Alice says, 'Did you have a theory? You know, if Mum knew something about Jean's disappearance, what did you think had happened?'

'No, I didn't know where Jean had gone, but I was sure that Violet knew more than she was letting on. I was too young to work it out, but when I think back, everything points to Violet.' I think a minute before adding, 'But I never thought it was murder. It never crossed my mind. Sounds daft but I thought maybe Jean was angry with me for not being at home that night; then I thought she'd had an accident and nobody had found her. This lot' – I flicked my thumb behind me towards the house – 'would have me believe she'd gone home. I thought for a time they must be right. But then in due course they'd have brought up her bones, along with Mam and…' My voice catches in my throat and she takes my hand, just holding it, until I can speak again. 'Oh, I don't know what I thought, but I never ever thought they'd done her in. If I'd been older I might have thought differently. Of course it occurred to me that she was dead, but...' I can't say any more.

'So you do think this –' She gestures towards the hole in the garden. 'This might have been your Jean?'

When I get my breath back, I say, 'I'm sure of it. And if what they said was right, and you were Violet's daughter, then there'd be another person in that shelter, wouldn't there? There'd be a baby.' She nods. 'And being as there isn't – well, that goes to prove it, doesn't it? You must be Elizabeth.'

I hear voices inside the house and stand up to look through the window. I can see my own reflection and coming towards it, like a procession of ghosts, I swear I see our Bill, and isn't that…

When I come to, I'm lying on the settee in the front room. It's that same, scratchy sofa I sat on back then. I look around and I'm reminded of the wedding day, and the day after Joe came back and found me. Alice-Elizabeth's bloke is standing by the window, watching me, looking anxious. I think maybe he always looks that way, that he's one of those fellas that does all the worrying for everybody. I sit up quick and feel a bit dizzy. He puts his hand on my arm to stop me standing up. He passes me a cup of tea. I tell him I must have been imagining things. I thought I saw some people I know. 'It's our daughter, Judy,' he says, 'and her son, our grandson, Adam.' And it makes sense.

Rob says, 'It's all too much, we think.'

Happen he's right. I should never have come. I say so.

'Yes, you should,' he says. 'We're glad you came. But it's too much, too soon. You need to rest.'

I tell him there's plenty of time to rest when they get me in a shroud, and I've a lot to do before then. I think he understands.

'Tell you what,' he says. 'I'll take Judy and Adam over to our house. Alice will stay with you and you can ring me when you're ready. You'll stay at our house, of course?' When I hesitate, he says, 'It'll be just you and Alice; I'll stay here with her mother – I mean…'

I know what he means. He leaves the room and I hear talking and rustling in the hallway and then the door closes, and it's quiet. I drink the tea – he's of the same school as Amy, it's got more sugar than tea in it.

After a few seconds, Alice comes in. 'Let's go and see her,' she says.

At the bedroom door he hesitates, looking down and shuffling his feet with a curious boyish shyness. Mum's eyes widen and fix on him while her lips move around his name.

He says, 'Violet.' It's a statement, not a greeting. With a deep intake of breath, he walks towards her.

'Can we come in?' She raises her eyebrows at me. I know, it's a pointless question, we are already in the room. Frank is now standing at the foot of the bed looking at her. I bring the upright chair from the window and place it next to the bed for him, and sit on the Lloyd loom. Mum looks from one to the other of us.

He sits and looks around. 'This room hasn't changed. When I came to see your father, when he was ill, in the other room, I came in here. That wallpaper…' The Australian intonation has fallen away almost completely.

Mum tries to sit up but falls back against her pillows. She tuts and flaps a bony hand at me, but doesn't resist as I help her to sit forward and fluff up the pillows. Her shoulders, even wrapped in a bed-jacket, are birdlike, fragile, and I'm afraid of breaking her. She no longer smells of tea rose, and although the fragrance that is left – it's a fabric conditioner, not unpleasant, but slightly chemical – this new loss adds to the impression that she is slipping away from me. Frank has taken up his waiting posture, hands hanging between his knees. Mum lies back and they look directly at one another, while long seconds pass.

I'm starting to feel uneasy, thinking how I can fill the silent space between them, when he says, 'You must have known I'd come, soon as I heard.' And when she doesn't react, he goes on, 'Or did you think I'd popped my clogs? Surprised I'm still alive? Well, the feeling's mutual.' She tuts at his bluntness. 'But given that I am here, let's have no messing about, I reckon the time's passed for all that. What's the story?'

Mum draws in a breath and says, 'Jean.'

Frank jumps from his seat as though an electrical charge has passed through him. Mum flinches as he walks past the bed. At the window, he looks down at the garden.

'Are you all right?' I ask him.

He nods. 'It's just the hearing of her name, after so long, from somebody else saying it.' He remains motionless at the window for maybe half a minute, then rubs his eyes with the back of a hand and returns to his seat.

Mum's fingers are fluttering in the air at her shoulder and she raises her head from the pillows. I start to fluff them up again, and she shakes her head, saying, 'Under the bed.' I pick up her handbag and hold it out to her but she shakes her head again. I open it and look inside, looking back at her, half expecting a sharp word, for the inside of her handbag has always been sacred, a place I have glanced but never dared go. In the bottom is a fat roll of pages held together by an elastic band. She flicks her fingers slightly in a 'go away' gesture and closes her eyes. I sit beside Frank and unroll the papers.

A sheet of her best writing paper is headed, '*Dear Alice*'. This, I think, is from the envelope that contained what I now know to be Jean's wedding photograph. There are several pages of the familiar neat handwriting with dates, which must be some of the missing diary entries. The final page is covered with scrawled, spidery writing, fragments of sentences that I can barely make out; names – Jean, Joe, and at the bottom, I think it says, '*all gone, what am I to do*'. I think it's Mum's handwriting, but quite unlike her usual script. I look at her for explanation but her eyes remain closed.

Dear Alice, you've read the diary. So she knows. No point, then, in waiting to see Frank alone. I tell him quickly about the diary, how it ended at the beginning of December when it seemed Mum was locked in her bedroom. Of course, he was the boy Mum wrote about, Jean's brother. Mum is silent, not looking at me. Frank nods and frowns, and smiles once or twice, but listens carefully and doesn't interrupt. Then we look at the letter together. The writing is spidery and shaky, but the words are articulate and confident, and I think she must have spent a long time composing it over the last few nights, when she wasn't sleeping, or when she was alone, before she was too weak. Looking at her fingers, I think she could barely hold a pen, today, and I realise how dramatic her decline has been.

Frank squints and holds the paper close. I think maybe he should wear glasses. 'Left them on the train,' he says, reading my thoughts. I pass him my vari-focals and he laughs, but puts them on and finds a way of reading comfortably by holding his head back and looking down through the reading lens. He studies it for a long time, then passes the specs, and the letter, to me and takes up the waiting pose that I already know to be part of the man he is.

Violet

Dear Alice,

You've read the diary. I don't approve of you invading my privacy in the way you did, but it's too late now. You never could leave well alone. You probably think you know all there is to know about what went on here in those terrible days. I have considered leaving it at that. The more I tell you, the more questions you will have. However, if I say nothing, you will fill in the spaces with your own imagination. I really don't know which is worse. I've lain here for hours trying to think what is best, and have finally decided to write the truth or at least enough of it to satisfy your curiosity at the same time as leaving the souls of others in peace. The lady in the shelter is Jean, Joe's first wife and your natural mother; of course this means Joe was your father. He didn't know this; you were born while he was fighting in France, and Jean had passed away before he came home. Everyone assumed you'd perished along with your mother and her family who were victims of the so-called Sheffield Blitz. I say assumed, but of course, I did nothing to disillusion them, even encouraged them to think that, for reasons that I will not say, as they relate to other people who cannot speak for themselves. I brought you up as my own and married Joe not for love – goodness me, my first marriage knocked any idea of romance out of me – but because I wanted you to be with your father. How Jean passed away is not important. It would be true to say that had it not been for me and my stupidity, it would not have happened. I have missed her very much, and regretted her passing every single day. I tried to make amends by looking after Joe and you to the best of my ability. Enough. For the lies I have told you, in fact or by omission, I apologise; it is against everything I brought you up to believe in. It was naïve of me to think my secret was safe. You deserved better. So did Frank. You have read the diary, you know who he is and if he is still alive and should you meet him, tell him I am truly sorry. It's unforgivable. The rest of the diary is yours, to do with as you will, though don't expect it to tell you any more than this.

Alice

The letter is unsigned and I can see why, for how would she address herself in relation to me, now?

Frank says, 'See where she says if it hadn't been for her it wouldn't have happened? Do you think she means it was because of her, but she didn't do anything to hurt Jean, not directly at any rate?'

'You're thinking Jean may have had an accident?'

'That kind of thing. It's what I always thought. But what accident? And how did Violet come to blame herself? And Jean must have been in this house, to have ended up out there,' nodding towards the window, 'and for you to have been here. Jean would never have left you. She never let you out of her sight.' His voice catches and when I put my hand on his arm, I think I can feel the depth of this emotion he has lived with for so long.

'That's what I think she means. If you read her diary, you'll see that she was having a bad time, she was pregnant and –'

'She was never expecting,' Frank says and I'm shocked. How would he know this? He was a boy. 'My friend Sam knew it. I think he overheard his mother saying it was one of those ghost pregnancies – all in her imagination – and I think that must have been right.'

I don't quite catch something Mum says. 'What was that?' I ask her. 'Something about one little lie?'

'Everything changed. Stupid. My fault.'

'What was the lie?' I ask her, but she shakes her head.

‘That she was expecting,’ Frank says, his voice matter of fact. ‘She’s admitting that she lied.’ I look at Mum, she looks away, and her silence seems to confirm what he says. He waves the letter. ‘Anyway, that’s not the point right now. Jean did come here that night, just like I always said, and she died here, and the police have said it was murder’ – Mum gives a start – ‘so we’re not going to get very far with this accident idea.’

‘Not Mum, no, I would never believe she could hurt anyone,’ I say, and inside my head a voice says ‘she’s not my mother’, but I can’t think of her as anything else. Mum is her name. She’s closed her eyes, but I’m certain she’s listening to every word. As I watch the bedspread barely move with her breath, it occurs to me she may have hoped to die before Frank arrived, or before we got to this point of the family secret. Of course – in her own fashion, she was starving herself to death. Taking control, even at the end.

Frank says, ‘I think you’re right. She was a funny lady – I suppose she was just a kid herself, really, though I was younger so she seemed grown up to me. I couldn’t imagine her hurting anybody. She was rude to Jean, and I heard her bad-mouthing her, but I guess that’s par for the course with women, isn’t it?’ He looks at me. I shrug. ‘Maybe I misunderstood, maybe they were bosom buddies even though they were catty about each other.’

‘Yes and no,’ I say. ‘She wrote about how disappointed she was that her wedding had to be shared with strangers.’ Frank is nodding. ‘A lot of the time she’s criticising Jean, but then there’s stuff that makes you think she really liked her, after she got to know her.’

He’s smiling into the middle distance. ‘When she came to our house for tea, she’d give Jean pamphlets about how to make do without sugar and how to cook with powdered egg.' He chuckles. 'We used to hide the butter and eggs when she came round.' The smile drops from his face. 'But this diary. Didn't you say she had a thing about our Jean having an affair with Richard?'

'That's the gist of it.'

'A bloody ridiculous idea. Our Jean was head over heels for Joe. And Richard – I mean, I'd have known if anything like that was going on.'

He must have been about ten years old at the time, so I think he is unlikely to have known the ins and outs of adults' romantic lives. Even so, 'I'm sure it wasn't true,' I say. 'There's a letter from Richard, that he wrote to Mum when he was in Dunkirk and of course he never came back. He told her he was homosexual, as good as saying he'd never loved her, and something about marrying her to cover it up. We think he admitted that he'd always loved Joe.'

Two things happen as I'm finishing the sentence. I'm startled by a cry from Mum, almost a wail, ferocious, animal-like. She presses her hands against her face so I can't see her eyes, and starts to shake. Frank has jumped up and is standing with his back to me, looking out of the window, his voice harsh as he says, loudly, 'Now that really is bloody ridiculous.' He smacks a hand against the frame. Mum jumps, keeping her face covered. 'Sorry,' he says, and sits down.

'We thought there might be something in it,' I say, carefully. 'I'll get the letter'. It's in the front bedroom. I'm back within seconds. Neither of them has moved.

He takes the letter from me, using my specs again to read it carefully, twice, then goes back to the window and stares out at the hill. 'Funny, all my life I've had an idea about Richard,' he says. 'I thought he was the bees knees. An all-out good bloke.' He leans his forehead against the glass and looks into the garden. 'I remember the day after Joe came back from Dunkirk and visited to give Violet something from Richard, it must have been this. But I don't understand why Joe would have brought such a rotten letter.'

'He probably wouldn't have known,' I think aloud. 'Knowing Joe, he wouldn't have set out to hurt Violet, and he wouldn't have shown it to her if he'd known what it said.'

Frank says, 'Hmm' and paces back and forth across the end of the bed, glancing at Mum who may be quietly weeping behind her hands, saying 'Hmm' again. Her shoulders are shaking. I'm struck by how, in the past few days, she has watched her life being taken apart and examined by strangers, remembered the death of a friend and all that came before and after it, including what sounds like two loveless marriages, and has remained stoic in the face of it all. What has brought her to breaking point is none of those awful events; it is that she can no longer hide the knowledge that her husband was gay, that this is no longer a secret. I think about my conversation with Judy and how unbearable life must have been for Richard, too, being gay in that time, being driven to a sham marriage in order to be respectable. I can't quite grasp how the shame would have led to lying about being pregnant, but this lie seems to have been at the heart of what happened next, and ultimately – for I think this is what Mum is hinting – to Jean's death.

Frank shakes his head and sits back beside me. He waves the letter towards Violet. 'She never let on. Well, she wouldn't, would she, me being a nipper and all. But

I'd bet my bottom dollar she never told Jean any of this.' It's hardly the kind of conversation people would have in front of a boy. As if reading my thoughts, he says, 'Our house was tiny, there were no secrets. No, if Jean had known this, I'd have heard her talking to my Mam about it.'

'She talked about Richard buying gifts for Jean,' I say. 'It made her think they were having an affair. That's how she dealt with him not being interested in her. But maybe Richard bought gifts for Jean to curry favour with Joe.'

'Yeah, I remember,' says Frank. 'He bought Jean a watch. I was here the day Violet found it. He gave Violet a locket.'

'I know it,' I say. 'She's always kept it in her handbag. I found it once, when I was little. She told me off, forbade me from touching her handbag. I've never known her wear it.'

'I think Richard bought Jean the wedding ring?' Frank asks, or rather says, but with that upward intonation creeping back. He opens the flap of his haversack and pulls out a parcel of black fabric, bringing with it a smell of mildew. Opening a corner, he lifts a piece of string with a green ring on it. 'It's a curtain ring – Jean wore it til Joe could afford a proper one. The next time he came on leave, he brought her a nice ring.' He looks at me. 'Have they found it? The ring?'

'The police haven't mentioned it. We can ask. They're coming round later.'

Mum is whispering something and when I lean over her, I think she says, 'Ring in Joe's pocket. With him always.'

'I think she put it in his pocket for the burial,' I say to Frank.

He's silent for some time, then shakes his head emphatically. 'But Joe, you know, he'd never have had anything like that – no – he'd have cut Richard out of his life if he'd had an inkling of any funny business.'

'I agree,' I say. 'Joe was my stepdad – my dad.'

He stares at Violet. 'Poor bugger. She had it rough, didn't she?'

'She certainly did. I can't see her doing anyone any harm, especially not Jean.'

He goes back to the window and looks out. The sun breaks out from behind a cloud, shining directly into the bedroom and turning him into a silhouette. I hear him say, 'Me neither,' and there is a long pause before he says, 'So, Jean died in this house, and Violet was here, but Violet didn't do it, so who–'

'It was Grandma.' As I say this, Mum takes her fingers away from her eyes and stares at me. I lean across and say to her, 'I'm right, aren't I? It was Grandma.' She looks at me but says nothing.

Frank makes a noise, halfway between a laugh and a snort, says, 'Strewth!' and stands at the other side of the bed, looking down at Mum, shaking his head in wonder.

I put my head close to hear what she's saying.

'What's she say?' Frank asks.

'She says it was her fault and we should blame her. I think she means she wants to take the blame. But that's not the same thing as being to blame. Is it?'

'So you reckon it was your Grandma? I remember her. A proper old witch.'

'A witch, a witch,' I repeat. 'The witch is dead.' He looks at me as though I've gone bonkers. I repeat what I told Rob about the man – I know now that it was Joe – coming to visit, taking me to see '*Over the Rainbow.*

When we got home, Grandma was angry that I was making a noise, dancing around and singing songs from the film.

Frank chuckles and says, 'That's our Jean up and dressed,' and I look at him, puzzled. He says, 'She could always remember the songs from the pictures, word for word. Drove me mad, singing and dancing all over the house.' He's lost in memory for a moment, then looks at me and says, 'See, I get why she might have married Joe, but why would Joe have married her?'

'Does it make you wonder whether he knew something – about me?' I ask him.

'Maybe. But maybe he was just worn down. I remember when I saw him, after the war, he did seem kind of hollowed out, exhausted, himself but not himself. Maybe he just wanted looking after.'

'But in return, Joe looked after Mum and me very well,' I say.

He comes round the bed, sits down. 'Go on, about the old woman.'

'It may have been later that night, or soon after. Mum had an argument with Grandma on the landing. I came out of my room and ran up to them. Grandma was standing on the top step. She fell down the stairs, right in front of me. I think I did it, pushed her, or knocked her off balance.'

'No!' Mum's voice comes from the bed. She is struggling to get up. 'No.'

'It's all right, Mum, I remember.'

Frank is chuckling. 'Well, I'll be damned, you pushed the old witch down the stairs?'

Mum's hands grasp at my arms; her nails scratch the skin through my sleeve. 'Not you.' I think she may be having a seizure and am about to ask Frank to run for Rob, to call the doctor, when I realise she's trying to speak, pulling me down, towards her. 'Me, I pushed– She – said she'd tell Joe I – I did it. If I – marry him, she, she would say– so I pushed her.'

'You don't have to take the blame, Mum. I was a child. It was an accident.'

Frank is standing next to me. He leans over her. 'She threatened you that if you married Joe, she'd tell him you killed Jean?' She lets go of my arm and falls back, looking at Frank with a slight nod. He says, 'What you're saying is, you didn't hurt Jean, your mother did. But if you married Joe, she would say you'd done it?' Her lips are blue. 'You argued, and that's when you pushed her down the stairs?'

'Like Jean,' she slurs.

I say, 'Is that what happened to Jean? Grandma pushed her down the stairs? And you feel guilty. You've kept the secret to protect Grandma.'

Frank has moved away from the bed. He is rubbing the piece of black fabric against his cheek, reminding me of Judy as a small child with her blankie. I sit down heavily. After the emotional see-sawing of highs and lows, from excitement to fear, from worry to confusion, over the past few days, my mind is wrung out, scrubbed out, empty. The silence is for so long, I think Mum is asleep. She is facing the window so I walk round the bed and see her eyes are open.

Although the slurring is getting worse, her voice is remarkably clear when she says, 'Jean opened the door. She said, why lock her in? Mummy said she can't be allowed out… the shame. You – Elizabeth – you were inside her coat. She said to Jean, get out, get out–' Her hands are moving as though she is acting out the pushing.

‘Stop it, you’re hurting Jean. You’ll hurt the baby. Hold the baby, then.’ Tears are coursing down her wrinkled cheeks and I search in my cardigan pocket for a tissue, can’t find one and see a handkerchief tucked into her sleeve. I put it into her hand and she dabs at her eyes, saying, ‘I’m sorry, Jean,’ and I’m not sure whether she’s calling me Jean because she’s confused, or because she is addressing Jean.

Frank is back beside me. He leans over Mum, and says, ‘But the papers talked about a fractured skull, a blow with something, lots of blows. What was it?’

Her eyes are unfocussed as she looks at him, whispering, ‘See what you made me do. Now you’ve got a baby. Hope you’re satisfied.’ It’s not like her own voice and I realise she’s back in that place, and Grandma is talking. Then she says, in her own voice, ‘Jean cried. She was hurt. Mother went downstairs. But–’

‘What did she do?’ Frank’s hands brush his face.

‘We don’t need to know.’ I lead him to his chair, press his shoulders until he sits. He rocks backwards and forwards. I keep a hand on his shoulder and he places one trembling hand on mine.

‘So my birthday is really the twenty-seventh of November?’ I say, almost to myself. Later, I will wonder why I focussed on the most unimportant detail. As if the date matters.

The door opens and Mum looks terrified, her eyes looking past us to the door as though the events she has been describing are happening now. Claire’s head appears.

‘What’s going on here? You all look as though you’ve seen a ghost,’ she says. How long has she been there? How much has she heard?

Mum taps my hand and I put my ear close to her mouth while she says, haltingly, 'Tell police woman. Give her papers. It's all there.'

Claire stands beside Frank, waiting for an introduction, but that can come later. I hold out my arm, ushering her in front of us down the stairs. Picking up his haversack and hanging it from his shoulder, Frank follows. Rob is sitting in the garden working on my Sudoku book. Hearing us, he comes into the kitchen, and appears startled to see Claire, so she must have walked in through the front door and upstairs without knocking, and I feel cross that she has tried to trick her way in to seeing Mum.

Claire places two plastic, zip-lock bags on the table. Frank picks one up and places it on his huge, calloused palm. He runs a finger along the narrow silver bracelet and round the small white stones that surround its face, repeating, 'Jean, Jean,' softly, as though he can feel his sister's presence. He turns it over and stretches the transparent plastic, pointing to the inscription which is now clear: *Jean Ibbertson, 16th September, 1939.*

'Jean is…?' Claire asks.

'My sister. The lady in the shelter.'

'Any relation to Mrs Ibbertson? Another cousin, perhaps?'

Frank misses the sarcasm. 'None. My sister's husband was Joe Ibbertson. He married this Mrs Ibbertson later.' Claire's eyebrows rise into her fringe. I'm grateful to Frank for taking responsibility for telling this. He adds, 'Joe knew nothing of this. Mrs Ibbertson has told us the story.' He sounds remarkably calm and matter of fact about it. I suppose he's lived with his questions for so many years he might be relieved to have some certainties.

Feeling stifled, I go into the garden and stand beside the crater, taking deep breaths, blowing my nose. I feel such deep loss, an emptiness, a longing for what might have been. Anger that she held on to all those secrets for so long. But at the same time, I feel the beginning of admiration for the woman upstairs who I will always think of as my mother. It's too early to know for sure, but I think I will look back and remember her for her courage.

Frank is beside me, holding out the zip-lock bag containing the torch. 'Tenth birthday present from my Mam and Dad,' he says. 'I came here with my pal, Sam, we were messing about in the shelter. I left it there. It was wet…' His voice catches and I put my hand on his arm. Claire is watching us from the doorway. As we walk towards her, he lifts the flap of his haversack and shows me the wodge of papers that we took from Mum's handbag, the cut-out diary entries that we haven't yet read. I stop and glance up at the window, half expecting to see her there, watching us.

ACKNOWLEDGEMENTS

I am grateful to my late next door neighbour for the idea: I was cutting the privet hedge in the garden of my home in Sheffield, when she called, 'Mind where you put your feet, we buried all sorts there during the War.' This was my 'what if?' moment. In Walkley Library, I found the voices of many men and women who lived through the Sheffield Blitz and they gave me both the inspiration and the knowledge to put the wartime experience into Frank's capable hands. I am grateful to them all for recording their memories in a way that has created an invaluable resource for future generations. In the plotting and crafting of this novel, a number of people helped me along the road to publication and I have appreciated their encouragement and feedback, and for their belief that the story should, could and would be told. They include groups of fellow writers and tutors of the Arvon Foundation and Sheffield Hallam University, particularly Mike Harris and Linda Lee Welch. Special thanks go to my home-grown team of experts: Hazel Mitchell, forensic bio-scientist, and David Start, archaeologist, for their advice on buried remains and crime scene investigation. Thank you to Clare Eastland for the vital, final edit.

A note from the author:

I hope you enjoyed reading The House Fell on Her Head as much as I enjoyed telling the stories of Frank and Alice, and trying to get to know the enigmatic Violet.

Please take a few moments to put a review on Amazon, or pop your thoughts onto Twitter or other social media. You can also tweet me, and follow my further writing on @k8swaby.

My next publications will be:

- 'Eclipsed,' a short story in 'The Day I Met Vini Reilly', a winners' anthology published by Cinnamon Press in March 2016.
- 'Flashback,' a crime novel, to be published later this year.
- A short story collection to be published in 2017.